As the helicopters to ___ ___ the deck, its passengers' u___ ___ sense of caution united ___ ___ ___ ___ ___ ___ ___ ___ darkness of the deck.

The only light came from the repeating flash of a helicopter's strobe, allowing brief glimpses of the machinery. The alternating bursts of red and green lent an eeriness to the derrick which loomed above them like a darkened monolith. The group started forward across the deck, but the specter of what they feared brought them to a halt: The first body had been spotted.

The expression on the dead man's face was bizarre, and his open eyes and bared teeth contributed to death's distorting work. The skin stretched over the bones abnormally. Dried, almost burned, it looked wooden to the touch.

The group advanced across the floor until another body was encountered, and then another. The men began identifying the workers one by one. "Here's Red Ferman!" someone yelled out. Then other names penetrated the silence. The unbelievable was being confirmed.

READ THESE HORRIFYING BEST SELLERS!

GHOST RIG

BY CLIFF PATTON, M.D.

ZEBRA BOOKS
KENSINGTON PUBLISHING CORP.

ZEBRA BOOKS

are published by

KENSINGTON PUBLISHING CORP.
475 Park Avenue South
New York, N.Y. 10016

Printed in the United States of America

With love, for

Haley
Kelly
Allison
Todd

our children.

We acknowledge assistance in various ways from many people: Trudie Broland, Mary Parker, Kim Turner, Lyn Dellosso, Gail Harrel, Molly Mehlich, Peggy Patton, and the ladies of the O.R. at Martin Memorial Hospital and The Hospital in Jupiter.

Special thanks for the enthusiasm of Jata Panaro.

PROLOGUE

. . . and, beware the stranger within.

April

It was the most exciting thing Jori Ashe had ever seen.
Entranced, she studied every detail of the majestic design
as her famous host waited, understanding her intense
interest. She knew immediately that she wanted it, more
than she had ever desired anything in her professional
life. It was everything she had dreamed of—a quantum
leap into the future. Very clearly, Dr. Adrian Sumter and
Florexco were light years ahead of everyone else. There
was nothing that could compare with it. Neither on the
drawing boards nor in the distant imagination of future
plans did her own company or any of the other big energy
conglomerates have anything even remotely similar.
This incredible drilling platform would signal the
dawning of a new era in offshore oil exploration. Like
nothing before, it would make possible the exploitation
of the theoretically huge petroleum reserves beneath
the continental shelf, a source of energy that had so far
proven more elusive than had been expected.

"I can see that you are as impressed with our new toy as I had hoped you would be," the tall, silver-haired man beside her said. His voice was deep and elegant, the accent distinctly English. The geophysicist was the chief of research and development of the Florida Exploration Company—Florexco.

"Incredible," she said, turning her gaze away from the detailed model in front of her. "It's a much more ambitious project than I had anticipated. I can see why you're keeping it so secret."

"You're quite right, my dear," he replied pleasantly. "It wouldn't do to have the opposition know what we're up to until we actually have our little endeavor under way, would it?"

He had lively green eyes and a handsome, well-structured face which he used animatedly as he spoke. She guessed that he was in his early sixties and, all in all, a very impressive man. An internationally recognized and honored scientist, he was known particularly for his studies correlating magnetic field forces with deep geological formations. Jori knew how close he had come to receiving the Nobel Prize two years ago for his revolutionary work.

"Are you really going to be operational in six months?" she asked.

"Precisely," he replied. "Every aspect of our time table is right on schedule. The construction of the platform itself will be completed within the next sixty days. That gives us four months to move it on site and initiate its maiden venture."

She nodded thoughtfully and glanced back at the engineering model placed in the middle of the small room. If Dr. Adrian Sumter said it was going to be ready,

8

then she was quite sure it would be. He usually accomplished what he set out to do and was known as an innovator in a field filled with brilliant men. It was his genius more than anyone else's that had helped change Florexco from a small drilling outfit into a large, multi-state exploration and development company now becoming recognized as a peer of the other major international petroleum corporations: the seven sisters.

She had studied his theories and published works in graduate school and followed his career ever since. Now after years of hard work, she was apparently about to be asked to join him. At thirty-two she had suddenly become a hot item, and her services were in great demand. With a Ph.D. in geological engineering and twelve years experience on offshore rigs, she had emerged as a successful young woman in an industry not only dominated, but absolutely monopolized by men. Her beauty made her seem even more out of place. She had a soft, almost aristocratic face highlighted by pretty blue eyes and light auburn hair, quite curly, which she wore down to her shoulders. On the job she kept it pinned up, of course, under her hard hat.

Adrian Sumter had moved around to the other side of the model and was pointing out features of engineering ingenuity. It was to be a tension-leg platform—TLP. The rig would actually be floating, held fast to the sea floor by a maze of steel cables and anchor pilings.

"What I have attempted to design," he said softly, "is a platform from which we can apply the most innovative accomplishments of drilling technology."

He stepped to a large relief map of the Florida east coast and adjacent sea floor. "Where we are going, my dear, is right there." He indicated a spot on the map at the

9

very edge of the continental shelf. "St. Lucie One will be capable of retrieving oil in deeper water than has ever been previously attempted. Our first project will be ten miles offshore near Palm Beach. The depth there is fourteen hundred feet, a mere test of what she can do."

She let out a soft whistle. Nothing that deep had been successful before near American shores. The man was either crazy or a genius. She wanted the job so badly she could taste it.

"Yes," he said slowly, "I can appreciate your astonishment." He walked back toward the rig. "But St. Lucie One can accomplish it, believe me, and more rapidly than anyone would expect."

As he gazed at her his voice took on a new intensity. "And that's only the beginning. This platform and others like her, within a few years are going to be drilling in waters five or ten thousand feet deep. I have no doubt about it. I have designed in every capability and systems redundancy needed to accomplish that goal." He turned back to the map. "The prophets of doom say that we're going to run out of petroleum soon—either that or be the slaves of Arab sheiks."

He shook his head and narrowed his eyes. "But not so. Three-quarters of the earth's surface has been totally untapped so far, and who knows what treasures await us there. With this creation, we will soon find out. It's simply a matter of technology, of course, and now we have it." He smiled. "I think there's enough energy out there to last ten thousand years if properly developed, and perhaps more."

His zeal moved her and increased her growing desire to work with this enthusiastic, charismatic man and help in the success of his bold undertaking.

10

Personally, he was very appealing; his brilliance in geology matched by charm of his personality. She had been told that he maintained a residence somewhere in the Bahamas and always wore white suits. He carried a handcarved mahogany cane and was prone to wearing Panama straw hats with a broad, black band around the crown. He was a master conversationalist and speaker: intent, reflective, and colorful in mannerisms and speech. She, like everyone else who met him, almost immediately had liked and respected the dignified, but warm and friendly, old gentleman.

It had been less than a week earlier that she had been invited to Florida. Had it not been for the opportunity of spending a day with the esteemed scientist, she would have refused the offer, just as she had rejected similar proposals from most of the other companies that were trying to hire her away from Gulf.

But now for the first time she was tempted. The command of this project, the experimental rig called St. Lucie One, would be a significant career leap. It would be the challenge of her professional life and was an opportunity she had waited for. It would establish her as a premier operations engineer throughout the industry. It was what she had wanted since that first teenage summer when her dad had given her a job on the rig he was running three miles offshore of Port Aransas, Texas. This would be the glory and recognition she had coveted ever since.

"Seeing this rig is like reviewing my own hidden dreams," she said to the scientist who was watching expectantly. "I'm very impressed. I have no doubt that what you want to accomplish can be done. I'm not so naive as to think it's going to be easy, even with this

11

magnificent design of yours. There are going to be immense difficulties, particularly with the coupling mechanisms in water that deep. And then there are the forces of the gulf stream to deal with. But I believe, with proper planning and skillful execution, you can pull it off. I have a lot of questions, though. For example, how are you going to overcome alignment problems between the well head and the drill platform when operating at such great depths?"

He smiled gently, acknowledging her engineering expertise. "As you said, my dear: planning. Detailed planning and advanced technology. I have used very little of the old in the development of my creation. Even the drill bits themselves are of a new generation. They will incorporate a gyroscopic attitude-control mechanism whereby at any moment the operators on the surface will know exactly their angle of inclination. Believe me, Jori Ashe, I have thought about this for years and this design is up to the task. There is nothing I have not anticipated. Whatever needs to be done, St. Lucie One can do it. My biggest concern now is the second half of what you just mentioned: execution. What I want now is skillful and imaginative execution. That is why I have brought you to Florida. I have a job for you. Very simply, I want your brains. As a member of our team, I believe you can make significant contributions to the operational phase of this program, both now and later when we move into the deeper waters."

He stepped closer to the model, resting one hand on the top of its tall derrick. "You see, Jori, not only are we going to be drilling in waters of greater depth than before, but this device is also capable of carrying us farther into the crust of the earth than has been previously done.

With this rig we're going to have it all. We are going to be capable of subsurface penetrations to distances beyond even your very vivid imagination." He gazed at her soberly for a moment. "Where there's energy to be found, we're going to find it no matter what the obstacle. The survival of our way of life depends upon it." He glanced wistfully to the window overlooking the sea. "I have visions of greatness for this machine. Not just for Florexco . . . but for all mankind."

The romantic connotations he used in speaking of this incredible undertaking exposed the true scientist in the man. Money was not his motive.

He led her into an outer room where a maid served them brandy in small snifters. She could hardly conceal her excitement as he prepared to discuss his offer.

She knew many companies were still made uneasy by her lack of testicles. Strong male-chauvinistic notions still lingered that offshore drilling was men's work. But she had proven them wrong, despite her soft feminine appearance, because on the job she was all business and the men around her rapidly learned it. She was tough and strict, perhaps more so than the average male. Anything less and she would have failed. Maintaining absolute discipline had been a vital tool of survival, and she had learned to use it well. She had to.

At five-six, she had a delicately slim build with long legs. Even the crudest and heaviest of work clothes could not hide her unmistakably feminine lines. Over the years she had come to dress in such a way that the roundness of her breasts and hips were somewhat hidden, but now that she had advanced to a position of authority, she no longer felt obligated to disguise the fact that she was a woman. As a consequence, she cultivated a more tailored look.

She rarely had trouble with men aboard the rigs. She had learned to handle that; but as a precaution, she had adopted a very cool, aloof behavior pattern—almost an unfriendly attitude toward the men around her. She always made it a point to fire the first man who gave her trouble on any new project. There was hardly ever a second one. One harsh example was usually enough. She knew some thought of her as a bitch, but that was their problem, not hers. She wasn't there to play games with them; she was there to find oil.

And find oil is what she had done. Four years ago, despite the objections of many, she had been given command of her first offshore drilling project. In record time she had brought the well in and had it operationally prepared to go on line as a producing unit. Even now she didn't know whether it had been mere luck or real skill. But her success had been followed almost immediately by other big scores and she had acquired a widely known reputation as a woman who gets the job done.

Her successful development of a modified and more efficient drill-initiation technique had brought her additional honors. But despite the offers that had come in, she had no desire to leave Gulf. She was good and she knew it, but fortune had played a role in her upward climb, and she had been boosted by the confidence and support of brave men within the company. Gulf had given her a chance very few other corporations would have and because of it her loyalty was strong. Only an opportunity like this one could lure her away.

Before they could resume their conversation, a large, handsome Negro man entered. He was totally bald with a noble black face and dark, deep-set eyes. Beneath his perfectly fitted suit, he was evidently muscular and well-built. He waited politely at the door until addressed by Sumter.

"Ah, Hex," the scientist said, "come in, my good friend. I want you to meet Jori Ashe." Sumter glanced at her. "My dear, you've not met Hex St. Claire, have you?"

"No, I haven't," she said, rising and extending her hand.

He shook it firmly. "My pleasure, Miss Ashe." The accent, much like Sumter's, was very British.

She knew immediately who he was, having heard much about him. Hex St. Claire was a native-born Bahamian, educated in England, who had become the scientist's almost constant companion. The man was considered a mystery by most of those at Florexco. He spoke very little and smiled even less. There were many rumors about the role he played in Sumter's life. Some said he was a bodyguard, others guessed he was a good friend, while some claimed he was merely a houseboy. Jori didn't know about the first two, but, as she studied the man before her, it was her impression that Hex St. Claire was not the sort of man to be anyone's houseboy. Whatever he did for Adrian Sumter, it was not in a servant's capacity. Over all, he presented a very powerful, somber, and mysterious appearance.

"Hex, I was just preparing to discuss our offer for this young lady's services as part of our little project. Please join us."

Silently, the black man took the brandy offered him and seated himself opposite Jori.

Sumter waited until they were both comfortable again and then began. "To make a long story short, we need someone like you with us. You have established an enviable record, especially for one of your age and sex,

15

and I have great admiration for your scientific accomplishments. We need a person to supervise the drilling operations who's not merely a mechanic—someone who can understand the complexities of what we are about— who can be flexible and innovative when the situation calls for it. In short, we need a scientist like you. It's a lot of responsibility for a young woman. Imagine it! You would be second in command on St. Lucie One." The intonation of his voice made it sound as if he were offering her the presidency.

Jori was shocked. She could hardly believe what she was hearing. Drawing in a slow breath, she tried to hide her disappointment. Second was not enough. The autonomy and professional authority to make her own decisions in the field was very important. She felt foolish at her own unwarranted excitement.

"There would be a chief of operations over me?" she asked. "I mean, my judgments and decisions could be superseded at any time?"

Sumter sat silently reflecting upon her question while Hex St. Claire gazed steadily at her, his face revealing nothing of his reaction both to Sumter's offer and her resultant inquiry. "Technically, I suppose you could say that," the scientist replied. "The chief of operations will have ultimate control. But for all practical purposes, you will be in charge of the drilling procedures."

Her hopes sagged. "I think I understand. You want me to do the thinking and the work. But someone else will be calling the shots, right? When the chips are down, I'll become the lackey."

"No," Sumter replied slowly, frowning slightly. "I don't see that as a problem. We have full confidence that you will handle yourself in such a way that no overriding

16

of your authority will be necessary."

So that's it, she thought. Once again I'm being offered a job with all the trappings of power and responsibility, but fundamentally it's not there. As soon as I make what someone else calls an error, they will be there to step in and correct me, however politely. It was another offer like many she had received, filled with glowing terms and semblances of authority, but devoid of the real power when push came to shove. Despite the intrigue of the new project, she couldn't accept it. For the sake of her career and the success she had already attained, she could not step down from where she was and once again play the role of the smart young woman who knew a lot about petroleum engineering, but who was not considered quite capable enough to be totally in command. God, how she hated sexual bias! If she had been a man with her record, the job would have been hers for the asking. She was convinced of it.

The two men were watching her intently as she replied. "Dr. Sumter, as much as I relish the opportunity of participating in what you're doing, I don't think you have a real need or place for me. You see, it's taken a long while to reach a position of full command on offshore rigs, and it's a job I dearly love. Gulf has been very good to me and they have shown a great deal of confidence to give me the chances I've had. To make a move now that takes me downward on the ladder of responsibility would be a betrayal of everything I have aimed for. I made a decision long ago to leave the company only to accept a position on a higher management level. What you are offering me, as exciting as it is, is not a move in that direction. I'm very sorry, but I'll have to decline."

Hex St. Claire's expression was unchanged. He

17

continued to watch her carefully, but Sumter's reaction was totally different. He was blatantly surprised. He had obviously thought she would go crazy at the opportunity to take the job.

"But, Jori, don't you understand what a terrific opportunity this is for a woman? You'll never get a chance to do something like this with another company!"

"Perhaps you've missed the point, sir," she replied softly. "I'm not looking for a great opportunity for a woman. I'm looking for a great opportunity for a geological engineer. I simply cannot accept anything that is not at least a lateral move. Career advances are too hard to come by in this industry."

Sumter rose and poured himself another brandy. "Maybe you don't understand how valuable we think you will be. I want you working with us. I think you can contribute. We don't have anyone else with the type of talents you could bring to this project."

"Then give me full authority over the drilling operations. I want autonomy." A tiny spark of hope was relit within her.

Sumter turned to face her. "Jori, why worry so much about who's in charge? You're a scientist. Bring your knowledge and skills to this task. Contribute things you can do best. By that I mean do some of the thinking for us. We don't need another person barking orders; we need someone who can analyze and make decisions."

"Making decisions doesn't count if they can be countermanded immediately by the man one rung up the ladder."

"Be realistic. You're a scientist, not a crew chief."

Jori smiled understandingly. She had dealt with dozens of oil executives with exactly his attitude about her and her career. "I know everyone likes to think of me that way, and that's what my training is—but in my heart, that's not me. I'm just an educated tool-pusher. I started out as one, and I'll always be one. Whatever the future brings me in this business, I want to be in charge of spinning the pipe, and I want to do it my way. It's the one thing I'm truly good at."

Sumter was clearly dismayed. "I don't want to do that. We already have a chief of operations. Winston Loggins is the most experienced man we have. He knows how to get a job done as well as handle the men."

"Then why do you need me?"

Rubbing his chin as he thought, Sumter considered the question from this obstinate but talented young woman. "I need someone with more of a scientific bent out there. All the experience in the world doesn't mean a thing when unexpected trouble occurs. You've established a reputation for trouble-shooting difficult situations. We want that. I need a highly educated analytical mind as well as an experienced man for this project to work."

"I understand your problem," she replied, "and I wish there was some way I could help. Truly I do. It's a magnificent thing you're attempting. But it doesn't look like you really want me specifically. I certainly hope you appreciate my needs to protect my own career." She rose and extended her hand to the scientist. "I suppose I should be on my way. I have an early flight to Houston in the morning. It's been a great pleasure meeting you, and I hope our paths cross again soon. My heart will be with you when you gear up this wonderful creation of yours."

Sumter remained seated. "I still can't believe you're turning me down. Is there anything short of making you

19

chief of operations that would persuade you to join us?"

She watched his face, wondering if she should pursue the topic with him. She paused a long while, considering her options.

"What can we do to compromise?" he said. She could sense his sincerity.

"Perhaps there is a compromise—unorthodox—but it might work," she replied. "Give me complete autonomy as to the drilling procedures, answerable only to you and the company executives. Leave the other man in charge of general operations at the well site, but not of my activities. We could function as co-chiefs. He could run everything else. I would merely be in charge of the actual drilling itself."

Sumter frowned and glanced at Hex St. Claire. "Winston Loggins would eat her alive," the black man said softly.

Sumter nodded. "Jori, Winston Loggins is a very tough and hard-nosed operator. I don't believe he knows how to share power. If he felt threatened by you or was insulted that we had given away responsibilities that should have been his, he'd make your life miserable."

"I understand. It was just a suggestion. I'm sure you're right. Please forget I even said it."

"No, I don't think you do understand. What you're asking is very difficult. A ship shouldn't have two captains. The complications it might provoke are immense. Human interactions are tough enough under stress as it is. Surely you can see that. Isn't there some other arrangement we can work out? I want you out there."

"I don't really think you do, Dr. Sumter. It sounds like you've got the man you want in charge, and I'm sure you have full confidence in his ability to handle whatever problems come up. I sincerely wish you good luck. And now, if someone will show me out, I'd be appreciative. It's been a pleasant visit."

Sumter rose and poured himself a third brandy. He was very distraught.

"You don't know Winston Loggins," Hex said quietly. "He's not a very gentle person, nor is he understanding of the rights of others. He's very egocentric and has a great love of power. He is not an easy person to deal with. If you were made co-chief with him, I doubt if you would be happy with what resulted."

Jori was becoming irritated herself. She realized fully that her chances of getting the position she coveted were almost nonexistent. The most important thing on her mind was getting back to Houston where she was respected and treated as a valuable engineer, irrespective of her sex.

"Why do you want me out there if this Loggins fellow is so good?" she asked. "He can handle the day to day management of the rig, and you'll be available to deal with any complex problems. How could I possibly be of any value with you around?"

"That's exactly the point! I don't plan to be around for the day-to-day occurrences," Sumter responded. "Other obligations are going to occupy my time. I will be spending much of the next year in Europe pursuing matters for the even more distant future. It is neither my role nor my intention to get involved in the management of a drilling platform. I am a scientist, Jori. I deal in research and ideas. My forte is planning and designing, not supervising workers. I need someone exactly like you on site to make sure that the full potential of St. Lucie

One is realized, because I won't be available much of the time."

"Then give me the authority to do the job right," she replied.

"Somehow I can't see you barking orders to a group of tough oil workers." He stared at her intently. "Do you really think you are strong enough to handle that?"

"I certainly do. My record proves it, and the men at Gulf Oil know it."

He took a deep breath, exasperated, and exhaled slowly. "You're a very determined lady, aren't you?" He stood and walked to the window while she waited.

Finally he turned back to her. "You're making it hard on me—surely you see that? I shall be honest with you, Jori. If I respected anyone else enough to offer them the position you've turned down, I would do it without hesitation. Unfortunately, there is no one else. It seems that I have no choice. I don't want to leave this project totally in the hands of Winston Loggins." He paused, gazing at her thoughtfully. "I hope you realize what you're getting into . . . and I hope to God you're tough enough." He took one more sip of his brandy. "They told me you would take nothing less than a command position, and I see they were right. I was prepared to give it to you if you absolutely insisted, as you have. You can have what you want. You can be chief of drilling operations, answerable to no one except the company. Winston Loggins will have no authority over you. All I demand is that you deliver."

He held out his hand. "Six months from now we'll be under way. The work we do is going to make history."

Startled at her sudden victory she felt a surge of exhilaration. She turned to Hex St. Claire who shook her hand firmly. His strong mysterious face revealed nothing of his inner emotions.

"God be with you, Jori Ashe," he said, "you're going to need him. From this moment on, consider me a close friend. In whatever way I can, I'll help you, believe me."

She looked into his coal-dark face and she did believe him.

For an instant she wondered if she were doing the right thing. But quickly the faltering self-confidence was banished. Whatever problems the mammoth undertaking threw at her she could handle. She knew she could— or she would die trying. It was going to be the greatest adventure of her life.

Adrian Sumter offered her another brandy. He seemed relieved that it was all decided. Hex St. Claire stood at the window, looking out to the ocean, seemingly buried in distant thought. He was indeed a curious man. She found his silence somehow disturbing.

ONE

ON EXPLORATION

(From *Seek the Distant Shore*—A compendium of scientific challenges and tragic misadventures.)

There inevitably will come a recognition that not all things are reasonably possible. For the present, our frail species—bold, energetic and adventuresome—is filled with dreams and visions of glory which we pursue with vigor. Sadly, however, there exist waters deep and dark across which we cannot and must not sail.

Like a child untaught, we blunder onward, not yet understanding the dangers of our limitless explorations. Some day we will learn.

Until then, like our fathers before us, we will seek the distant shore.

by Adrian Sumter, Ph.D.
Geophysicist
Florexco

TWO

October

A stiff breeze had come from the east in the last few hours since sunset, and the sea was beginning to build. It had already become quite choppy, and a heavy rain was falling. Standing on the afterdeck of the large transport boat which had brought her to the base of the giant offshore oil rig, Jori Ashe carefully appraised the motion of the vessel and then deftly stepped onto the landing platform. She was immediately drenched by a cold wall of salt spray which swept across the slippery deck, inundating all those standing there. The young woman quickly crossed the loading area and hurried up the stairs to the main deck of the mammoth rig above. After a last look at the big boat bobbing and tugging against its restraints, she stepped through the portal onto the brilliantly lit drilling platform where just three days earlier operations had commenced exactly on schedule.

George Elkins, the aging crew chief, was waiting for her. "I didn't know whether you were going to make it in time, with the wind whipping up like this," the heavy-set, gray-haired man said loudly above the splattering noise of the rain against the steel deck. His normally warm eyes and friendly face showed deep concern. He was obviously very worried. "You'd better get on up to the control booth. Loggins is waiting for you."

"Great. That's just great," she replied sarcastically, frowning. "Where do we stand on pulling the pipe?"

The old man wiped the rain off his face. "We've got most of it out. We should know the answer in a few minutes."

"What do you think, George?"

He shook his head. "I don't know. I've never seen anything quite like it. It's the hardest stuff I've ever tried to drill through. It just shouldn't be there, especially not now, not this early. We're only three hundred feet down."

She nodded, frustrated. "I guess I should have had you make the change an hour ago."

"Yep. In retrospect, I think that's right," he said, looking in the direction of the drill table, where the crew was removing one more section of drill pipe. "But how the hell could you have known? Who would have guessed this would happen? I've never seen anything like it in thirty years of offshore work. If you ask me, there's something awful strange down there."

"What's Loggins's attitude?"

"He's pissed as usual. Blaming you. Saying that you're incompetent."

"Typical," she replied. "He hates me."

"That's for sure, but I'm getting tired of it. If he was so all-fired great, why didn't they put him in charge of the drilling instead of you? I'm sick of his bitching and moaning."

"He won't stop that until he gets rid of me," she said and glanced up at the control booth two levels higher.

She could see Winston Loggins standing in front of the large window, watching them. "I might as well go up there and face him now—and get it over with."

"Be careful," Elkins said, and started back toward the drill table. "He's a callous bastard."

She walked across the main deck and up the stairway leading to the control room. The rain had slackened somewhat, and she stopped momentarily to look down at the men and equipment. The crewmen not involved in the pipe-withdrawal operation had wandered out onto the main deck and were milling around nervously. They were unusually quiet, almost somber. She sensed a peculiar feeling of uneasiness, and she didn't like it. It was too early in the drilling to be having problems, particularly strange troubles like this. She didn't have any idea what they had hit or why they couldn't get through it. It didn't make sense.

But that was why she had returned to the well tonight. For the moment, drilling had stopped, but it was her intention to get it started again. She noticed the new drill bit, still in its wooden crate. It had been moved into place, ready to be put to use should she give the word.

As she continued up the stairs, dreading another battle in her perpetual conflict with Loggins, she could feel the intense scrutiny of the unoccupied crewmen. They were waiting, ready to judge her. To them, she was still unproven and her presence on the project had added an extra element to the ever-present anxieties of offshore workers. For some of them it was difficult accepting a woman as boss. It was something unusual, something different—and old suspicions die hard. But suspicions or not, she was in command, and the problem was going to be solved her way.

At the top of the stairs a door led into the large control room. Loggins was sitting in front of the monitoring equipment. He spun around to glare at her with blatant disdain. "Looks like you were wrong again," he said caustically. "I told you to switch to the other drill bit. If you weren't so stubborn, you'd take good advice when it was given."

He was tall and muscular, about forty years old, and if she hadn't disliked him so much, she would have found him handsome. He had well-kept black hair which he wore down over his ears. A bushy black mustache curving past the corners of his mouth added to his very masculine appearance. His eyes were a dark gray, widely set in a strong, square face. Although he could display a pleasant smile, his frown was cold, at times cruel.

"Winston," she said, "I make decisions just like you do. I have to play the odds. In this case I might have been wrong, but I'll get it straightened out."

"You're just going to have to learn to share the responsibility for some of the major decisions," he replied. "If you had just listened to me, this wouldn't have happened. This kind of crap costs the company a lot of money."

"There comes a point when a decision can't be shared," she responded coolly. "It's either black or white. My way or yours. In this case, since I'm in charge of drilling operations, we'll have to do it my way."

"Don't give me that! You don't have complete autonomy to do whatever the hell you want to," he said, obviously irritated. "We've only been drilling three days and you've already screwed us up. As overall chief of operations, I have the authority to insist on some shared responsibility in certain critical areas."

"Look, Winston, you and I both know now that it was a mistake to divide authority on this rig. But there's nothing we can do about it. We've got to live with it. So you do your thing, and I'll do mine. If the company had wanted you to make all the decisions, they wouldn't have put me in charge of the drilling."

As she said it, she thought again about the day she had insisted on the novel command structure. Unfortunately, it just had not worked, despite an enthusiastic effort on her part. Loggins had reacted exactly as Sumter and Hex had predicted. He was in charge of overall operations and she controlled the drilling. But Loggins, who had expected to be totally in control, was bitter and hostile and resented her presence. He was doing everything possible to undermine her authority and humiliate her. She was determined, however, to run the drilling exactly as she thought it should be run—exactly the way her father had taught her. She was going to drill and drill hard.

"Kid yourself as much as you want to, Jori," Loggins said, "but I'm putting you on warning right now that I will countermand anything you do from now on that I think is to the detriment of this operation. I gave you your chance and you blew it."

She ignored him and stood in front of the big window looking down at the workmen surrounding the drill table. A soft bell rang and the intercom relayed George Elkins's voice.

"We're getting ready to pull this drill bit out. If you two want to come down and take a look at it, it's just about time."

She walked across the room and pressed the talk button. "Thanks, George, we're on our way." Loggins

29

rose and left the room without a word, but she paused in front of the large geological drawing above the intercom, staring at it in dismay. How could Sumter have made such an important mistake? she wondered. The chart, drawn under his supervision, indicated no evidence of major rock formations until at least seven hundred feet—a tremendous misjudgment proven by tonight's problem. Just beyond three hundred feet, they had drilled into it less than two hours ago. Even more surprising than the abnormal presence of rock at this unexpected depth was the hardness of the layer they had reached. After two hours of intense effort, they had, incredibly, made no progress and quite probably had done extensive damage to a very expensive experimental steel bit.

It had been her decision to continue drilling with steel as opposed to changing to the tungsten diamond bit—which was somewhat harder and more appropriately designed for this sort of task, but which resulted in a loss of efficiency and speed. She had hoped to break through the layer quickly with the steel and then proceed on at a rapid clip, avoiding an early change to the slower tool, but it was not to be. Now, to her chagrin and Loggins's hidden delight, they were waiting to see what damage had been done as a result of her decision.

She turned away from the chart and went down the stairs. Two stories below in the center of the football-field-size main working platform was the drill table, the actual heart of the operations. The spinning drill pipe passed through an opening there into the dark waters below and descended through 1,400 feet of Atlantic Ocean to reach the sea floor. The giant engines that turned the pipe lay to the left, one level above the drill table. The derrick itself towered over the main deck, which stood ninety feet above the water. The huge structure was a complex maze of latticework and steel, efficiently designed for maximum utilization of the space housing the equipment, tools, and engines, as well as the living quarters for the men themselves. Scattered over the seven different levels on the rig were men and the machines they worked. At the moment, however, most of the crew and their equipment were stilled as they awaited her decision.

The tool pushers were removing the last section of pipe as she approached. Most of the remaining crew were crowded around, anxious to see what had happened to the drill bit in its encounter with the strange rock. Without a word they parted and allowed her to pass through to stand just at the edge of the clearly marked off no man's zone, which was entered only by the tool pushers when the rig was in operation. She stood by George Elkins and waited passively along with the others as the machinery was prepared to pull the instrument clear of the casing so that it could be inspected. The chief tool pusher was making a final inspection of the giant clamp holding the bit prior to ordering it withdrawn.

A few yards away stood Winston Loggins, folding and unfolding his arms repeatedly. His impatience was obvious. The rest of the crew, mindful of his unpredictable temperament, were standing well clear of him, not wishing to become victims of his wrath. "Come on! Goddamn you guys!" he finally yelled. "Quit screwing around and get that thing out here where we can look at it. We don't have all night!"

The chief tool pusher, a tall, gaunt, older man, cast an angry glance in his direction and started to speak, but

31

then thought better of it and ordered the bit pulled.

Slowly the five tons of steel, the essence of the drilling, was lifted up and swung away from the drill table and then lowered to within five feet of the platform where it could be easily examined. Even before the huge engine of the winch had been shut down, the crew, filled with anticipation, surged forward to get a better look at the giant blades, the biting edge of the bit. What they saw shocked even the most experienced of the men. Jori was dumbfounded. Even Winston Loggins was uncharacteristically silent. The cutting edge of all six blades had been ground completely off. What had been a razor-sharp, precision-crafted tool designed to chew its way through the hardest of earth had been reduced to a ragged mass of worn-off, broken, and bent pieces of metal. The bit had been destroyed.

The silence was rapidly broken by the excited talk of the men as they each shoved forward to get a look. The chief tool pusher and George, along with Jori and Loggins, stood silently examining the remains of the device. They ran their hands along the destroyed blades, oblivious to the exclamations of shock and amazement being uttered all around them.

Loggins took his hands off the broken metal and angrily pointed a finger into Jori's face from little more than a foot away. "It's your stubbornness that did this." His voice was filled with hostility. "If you had listened to me, it would never have happened. If you were a man, I'd punch you right in the nose."

Overwhelmed, she stared coldly back at him. The confrontation with the disastrous results of her misjudgment combined with his continuing belligerent attitude was too much. Reflexly, she struck back. "Don't

32

start that macho crap with me," she said bitterly. "If I were a man, I know what you would want to do to me."

He looked stung. The surprising reference to his personal life had found its mark. His face went white. "You little bitch," he muttered. "I'm going to get you for that." He turned to the crew chief and spoke more loudly, "George, I've seen enough of this screw-up. Get the drilling back under way as soon as possible and keep me informed." He started to leave, but then turned back to her. "Whatever you do, you damned well better take it easy. I don't think the company can afford much more of your stupidity."

He strode quickly through the crowd, pushing a small Mexican worker roughly to one side as he went. The rest of the crew gave him wide passage as he stomped away from the drill table toward the helicopter waiting at the far end of the main deck. A few minutes later the craft's engines had been started, and it slowly lifted away from the helipad and disappeared into the night.

With Loggins's departure the crew began to scatter while Jori, still bewildered by the unexpected extent of the damage to the bit, continued her inspection of the crumpled steel. George Elkins stood by, waiting.

As the area around them cleared, Red Ferman, the chief engine mechanic, came down from his post on the level above to inspect the damage for himself. He was in his mid-thirties, short, stocky, with a ruddy complexion that matched his thinning red hair. He whistled as he ran his fingers along the twisted edge of one blade. "Holy smoke," he said, dragging out the words for emphasis. "That's some kind of rock we're trying to bust through. I don't ever remember seeing one torn up like this."

Jori gazed thoughtfully at Ferman and then turned to

33

the crew chief. "I don't understand it, George. What could do this to solid steel?"

Elkins shrugged. "I don't know. We drilled pretty hard, damned hard, for almost two hours without making any kind of progress at all. That sort of thing can be rough." He put one hand back onto the twisted metal. "But I've never heard of anything like this. I've never seen a bit get messed up this bad in that short a period of time, regardless of what we were drilling through."

She looked again at Ferman, who was obviously waiting around to hear her decision. He had been the chief mechanic on a couple of wells before, working for Loggins, and she didn't exactly trust him. He knew his business, though, and was a very experienced drill mechanic. "You're not having any mechanical problems, are you, Red?" she asked.

"No. Nothing's wrong. These babies are humming."

"Good, because we're going to need all the muscle you've got. When we start up again, I want to throw every bit of weight and power that you can muster out of those engines to punch through this layer, whatever it is. I want an all-out effort, maximum plus. We're going to get through this stuff quick and get on with it."

Ferman was puzzled. "But I thought Loggins said for us to take it easy, go slow on this thing."

"It doesn't make any difference what Loggins wants. I'm in charge of the drilling," she responded tartly.

"But I thought—"

"I don't care what you thought," she interrupted. "Just get ready to give us maximum output."

Frustrated, Ferman glanced back and forth from George to Jori. "But, Miss Ashe, Mr. Loggins clearly said that—"

"Save it, Red," Elkins stopped him. "Jori's not interested in what you thought Mr. Loggins said. She's calling the shots. Just make sure your engines are ready to go."

Ferman stared at both of them in disbelief. "All right, goddamn it! But I don't like it!" He stalked toward the ladder leading up to the engine deck.

Jori and Elkins walked slowly away from the suspended bit and up the stairs to the control booth. "I just don't understand this, George," she said. "Geologically, it doesn't make sense. Something must be wrong."

Elkins grimaced. "I'm not sure. The mud washings don't have any chips at all. There's no way to know what's down there without more information."

"It must have been a defective bit. It just has to be. There's no other reasonable explanation." She was profoundly puzzled and concerned.

"Maybe Sumter just made a mistake," Elkins replied. "Nobody's perfect."

She turned to look at him. "Do you really believe that? Sumter making a stupid error like this? I sure don't."

"I guess not." He shrugged. "He's worked too hard on this one. What are we going to do now?"

She was surprised at the question. "Put on the diamond. What else? Let's get started as soon as we can."

Elkins frowned. "It's a risk. If we charge into that rock full steam, we might just punch through it. On the other hand, there's a chance we might not. We could tear up the diamond—just like this one."

"We're just going to have to take that chance. A halfhearted effort might put even more strain on the machinery if we don't get anywhere. I think it'd be better to go all out and just get it done."

"All right. Loggins won't like it, of course, and if we have any more trouble, there's going to be hell for you to pay."

"I'll face that when I get there," she said. "Loggins's problem is that he's too conservative sometimes. I may have made a mistake at first, but I can't let that keep me from doing what I think is best now. It cost us a lot of money to tear up that bit. But, for the company's sake, we just have to cut our losses and keep going. Standing around wringing our hands is not going to get us anywhere. It's just bad luck that we hit this stuff so soon, whatever the hell it is."

"Jori, it's your decision and I'll do what you want. You know what you're doing, but I want you to understand that you're taking a risk, pushing this equipment that hard. That diamond's quite a lot tougher. It may just hold up under the strain until one of the engines fails. We could burn up a main bearing. If that happens, Loggins is going to have your hide."

"Come on, George! For Pete's sake, don't you start getting on me, too. I have enough trouble as it is. Sumter's going to be all over me if I don't get moving soon. It costs too much money to have this rig in operation and not be making progess. So let's do it my way, all right?"

Elkins looked hurt. "Okay," he said quietly and turned away.

She was immediately sorry for her remark. The old man was the best friend she had on the well. He had worked with her father before he died, years ago. "Wait a minute, George. I didn't mean that like it sounded," she said. "I'm just under stress, okay?"

He smiled understandingly. "I know. It's this running

battle between you and Loggins. It looks like it's getting pretty rough. I don't know how much longer you two can keep it up."

She shook her head glumly and sat down. "It's taking its toll on me. I guess I can't hide it. The stresses of this job are enough on their own without having him on my back all the time."

"I want to warn you about him," George said. "You haven't known him as long as I have. He's a very ambitious man, and he can be extremely vicious. He's vindictive, too. I think it's dangerous for you to push him like you did down there. He's got a violent streak that slips out every now and then."

"You meant about the macho stuff?"

"You know what I mean. Nobody talks about it, but he's got his problem. I've seen him do some very cruel things. I wouldn't bait him if I were you."

"Nobody knows about him better than I do, believe me," she replied.

Elkins raised his eyebrows in curious interest. As he continued to eye her expectantly, she stood up and forced a more cheerful expression.

"Well, there's nothing I can do about that now," she said. "I'm afraid the die is cast between the two of us. I'll just have to live with it. But one thing's for sure! I asked for this job and I'm going to finish it. I can't quit now, no matter what. I'm going to see this job through to the end."

"Just be careful. That's all I'm asking," he replied. "Now, in the meantime, go get some rest. If anything comes up I can't deal with, I'll get in touch with you."

"Maybe I should stay until you make sure that we're okay."

"No, I don't think that's necessary," he said. "It's going to be a couple of hours before we can start again anyway, and you've got to be back here early in the morning. There's nothing you can do just standing around out here waiting. We can handle it."

"All right, George. I'll call you before I go to bed." She headed down the stairs, as he gave the appropriate orders to prepare to restart the drilling.

On the main deck, a group of men began to uncrate the new bit. It was an impressive instrument. The shiny new blades gleamed and sparkled in the glare of the intense lighting. Even more awesome than the huge steel bit, this new tool would do it. She was sure of it. The question remained, though. Why? Why was this change necessary so soon? Her lack of understanding fueled her sense of defeat at what had happened. She knew she couldn't afford any more big mistakes if she were going to maintain her credibility with the crew. She wished Sumter were around to give her advice. But as usual he wasn't. He certainly had not exaggerated when he said the routine functioning of the rig would be up to Loggins and her. The scientist, brilliant as he was, evidently hated day-to-day responsibility.

By the time she reached the loading platform, the captain, anxious to get on his way, had already started the big boat's engine. The vessel, shielded from the waves by a steel jetty, rocked slowly as the ocean swells passed beneath it. Three of the drill crew were waiting to help her aboard and to handle the dock lines. There was the small young Mexican Loggins had pushed earlier, a short fat man, and a tall skinny one. They made a motley group. She felt them staring at her, but no one spoke as she carefully climbed aboard and stepped down into the cockpit at the rear of the boat. She glanced back at the three men and became annoyed with the way they were still looking at her. She glared at them until their eyes turned away, and then she disappeared into the cabin.

On a signal from the captain, the three men loosened the lines and tossed several of them to the mate standing in the cockpit and then coiled and stowed the others. They stood together, watching as the boat slowly edged away from the rig and threw up a huge line of spray as it roared off into the night.

"How would you like to get a hold of a woman like that, Paco?" one of them—the short, middle-aged, beer-bellied man with the dirty T-shirt—said to the young Mexican standing beside him. The Mexican didn't speak, but smiled broadly while continuing to watch the boat. "She's one hell of a tough, good-looking bitch, ain't she?" the fat man said.

"Shit! She ain't as tough as she thinks," the tallest of the three said, taking off his hard hat and wiping his grease-smeared face with a handkerchief. He smiled and showed his rotten teeth. "I'd like to have about an hour to get my hands all over those nice round tits and that cute little ass. She'd be singing a different song when I got through pumping it to her. She wouldn't be so worried about drilling wells as she would be begging my sweet ass for more."

The fat man bellowed with laughter. "Paco, you hear that stupid turd? A woman like that would eat him alive." He turned to the tall man and slapped him on the back. "Duaine, you'd better get a hold of your senses. That lady'd kill you. She'd hang your balls on the wall. There ain't no man around here that could handle her, except a few of them oil execs, maybe."

39

"Screw you!" Duaine responded. "I'd like to get my mouth on those tits for a minute and let that long hair of hers hang down all over my face."

"You dirty-mouthed bastard!" The fat man laughed uproariously, and the three went up the stairs with Paco leading the way. Their light mood soon vanished, and they walked soberly across the platform to join the drilling crew. Twenty feet higher, up on the control deck, they could see the chief mechanic, Red Ferman, standing with George. The two men were obviously in disagreement. The mechanic was waving his hands wildly and pointing in the direction of the main engines.

"What's going on up there?" the fat man asked one of the tool pushers standing nearby.

"They want more power to get through this rock," the man answered. "Red says we're going to burn up an engine if we push it any harder."

"Shit! Work will sure stop then," the fat man said. "I can't afford no layoffs right now."

"Don't matter," Paco said. "Work's going to stop anyway."

"What do you mean?"

"That ain't no rock we hit. Ain't no rock that hard. We ain't gonna get through it. We gonna have to quit."

"You stupid Mexican!" the fat man said. "What the hell do you know about drilling? Ain't nothing we can't get through with this equipment. I mean nothing."

"Tiempo lo dira," Paco said.

"Cut out that Mexican shit. What'd that mean?"

"Time will tell," Paco answered.

"You got a lot to learn, Paco," the fat man said and walked away. He stopped for a moment and looked back toward the Mexican and shook his head. "You got an

40

awful goddamned lot to learn about drilling oil wells."

Paco stood staring at him, his expression unchanged, and then glanced up to watch the chief mechanic leave the control platform and return to the power deck. The roar of the giant diesel began to increase.

"Tiempo lo dira," Paco said again quietly to himself.

"Shut up, Paco, and get to work," the chain man said, pointing to the drill table. Paco eyed him resentfully, but did as he was told.

Harpoon Harry's nightclub and raw bar restaurant was one step above being a crummy dive. Barely one step. But the garishly lit place along the Florida ocean front was an extremely popular hangout for the local singles set. The layout of the club allowed easy circulation and social mixing. Jori had spent a fair amount of her free time in Harry's, and on occasion it had paid off handsomely. In the past few years, she had become an expert at the singles game, and Harry's was just the sort of place to play it when one was hungry for that sort of thing. The more she thought about it, the better the idea sounded. She needed something to get her mind off the well and its problems. And besides, the seafood at Harry's was great.

She swung her Datsun into the restaurant's crowded parking lot. The joint was divided into two halves: the restaurant to the north, the night club to the south. She chose the former. One customer was sitting at the raw bar viciously attacking his oysters, but the rest of the nautically flavored room was deserted—with the exception of a waiter, who was sweeping.

Benny, the oyster expert, the man who ran the raw bar, greeted her with a smile which she returned. The darkness of the room made his white teeth shine brightly against the background of his black face and the dark rubber apron he was wearing. He was a prototypical old-fashioned black man, subservient and almost obsequious to whites. He worked hard and wanted to keep his job. But honestly, she sometimes felt as if he were about to break into a tap dance or try to shine some shoes. She held her hand up in greeting as she walked past. "Good evening, Benny. How about a dozen when you get time?" The man bowed politely as she continued through the restaurant to the open deck at the back. The throb of the rock band next door seemed louder than usual. So did the noise of the crowd. Just being in the place made Jori feel better. She definitely liked Harpoon Harry's.

The deck was large and extended out over the beach below. It opened to both sides of the establishment. There were about a dozen round tables that resembled power cable spools. Seven or eight high stools were around each of them. She sat at her usual table against the railing where she had a commanding view of the nightclub area. Anchors, old buoys, crab traps, and other seagoing paraphernalia were scattered here and there throughout the old wooden building. The sliding glass doors were pushed wide open, and the overhead fans on both sides of the place were going full blast. The open deck area was a little chilly, however, as there was a good breeze from the sea. Her oysters arrived shortly, along with a Margarita on the rocks. As she ate, the noise quieted down with the band taking a break. A handful of dancers drifted out onto the deck, occupying several of the tables around her and leaning against the rails looking out over the dark sea.

Overhearing isolated bits of conversation here and

there, watching the couples enjoying each other's company, she experienced a surge of loneliness. It was a hard life she was leading. Separated from the people with whom she had grown up back in Texas, both of her parents dead, and no siblings or close relatives, she felt alone. For the first time in a long while, she thought of the only real love she had ever had.

She had been seventeen at the time, a freshman at college, and it had been the happiest year of her life. She had given the boy her virginity, and he had done for her first what no one since then had ever done better. It was a bittersweet memory, but she was glad her father had kept her from the marriage she had thought she wanted. She knew now that she wouldn't have been happy married to Johnny. But she had been so contented during the year she spent with him—secure, dependent upon him, and enjoying their young adulthood and sexuality. It seemed so strange to compare herself now with herself then. She couldn't remember when she had emerged from a soft-spoken, sweet, and completely giving person into the woman she had become. Sometimes, on nights like this one, she longed to go back. As crazy as it seemed, she envied the girls she saw around her, the ones who could lean on and draw strength from a dominant male. It's the booze, she thought, looking down at her drink. The booze and the unnatural stress of fighting men every minute of her day that made her feel this way.

Anxious to snap out of her self-pity, she looked up and down the empty beach behind her and gazed out over the ocean. The sky was still overcast. The moon was not visible, but the weather was more pleasant than earlier in the evening. In the distance, almost ten miles away, the lights of the St. Lucie One rig could be seen clearly.

When she turned back to the dance floor again, she saw the most handsome man she had seen in a long while. The blond, slightly older Adonis came out from the club to the edge of the deck. Like all women, she had an eye for good-looking men, but this one had special appeal. He stood for a moment looking around, obviously on the hunt, and then took a sip of his drink. She watched him, debating whether he was a sailor or surfer, or perhaps a combination of the two. He was a definite golden boy just beyond the radiance of his youth, maybe in his mid-thirties, but he was still beautiful. Probably six feet tall, she judged. He was built slim, but muscular. The most appealing thing about him was his hair and beard. He had a thick, curly head of blondish-brown hair with streaks of gray. His beard was the same, but with a little more gray. It was a full one, clipped closely, neatly following the angle of his jaw. It looked soft and velvety. He had a narrow face and slightly hollow cheeks that made him seem a little hungry. To her, he had big beautiful blue eyes that looked warm and alive—and slightly lonely. He was, all in all, very masculine appearing and very attractive. He was wearing long white pants with a thin belt and old-fashioned penny loafers. His shirt was light blue with an open collar. Just watching him made her feel better, and she smiled.

He continued to look around the deck, and then his eyes fell on her, and her grin grew broader despite her efforts to control it. He came immediately toward her.

"Hello," he said when he reached her table, his voice deep and strong with a very subtle hint of a southern accent. "You're one of the geologists from Florexco?"

His knowledge caught her by surprise. "Yes, but how—"

44

"I heard you talk at the Ecology Club," he interrupted. "I would've asked you out, but I'm afraid of smart women."

"What makes you think I'm so smart?" she said, smiling.

"Because you're good-looking."

She felt as if she were going to blush, but hoped she wouldn't. "What has that got to do with it?"

"You see, I have this theory about women," he began, his tone warm and friendly. "When you see a successful career girl—I don't mean the secretarial types—I mean the one who's had to really do something to get where she is, a professional, so to speak . . . there are only two types: the pretty ones and the two-baggers." He paused, looking at her, obviously waiting for a response.

"All right. I'll bite. What's a two-bagger?"

"The two baggers are the ones who are so ugly that, if you take them to bed, it takes two bags. One to put over her head and the other to put over your own, just in case the one on her head falls off." He grinned.

"Oh Christ!" she said, continuing to smile. "I hope there's not more where that came from."

He continued. "So much for that story. But anyway, back to my theory. The ugly ones aren't necessarily smart. It's just that they had to succeed in order to get anywhere in life, so they were willing to work real hard. Sometimes even the dumb ones can make it, just on effort. But the good-looking ones—that's a different story. They have it made anyway. They don't have to do a thing. So, odds are, they wouldn't be willing to work too hard or make very much sacrifice. So if they make it big, the only conclusion is that they must be so smart it all came easy." He smiled and shrugged. "So . . . when I see a very successful, very good-looking lady I know that she must be damn smart."

She nodded slowly with a chagrined expression. "That is about as distorted a bit of male chauvinism as I've ever heard. But I've got to admit it's original." She was liking him more and more every minute. "So what is it about smart women that makes you afraid?"

"A smart woman likes to emasculate a man, put his testicles in her back pocket."

She laughed. "These pants don't have any back pockets. So you're safe. What were you doing at the ecology meeting, anyway?"

"I'm big on the environment. Mostly I'm against nuclear power plants, but I don't like oil companies either. I sort of participated in the effort to keep Florexco from drilling out there."

"Score one for the oil companies."

"Yes," he muttered. "Can't win them all. But we're watching you guys, so be careful." The waitress arrived and he reordered a drink for each of them. "I'm Blain Robson," he said when she had left.

"And I'm Jori Ashe." She held out her hand which he grasped and held a bit longer than cordiality required. She found him definitely very attractive. "You seem to know a lot more about me than I do about you," she said. "Do you ever have to work?"

"Yes, unfortunately. What do you think I do? Take a guess."

She smiled again. "All right. Let's see. I'll bet that you teach surfing lessons by day, and at night you bring in loads of cocaine in small sailboats through the inlet."

For the first time he laughed, and she knew she was beginning to charm him. "No," he replied, and rubbed

46

one hand along the side of his beard. "I'm too straight for that. I'm a surgeon."

Her mouth dropped slightly open in surprise. "A surgeon!" she said. "You're a surgeon? You don't look like a surgeon."

He seemed pleased. "I don't? What do I look like?"

"I just told you, a surfing instructor. Maybe a little beyond your teenage prime, but you don't look like the average doctor, that's for sure."

"What are doctors supposed to look like?"

"I dated one once, an anesthesiologist named Melvin, and he didn't look like you. He was more of a two-bagger type."

He laughed again. "Melvin," he said. "That's a good name for an anesthesiologist."

"He didn't like surgeons too much. He told me most of them were dumb bunnies. Guys that should've been carpenters or mechanics, but somehow lucked their way into medical school and then realized they weren't smart enough to cut it. So they stayed away from the tough stuff like internal medicine."

He chuckled. "It's sort of true. I do feel like a carpenter sometimes, or maybe a seamstress, leaving all the deep thinking to the medical boys. I'll concede the point. As a group, the surgeons aren't the smartest guys in medicine. I can't believe you went out with a guy named Melvin, though. He doesn't sound like your type."

She grinned. "He wasn't. But I was short on men at the time. He told me a good story about surgeons though."

"Let's hear it."

"Well, it seems that it took place in the future in the days of popular transplant operations when almost anything was possible. They were transplanting hearts, livers, brains, anything, and whenever someone wanted to change his occupation he went into the brain transplant shop and picked out one of the available brains and had it put in."

Blain nodded, pleasantly suspicious. "Go on."

"Well," Jori continued, "this particular guy was a draftsman, and he was unhappy with his work. So he went in and looked over what was available. The first brain he looked at was an architect's brain, and it was three hundred dollars a pound. The next brain he saw was a geologist's brain. It was three hundred and fifty dollars a pound. Then he came across an anesthesiologist's brain for four hundred dollars a pound. And finally, there was one container with surgeon brains and it was two thousand dollars a pound. So he called the proprietor over and said, 'Look here, buddy, how come for anesthesiologist's brains it's only four hundred dollars a pound and yet for surgical brains it's two thousand dollars a pound?'

"'Listen son,' the proprietor said, 'do you know how many surgeons it takes to get a pound of brain?'"

He laughed as she smiled. "That sounds like a joke a goddamn anesthesiologist would tell," he said. "Now let me tell you one. It seems that they were having this combined meeting between oil company people and some environmentalists, and they were holding it in Egypt. One day after the meeting a couple of these oil company execs decided to go see a soccer match, so they rented this camel to ride over. So while they were both riding on this camel over to the match, they saw a couple of the environmentalists and waved at them. Then they went on to the game. Afterwards, when they came out the entire

48

stadium was surrounded with camels, and they couldn't figure out which one was theirs. Finally, one of the oil company guys was walking around behind each camel lifting up the tail looking at the rear end. And the other guy says, 'What're you doing?' The first guy says, 'Well, I think I can figure out which camel is ours. Don't you remember a while ago when we were coming to the game we saw those two environmentalists and they waved at us?' The second guy says, 'Yes.' So the first guy says, 'Well, I heard one of them say, "Hey, look at those two assholes on that camel."'"

She grinned with him and they both took sips of their drinks and watched as the crowd moved back out toward the dance floor. The band had started again, and it was better than most at Harry's. The kid playing the electronic synthesizer was a good musician.

With three Margaritas inside her, good music in the background, and this new, very interesting man beside her, Jori was slipping into a mellow mood. The last person in the world she wanted to see was Winston Loggins, but as she looked across the deck that's exactly who she saw emerging from the club and coming straight toward her. She felt at once agitated, resentful, and angry.

He looked and sounded as if he had been drinking. His expression was wild. He seemed totally oblivious of the people around them. "I've been looking for you, goddamn it," he said. "Sometimes the things you do surprise even me, and I'm getting pretty used to your stupid stunts."

"Winston," she said quietly, remaining seated, "this is not the place. If there's something on your mind, we can talk about it in the morning."

"Screw that," he said angrily. "You're going out to the

49

office right now and call Elkins and tell him to slow down on the drilling. I won't have you tearing up another bit."

Everyone around them became quiet. He was attracting a great deal of attention. She felt embarrassed and hated him for humiliating her like this. Blain had pushed back his stool and was now standing beside her. "I'm not going to do anything of the sort," she said softly. "I've made my decision and we'll stick with it. Now, please, go away and let me alone. You're making a spectacle of yourself."

"I'm not going away, and you are going to do as I say. Now get up!" He put one hand on her arm as if to lift her from her chair.

"Get your hands off me!" she said, pushing his arm away and standing up immediately beside Blain. "You don't have any authority over me. I'm in charge of the drilling, not you."

"Don't give me that, you little bitch. I've worked too long and too hard on this project to let you ruin it. You're going to do it my way or be sorry."

People were beginning to stand around them now watching the bizarre scene. She wished desperately that he would go away.

Blain had an angry puzzled expression. "Just a minute, buddy," he said. "You better lower your voice a little bit and calm down. This lady's not doing anything to you."

"Keep out of this, asshole," Loggins said, casting a furious glance in his direction.

"Winston, please. You're causing a scene. I think you're drunk. If you don't stop they're going to call the police. Let me alone. I don't want to fight with you. I don't even know how you found me here."

"You little piece of trash. Don't you know how I knew

you were here?" His expression became a vicious smile. "Every man in town knows where to find Jori Ashe. The problem is getting here early enough, before you've already sunk your teeth into some guy's cock."

Her eyes filled with tears, and her head swirled with rage and hostility at his verbal assault. She became totally oblivious to the people around her. She would've killed him if she could. She leaned forward, pushed him in the chest with her index finger and insulted him in the worst way she knew. "That's the one thing you and I have in common, isn't it, Winston?" she said bitterly. "We both love men."

As she said it, she realized it would've been best left unsaid. Loggins's face reflected an uncontrollable, almost animal-like rage. She never saw his right hand coming up toward her, but she felt the smashing blow against the left side of her face. Her head jerked around. For a moment the room spun and there was a roar in her ears as she careened backwards, knocking over several chairs and rolling to the floor. She felt dizzy and confused. Where was she? Her mouth was filled with blood. She heard a beating in the background and wondered if it was her heart or the band. Everything was black, and her eyes wouldn't focus. She heard girls screaming and felt herself being stepped on as people jumped away from her.

An instant later she realized what had happened. She propped herself up to a sitting position and spit out a mouthful of blood. Loggins, wild-eyed, was standing above her. Everything seemed to be moving in slow motion. Blain Robson had drawn back a fist to hit Winston Loggins—and would have if the dark night around them hadn't been turned into day by a

51

tremendous flash that came from the ocean.

At first, it was almost as if a huge strobe had gone off. The entire sky and sea around them had been turned into the bright glare of midday for almost a second. As rapidly as it lit up, it turned dark again. The band immediately stopped, and the stunned crowd stood quiet and motionless.

Several empty seconds later, the bizarre flash came again. The night was transformed into day. The beach was as bright as noontime, and the ocean was visible for miles. The clouds were lit up in perfect detail. The darkness was totally gone. Again, it lasted for almost a second, but this time when it faded, it took with it all the lights. The electricity went off.

Jori, coughing and choking on the blood in her mouth, remained on the floor propped up on hands and knees, crying uncontrollably. She was still disoriented and frightened. Tears mixed with blood and saliva fell in large drops onto the wooden deck in front of her. More than anything else, she wanted her father. As she slowly pushed herself to her feet, still sobbing, the people around her began to shout and point in the direction of St. Lucie One.

There on the horizon was a bluish-green, shimmering, fiery ember. The crowd lunged toward the railings, chattering excitedly. The glowing ball in the distance seemed to be pulsating and throbbing. Its size grew slowly into a large sphere of glimmering green. It seemed to pulsate for a moment, and then, after a burst of brilliant light, it flickered back to its earlier size before it slowly grew once more to explode in a shocking brilliance. The ocean around it lit up, and then suddenly the inferno was gone.

The sea became instantly dark again. The night returned, but the lights of St. Lucie One were gone.

Everyone in the crowd was talking and shouting as Jori's head began to clear. Winston Loggins was gone. Her mouth tasted of blood. She felt a hand on her arm and turned to Blain.

Before she could speak, the lights came back on. "Are you okay?" he asked. Her shirt was spattered with blood.

"I think so," she said thickly. Her tongue felt numb and swollen. "Am I bleeding?" She buried her face in her hands and began sobbing again as he put his arms around her.

"You're all right," he said. "Everything's going to be okay." She looked up at him, trying to regain her composure. "Your face is fine," he said. "It must be inside your mouth. Let me see." She dutifully opened wide while he examined her. "There's a laceration of your tongue and the inside of your cheek's torn up, too. You're going to need some stitches."

"What happened?" she said. She still felt confused.

"That bastard hit you. Who was he?"

"No. I mean those lights." She stared in the direction of the rig. "Something's happened on the well. It must have been an explosion."

"I'm more concerned about you. Are you going to be all right?"

"Yes," she responded and glanced around. The people not looking out over the ocean were watching her. She felt like a side show. "I've got to get out to the well. Something terrible's happened."

"You can't go now," he said. "You've got to let me patch you up first. You're bleeding too much."

She shook her head. "No. You'll have to fix that later.

I've got to go out there. They might need my help."

"Don't be crazy. You're injured, Jori. You could be hurt worse than you think."

"Okay, as soon as I find out what's happened out there, I'll get it fixed. I think the bleeding's stopping now, anyway."

She stood at the rail, studying the dark horizon. There was nothing, total emptiness. "I can't believe it," she said. "It looks like the rig is completely gone." She began to wipe the tears from her eyes and then, unexpectedly, began to cry again.

He put one arm around her, gazing alternately at her bleeding, puffy mouth and out over the empty, silent sea.

THREE

The headquarters for Florexco's St. Lucie One drilling operation was just inside the inlet of the St. Lucie River at the tip of Hutchinson Island, thirty miles north of Palm Beach. It was bordered on three sides by water—the ocean, the river, and the inlet between the two. A number of large docks, loading platforms, and supply storage areas, as well as the headquarters building, were spread over the isolated tract of beach front. From Harpoon Harry's it was five miles south, down the narrow strip of land between the ocean and the river, to the company's security check point. The desolate stretch was almost entirely undeveloped, except for Jori's small rented home on the beach between the two.

When she reached the Florexco compound, the place was in a state of pandemonium. People were running back and forth between the main building and helipads, as well as the dock area. No one seemed to know what the hell was going on. The first helicopter lifted off before she had a chance to get aboard. Presumably Loggins was in it. A small group of men were out on the docks preparing one of the crew boats to go. As she started toward them, she spotted Daryl Hayes, one of the helicopter pilots, coming out of the main building. She ran quickly across the parking lot and caught him just as he reached the remaining craft.

"What happened out there, Daryl?" she asked the short-haired Vietnam veteran.

"I don't know," he answered, frowning, "but we're going to find out in about ten minutes. They won't answer their radio call at all. It doesn't look good."

She climbed in beside him. "Has the Coast Guard been notified?"

"I just did," Hayes responded. "They're going to deploy a rescue copter and one of their big cutters right now. We may need all the help we can get if there's any survivors." As he started the craft's engine, four other men left the building and came toward them. As soon as they were aboard, the helicopter lifted off, swung out over the ocean and headed east into the darkness. In the distance ahead of them, she could see the blinking lights of the first helicopter.

"Who's aboard that one?" she asked.

Hayes shook his head. "I don't know."

"I saw Mr. Loggins get on, but I don't know who else," Skip Majors, the assistant chief mechanic said. He was sitting just behind her. "Does anybody know what happened?"

No one responded. Except for the rush of the air past the craft and the throb of its engine, they sat engulfed in silence, waiting nervously to see what lay ahead.

Tony Torres, the quiet, hard-working Mexican, was fingering his prayer beads and murmuring to himself. "My brother's out there," he finally said softly. "Paco was working this shift."

Jori looked compassionately into his youthful face. The man's anxiety and fear were not disguised. "I'm sorry, Tony," she said. "Maybe he'll be all right."

Torres nodded and continued moving the beads through his fingers.

As the silence returned, she stared ahead of them, watching the lights of the other craft. Her mouth still tasted of blood. She swallowed large mouthfuls of the thick, salty fluid. Her tongue felt as if it had been ripped open. It was definitely continuing to swell. The bastard, she thought. The sorry bastard. If she hadn't before, she hated him now. Her feelings toward him had always been more defensive, because of his loathing of her, but now the feeling was absolutely mutual. No one in her life had ever hurt her physically like he had just done. At that moment she wanted to see him dead. Again she swallowed, again the lumpy sensation of her own partially clotted blood.

"We should be getting close," the pilot said. "Help me watch for it. Without lights, this could be tricky." The helicopter far ahead of them seemed to have stopped. It had probably reached the well.

At last, out of the darkness they could see the rig. The structure, which up until this moment had been the pride of Florexco, was totally without sign of life. The contrast of its now-darkened hulk with the way it had appeared just a few hours earlier was overwhelming. The first in a whole new breed of offshore drilling rigs designed for truly deep ocean oil exploration, it was an engineering marvel from the top of its derrick to its innovatively protected docking area below.

In the process of placing it over the drill site, the five huge buoyant steel legs had been partially flooded with water, and then, with the use of small two-man submersibles, a maze of steel cables had been hooked to previously placed pylons on the sea floor. Water had been pumped from the hollow legs, and the increased buoyancy of the platform caused it to rise and pull taut against the cables. While the platform was technically floating, it never moved or bobbed with the movement of the sea. It was constantly pushing upward against the resistance of the one hundred steel cables holding it in place. The design was such that after the drilling was done the rig could be moved to a new site for additional explorations.

But now, instead of an immensely impressive example of technical might, the rig looked dead and empty—a mere shadow of what it was meant to be.

While they watched, the first helicopter started down toward the main deck. Its running lights danced in eerie reflections across the darkened structure. After the first craft settled into place, Hayes inched his copter over the main deck and skillfully landed not far from the first one.

As they touched down, Jori had the uneasy feeling that she was in a foreign place. St. Lucie One was no longer a friendly safe haven. An aura of death hung like a thick cloud around them. A sudden sense of foreboding gripped her and she felt an unfamiliar sensation: a feeling of profound anxiety—fear of the unknown.

The door was opened and they stepped cautiously out onto the darkened deck. The only lights came from the helicopters. Blinking steadily, the flash from the strobes allowed weird brief glimpses of the machinery and structures. The alternating bursts of red and green added to the haunting mysteriousness. The giant derrick stood above them like a darkened monolith marking the place of danger and death. The two groups huddled in uncertainty near the safety of the crafts which had brought them to the well, but then finally, with swinging flashlights illuminating patches of the steelwork around them, they started forward across the deck. When the first body was spotted the entire group froze, spellbound for an instant at the specter of what they knew they would find. One of them finally stepped forward to shine his light into the face of the victim.

The dead man's face was contorted into a bizarre expression of fear or pain. His eyes were open and his teeth bared in a tense grimace. For a moment they stood over him, and then Jori bent down and looked more closely at the lifeless form. It was not a face she recognized. At first she thought it was because of the distorted expression, but then she realized how abnormal it appeared, even for death. The skin had been stretched tight over the bones. It looked dried or, in a peculiar way, burned. It was almost as if he had been dead for a long, long time. She carefully touched the skin over the man's cheek and quickly pulled back her hand in surprise. It was hard and leathery, dried out. It seemed stiff and almost wooden to the touch. The others bent down and looked with her, but no one spoke as they stared into the dead and dry eyes of the victim.

Without a word the group moved slowly forward toward the drill table. They soon came across another body. Shining their lights ahead of them, they could see many more scattered across the deck. They went from victim to victim, growing more bold with each discovery, becoming resigned to the devastation before them. Strangely silent, one by one and in small groups of two or three they began to explore the rig, still startled by the bizarre appearance of the dead men.

A startling outcry of grief came uncontrollably from Tony Torres as he discovered his dead brother along the edge of the turntable. Jori was quickly at his side as he knelt over the destroyed body, sobbing and moaning. She looked down into the face of the young boy. Just a few hours ago he had been one of those who helped her into the boat when she had left the well. His face, like the others, was dried. The skin was stretched, his features distorted—his eyes pulled open and teeth bared. The leathery feel of his dehydrated skin made her shudder with a deeply felt sense of horror.

She turned away from the sobbing Mexican and stepped up onto the drill table and crossed over to the body slumped near the now-stilled drill pipe. She carefully pulled on a limp arm turning the body over onto its back and looked into the gaunt, dried face of the chief tool pusher. It was almost more than she could take. Death was everywhere.

The men were beginning to talk and shout as they identified the workers one by one. "Here's Red Ferman!" someone yelled from the engine deck above her. Other names were called out. She felt numb. It seemed impossible. What could have caused this?

As she looked around her, the physical aspect of the well itself appeared untouched. There was no evidence of fire or explosion. It was almost as if the lights had been quietly turned off and the rig put gently to sleep. Nothing on the surface was damaged. A few of the others with her were drawing the same conclusion. Nothing else was wrong—except that the men were dead.

The others were walking around in stunned horror when suddenly she remembered old George in the control room. She dashed across the deck and started up the stairs. She had to step over a body on her way up, but then she reached the door and opened it. There was

George, slumped motionless across the control panel. At first she thought he was dead, but as she pulled back his head she saw his eyes move and saw him take a breath. His face looked normal; his skin was not changed. She yelled his name—but nothing. He lay silently in her arms. His eyes seemed dull and unseeing, but he continued to breathe.

Someone came in behind her, and she looked up to see Daryl Hayes. "He's alive," she said. "We've got to get him to the hospital." Hayes nodded and stepped back out through the open door and called for help. Two others soon joined them, and struggling with the limp form of George Elkins they carried him down the stairs.

Jori watched his face closely. He was barely breathing; he made no noise. Watching her dear friend so near death, she felt a flood of emotion which she could hardly contain. Her eyes filled with tears.

A voice rang out from the top of the derrick. It was that of Carl Slagger. Being a derrick man himself, he had been the only one who had thought to go to the top. "Blake's up here!" he yelled. "Jim Blake. It looks like he's alive!" There was a quick scramble as several others hurried up the stairs. Soon they were coming back down, bringing the second survivor.

He looked worse than George. He was breathing noisily, making a funny sound with his tongue. He seemed to gurgle. Although not as gruesome appearing as the dead men, Blake's face had a peculiar, slightly parched appearance. She watched silently as they loaded him into the helicopter beside George.

"I think that's it," the pilot said and climbed into the craft to start the engines. She entered and sat between the two survivors, wishing there were something else she could do for them.

Skip Majors climbed in beside her and was starting to close the door when Winston Loggins pushed his way through the others and stopped at the doorway, staring at her. His face was contorted with hostility and bitterness. He was shaking with rage. The vicious tone of his voice cut through her defenses as much as did the things he said.

"These men belong to you." He pointed at her. "You put them in their graves." His voice trembled slightly, and then he spoke more quietly. "You've played a game with this job, Jori Ashe, and because of you, people are dead. Goddamn you for that. Goddamn you! I hope you rot in hell!" His stare pierced through her as she sat in numb silence. The men behind him stood motionless. "You did it your way," he said. "I hope you're happy with the result."

She didn't move; she hardly breathed. She stared into his dark eyes, and she hated him more than she had ever thought possible. The faces of the men behind him were frozen in horror and despair.

Mercifully, Skip Majors pulled the door shut on the craft, and it immediately rose up and away from the well. Her last view was of darkness and quietness and the ten men left standing on the open deck as they departed with the only survivors of the unexplainable disaster.

She felt hollow and empty. Her mind no longer seemed to function. It was as if she were in a haze through which she could barely see. She sat dazed by what had happened, consumed by recurrent feelings of guilt and gloom, and waited for an eternity while they crossed over the dark ocean below toward the lights of the small town of Stuart beyond the beach in the distance.

Her tongue felt worse, as if it didn't belong in her mouth. She continued to swallow blood which tasted very salty. Then she began to feel weaker and slightly dizzy. An intense feeling of nausea swept over her. She was sick and scared. The craft landed alongside the hospital, and Skip Majors opened the door. She leaned forward and vomited what looked like quarts of dark, clotted blood onto the ground beneath them.

Nurses and orderlies quickly took George and Jim Blake away and then insisted that she lie on a stretcher. They were wheeling her toward the emergency room when she vomited again. It was more blood than she had ever seen. She looked up into the face of a young R.N. "Dr. Robson," she whispered. The girl nodded.

Her mind filled with the image of the face of the young, dead Mexican boy and his sobbing brother, and then she saw again the hate-filled glare of Loggins blaming her for the deaths. Oh, God, she thought, it can't be true. Please make it not true!

After a long while Blain entered the small room into which the nurses had placed her. "Are you all right?" he said, putting his hand to her wrist to feel her pulse. Her eyes were puffy, and he could tell she had been crying.

She shook her head, "I don't think so. I've been throwing up blood, and I feel like hell."

"I could have predicted that. Let me take another look at you." He adjusted the overhead light and then carefully examined her mouth and tongue. He turned to the nurse who had come in with him, "I'll need a minor suture set and some Xylocaine." He looked back at Jori. "It's a pretty bad laceration, but you'll be all right. I'm more concerned about the amount of blood you've lost. I may want you to stay in the hospital tonight."

"No," she said, shaking her head. "I don't want to. I'll be okay. Just sew me up. I've got to get back out to the well. We've got to find out what happened. It was horrible." Her voice began to tremble and she buried her face in her hands. Her shoulders were shaking.

"All right," he said softly and put one hand on her back. "Just take it easy now. Try to get yourself calmed down." He waited for a moment, and she seemed to regain her composure. "Let me get you sewed up now, before you lose any more blood. Open your mouth. Okay?" She put her hands back down into her lap as he took the syringe handed him by the nurse and carefully injected along the edges of the wound in the back of the tongue. She lay very still as he worked, and he spoke to her quietly, attempting to soothe her. "These things happen, Jori. Sometimes there's nothing that can be done to prevent them. You've got to try and keep yourself calm while everything gets sorted out."

She nodded as he continued injecting her. "They told me it didn't look like a fire," he said.

"It was horrible," she said again when he had finished with the needle. "I've never seen anything like it. Almost everyone was dead." She paused and tears again filled her eyes. "And they looked so terrible, so dried up." Her voice trembled. "And he wants to blame me," she blurted out and once more covered her face, sobbing. "It wasn't my fault. It couldn't be," she mumbled, the tears rolling down her cheek.

He put one arm around her shoulder again and supported her as she cried. "You're going to have to try to relax, Jori. Come on now. Just take it easy. It couldn't possibly have been your fault. No single person is ever to blame for something like this."

She looked up at him. "Everyone's dead. Everyone except for George and Blake—and they looked so bad." She struggled to fight back the tears. "I just don't know what happened. It must have been some sort of electrical thing."

"The pilot said it might have been lightning," Blain said.

"I guess it could have been, but the rig is supposed to be protected against things like that. I don't understand it. It's the strangest thing I've ever seen or heard of. How's George, and what about Blake? They're not going to make it, are they?"

"It's too soon to say. I don't think the young guy has any chance at all. He's barely alive. Elkins I don't know about. He moans every now and then, but he's not responsive in any other way. His respirations are good though."

"What's wrong with them?"

"It's hard to say. I guess it could be lightning or something like that. They seem to have mild first-degree burns—very, very mild though. It's unusual. I don't understand the unconsciousness. We're going to have to know exactly what happened to them before we can predict how they're going to do, but they both look real bad right now." He opened her mouth and began to suture her tongue.

"Can I see George?" she asked when he finished a few minutes later.

"Not tonight, there's nothing to see. They still look the same, and besides I think you need rest. You've lost a lot of blood. Why don't you stay in the hospital, just

65

overnight?" He looked concerned.

"No, I don't want to." She sat up on the bed and was immediately overwhelmed with nausea. She turned quickly to her side and threw up—again, more clotted blood. "God, I feel crummy," she said, "but I'll be all right. There's so much to do out there. I've got to get back. They'll be needing my help."

"No, Jori, you can't." His voice took on a stricter tone. "I'm not going to let you go back out there tonight. This injury is more significant than you think. You've lost a considerable amount of blood. You're going to have to stay in the hospital, or at the very least, go home and go to bed. They can get by without you tonight. Believe me, when something like this happens there's plenty of help."

"I'll be okay. I need to go, Blain. Really, I do. You don't realize what this well and those people mean to me."

"Yes, I do. But you're not being very rational at the moment. You're under a lot of stress. I feel strongly enough about this that I'll call the company myself and tell them you're not fit to work out there if I have to. I can't let you take a chance with yourself, Jori. Please, cooperate with me."

She sat looking down at the floor for a few seconds. "All right," she said finally, very softly. "But let me go home. I don't want to stay in the hospital."

"Okay. But I want to see you in the morning. We can talk more about George then. I'll have a police car take you home, but go straight to bed and stay there tonight. Don't try to go back out to the well."

She sighed. "I understand."

"I want to see you tomorrow morning before you do

anything else. If you have any problems during the night, anything at all, call me."

"Okay."

"You better. You're pushing yourself pretty hard."

"I'll be careful, honest I will."

"All right. You're under a lot of tension right now. I'm going to have the nurse give you a very mild sedative. It'll help you to sleep." He put one arm across her back, patting it gently. "I'm going to go back up to see about the other two." She didn't reply as he stood by her, and then he started to leave. "Good night, Jori. Be careful, please." She could see in his face that he really meant it. A moment later he was gone.

After a short while, she was helped into a sheriff deputy's car and taken home. She lived in an old white house along the beach, which she had leased for the season. It was an old-style frame structure with a small front porch and a much larger one in the back with a view looking out over the ocean. After the deputy had gone, she went through the kitchen and out to the back. Looking to the east, the lights of St. Lucie One were absent. As she watched, a helicopter to the south of her flew into the darkness toward the silent rig.

She felt exhausted and weak and, after vomiting one more time, undressed and got into bed already feeling very sleepy from the sedative. She was depressed, still horrified at what she had seen, but she was beginning to believe one thing. No matter what Loggins had said, it wasn't her fault. She had done nothing wrong. She had not sent all those men to their graves. Something she didn't understand had happened—maybe it had been lightning, maybe not.

FOUR

THE RUSSIAN EXPERIMENT

(From *Seek the Distant Shore*—A compendium of scientific challenges and tragic misadventures.)

Extremely deep drilling has always been a problem. It is, first of all, very expensive and complicated. Above and beyond these not inconsequential matters stands the risk. Probing the depths of the earth, forcing one's way through unknown regions of subterranean structures, poses great hazards, to say the least. It is, quite frankly, dangerous, as excursions into the unknown ultimately always are. Largely because of this and the potential political ramifications, deep exploratory efforts by the Western countries have ceased. There have been a few gallant attempts to perforate the earth's crust into the fringes of the mantle below, but after great effort and cost in labor and materials, they were abandoned—given up for the most part prior to the development of any adverse consequences.

Within the Soviet Union this may not have been

the case. The reports are, of course, very sketchy and at times conflicting. The Soviets have never been ones to freely exchange information about anything except triumphs. The drilling disaster in Central Siberia has been shrouded in even more secrecy than the nuclear accident at Kyshtym, in the southern Urals. The latter reportedly caused the death of nearly 8,000. Perhaps, because of the rapidity with which the CIA and other intelligence agencies gained information about the accidental detonation of the nuclear power plant, security involving the drilling project was tightened. The information that has been uncovered, although very sketchy, is tremendously interesting.

It apparently was a massive, well-equipped undertaking. With the exception of several relatively minor accidents in the very early stages, the drilling had gone well until somewhere beyond 52,000 feet when the tragedy occurred. Exactly what happened is not known, only that there were a large number of deaths and near total destruction of the drilling apparatus.

Rumors spread throughout the scientific community, but few of them were based upon fact. A number of very serious questions remain unanswered to this day. First of all, why would the project have been located in Siberia? It seems very strange that an attempt to drill through the outer crust of the earth and into the underlying mantle should have taken place at a point in the center of a continent where the crust itself is at its thickest. It would have seemed more rational to locate the exploratory effort in a more amenable location.

The core of the earth, as is well known, extends more than 2,000 miles outward from the center and seems not to vary from point to point around the globe. Its make-up is totally unknown. The mantle, an eighteen hundred-mile-thick layer, completely surrounding the core, is equally invariable and unexplored. It is only the crust, a rather superficial layer covering the mantle, about which we have some sketchy knowledge. Composed of a variety of minerals and geological formations, its thickness varies from point to point. Under the great land masses, it may be as deep as forty to fifty miles, while becoming as thin as five to six miles under certain areas of the ocean floor.

The question remains then. Why would the Soviets drill in the thickest area of the crust instead of making the attempt through a thinner region? Secrecy? Perhaps. It has been postulated that they somehow were able to discover a thinner spot in the crust or perhaps even one that was softer and more easily perforated. Are these overly imaginative answers? Probably yes, but nevertheless, the fact is the Russians drilled where they did. They must have had a reason.

The second, and in some ways, even more puzzling question raised by the incident is one regarding the motivation of the Soviets for engaging in the effort at all. The history of the Russian government has been one of pragmatism. It is true that over the last two decades they have engaged in a great deal of research, but only in areas where the fruits of such efforts promised to be of economic or *military benefit. An attempt to explore the mantle of the earth forty miles below the surface is one which is ordinarily thought of as having only scientific merit. Why the Russians would engage in it, completely contrary to their usual policy in every other scientific endeavor, is indeed a mystery. It seems reasonable, to me, to conclude that the Soviets were working in the belief that there was something of pragmatic value to be found.*

When knowledge of the project first came to light, the hypotheses working in the scientific rumor mill were many. All but one of these has subsequently been dispelled. The remaining notion is one of such bizarre consequences that it is spoken of only in whispers and nervous jests. The theory has not yet been published. However, informal papers and calculations have passed from hand to hand through the upper echelons of the society of geophysicists.

It is beyond the purposes of this report to delve into this matter any further than this. The real truth of what happened to the Russians shall perhaps never be known in the West until a major scientific defection brings with it the news. Considering the rumored consequences of the accident, it is possible that no one, even within the Soviet Union, has a real grasp upon what happened. Knowledge of what lies beneath the crust of the earth must presumably now wait until time and circumstance give us the opportunity to extend the reach of man that far into the bowels of our planet.

What we will find there is anyone's guess, but

71

considering the theoretical possibilities and the consequent ramifications, it is a mission we must eventually undertake, whatever the cost or undeniable risk.

by Adrian Sumter, Ph.D.
Geophysicist
Florexco

FIVE

She awoke at the sound of a car pulling onto the gravel in front of her house. She was miserable; her tongue was hurting and she was nauseated. Her pillow was splotched with clotted blood. She tried to open her mouth and felt a stiffness in her jaw. Her tongue was still swollen, and the stitches irritated the inside of her cheek. She tried not to think of the horror on the well.

It was after nine o'clock. Getting slowly out of bed, she walked into the bathroom and stood before the mirror. She was a mess. Her cheek and chin were sticky with dried blood. But fortunately her face was not too badly swollen. After she washed off the residue of what she had bled during the night, she appeared almost normal. Only her pain and the thickened fullness of her tongue reminded her of her injury. Although she no longer tasted blood in her mouth, she still felt faintly queasy. A good breakfast would take care of that, she told herself. As she brushed her hair back quickly, she heard footsteps on her porch and then the doorbell.

A moment later she opened the door to face Wally Jenkins, the big, burly sixtyish vice president and chief of operations of Florexco. He seemed tired and tense. "Where have you been?" he said as he followed her into the house.

"Sick," she replied curtly. "That wonder boy of yours busted up my mouth last night."

Jenkins frowned. He had a ruddy, sun-weathered complexion with thinning brown hair which he kept cut close to his head, military style. "I suspected as much. Skip said they had to sew you up in the ER last night."

"It doesn't matter much now though. I'll be all right. What's happened on the rig?"

"That's what I wanted to ask you. I just got in from Pensacola a couple of hours ago. I was out there a little while, and I've talked to Loggins, but I still can't understand it. It's a total disaster. A wipe-out. Twenty-two men dead and two more dying. The morgue is swamped. I just don't have an adequate explanation for it."

"What about lightning?"

"I guess so. It's the only thing that makes any sense at all. Winston doesn't buy it, though. He thinks it's some kind of electrical failure. He wants to put it on your back."

She looked annoyed. "I could have guessed as much. But I refuse to accept the blame, Wally, no matter what he says."

"I know. It wasn't your fault. It's some kind of design defect. I think Adrian Sumter is going to have to take the blame; it's his baby. Funny part is there's almost nothing wrong with the rig. The breakers are all tripped, and a couple of electrical connections have been burned, but everything else is perfectly fine. I think Loggins is off base, and I told him so. It must have been just an unlucky fluke hit by lightning—nothing else fits. I've never seen anything else like it. . . . We lost so many men."

His face mirrored the pain she knew he was

experiencing. Jenkins had been with the company from the beginning. He was a tough-minded worker from the old school who demanded one hundred per cent from the people below him, but he gave a lot, too. He knew many of the workers by name and was concerned about their welfare. He was compassionate and well thought of by everyone throughout the organization.

Because he had been preoccupied with difficulties in other areas of Florexco's expanding exploration program, he had taken almost a "hands-off" approach to St. Lucie One, having turned operations almost completely over to Loggins and her. On paper, Wally ranked second in the organizational structure of the company just below the aging president, Matthew Downing. But in reality, he was in charge of everything on a day-to-day basis, answering only to Sumter. Technically, he didn't even have to do that. Adrian Sumter was only in charge of research and development—though everyone knew that the scientist was the moving force behind Florexco's recent growth. And on a practical level he had more influence with the board of directors and stockholders than anyone else.

So, as a consequence of Sumter's influence, he was consulted frequently when Jenkins had major decisions to make. But Wally remained responsible for ordinary exploration and production activities.

Now, with Florexco's most expensive venture ever in trouble, Jori knew Jenkins had to be concerned about more than just the deaths of the workers.

"What do we do now?" she asked. "Have the families been notified yet?"

He nodded slowly. "Yes. They've been doing that this morning." He paused, seemingly buried in thought while

75

he took a deep breath, letting it out slowly. "This is a dangerous business, Jori. I've seen so many accidents on oil wells it's incredible. But this one shouldn't have happened. It's a crime to lose lives when we could have prevented it. I don't think I can face these men's families." He stood up and walked nervously across the room. "Do you have any coffee here?"

She led him through the dining room into the kitchen where she put on a pot of water. "We've got to find out exactly what caused this, Wally. I don't care if we have to take that rig apart piece by piece. I won't be able to relax until I know we've solved it. We can't go on until we're positive it'll never happen again."

"I understand your feelings, Jori. You've been a lot closer to this project than I have. But we may not ever come up with anything more than we've got right now. There's nothing out there to find. There's just not a damned thing wrong with the rig. The Coast Guard's been out there since sun-up and the company's design engineers. They just can't find anything to explain it, except maybe lightning."

She looked skeptical. "There has to be a better explanation. We can't just close our eyes to the fact that these men were killed and go back to work as if nothing were wrong."

"I know it seems callous to talk about starting up again," he said almost defensively, "but we've got to. We could wait forever and it wouldn't bring those men back."

"You should've seen the way they looked," she replied angrily. "It was awful. Their faces were . . . I can't describe it. It was too horrible."

"I know," he answered softly. "I saw them myself this morning. I don't know how it could've happened." He gazed at her quietly for a moment.

"How long do you think it'll be before the investigation is over?" she asked.

He sighed again. "Jori, I think the investigation's almost over now. Prolonging this thing is not going to do us any good. Today we start the repairs. We're beefing up the lightning protection system and a few things, and I want to start the drilling again at eight o'clock Thursday morning. We've already got more men coming in, and I think we should be ready to go."

"Get serious, Wally! We had men die out there! Last night Loggins was trying to blame me for everything, and now you say you want to start again. You mean that's it? Just crank up the engines and go? I don't believe it!"

Jenkins appeared irritated. "Look, Jori, I'm as sorry as anyone that the men are dead, but there's nothing we can do about it now. We just have to regroup and get going. We don't have the leisure of waiting."

"What are you talking about?"

Jenkins's voice softened and his expression changed to one of concern. "Whatever happened out there, we've got to get it straightened out—and quick. You may not know it yet, but Florexco is in real trouble. We're at the point of economic collapse. That's why we have to pick up the pieces and start moving again."

Jori looked surprised. "Are you kidding?"

"No. We're on a razor's edge. This project has got to be a success or we're dead. You wouldn't believe how much money we have riding on this thing. I won't kid you. My neck's on the block just like everyone else. The company's in deep financial trouble."

"But I thought Florexco was bringing in wells all over the place."

"We are, but most of that is contract work for other

companies. The seven sisters have been good to us. We've made a lot of money in subsidized operations drilling offshore rigs for them. But they're not our wells. They belong to the other companies. We're not getting the steady income from them that we need.

"We've had a couple of pieces of bad luck ourselves recently. Some of our own ventures have gone sour, and things are getting tight. If St. Lucie One makes it, we'll be all right. Actually, even if we don't hit paydirt, if we can just show how efficient this new type of drilling platform is we'll be able to get a lot out of it. We have three more of these things under construction. We can put them into subsidized operations for a while and recoup some of our losses, but if this thing doesn't make it we're in trouble.

"That's why we wanted you in charge of the drilling. We can't be conservative. We need a quick score. Then we'll replace the rig with a small pumping platform, tow it to a new site and start up a new operation. What we want to do is show that this is the best goddamn offshore rig that's ever been built and demonstrate that we can put in two or three wells during the time it would take an ordinary rig to just get one pumper going. That's the bottom line, Jori. We've got to get somewhere quick. If we don't, the company could collapse."

She was dismayed. "I can't believe it. I just can't believe it. I thought Florexco was booming."

"We will be if everything goes okay from now on."

She went to the coffee pot and poured herself a cup. "And so, because the company's in trouble, we've got to cut our losses and keep moving. Right?" she said, frowning.

"It's the only thing we can do. Otherwise we're finished."

She took in a deep breath and let it out very slowly,

almost sadly. "Okay. I understand. What happens next?" She felt tired and discouraged.

Silently he unrolled the papers he had brought in with him and spread them out on the table. "Look at these graphs, will you? There are a couple of peculiar things here I don't understand." She looked down at the graph tracings that he had brought from the well's control booth. "Now, right here is where you changed to the diamond bit, right?" he said.

She glanced at the flat line on the depth indicator chart. "Yes, we had been stuck at three hundred feet for a couple of hours."

"Why?"

"I don't know," she responded. "I just don't know. It was a very hard layer."

"Whatever it was, according to Sumter it shouldn't have been there at all," Jenkins replied. "But here is the interesting part; look at the temperature graft. Right after they'd started the drilling for the second time, the temperature at the bit starts to go up, and then it skyrockets about ten seconds before the shutdown. And look at the depth indications—no progress at all until just about the point when the well shuts down and the drill pipe plunges forward ten or fifteen feet."

"That is interesting," she said, examining the graphs more closely. "It's a peculiar coincidence that the lightning would have struck just as we started to make progress for the first time in hours."

"Yes, that's what I think. And what about these electromagnetic field measurements. Everything's normal, and then, all of a sudden, the forces change almost 180 degrees—just five or six seconds before the shutdown, at almost exactly the same time that the drilling started to make progress. What do you make of

79

that?" he asked.

She continued studying the charts. He fixed himself a cup of the coffee. "This is really strange," she said. "It's a phenomenal coincidence that all these things could have happened just as the accident occurred." She looked puzzled. "This data could be erroneous, you know. It could be false readings caused by static electricity build-up just before the lightning hit."

"Yes," Jenkins replied, and he took a sip of his coffee. "Maybe so. In any event, I'm going to send this to Sumter. He doesn't know about the accident yet. I'm going to call him as soon as I get back to the office. He's going to have to come back from Europe and help us with this thing."

She agreed. "I think so." The scientist had been gone for almost two months, but she was quite sure he would have an adequate explanation for the inaccuracy of his geological tracings as well as the cause of the tragedy.

"I just wish he'd stay home and do a little work for us some of the time," Jenkins said, irritated, "instead of running around to so many of these blasted scientific meetings. He's presented so many papers in the last few years, it's incredible. It's like he's still chasing a Nobel Prize or something. As much money as the company pays him, you'd think he would be here twenty-four hours a day."

"He's a scientist, Wally, and what scientists want more than anything else is recognition from other scientists. That's the driving force behind almost everything they do. He'll have to come home now, though."

"For sure. I doubt if he can make it by the time we're under way again, but we need him as soon as he can get here. I just hope we don't have any more bad luck, though. You know everybody is sick this morning."

"Who's sick?" she asked.

"Everybody who worked out on the well after the accident—even Loggins. They've all got diarrhea and vomiting. They look like a bunch of sea-sick ninnies this morning, every five minutes somebody barfing over the rail. Dr. Thompson has been earning his money for the first time ever. They even had to put one kid in the hospital, he got so dehydrated. Torres, I think it was, but that may be partly psychological. His brother was one of the men who died."

"What's causing that?" she asked.

"I don't know," he said, disgustedly. "Some kind of virus maybe. The doc thinks it may be food poisoning. The jerk cook probably wasn't careful enough with some sandwiches he put out for them about three o'clock this morning. You're lucky you left and didn't eat any of it. Everybody else who went to the well last night got it."

He glanced at his watch and then back at her. "Now listen, Jori, there's something else we need to discuss." He looked at her thoughtfully.

She knew immediately what he meant. "Are you talking about this thing between Loggins and me?"

"That's exactly what I'm talking about. It can't go on. It's all got to change, and it's got to change quickly." He seemed to grow angry. "I talked to Matthew Downing this morning, and he wanted to replace you. I told him I'm not ready for that. I still think Sumter was right in bringing you in." He glared at her sternly, pointing one finger for emphasis. "But I'm tired of this horseshit. I told Winston the same thing this morning, and I'm telling you now. Cut out this high-school crap. I'm out there working my butt off trying to keep this organization together. We've turned over the most expensive operation this company has ever tried to you two. And I've been getting nothing back but bitching and moaning ever since." He glanced out the window to the ocean and then back to her. "I'm telling you, Jori, I'm sick of both of you. If it was up to me, I think I'd yank both of you right off the job, but I can't do that—the company needs you. But all this childish squabbling has got to end, and it's got to end now. If it doesn't, I don't know what's going to happen."

He paused, watching her closely and then his face softened. "I know it's mostly Winston's fault. He doesn't like working with a woman, and you're getting in the way of his ambitions and all that. But right now, besides me, he's the most experienced man in the company for this sort of thing. He's getting very, very powerful. I couldn't get rid of him even if I wanted to. But I don't want to let him crush you if I can help it. I personally need you to do well here, believe me. So, please try to work this thing out. We both are going to lose if you don't. Right now, if push comes to shove, he will beat you. So ease off on him, would you?"

"Wally! He's the one on my back. The problem is not me, it's him. It's a two-way street, you know. I can't just stay out there and let him abuse me. I ought to put him in jail for what he did last night, the son of a bitch!"

"I know. I understand a lot more about what's been going on than you think, really I do. But try to work it out, please. We need the problem solved. We've got too many other problems." He looked at her hopefully.

"All right," she said finally after a long pause. "I'll give it a try, but if he so much as touches me again, I'll shoot him."

Jenkins nodded. "You'll have every right to, but there won't be much left of him when I get through if he does that again. I told him that this morning, and I think he understands that I mean it—and I do."

"One more thing, Wally, and this is important. I think it's crummy that we're restarting so soon. I don't care what the money problems are. I'll do it because it's my job. But, if Loggins says one darned thing about it being my fault, I'm going to explode. I feel bad enough about this as it is."

"I understand," Jenkins replied. "He won't. I'll see to it." He looked at his watch again. "Well, I've got to get back. When do you think you can come to work?"

"I've got to check with the doctor who sewed me up, and I want to see about George—so I should be out there after lunch."

Jenkins moved to the door. "That'll be fine. I need to get by the hospital myself and see George. Give him my blessings, the poor old guy." His face reflected the sadness Jori knew he was feeling. "Maybe I'll go over there tonight."

She stood silently as he walked down the steps, across the sand and got into a company car that had been waiting for him. "I brought your truck down to you," he called. "I guess you forgot about it last night. The keys are in the ignition." He paused. "I appreciate your help, Jori. It's a tough situation." She said nothing, but continued to gaze unhappily at him as the driver started the car, made a U-turn and headed south toward the Florexco compound.

She walked back up onto the porch and went inside. It was still hard to believe twenty-two men were dead and maybe two more. Her cut tongue and bruised ego didn't mean too much by comparison. It seemed disrespectful to start up again so soon, and she resented it. But who was she to argue with big money.

SIX

"That's it," Blain Robson said as he finished the last stitch, closing the wound across the woman's chest where once a breast had been. "Put a dressing on it." He stepped back from the operating table and took off his gloves and mask. He picked up the patient's chart and sat on the stool in the corner writing out a post-surgical note while Richard Mason, the chief of anesthesiology at Community General, began the process of reversing the effect of the anesthetic. Blain hated mastectomies, even the modified radical procedure which he usually performed. But cancer of the breast was a deadly disease and justified the mutilation.

When he was certain the patient was going to awaken satisfactorily, he left the OR and walked down to the family waiting area where he discussed the unfortunate situation with the stunned husband. A few minutes later he turned into the recovery room just as Dr. Mason was bringing his patient in. He sat down at the nurses station, wrote a few more orders and then closed the chart. Richard Mason, a very short, stocky man whose totally bald head was covered with a surgical scrub hat, came across the room toward him. Neither of them was in any mood to discuss the case they had just completed. Removing the breast of a 40-year-old, otherwise healthy and happy woman was not the sort of thing they enjoyed or took pride in.

"Well, Rich," Blain said, "I guess I'll go up and see that little appendectomy we did last night."

"You do that." Mason smiled and rubbed his eyes. "When I finished that damnable case, I had to do two C-sections back-to-back. I haven't been asleep all night."

"Hazards of the trade, my good man," Blain said jokingly.

"No," Mason replied, his face becoming more serious. "That's not the hazards of the trade. The hazard is this pitiful malpractice problem. I just heard from my insurance carrier that they're going to sue all of us over the Pendleton case."

"That's ridiculous. What can they sue us on that one for? We're not the ones who screwed him up."

"It doesn't matter in this situation," Mason answered. "That's the trouble with the whole system. Whether you help somebody or hurt them—if anything goes wrong, everybody involved gets sucked into it."

"I don't see how we can get stung on that one. We did that guy a lot of good whether he likes it or not."

Mason shook his head. "It doesn't make any difference. When they go to the lawyers, it costs us money, right or wrong."

"That's the sad truth, isn't it?" Blain responded, disgustedly, and left the recovery room, heading down the hall to the ICU where the two men from Florexco were dying despite everything he could do.

But the Pendleton case was another matter. Blain had been forced to perform bilateral below-the-knee amputations on the unfortunate man because of another

85

surgeon's botched attempts at vascular surgery. The patient, who had nearly died, was livid about the loss of his legs. However, Blain felt sure that if Pendleton's lawyers attempted to sue him for malpractice, they would get nowhere with it. The man had a very good result considering the gravity of his complications. But then again, he worried, if Mason was upset there might be some risk to it. Mason had been around quite awhile and had had his share of knocks, and although he had never really lost a malpractice case, he had been involved in several. It was a rare anesthesiologist who had not. Any bad result by an anesthesiologist was usually a very bad result. And, unfortunately, sometimes they were just impossible to prevent.

Mason had pulled quite a few surgeons out of bad situations in the OR though, and everyone knew it. Most of the men on the staff were very glad to have him. Even Stanford Wilcott, the pompous chief of surgery, respected him despite Mason's general unwillingness to remain subservient to him. Blain had witnessed several incidents where Mason had told Wilcott to get screwed.

Blain loved to see it. Stanford Wilcott and his two junior surgical associates had tried hard to keep Blain from coming to Community General. The reason was money. Until Blain's arrival, Wilcott's group had had a monopoly in the county for over twelve years. The chief of surgery was part of the old guard. He and the older men formed a small but very powerful group that still seemed to have a stranglehold on the hospital and the referral relationships within. Some of this was being broken down with time and the arrival of new doctors. But the general surgeons were resisting it, and Blain was having a hard time because of their antagonism. Good referrals were few and far between. After six months in practice, he was still getting most of his cases through his emergency room call. Just as he had gotten the two patients he was now going to see in the ICU. Strange cases indeed.

He pushed through the double doors into the large surgical intensive care unit. There were beds for eight patients. Each was separated from the others by a wall studded with monitoring devices, oxygen supplies, suction equipment, and other medical machinery. It was a large room, but each cubicle could be viewed from the central nursing station.

He stopped at the bedside of George Elkins to observe him, watching the nature of his respirations, the movements of his eyes and facial muscles. The man seemed to quiver slightly, intermittently, but he was breathing well. His pulse felt fine. Blain pulled back the sheet covering the chest and abdomen. There was a faint erythema, a redness, that involved his total skin surface. It appeared almost like a mild sunburn, not a significant thermal injury, but distinctly abnormal. Blain examined again the ends of Elkins's fingers and his toes, carefully looking for evidence of the more serious burns which are common with lightning or electrical injuries, but found none. He listened to the man's heart and chest; he palpated the abdomen; he opened the eyelids and looked into the pupils which reacted normally to light. He bent down at one end of the bed and looked at the urine container, noting the times and volumes. At the nurse's table just to the left of the bedside, he studied the patient's temperature chart, his blood pressure, and other vital signs. Finally, he paused to watch the electrocardiogram on the screen above the bed.

He went to the nurses station, pulled down the chart and looked at the laboratory data accumulated there. Very perplexed, he went back to the bedside of George Elkins. He made his hand into a fist and dug his knuckles hard into the front of the man's chest, pushing against his sternum. This elicited a dull moan and a movement of the four extremities, but nothing more. At least he responds to deep pain, Blain thought, as he went next door to see his other patient.

As bad as George Elkins looked, this man was worse. He had the same slight redness of the skin, but it was more dry and thickened—almost tough. His respirations were irregular, the pulse weak and thready. His pupils were wide open and fixed—a sign of neurological death. He did not respond at all to the pain maneuver. The record of his temperature and other vital signs showed ominous irregularities. Jim Blake wasn't going to make it. Blain was sure of it. He wished he knew how to help the poor guy, but he didn't. It was a confusing and peculiar situation. Blain wasn't even sure what was wrong. The clinical picture didn't fit into any reasonable pattern. It made him worry that he was missing something, some little piece of the puzzle that would tie all the various abnormalities together.

"Good morning, Dr. Robson." The pretty nurse appeared from one of the other patient's cubicles.

"Hi, Jan," he said, turning to look at the short brunette girl with a dynamite figure barely hidden beneath her uniform. "What's new?"

"Nothing, except Dr. Wilcott's on the rampage again."

"What about this time?" he asked.

"He doesn't think your patients ought to be in the

surgical ICU. He says they're medical problems. He says they should be in the medical intensive care unit."

"Where the heck does he get that idea?" Blain said indignantly. "Burns have always been surgical problems."

"I know," she said and made a facial expression of mock exasperation. "He says they don't look like burns to him and that you are just case hunting."

"Baloney!" Blain said. "I don't know what I have to do to get him off my back."

"Don't ask me," she answered. "Do you think their real problem is burns?"

"I'm not sure. I've never seen anything exactly like this. It's the diffuseness of their skin changes that puzzles me, and I don't understand the neurological depression. Why should they be so deeply in a coma without more evidence of injury? I'm going to have a neurologist see them, but I don't guess it makes any difference. Blake is not going to make it anyway, no matter what we do. Elkins might have a chance, but I doubt it."

"What do you think about their low white cell counts?" she asked.

"It's distinctly unusual," he replied. "The counts should be going up, not down. Has Elkins had any bloody diarrhea like Blake?"

"No, not yet. But Blake's getting worse. We're getting blood out of his stomach, too. The N-G suction is filled with it."

"That's bad. Type and cross both of them for six units of blood. Let's get some clotting tests on them, too."

"Whatever you do, watch out for Wilcott," she warned. "He wants those beds. Needs to put some of his gallbladders in them or something. You know, something real important."

He smiled, but said nothing. The chief of surgery was famous among the nurses in the ICU for abusing them with his "rich bitches" as they called them. Well-moneyed ladies from along the Palm Coast who needed various procedures—mostly having their gallbladders removed—whom he treated with loads of TLC. He made an elaborate deal of a routine operation, running each of them through the ICU for two days post-op and in general *ooh*ing and *aah*ing over them. His surgical fee for such cases was reputed to be twice or three times the standard. In any event, when Wilcott couldn't get a bed in the intensive care unit for one of his "ladies," he was always pressing to clear "graffiti" out of the ICU, many of whom were seriously ill and truly needed the care.

He isn't getting these two beds, Blain said to himself, at least not for the moment, and glanced back at his patients. He didn't have much hope for holding both of them together for much longer, however.

Still trying to decide what to do for the two, he left the ICU and stopped in at the doctors lounge, a few feet down the hall. He had no more than mixed his coffee when the door swung open and Stanford Wilcott appeared in the doorway, holding it open with his foot, a stack of charts under each arm.

The chief of surgery was a tall man and big. He had a full head of flowing silver hair and a very strong face with piercing, slate-gray eyes. He had broad shoulders and hands with long, slender fingers. He looked to be in excellent physical condition and his voice had a booming, authoritative quality which was used unsparingly. Almost the perfect picture of the steely eyed, godlike surgeon, he played the role perfectly. Being such an imposing figure, patients seemed to melt in his hands. He had been able to convince the board of directors and other financiers that he was, indeed, a surgeon of surgeons. He was well respected by all who knew him, except those who knew him very well. From the old guard, he was a man very obviously in command of himself, his environment, and the hospital around him. Few people stood up against him and survived. Mason was one and now Blain was trying to be another.

"Robson," the strong, dignified voice began, "when are you going to get those two medical patients out of the surgical ICU?"

"I didn't know there were any medical patients in the surgical ICU," Blain replied, without looking at him, continuing to stir his coffee.

"Cut the crap, Doctor. You know exactly which two patients I'm talking about."

"You mean my two patients?" Blain said, turning to look at him. "They're not medical patients; they're surgical."

"Since when has coma of undetermined etiology been a surgical problem, Blain?" Wilcott continued, still standing in the doorway.

"Those patients are suffering from some sort of energy related trauma, Stan, maybe lightning or electrical."

"Nonsense!" Wilcott retorted. "There's not a second degree burn on them. I looked at them myself."

"Well, what do you think the problem is, since you've obviously examined them?"

"Don't get smart with me. I just looked at them enough to determine that it's not a surgical problem that they've got. You'd better get an internist to take care of

91

them and get them out of there."

"Don't worry. I think one of them is going to be leaving soon, anyway."

Wilcott's voice became slightly more conciliatory. "Oh, well, good. Now see what you can do about getting rid of the other one. This is a busy surgical hospital. We can't fill up our surgical beds with medical problems."

"I'll see what I can do, Doctor," Blain answered, mockingly polite. With that, Wilcott removed his foot from the door and it closed between them.

"Jackass," Blain muttered to himself and took a sip of his coffee just as his name was paged overhead. He picked up the phone and dialed the appropriate extension. "Tell her I'll be right down," he said after a brief interval.

He finished his coffee quickly and left the lounge, heading for the family waiting area near the ICU. His bad mood was already starting to improve by the time he met Jori standing in the hall waiting for him. She looked great, considering everything. The woman was really a looker. He couldn't keep himself from admiring her nice breasts and attractive little bottom. Her auburn hair hung in big curls all the way to her shoulders. She just didn't look like a geological engineer.

"Hi. The nurse said I could probably still catch you here," she said. "How are George and Blake?"

"Not too good. But how are you doing? You look a lot better than last night. How's your tongue?"

"Sore," she answered. "And it feels very big in there."

"Have you been vomiting any more?"

"No. I'm much better. I still feel nauseated, but I'm much better."

"Good," he replied. "Open up. Let me take a look." She did as she was told and he peered into her mouth.

"Everything looks fine," he said. "I think it's going to heal okay. Did you follow my advice last night?"

"Yes. I stayed home. I haven't been out there yet. I feel like I'm not doing my share of what's necessary, considering the circumstances."

"I think you were wise to do it. I can promise you, you wouldn't be feeling as well today as you do. You shouldn't have any more problems now, though. You can go back to work whenever you're ready. Look, if you've got a few minutes, why don't we go down to the cafeteria. We can have a cup of coffee and I can tell you the whole story about Elkins and Blake. It doesn't look good for either one of them."

She agreed and they started down the hall. In the cafeteria, he poured another cup of coffee for himself and one for her. They took a table in the far corner of the room near a window overlooking the river. "I don't know how close you are to these two, but I'll tell it to you just like it is," he said. "Blake looks like he's going to die real soon. Mr. Elkins is not quite that bad off, but close. Neither one has regained consciousness at all. They're almost totally unresponsive to anything except intense pain. I am not optimistic at all. It's a very bad situation."

She grimaced unhappily. "What's wrong with George?"

He glanced out the window for a moment, hesitating. "That's the problem. It's hard to evaluate the extent of his injuries because I don't really know how they occurred. The circumstances seem to dictate that this was some kind of electrical injury, but quite frankly, he just doesn't look like it, Jori. I've had lots of experience with that type of pathology and this is atypical. Usually, with either electrical accidents or lightning, the patients have severe burns of their extremities where the electricity entered and left the body. Patients hit by lightning can even have an arm or a foot burned completely off. The point is, lightning accidents are very damaging. High-wire accidents with linemen are the same way. They lose fingers and hands. The strange thing about these two is that they seem to have an extremely mild burn over their entire body. There's no area where it's any worse than others."

"I don't understand what you're suggesting, Blain. Are you saying that you don't think it was lightning that injured them?"

"No. I'm not saying that at all," he answered. "I can't make that judgment. All I mean to say is that this is very unusual and it's hard to understand. There are several mysterious things. One of them is their unconsciousness. Usually when a patient is in a coma from electrical injuries, he has sustained severe burns. Neither one of them looks like that. It's more like they've sustained severe internal injuries to their GI tract and their nervous system without actually doing that much damage to their skin. I've never seen any cases exactly like these."

"What are you going to do?" she asked. "Is there a chance that George will be okay?"

"I just don't know. I'm being honest with you. I do not know. There's several other things that are peculiar: some of their laboratory work. Their white blood cell counts have dropped way off. This is very unusual for burn victims. You know what the white blood cells are, don't you? They're the ones that combat infection. Normally, the count rises after any kind of trauma like this. In the case of Blake and Elkins, the white counts this morning have fallen below normal. Blake has started some internal bleeding, too. I just can't put it all together yet. I wish I could tell you better news, but I can't."

She took a deep breath and sighed. "I understand. Do what you can. I know that something terrible happened out there. I think it's a miracle that these two are even alive considering what happened to the others."

He could see pain in her face as she looked down and stirred her coffee. "How are you feeling about that now?" he said quietly. "You're not still blaming yourself, are you?"

"No," she replied and looked up at him. "I know it's not my fault. I'm sure there's nothing I did wrong. I just feel so guilty being a part of something that's taken this many lives."

"That's understandable. The company's not trying to blame you, are they?"

"No. Just that jerk Loggins, and I think they're going to get him off my back now."

"What was it like out there last night? What do you think happened, really?"

She shook her head. "I'll never forget it. It was the most horrible thing I've ever seen. The well was pitch black, the bodies everywhere. Some of them looked so mutilated, so strange. It was almost more than I could take. Have you seen any of the bodies?"

"No."

"I'll never forget what they looked like. Will they be doing autopsies?"

"Not likely," Blain responded. "It wouldn't really give us any additional information. The results are just not that specific. And besides, families generally are opposed to autopsies. No widow likes the idea of having her

95

husband cut up in a laboratory. If there was some question about how they died or if the coroner disagrees with the cause of death listed by the physician who pronounced the deaths, then he would intervene. Otherwise, it wouldn't be done."

"Who pronounced these men dead?" she asked. "There was no doctor on the well when I was there."

"That was Dr. Thompson. Your Dr. Thompson."

"Adam Thompson?" she asked, puzzled.

"Yes. What's so strange about that?"

"I guess that's about all he would be good for—to pronounce someone dead."

Blain smiled curiously. "What are you talking about?"

"I don't know," she said and shook her head. "Old Dr. Thompson—he's drunk half the time. Sometimes I've wondered if he's really a doctor at all. He's retired from the military, I think. He doesn't care about practicing medicine. He just has a nice easy job doing physicals for the workers and taking care of a cold every now and then. I think he's put a few stitches in here and there, but I just can't imagine trusting his opinion on something this important."

Blain shrugged. "Well, that's what happened. The company took all the bodies to the Florexco headquarters and set up a temporary morgue there. They got Thompson out of bed. He came over, declared them all dead and has apparently cited lightning injuries as the cause of death. So now it will be up to the coroner to decide if he wants to challenge that."

"It's a screwball system if you ask me," she replied, slightly irritated. "I would think that when an important decision like this has to be made, someone who knew what he was doing would make it. Don't any of the doctors around here care enough to want to know why all these men are dead?"

"Jori, it doesn't take too much talent with twenty-two bodies after some kind of flash on an oil well, with no evidence of fire or explosion, to put two and two together to figure out they were killed by lightning. It sort of makes sense you know. Particularly when there's no other damage to the rig itself."

"How'd you know that?"

"It was on the radio. The news said that the company had determined that the rig sustained only very minor damage. Apparently they're going to improve the lightning rods and go on. Don't you know all that? I thought you were one of the bosses out there."

"Right," she replied, chagrined. "But I haven't been out there since last night. You told me to stay home. Don't you remember?"

"True. I'm glad you did. What do you plan to do about the guy who punched you, anyway? He's one of the ones you work with, right? Seems like a real swell fella, even-tempered and all." He smiled sarcastically.

"There's a long story behind that."

"Are you going to press charges, or is the company going to do something about him?" Blain asked.

"Ordinarily I would've, but not now. We've got enough problems as it is without getting into some kind of a legal hassle."

"I hate to see bastards getting away with stuff like that," Blain responded. "Another second and about five of us would've decked him after he hit you. Southern boys, me included, don't really care too much for men who go around punching out women."

She shook her head. "I guess I sort of had it coming."

"That's ridiculous. I think you should press charges, teach him a lesson."

"No," she said, tight-lipped. "That wouldn't work."

"I don't see why not. I'd go after the son of a bitch if I were you."

"Well I'm not, so let's drop it, okay?"

He nodded. "It was none of my business anyway. You've got enough things to think about without having to listen to my advice. Anyway, I'm glad you're okay, Jori. I was worried about you last night. It's got to be hard being involved in a tragedy like this."

She grimaced. "Just yesterday I was out there with those men, talking with them, working out the plans to overcome some of the problems we were having—and now, for no reason at all, they're dead. I don't know how to cope with it. Really, I don't. I'm just trying to blank it out and keep functioning. I still feel numb, in a way."

"That's normal. The main thing to do is keep going. You can't just stop and dwell on this. You've got to figure out what went wrong and proceed. Life goes on."

She looked tired and sad. "That's what the company says. They want to start the drilling as soon as they can. Apparently the Coast Guard and the engineers who helped design the rig have given us the okay and so, with very little change, we're going to go back to work. I don't see how I can do it, but I guess I will."

He looked at her thoughtfully. "I guess you have to, unless you just want to quit. I face something of the sort every now and then when I lose a patient. Sometimes I feel so guilty about it, I'd like to hang it all up and go sell insurance or something. But, after awhile, I get myself back together and go on. You never get used to it, though.

You just learn to block it out."

They sat silently, each absorbed in thought. Before the conversation could continue, they were interrupted by a page overhead calling Dr. Robson to the ICU.

He stood up. "I've got to go. I'm glad to see you're looking better, but you still look a little pale. You may have bled more than we thought. I'd like for you to get another CBC on the way out of the hospital. Stop by the emergency room."

"Fine," she said. "Oh, by the way, have you heard anything about what's going on with the rest of the men who were working on the well last night?"

"No," Blain answered. "What's happened to them?"

"I was told that they were all sick, a virus or something, or maybe food poisoning. They said that everybody who worked on the well last night, except me, came down with nausea and vomiting and even diarrhea."

"That sounds unusual. It's not seasickness or something, is it?"

"No, not these boys. They must really be sick. They had to send some of them home. I heard they even put one man in the hospital."

"That's an interesting coincidence. I'll ask around," he said. "Let me see you in a couple of days. I'd like to check those stitches. Now be sure and get that blood drawn on your way out. I'll let you know if there's any change in George."

"Okay," she replied. "Take care of him. I'm awfully fond of the old man. If there's anything you can do for him, please do it."

"I will. Now you take care of yourself." He turned and walked away.

She sat finishing her coffee, thinking about the whole situation for a few minutes as she watched the river beyond the window. She pondered over what he had told her he went through when he lost a patient, particularly the part about blocking it out and going on. She supposed he was right. She couldn't just quit. She had to get herself back together.

Finally, she rose and went to the ER and had her blood drawn, as she had been instructed. After that she headed out toward the Florexco compound, despite the fact that she was beginning to feel more distraught and tired.

As Blain pushed through the doors into the ICU, he heard his name being called again over the paging system. This time it was followed by "Stat to ICU," meaning that an emergency had arisen and that he was needed immediately.

He knew why a moment later. Almost the entire nursing staff was huddled around Jim Blake's bed. One was giving him external cardiac massage, while several others were drawing up medications.

Jan, who was Blake's primary nurse, had the defibrillator paddles in her hand and was preparing to administer electroshock. She looked up as he approached. "Oh, thank God you're here. He's had a cardiac arrest. We're getting ready to shock him."

He motioned for them to stop for a moment. He listened over the man's chest with his stethoscope and felt in his groin for the pulse of the femoral artery. Nothing was present. He pointed at the nurse who was doing the cardiac compressions, indicating for her to continue. "Let's go ahead and shock him, and we need to get him intubated. Has he had any Atropine?"

"He's had one ampule," someone said. "Shall I give him another?"

"Yes, might as well," he said. "How about a Dopamine drip?"

"Right," someone answered.

Blain looked at the EKG monitor. It was flat. The man was definitely in cardiac asystole, the hardest kind of cardiac arrest to deal with. Fibrillation, where the heart muscle went wild with irregular electrical impulses could usually be shocked back into normal electrical function, but in asystole the heart just stops. No electrical activity at all. It usually did not respond to electical shock.

"Want me to intubate him?" a familiar voice said behind him, and he turned to see Dr. Mason, who had responded to the cardiac arrest call as he usually did because of his skill in handling such problems. He, like most good anesthesiologists, was an expert in cardiac resuscitation and was able to skillfully place a tube into the trachea of a patient in order to easily give him oxygen through direct inflation of the lungs.

Mason opened Blake's mouth with a laryngoscope and carefully passed the tube between the vocal cords into the trachea. He gave him a couple of quick puffs of oxygen, and then Jan applied the electrode paddles across the man's chest.

"Everyone stand back," she said and pressed the discharge button. There was a thump and the man's body heaved. His arms swung forward across his chest and then they fell back onto the bed again, limp. Everything stopped for a few moments as they studied the EKG screen.

"Nothing," Blain said. "Let's pump him some more.

Give him bicarb and turn that Dopamine drip wide open."

Dr. Mason continued to ventilate the man's lungs. "How about some intracardiac adrenalin?" he suggested.

"Good idea," Blain replied and took the syringe with the long three-inch needle that the nurse handed to him. The nurse rhythmically compressing the man's chest stopped and leaned back as he slid the long needle just under the rib cage, up through his diaphragm and toward Blake's heart. As Blain applied suction to the needle, the syringe suddenly filled with bright red intracardiac blood. Recognizing that he had found his target he emptied the syringe into the still heart. "Pump him some more," he said and the cardiac massage continued.

They watched the EKG, waiting, hoping. But nothing appeared. The straight line persisted. "Goddamn," Blain said. "I think his heart is dead."

"I agree," Mason responded. "Let's shock him one more time."

The paddles were again placed across the chest and the warning given. Again the loud thump and the jerking motion as every muscle in his body contracted once more, due to the tremendous electrical stimulation. Again they waited and watched the EKG monitor with no result.

"I don't think you've got a chance," Mason said, indicating the man's pupils which were dilated wide open. "I think he's dead."

Blain didn't respond but continued to watch the EKG monitor another minute. "All right," he said finally. "Let's quit."

The nurse doing the massage immediately stopped. She was tired and sweaty from the hard work. The others turned away from the dead body, each reflexively finding something to occupy their minds rather than think about the death they had just witnessed.

Blain walked out into the main area of the nurses station and stood washing his hands. Stanford Wilcott was standing at the far end of the long counter in surgical greens looking through Jim Blake's chart. It instantly irritated Blain to have the man looking over his shoulder, although he realized that it was his right under the system. Blain was not yet a permanent member of the staff. He would remain on provisional status until he had been there for one year. During this period he was theoretically under constant surveillance from the other staff members, to assure that he had the competency level expected in the community. It was usually a nuisance situation that failed in its purpose of keeping out inferior physicians, and it was also occasionally abused to eliminate unwanted competition.

Wilcott was shaking his head back and forth as he read, flipping through the various sections of the chart.

"You got your bed!" Blain spat.

The chief of surgery closed the chart and flipped it onto the counter. "He should never have been here in the first place."

"Yes," Blain answered sarcastically. "I guess I should have treated him as an outpatient and just seen him in my office."

Wilcott glared at him. "I find your humor deplorable and unprofessional. Considering the gravity of this situation, I would think you'd be a little less flippant about this." He waited, but Blain didn't answer. "Dr. Robson, I think you're going to have to learn the limits of your ability. Unfortunately, it appears that this case

103

was mishandled."

"What do you mean?" Blain said, turning to stare at him.

"The man was seriously ill, yet he was not on antibiotics; he was not on steroids; almost nothing was being done. I think your work-up was woefully inadequate."

"What do you think I should have been doing? He was practically dead when he got here."

"That's exactly the point I'm trying to make. None of us will know what should have been done with this patient because no one else was allowed to examine him. You should have called for consultation. This was a problem that seems to have been above your ability."

"Don't be ridiculous!" Blain responded.

Wilcott's voice was cold and authoritarian. "I am not being ridiculous. I think it is an unfortunate tragedy that you persist in thinking of yourself as super-Doc. You consistently fail to ask for help. You attempt to manage problems beyond your level of expertise. You pursue radical and untried therapies. And in general, you do not conduct yourself as a mature, responsible surgeon."

"That's the biggest crock of horseshit that's ever rolled out of your mouth, Wilcott."

"Call it what you may, Blain, but as chief of surgery, I'm telling you right now that I am initiating a formal inquiry into your management of this and several other cases with which I am familiar that have ended in a poor result. You may consider your status here in jeopardy."

Blain was furious. "You can take your goddamned inquiry and shove it right up your ass, as far as I'm concerned. I'll match my ability against you or either of your shithead associates at any time. You can't run me out of this town just because you don't like the competition."

A smirk crossed Wilcott's face. "Slandering me or my colleagues will not accomplish anything. Your own actions have gotten you into trouble around here. I just wish you had learned something from the Pendleton case."

Blain's jaw dropped open at the mention of the case. It was incredible to him that someone could even suggest that his handling of that case had been less than competent. The man was alive due to him and to no one else. "I can't believe you said that."

"Believe what you want," Wilcott said. "But you've been warned." He turned and briskly left the ICU.

"What was that all about?" Mason said from behind him.

"That son of a bitch wants to bring me up for review because this patient didn't make it."

Mason's expression didn't change. "I can't think of any reasonable grounds for that. I wouldn't worry about this case. But I'm telling you one thing, you'd better watch out for him!"

Blain shrugged. "I know, he wants my ass."

"He didn't want you here in the first place. That was clear. But I think when he really got on your case was with the breast biopsy snafu. It gave him some real ammunition to paint you black with."

"It's true," Blain responded. "The incredible thing is that I was absolutely right in what I did."

"Maybe, but he made you look exactly like a hungry new surgeon trying to steal cases."

Blain sighed. "I don't know what to do. I guess I just have to keep rolling along and taking everything he dishes out."

"You don't have any choice. When you crossed both Hoyt Fieldman and Wilcott in one swoop, you bit off a chunk that I don't think anybody could chew very easily. Those two guys have this hospital in their back pockets. The board will do exactly what they ask, nine times out of ten." He paused. "Look, I've got to get back to the OR, but remember one thing. You've got a few of us on the staff here who will back you, but it's hard to fight those guys. If he really gets an investigation going, step very carefully and watch your tongue."

"Thanks, Rich, I will. See you later." As the anesthesiologist crossed the room and left, he stood idly watching the nurses continuing to clean up the dead man's body and go through the ritual required at the time of any patient's death. Mason's right, he thought. I've got to be careful. With Wilcott and Fieldman both after me, it's an uphill climb.

Hoyt Fieldman was an older general practitioner who also just happened to be chief of staff. It had been his patient upon whom Blain had performed the breast biopsy at the patient's request, not long after arriving at Community General. He had not known that Fieldman had wanted the patient to be treated by Wilcott. They had both been furious about the case and a big, big stink had ensued. Fieldman had not said a friendly word from that day on. He was a feisty little son of a bitch who had been in practice here almost twenty-five years and had been chief of staff for the last five of those. He was a very influential man in the community and was well thought of by almost everyone. But when anything at all troublesome or insulting or displeasing to the man arose, he displayed the most virulent meanness that Blain had ever seen. He could turn into an absolute banshee of a fighter. Blain admired the man in a certain way, and regretted having made an enemy of him.

"What the hell," he finally muttered to himself and sat down to write a death summary on Blake's chart. By the time he was through, the nurses had completed most of their work. The dead man had been placed in a zippered plastic bag. Jan Hendricks had gone back to the care of her other patient, George Elkins, and she seemed to be having some difficulty.

Blain walked past her on his way out. "He's doing okay isn't he, Jan?" he asked.

"About the same," she said, "except that he's starting some rectal bleeding. He's doing just like Blake did."

"Go ahead and start a couple units of blood. I'm going to get an internist to look in on him, too."

Jan nodded and continued changing the sheets which were soiled with the bloody diarrhea. She looked up and frowned sheepishly. "Sometimes I hate this job," she said.

"I can understand that," he responded. "Sometimes I hate mine." He turned and left the room. As he descended to the first floor in the elevator and then went down the hallway toward the laboratory, he worked hard to calm himself down and let his hostility ease away. Fortunately, he had no patients to see in the office that afternoon. He turned into the lab and went past the front desk straight back to the hematology section.

"Hi, Carol," he said to the middle-aged, slightly fat technician working there. "I sent a patient in earlier for a CBC; her name is Jori Ashe. Do you have anything on her yet?"

"I'm through with it. It should be on the list there.

You want me to get it for you?"

"No, I can get it myself." He went to the table where the results were tallied on a large sheet. He quickly found her name and followed the line across the sheet to the results. The hematocrit and hemoglobin were almost normal. Good, he thought. She probably hadn't lost as much blood as he had figured. As he followed the line across to the white blood cell count, he thought he had made a mistake. He repeated the process and once again looked at the same figure—"1200 white cells."

"Carol," he said to the technician, his voice carrying a note of concern. "What's with this white count of 1200? I had one on this girl last night and it was 8500."

"I saw that," she answered. "It's kind of peculiar, isn't it? I double checked it and it's right. Her count's only 1200."

"Jesus Christ!" he said. "She's supposed to be as healthy as a horse. All she's got is a cut on her tongue. There's not a reason in the world for her white count to be that low."

"That puts her in there with the other ten, doesn't it?" she said.

"What do you mean?"

"Look at some of those figures. We've had almost ten patients in the last four or five hours that have come through the emergency room with super low WBC's."

"Show me."

"Look down the list." He glanced back at the tabulation. As he looked at the figures, he was astonished. Ten out of the last twenty-five patients who had their blood drawn in the emergency room had white counts of less than 1500. One of them was down to 600. A count of less than three to four thousand was distinctly

108

abnormal and usually only seen in severe cases of anemia or bone marrow depression, or in cancer patients being treated with powerful drugs or radiation.

"What was wrong with these guys?" he asked.

"I don't know," she responded. "As far as I know, none of them was too sick when I drew their blood. I think they all went home except for maybe one, Tony Torres, the one with the lowest white count of all."

His eyes followed the lines across to the far right hand column where the names of the primary physicians of the patients were reported. One by one, he picked out the patients with the lowest counts and he looked to see the name of their doctor. The first one was Adam Thompson and then the second and the third. It finally became apparent that every patient with a low white cell count, except for Jori, had been sent to the hospital by Dr. Adam Thompson, the Florexco G.P.

Stunned, he started out of the lab trying to digest what he had just learned. This was far too much to be just a coincidence. Ten patients come to the hospital emergency room and are found to have severely abnormal white blood cell counts, and they're all patients of Dr. Thompson's. That meant they must be Florexco employees. The old G.P. only treated workers for the company. And then his own patient, an otherwise healthy young woman with no history of hematologic disease, is found to have a very low white count—and she too works for Florexco. Finally, his two patients in the hospital—one now dead—both were Florexco employees, having been injured in some sort of peculiar accident, and each having extremely low white cell counts. It was too much to be a coincidence, but it didn't make any sense. He turned into the emergency room.

"Rita," he said to the chief nurse of the ER, a portly but very competent nurse, "I'm curious about something. Has Dr. Thompson, the Florexco doctor, had a lot of patients in here today?"

"He sure has. Thirteen, I believe."

"What's been wrong with them?" he asked.

"Not too much," she said. "Diarrhea, lots of nausea and vomiting. Dr. Thompson said it was a flu virus going around the company. Except for that one guy, what was his name?" She turned to look through the log sitting on the desk. "Oh yes, here it is . . . Tony Torres. We admitted him. He was just too sick to go home."

"What was wrong with him?"

"Same thing, profuse vomiting and diarrhea, getting dehydrated."

"Who's the admitting physician?" Blain asked. "Dr. Thompson doesn't have admitting privileges for inpatients in the hospital, does he?"

"No, he just takes care of his own patients in the emergency room. But if they're sick enough to come into the hospital, he has to turn them over to someone else. I think Dr. Fieldman took over this one. He usually does for Florexco."

"Thanks, Rita, I appreciate it. Oh, one more thing. Are any of them still here, other than the one that got admitted?"

"No, the rush is over," she smiled. "Dr. Thompson was glad too. He seemed to be real irritated at having to spend his whole morning here."

"I don't blame him," Blain answered. "It's probably a lot more pleasant sitting over at the company headquarters drinking coffee and talking with the secretaries."

"If that was all he drank," she responded with a smile.

"But the way I hear it, he hits the hard stuff pretty good."

"Come on now, Rita," he teased. "A little drink now and then never hurt anybody." She grunted in mock indignation as he waved goodbye and continued on through the ER to the parking lot outside.

It was warm and sunny and almost midday. He felt tired. He had been up most of the night taking care of an emergency appendectomy and his two critical patients. He decided to go home and try to get a few hours nap before coming back to the hospital to check on Elkins. But he knew he probably wouldn't be able to sleep. Too many things were swirling in his mind.

The incidence and similarity of the abnormal white counts fueled an uneasy curiosity which he could not suppress. He thought about Jori and wondered what it all meant, but there was nothing that he could do except watch and wait. He would call tonight and check on her. He was sure she would be fine. The whole thing probably meant nothing, but he couldn't escape the vague sensation that there was more to the well accident than met the eye.

SEVEN

Thursday morning, the day of the scheduled drilling, dawned overcast, rainy and gloomy. Jori stood on the deck outside the control booth watching the early morning light in the east as it spread into the sky above the rig. She was wearing a yellow rainsuit and her hard hat as were the other workers on the rig. It was 6:30. In less than ninety minutes the plans called for her to begin the drilling operations. She didn't think she would make it.

The miserableness of the day matched the mood of the men, as they unenthusiastically prepared to restart. Nothing was going right. The check-out of the electrical system and the monitoring electronics had taken twice as long as expected. The technicians in the control booth were still fiddling with the wiring, replacing fuses, and checking the circuitry. Hopefully they would be through soon.

To the north about five hundred yards away the company's well-tending ship, the three hundred-foot *Florexco Lady*, was just getting into position to lower the submersible vessel which was to inspect the underwater portions of the platform. The workers on board the vessel were struggling in the rough seas to get the small yellow submarine safely into the water. When the difficult problem was solved, the small craft disappeared beneath the sea. The inspection would take slightly more than an hour, assuming no new problems were found. She expected none.

She glanced back down to the main deck where more pipe was slowly being moved into the ready storage position near the drill table. At least that was going without a hitch, but even at the distance from which she was viewing the work she could feel the lack of enthusiasm of the men. In fact, almost everyone was unhappy. The crew was under intense stress, understandably. The shocking deaths of their friends had left many of them fearful and on edge. The long parade of hearses entering and leaving the Florexco compound had been unnerving as had been the emotional, frequently tearful, interactions with the wives and children of the dead men. The horror of it all hung thickly around them.

The knowledge that the caskets had all been sealed, barring family viewing of the deceased, festered in their minds like an open sore emitting a foul stench of suspicion and despair. What had really happened to their comrades now lying twisted and contorted, faces destroyed, in those thick wooden boxes from which they would never leave?

The lingering notion that the well was snake bit was in the minds of many, particularly considering the strange illness some of them had experienced the morning after the rescue operation which left them still feeling weak and run down.

Surprised at the callous plans to renew the work so soon, a small number had quit, but the men who had agreed to stay on were trying hard to cope with their problems. They were irritable and nervous, though. In

113

addition, there was the difficulty of functioning as a smooth team because the men, as a crew, had not worked together very long. The surviving experienced members of the original work force had been spread over the three new crew shifts that had been formed.

Jori had done very little over the previous two days, Loggins having been in charge of the start-up preparations. She had spent the time brooding, wondering and worrying. But now with her work about to begin, she was doing what Blain had suggested. She was putting her feelings behind her. Soon she would be taking command again, and for this reason she was anxious for a final conference with Eric Duval, the new crew chief. As she had requested, he was coming up the stairs to meet with her now.

"You wanted to see me, Miss Ashe?" he asked in his hoarse voice. In just the two days that she had known him, she had become aware of what a heavy smoker he was.

"Yes, I did," she said. "I wanted to have a little talk before we actually start up."

In his mid-forties, he looked like he had been around. He was of average height, but thin, although he appeared strong. He looked like one of those men who never got quite enough to eat. The muscles of his arms and neck were too easily outlined beneath his skin, as were the veins. He had no fat at all. His temples and cheeks were hollow. His thinning, slightly greasy hair was combed straight back, and his face was pockmarked from acne years ago. He was missing two of his bottom teeth. All in all, he was very unattractive.

"What do you think about the men's attitudes?" she asked. "Are they going to be all right?"

"I'm not so sure I'm reading you, ma'am," he replied, flicking his deep-set, brown eyes back and forth from her to the platform below.

Her voice grew more authoritative. "I'm referring to how nervous they are—how they feel about working on the rig since the accident. I want to know if you think they're going to do their jobs efficiently. I don't want any problems."

"I think those are questions you're going to have to ask the men themselves," he answered. "But as far as I'm concerned, there won't be any trouble. If there's anybody who gives me or you any lip, or seems like he doesn't want this job, I'll have him off this rig quick. That's what I'm here for."

"You've had a lot of experience on offshore rigs, haven't you?" she said. "You may need every bit of it."

"I've been at this for a long time. I think I know how to do it. You just tell me what you want, and I'll guarantee you I'll have it done."

She wasn't really happy to have him as her new crew chief. He had loyalty ties to Loggins. Winston, who had never particularly cared for old George, had brought Duval in to take over almost immediately after the accident. She was quite sure that this man was his lackey.

"That sounds reasonable enough to me," she said. "You keep these men working hard, and you and I'll get along just fine. Now, there's one more area related to this project that might get us in trouble, and I think you need to understand it clearly. I'm chief of drilling operations on this project, not Mr. Loggins. I know he's overall supervisor of the rig, but not of the drilling itself. Is that your understanding of the situation?"

"Yes. That's what I've been told."

"Does that give you any problems?"

"No, not at all. Like I said before, I've done this lots of times and I know what I'm doing. You give me the order, and I'll make sure it's done."

"Has Mr. Loggins given you any instructions about when not to obey my orders?"

"No. He wants to know any time I think something wrong is being done, but I'm supposed to follow whatever orders you give me."

She concealed her annoyance and pressed on, "Do you think you will have any problems taking instructions from a woman?"

"I've never had a woman boss before, so I can't say. I don't plan to have any, though."

"What about the new men? Can they handle it?"

"They'll do what I say, Miss Ashe. I don't know what they think about you, and I don't care. I just want them to move their butts when I tell them."

"All right," she said. "We should be getting ready to roll in a little while. I'd like a good, clean beginning."

"We'll get it," he responded and went quickly down the stairs.

Instinctively, she didn't care for Duval. But that was all right, she told herself. It would make it easier to give him orders. Sometimes it had been tough to supervise George because of the close feelings between them. She looked back into the booth and the workmen were finishing up.

"You're ready to go from here," one of them said, and she thanked him and started down the stairs toward the work deck, intending to make a final check of the preparations. The rig was still very quiet compared to the way it would be shortly, when the big engine was started.

She could even hear the sound of a flock of gulls scattering and taking flight from the top of the derrick, spooked by one of the men ascending the stairs. As she looked around approaching the main deck, she had the feeling that, with the exception of the mood of the men, everything else was ready. The drill crew was moving one last set of pipe into place near the drill table. They looked ready to go. Good, she thought. That'll give the tool pushers time for a break before we start.

Their job was the toughest. They were the most respected and certainly the best paid of the team. It was their job to swing each new section of pipe over the drill table, engage it into the section before it, reset the giant power clamp, and then, at the last minute, disengage the chains holding the pipe as it was set into motion by the engine. A wrong step or a poorly placed hand at that moment could be dangerous, even fatal. Tool pushers had lost hands, arms, even legs in the bizarre accidents that happened when carelessness crept into their work.

She walked across the deck and then up the short flight of stairs onto the work area surrounding the drill table. She was met there by Jimmy Jones, the chief—a tool pusher par excellence. He was a black man, about forty, and extremely experienced. He had even spent time drilling in the North Sea where working conditions were always more harsh than anything off the coast of Florida. He knew what it was like to work hard, and he expected his team to work with him.

"How's it look, Jimmy?" she said.

He turned away from the pipe that was slowly lifted off the deck and swung into the air and stepped toward her. "Darn good," he replied. "I think we're in good shape. I'll have my section ready to go in another hour. All

117

we've really got left to do is reinspect the equipment and we're ready."

"Great," she replied. "We need a nice, smooth, trouble-free start-up."

They were interrupted by the urgent voices of another worker. "Hold it!" the man yelled. "Stop that winch, and be quick about it!" They both turned toward the man standing almost in the middle of the drilling platform, peering down into the mechanism of the table. He waved to them. "Jimmy, come here. Come see this!"

The chief tool pusher walked rapidly across to the man and Jori followed. "What's the matter?" Jones asked. "What are you doing?"

Bobby Ford, the young aggressive assistant tool pusher looked angry. "Look right down there. Goddamn, one of us could be killed, Jimmy. You told me this thing had been inspected."

"What are you talking about?" Jones asked impatiently. "What's the problem?"

"Look right down there through that pulley. Don't you see it? Look at that friggin' chain."

Jones and Jori peered carefully down through the opening in the deck where a large chain was running down and engaging in the gear. The rest of the chain was sliding in a long groove in the floor of the drill platform toward another set of gears and a winch at one side of the rig. It then arched into the air high overhead and hung down loosely in a loop, which was to be wrapped around the pipes as they were being applied to the drill. The tool pusher's task was to engage the chain to help with the manipulation of the pipe and then, as the bit started to turn, to disengage the pipe from the chain and swing it away. It was the critical part of the job. The part where any sort of accident could lead to disaster.

"I still don't see what's wrong, Bobby," Jones said.

"Just back that son of a bitch out, and let's look at those links real close. One of them is broken," he said angrily. He was tall, bare-chested, and skinny. He was a good worker and smart, but a hothead. He was also very safety conscious. Jones signaled to the winch operator, who put the chain into reverse, and it slowly edged up and through the pulley and slid across the deck. Suddenly they all saw what Bobby had been upset about.

"Hold it!" Jones said and waved his hand to the operator, who shut down the engine. "Would you look at that," he muttered as the three of them bent down to examine the chain. The other members of the tool pushing crew gathered around. "Mother of God!" Jones said, picking up the chain with his hands and examining a large link, which had obviously twisted loose its welded closing point and had now been sprung open under the pressure of the load. The gap was not quite wide enough yet to allow the other link to slide through, but it was not far from it.

"See what I told you," Bobby said. "One good yank on that thing and it could have come loose and cut our friggin' heads off!"

"Damnation!" Jones said. "Where is Lockhardt?"

"Did he inspect this?" Ford asked.

"Yes," Jones replied without looking up. "Where is he? Lockhardt!"

"He's in the john," someone answered. "He'll be back in a minute."

"Back in a minute, hell," Bobby snarled. "I'll get that son of a bitch back here right now. I want him to see this." He stormed across the deck, took the stairs in two

119

steps and headed for the toilets.

"Wait just a minute!" Jones yelled. "I'll take care of this." But it was too late.

The unsuspecting Ben Lockhardt was just emerging when Bobby Ford reached him. "You son of a bitch!" he yelled and grabbed the surprised man by the chest and threw him against the wall of the small building. "You could have had our asses killed, you good-for-nothing bastard."

The startled man looked as if he had no idea what Ford was saying, but he reacted reflexively. He was a strong, burly man, and his big fist came up quicker than Bobby could move. It caught him right underneath the chin and set the skinny man sprawling.

"You cock sucker, I'll kill you!" Lockhardt screamed as he stepped toward Ford, who was back on his feet in a flash and had delivered two powerful blows into the heavier man's abdomen before he could respond. The big man grunted and bent over slightly but swung his left arm around in a punch to the center of Bobby's chest. Ford swayed slightly, but came back with a round house from the right, catching the breathless Lockhardt squarely in the face. Blood erupted in a big spray from the man's nose, and he staggered back and crashed heavily into the door of the toilet.

"Get up, you bastard!" Bobby yelled, as the men on the platform, led by Jimmy Jones roared off the deck toward the fight.

Jones quickly put his arms around Bobby to keep him from hitting the downed man, but it was a mistake. Seeing his opening, Lockhardt, whose vision was obscured by blood, was on his feet to deliver a resounding blow deep into the restrained man's abdomen. Ford let out a bellowing grunt and sagged forward almost unconscious.

Enraged at the unfair punch, Leo Silversmith, the giant Seminole Indian, attacked from the right. He grabbed Lockhardt about the neck and swung him around, slamming him once again into the wall of the building, and then heaved him across the deck and into the railing of the stairwell. The bloody man staggered, completely disoriented, as Silversmith jumped from six feet away and landed on him with almost his full weight.

Lockhardt grunted and then lay motionless. The Indian pushed himself up and stood above him, watching the downed Lockhardt groan and flop over onto his back moving his head from side to side. For a few seconds, everyone was silent, but suddenly Lockhardt's feet began to jerk and twitch. The peculiar movement spread to his whole leg which began jerking and kicking. His back arched and then, as all of his extremities began to twitch and tremble, he pulled his head back, repeatedly banging it against the steel deck. His eyes rolled upwards and he began to gnash his teeth—biting his tongue and lips, which started bleeding profusely. A foamy discharge frothed from his mouth. The clattering and clanging from his boots and belt and head against the steel of the deck was ominous as the man continued to jerk and jump.

"My God! He's having a seizure!" Jori yelled. "Somebody do something! Get the first-aid kit."

Two of the workers knelt down beside him, attempting to restrain his jerking motions, while a third took off toward the crew building. He was back quickly with a large kit which they opened. Carlos Hector, a Cuban immigrant and ex-paramedic, grabbed a large bite block and attempted to place it into Lockhardt's mouth. But _suddenly the jerking stopped and the man lay motionless.

"He's not breathing," Hector said.

After what seemed to be an eternity, with a deep tortuous sigh, Lockhardt took a breath and then slowly resumed a more normal respiratory pattern. He began to moan and finally opened his eyes, looking around with bewilderment and confusion.

By then, the entire crew, including the men high on the derrick had arrived and were all standing around, morbidly entranced by the convulsion.

"What the hell is going on here?" Eric Duval growled angrily as he arrived. "You bunch of stupid shits!"

Carlos Hector, still bent over the prostrate Lockhardt, looked up. "Ben's had a convulsion. I think he's hurt bad. I don't know about Bobby; he took some pretty good hits, though."

"Jones," Duval said, looking toward the chief tool pusher, "if you can't keep your goddamned crew in line, I'm going to get somebody here who can. What the hell have you been doing down here?"

"I didn't do nothing!" the black man yelled. "I can't help it if these stupid asses—"

"Oh, shut up!" Duval interrupted. "Get your men and get back to work." He looked around at the crowd. "The rest of you guys get to your posts. What do you think this is, some kind of circus?"

He walked over to Ford. "Are you okay?" he said.

"I think so," the man responded weakly.

"All right, then get your butt into my office. I'll talk to you in there." He turned and looked at Lockhardt. "Hector, get this man into the first-aid station. I'll call in a chopper. We'll send him to the hospital."

Hector nodded as the workers scattered, a few

remaining behind to help.

"Goddamn," Duval said again as the crowd thinned. He bent over and felt Lockhardt's pulse. Apparently satisfied, he stood up and looked around. Jori was still there as was Jones. "Now what was this all about?" Duval said, scowling at the chief tool pusher.

"Lockhardt screwed up. He was supposed to inspect the drive chain and he botched it. Bobby came along behind him and found a broken link and got pissed off. So they had a fight. Damn it, I can't be watching these guys all the time. I'm not their babysitter."

"When they screw up, you screw up," Duval said. "Now you're going to be short two men. Ben is sure as hell in no condition to work, and Bobby doesn't look like he's ready either."

"Bobby's all right," Jones argued. "Let him rest a few minutes, then he can get back to work. We can get by without Lockhardt. I don't want him around anyway, after this."

"Wait a minute," Jori interrupted. "I don't want Bobby Ford around either. I'm not going to have anybody working under me that's got that kind of temper. This isn't a high-school football game. He could've killed someone. He's through. Get rid of him. And Lockhardt, too, for that matter. I don't want either one of them around here when the drilling starts. I won't have this kind of thing on my well."

"Now wait a minute, Miss Ashe," Duval said. "This crew is my responsibility, and I'll get this straightened out. We won't have anything else like this, I can promise you that. But it's my job to hire and fire these boys if they cause trouble."

Jones lifted his arms in exasperation. "You can't get

rid of Bobby," he said to her. "He's my best man. I need him. I'll keep him under control, I promise. But don't fire him right now. I'm too short as it is."

"Shut up, Jimmy," Duval said angrily. "I'll take care of this. Just get back over there with your men where you belong."

The black man whirled around and stared at him. "Shit!" he said, kicking the deck and then turned and walked toward the drill table.

"Eric," Jori said forcefully. "I don't care what anyone thinks; Ford's out. I will not have that sort of behavior when I'm in charge."

"Damn it, Miss Ashe," he responded. "You're undermining my authority by doing this. I don't think he needs to be fired, just disciplined. It's Lockhardt that we ought to get rid of. These men are nervous enough and scared. We can't have incompetence like this going unpunished."

"Get rid of Lockhardt, too. I don't want to see either one of them and that's the end of it." Duval was extremely annoyed, but said nothing, as she went over to Lockhardt.

He was sitting up unsteadily and Carlos Hector was talking to him. He looked bad. There were big bruises on his cheeks and his left eye was almost swollen shut. A deep cut on his bottom lip was continuing to bleed as was his nose. The massive gushing of blood seemed to have slowed down, however. He was absent-mindedly staring at his knuckles, which were covered with what appeared to be big blood blisters. The man looked like he had been hit by a truck.

"Is he okay, Carlos?" she asked.

"I think so. He sure does bruise easily though. He

looks a lot worse than the fight was."

"How do you feel?" she asked Lockhardt.

"All right," he mumbled. "I'm just a little dizzy."

"You'll be all right. We'll get you to the hospital."

He shook his head. "I don't want to go to no hospital. Just let me go see Doc Thompson. He can bandage me up okay. I'm all right. I sure don't want to go to no hospital."

She frowned. "I think you might need to, but Doc Thompson can look at you first. Whatever he says is what you'll do."

Lockhardt grunted as she started toward the stairs to the control booth. She felt disgusted and sick about the fight and having to fire the two men. She understood Bobby Ford's feelings. His job was dangerous enough without the risk of accidents caused by incompetent maintenance. But, damn it, she wouldn't allow this kind of violence. It wasn't right and had a bad influence on morale. She hoped that Lockhardt had not been seriously injured, but the mental image of his convulsion gave her adequate cause for deep concern, although there was nothing she could do about it now.

Jori went back into the control booth and spent the next fifteen minutes running through her own checklist of the monitoring equipment. At almost exactly a quarter after seven an incoming helicopter flew over the rig. As she was watching it land, the intercom from the crew chief's office came to life. It was Duval.

"They're pulling the submarine out of the water now," he said. "The inspection went okay. The rig's all set."

"Good," she replied as she glanced out to the north where she could see the small yellow vessel being slowly hoisted aboard the *Florexco Lady*. "How's Lockhardt doing?" she asked.

125

"About the same. He's sure turning black and blue, but I think he's all right."

"Tell them that if he has to go to the hospital I want him to be seen by Dr. Robson, okay?" she replied.

"Whatever you say. I'll tell them." The intercom clicked off and she stood watching through the window as the giant propeller of the helicopter slowed to a stop, and they helped the defeated Lockhardt across the deck.

She went down the stairs, crossed the main deck again and climbed up to the drill table. Jones and his crew were all standing over the infamous chain with coffee cups in hand. A portable welding unit had been brought onto the deck, and one of the other workers wearing a welder's helmet propped up high on his head was inspecting the freshly welded chain.

"That son of a bitch'll hold," he said. "Those other links will break before this one goes."

"It better," Jones said. "Because if it doesn't, Bobby Ford is gonna whip your ass."

The man chuckled, and the others smiled. The attempted humor was lost on Jori. "Everything all set here, Jimmy?" she said shortly. "You have enough men left to do your job?"

"No problem," he answered quietly. "We'll get it done."

She walked across the deck and went up the stairwell toward the mechanic's deck. Skip Major met her as she arrived and stood beside the huge engine which powered the rig. He was the youngest of the team chiefs, but at 26 the black man was experienced and capable. His hands were greasy, and he was wet with perspiration.

"We're all set if you are," he said and picked up a greasy rag, vainly attempting to wipe clean his hands.

"Fine," she responded. "Have you double-checked everything? I don't want any accidents."

"You bet I have." He pointed toward one of his men who was leaning down into one of the engine compartments. "And we're still doing it. My section is ready to go."

"Okay. It won't be long now. Get another cup of coffee before we start." She went back down to the main deck.

She caught Duval as he was reentering the crew chief's office. "What have you done about Ford?" she asked.

"Nothing yet. I've just got him sitting in the first-aid office. I haven't talked with him yet. I keep hoping you're going to change your mind."

"I won't."

"Look Miss Ashe, the men got a little tense. They had a fight and somebody got hurt and that's all there was to it. What do you want me to do, go around and play policeman?"

"That was more than just a little fight, Eric. Someone could have been killed."

"This is a tough job. This kind of thing is going to happen from time to time when the stress level gets pretty high. Lockhardt just should've done a better job on that inspection."

"That's not enough. I won't let a man as volatile as Ford work out here. And I want you to do more than even that. For one thing, you've got to make sure that anything as critical as that drive chain gets double-checked—triple-checked. We've had enough unavoidable accidents out here. We can't let something stupid like this happen. We don't need any more injuries."

"I've already reamed out Jones for not doing that inspection himself."

"I don't care what you do. I just don't want it to happen again. Do whatever is necessary, but I don't want any more trouble."

"I've kicked enough rear ends already. I don't think there'll be anything else like that."

"There better not be."

"Anything else?"

"No," she answered and looked around. "I'll see you up in the control booth in half an hour." Without responding he disappeared into his office.

The helicopter carrying Lockhardt was already gone, but as she reached the top of the stairs she heard the sounds of another incoming craft. She stood on the platform and watched it land. A moment later Jenkins and Loggins emerged. Wally looked up toward her and waved. She could see him smile. Loggins glanced in her direction and held up one hand in sort of a passive salute, but did not smile. After a quick stop into the crew office to get their hard hats they started up the stairway toward her.

The relationship between her and Loggins seemed to have improved immensely on the surface. She had worked very hard at trying to deal with him on an even-handed, nonemotional basis and it appeared to her that he was trying to do the same. His conversations with her were still strained however, but that was an improvement. It was clear to her that Wally had gotten his point through to Loggins about the necessity of ceasing the hostilities. The man was, for the moment, attempting to obey the orders, although it was apparent to everyone that there was no love lost between the two of them.

Jenkins hailed her as he reached the landing just below her and continued to come up. "What's the holdup?" he yelled. "I thought I'd see mud flying by now. What are you guys doing out here, just sitting around?"

She smiled. "We've been waiting for you. We could have been started an hour ago. We've been ready to go; it's just that we've been waiting for the executive types to get here."

Wally snorted as he stepped up beside her. "Very funny. I could still outwork any man on this crew and you know it."

"You may get a chance to test that theory if we keep losing crew members," she replied, her face becoming more serious.

Jenkins frowned as did Loggins. "Yes, that's what I heard. What happened?"

"The men are just a little too tense," she answered. "It's been a rough forty-eight hours getting this place ready to go. You know how they all feel about the accident."

Jenkins nodded. "I just hope we don't have any more problems. That would spook them for sure."

"What caused the fight?" Loggins asked. "Something about the chain?"

"Yes," she replied. "Bobby Ford found an open link in the drive chain. They blamed Lockhardt for it, so Ford jumped him."

"How badly was he hurt?" Jenkins asked.

"He must have gotten hit in the head or something," she answered. "He had some kind of convulsion, but he looked okay when he left here. I guess he's going to be all right."

"I hope so," Loggins responded. "What did you do to Ford?"

"Fired him."

Loggins frowned, but said nothing. Jenkins glanced back and forth at the two and then changed the topic. "So everything else looks like we're set for a good start, huh?"

"Yes, I think we're ready." She led them into the control booth where they removed their hats, set down the cases they were carrying and looked around.

A few minutes later, Duval came in and greeted the two.

"Eric, why don't we power up the electronics?" she said. "Let's see what our monitors are reading."

He flipped the large switch at one side of the control panel. One by one, he began to turn on the monitoring circuits which fed power into each of the data-gathering transducers located in the drill head far below. The gauges lit up and the needles slowly swung into position. To their left a print-out tape with twelve stylets came into life and foot-wide paper began to roll slowly across the display panel.

As they waited for the instruments to warm up and the dials and meters to reach a stable base line, Wally walked back and forth studying each indicator with obvious fascination. "Everything looks all set," he said.

She glanced at Duval. "Why don't you tell Skip to start his engines."

He flipped an intercom button and spoke to the chief mechanic at his station one deck above the drill table. A few moments later, they felt the vibrations of the giant engine beginning to turn over, and several lights blinked on in the upper left-hand corner of the control panel. A tachometer slowly worked its way up to 400 r.p.m. The distant rumbling of the engine was a comforting and familiar sound to those in the control booth. They knew it was one they would hear continuously for weeks to come.

The intercom came on. "Looking good," Skip Majors's familiar voice told them. "Looking real damned good."

She turned to Jenkins. "I think we're ready to go. Right now we're at 328 feet, fifteen feet beyond where we hit the rock layer. What I plan to do is pull the bit, inspect it, and if it's okay, then drop the pipe back down to this level and start drilling. What do you think?"

Loggins answered. "Let's go."

She flipped on the loudspeaker system, pressed a red button which sounded a loud horn, and then spoke into the mike. "Operations beginning; we're going to pull the bit." She then replaced the mike, went to the intercom, and spoke directly to the chief tool pusher. "Jimmy, go ahead and get started at will."

"We're on our way," he responded, and the intercom clicked off. She glanced at the clock above them. It was 8:22.

The big engine began to rev up and pipe began to rise from the platform floor. Very quickly a 100-foot section had been pulled up out of the well. It was disengaged, swung out to the side and placed in the storage pile. A few minutes later, another section had risen, and it too was removed, while Jori monitored the readings on the big board.

It took almost two and a half hours to get the bit to the surface, considering the total numbers of 100-foot lengths which had to be removed to pull the tip of the drilling apparatus up from 328 feet below the ocean floor and through the 1400 feet of water between the rig and the sea bottom. Jori concentrated mainly on watching the instrumentation and checking machinery functions, while Loggins and Jenkins occupied themselves with an extended tour of the rig, observing the operations carefully.

By eleven o'clock, the bit had been inspected and reintroduced into the main casing, and the reverse process begun. A section of pipe was swung over the drill table, quickly attached to the one preceding it, and then lowered into the casing of the well which had been placed along with the initial drilling.

By noontime they were within one section of pipe of reaching the level at which the drilling had been interrupted. The monitoring instruments indicated all was well as the last 100-foot length began to advance rapidly.

"Hey! Look at this," Duval said as the 280-foot mark was passed. They looked at the electromagnetic field indicator. The instrument was an elaborate compasslike device that measured the directional angle of magnetic forces at the drill bit. A second circuit measured the amplitude of the magnetic field as compared to the base line at sea level. The magnetic force direction was fluctuating wildly, having switched from a bearing approximately north to an almost 90 degrees due east reading. It began to gyrate back and forth in a random, erratic pattern. The amplitude of the magnetic field had surprisingly risen to double that of the surface reading. The amplitude indication then tripled, quadrupled, and went to the maximum reading. At the same time, the angle indicator became even more wild in its movements. As they watched, startled at the bizarre readings, the depth indicator rushed past 315 feet, and both readings abruptly swung back to normal, where they stayed until the drill process stopped, as planned, at 328 feet—the exact depth from which they had begun that morning. The crew was now waiting for orders from her to proceed with new drilling.

"Wait a darn minute!" she said and walked to the recorded tracings on the paper at the left side of the control panel. The ink lines corraborated what they had just witnessed. At slightly beyond 280 feet the magnetic field indications had gone crazy, but had returned to normal 35 feet later.

"What the hell was that?" Loggins said, standing beside her. Jenkins looked puzzled.

"I don't know," Jori answered as she examined the other readings. "Everything else is okay."

"It must have been some sort of interference," Loggins said. "The magnetic field couldn't have changed that rapidly."

"Let's proceed," Jenkins interjected impatiently. "You guys can let Adrian Sumter worry about that when he gets here. It certainly doesn't mean a damn thing to me. I just want to get going."

She frowned at him and then walked back to the window overlooking the rig, all the while thinking about the magnetic field changes they had seen in the tracings from just before the accident. The men below were standing by, several of them looking up toward the control booth, waiting. Everything seemed fine. They knew that now was the moment. Real drilling was set to begin.

"Okay," she said quietly, glancing at Duval. "Let's go. Quarter speed."

He turned to the intercom and spoke with Jones. A few moments later the r.p.m. of the big engines picked up somewhat and they could see the pipe again beginning to slowly descend.

The pressure indicator rose slightly as the bit began to dig into the virgin earth for the first time in days. After a few minutes time, they had progressed ten feet and the drill bit temperature was beginning to rise modestly. All other indications were normal. The instruments indicated that drilling was going easy and with little resistance.

"Looks like we're in sand," she said to the others and then turned to Duval again. "Let's go to half-speed." He quickly spoke to Jones, and the r.p.m. of the engine increased once more. Another minute went by. Twenty-five more feet had been attained, and the operations stopped as a new section of pipe was swung into place.

The drilling was going spectacularly easy. Within twenty minutes, two more sections of pipe had been consumed, and they had progressed almost a total of 300 feet in less than half an hour from the time that the new drilling had been initiated. "This is incredible," Jori said as they watched the fourth section of pipe being swung over. "And we're only going at half speed."

"Well, don't get too excited," Loggins said. "We won't have soft sand like this for very long." He walked toward the far wall of the control booth and examined the geological drawings prepared by Adrian Sumter prior to the onset of operations. "He thinks we'll hit bedrock at 700 feet. That's not far so you might as well get set for it."

No one spoke as the engine revved up and the next section was quickly pushed through. Jori studied the gauges. Everything looked absolutely perfect. The bit temperature was ridiculously low, considering the progress they were making. Pressure was neglible. Magnetic force was normal. Everything was going beautifully.

"Tell you what let's do," Jenkins said as they watched one more section of pipe being put into place. "Soon as we get that rock, and that should be any minute now, let's have lunch to celebrate." The others agreed.

Two hours later, however, they were still waiting. The expected bedrock never materialized. By three o'clock that afternoon the drilling was still going easy and unhindered past 1500 feet—more than twice the depth at which rock was expected. The attitude in the control booth had become one of quiet concern. It was disconcerting to have a geological opinion be so awesomely in error over such a basic matter as bedrock depth.

"We've made a lot of mistakes in the past," Jenkins said, "but I don't see how we could be this much wrong." He glanced at Jori and she shrugged.

"It's obvious that someone made a mistake," Loggins said. "It's not the first one Sumter's made in his estimates for this project."

"That's the point," added Jenkins, "and this is the simple part. If we've got a mistake in these calculations then what might be wrong with his other projections?"

"I'm sure we're jumping the gun a bit," Jori interjected. "We probably just stumbled into a minor aberration in the sea floor. We'll be hitting that rock any minute now. I'm not inclined to complain about a gift horse. If we get a few hundred feet of easy drilling that's okay with me. We've got enough hard stuff ahead to make up for it. I can guarantee you that."

Jenkins nodded. "I just don't like having anything unpredicted happen when you're talking about a million-dollar operation." He laughed sarcastically. "Or rather a hundred million-dollar operation."

The conversation was interrupted by the intercom from the crew office below. "Mr. Loggins," the voice said, "headquarters just radioed in and wants to know when you're coming back. You've apparently had some calls."

Loggins turned to Jenkins. "What do you think, Wally, do you want to go on in for a while?"

"Might as well," he responded. "We can come back later."

Loggins turned to the intercom. "Tell them I'll be there in a half hour." He looked back at Jori. "Keep me informed. I want to know when we reach bedrock."

The tone of his voice irritated her. It was neither a question nor a polite request. It was obviously given to her as an instruction, a command perhaps. She didn't answer but glanced at Wally, who was watching the two of them carefully.

Loggins picked up his hat and opened the door, stepping out onto the deck. Jenkins did the same. "Take care of this rig now," he said.

"Right." She stepped to the door and looked toward Loggins. "Be sure to get me more pipe. At the rate we're moving, we're going to be out by morning."

"It'll be here," he said, and stuck his head back inside the room. "Eric, come on down for a minute. I want to talk to you about some of these crew problems." Duval rose and followed him out the door, and the two of them went down the stairs with Jenkins.

She went back inside, idly watching as another pipe was swung into position above the well. Jenkins went straight to the helicopter while Loggins and Duval stopped at the base of the stairs and engaged in a very intent conversation. She watched them as it appeared to grow heated at one point. Loggins finally shook his head back and forth and pointed with one hand to the control booth while Duval held both hands up in exasperation. Then, Loggins went to the helicopter and Duval turned into the crew office.

Duval definitely needed to be watched closely, she

decided. It seemed likely that his relationship with Loggins was going to be troublesome for her.

She looked out over the rest of the rig where the men were working busily. The tool pushers finished engaging the segment of pipe and then stepped back from the drill table as the rotation commenced. The three of them leaned against the railing surrounding the work area and then spontaneously, all at once, turned and looked up toward her. She gave them a thumbs-up sign, and they smiled and returned it.

She glanced back at her gauges. The depth indicator read 1,612 feet and rolling. The resistance to the drilling was remaining absolutely minimal. It was unusual. Awesome might have been a better word to describe the progress they were making.

She walked across the room and studied once more the oscillating lines produced by the needles on the advancing papers. Taking the connecting roller loose from its carriage, she unrolled the paper back to the point at which they had seen the strange fluctuations in the magnetic field. She stretched it across her desk and reexamined it carefully. Opening the desk drawer, she pulled out the recordings from the minutes immediately preceding the well accident. The paper was unrolled and carefully aligned just beneath the current tracings. She looked again at the strange sudden rise in temperature of the well head which seemed to occur, seconds before the drilling was stopped, presumably by the lightning. But more interesting were the irregular changes which had taken place in the magnetic forces. The contour of the tracings was very dissimilar, and the time intervals were different, but in studying and comparing the two tracings she could see that the exact angles of change in the magnetic force, as well as the magnitude of changes in the amplitude,. were almost identical. It was as if they had both been caused by the same changes in the magnetic field. The only difference being that the first one had occurred much more rapidly and precipitously than the slower changes that had occurred when they pushed the drill bit slowly past the area of earlier resistance.

She rolled up the paper from the accident and tucked it away again in the desk drawer. She didn't know what to make of it. It was definitely strange. She would have liked a reasonable explanation, but she didn't have one. Perhaps Dr. Sumter would.

The depth indicator had advanced to 1,800 feet and was still going. Where was the bedrock, she wondered. Why was the drilling going so easily?

The door opened behind her, and Duval came in. His face showed concern. "The men are getting edgy," he said. He did not elaborate, but she knew what he meant.

"Tell them just to relax," she said, standing up. "Tell them we've lucked out and come across some sort of flaw in the bedrock, but we'll be getting to it soon."

He stood silently observing her for a moment. "Do you believe that?" he asked.

"Of course I do," she snapped. "Do you have a better explanation?"

"No," the man said, turning his eyes quickly away from her. "I'll tell them what you said." He opened the door and once again descended to the main platform.

She looked out the big window and watched him going down the stairs. He immediately went across to the tool pushers' work area where they were just swinging a new pipe into position. Then she checked the depth indication again: 1,925 feet. My God, she thought, we're going to hit two thousand feet without rock!

138

EIGHT

The death of George Elkins came as no surprise to Blain Robson, but the peculiar manner in which he expired did. The man died quietly the morning that drilling operations restarted. Although there was nothing that could be done, Blain stayed with him to the end, as always with patients he lost. He stood at the side of the bed, leaning against the wall, waiting, listening to the hypnotic, rhythmical sound of the automatic lung ventilator. Impervious to the man's dying, the machine ponderously worked on, repeatedly filling George's lungs with life-sustaining oxygen. It had become necessary two days earlier when Elkins's own normal breathing failed him.

The patient's face was puffy and swollen. The skin, bruised and strangely discolored, had broken open in several spots. It had developed an unusual, thick, roughened texture, one of the many unexplainable elements in the bizarre case.

Neurologically, George had died days earlier. The causes of the coma could not and had not been diagnosed, just as many of his other injuries defied explanation. But the most complicated and bewildering factor had been the strange hematologic syndrome that had developed. By the morning after his admission, George Elkins's white blood cell count had plummeted to an amazingly low level from which it had never risen. The platelet count, critical to the ability to clot and stop bleeding, had followed within a few hours and had fallen to an almost zero level and never rebounded. It had become apparent very early that the man's bone marrow, the normal producer of blood cells, was no longer functioning. He had developed a form of aplastic anemia—a state in which the many blood cell types normally present are no longer produced. The case was very mystifying. No one around had ever seen or heard of such a precipitous bone marrow failure.

It had been a heroic effort to keep the old man alive. But finally, exhausted and defeated, with all hope gone, Blain stood by and let death gently come. By nine o'clock, he had begun to bleed rectally again. At first just a little, but later, massively. The decision had been made the night before not to transfuse him any more. More than thirty units of blood had been poured into the dying body in the previous two days, along with multiple platelet concentrates. In addition, packs of white blood cells and units of fresh whole blood had been administered. It was fruitless, but it was all that could be done to combat the clotting defects that had developed.

Elkins had finally come to the inevitable curse of the intensive care death: to die organ system by organ system, until the total organism was destroyed. Tubes everywhere, needles, electrodes, catheters, the whole nine yards. But mercifully, this time the patient had never known agony because the brain had died first. Blain wished now that he had let the rest of the body go as quickly.

Bill Hallam, an internist consulted for assistance with the complicated case, stuck his head into the room.

"How's it going?" the tall, slender man said, adjusting his horn-rimmed glasses. He was scholarly appearing with light sandy hair, a Harvard man, well-respected, talented, and very compassionate.

"Badly," Blain answered. "I'm letting him go. I don't think it'll be long now."

"Just as well," Hallam replied smiling sympathetically. "You can't beat aplastic anemia, particularly with all the other problems he's got. I knew day before yesterday when we looked at his bone marrow that he was finished. He just didn't have anything left there."

Blain shrugged. "I guess it was hopeless. It's too bad."

Hallan nodded. "It's been a strange one. I sure as hell don't understand it. I've never seen lightning injuries cause aplastic anemia like this."

"Neither have I, but there's just no other explanation."

Hallam agreed. "Well, see you later. Sorry I wasn't more help."

"Don't worry about it. There was nothing we could do. I just wish we could have understood the pathology more."

After Hallam had left the room, a red light flashed on above the EKG monitor to the left of the bed. The heart rate was getting slower and slower. Blain put his hand on George's wrist and felt the pulse fade away. Soon there was nothing, and the EKG had flat-lined. He put his stethoscope across the man's chest and listened, but heard nothing except the ventilator continuing to expand the dead man's lungs. A high-pitched alarm sounded from the EKG monitor. Blain flipped the switch to off along with the ventilator, which quit with a loud, sighing hiss. The room was suddenly silent.

The nurse came immediately into the room. "He's gone, Jan," Blain said. "Tell the girls they did a super job. We held him together as long as we could."

"Thanks," she said. "I'm sorry we couldn't do any better."

"It doesn't matter. I don't think we had a decent chance from the beginning on this one."

She pulled the sheet up over the dead man's head. "The part I hate about these is that we work so hard and then it's all wasted. That's what's discouraging."

"I agree. Incidentally, I'm going to try to get an autopsy on this one, so don't let them move the body until I get that worked out." He started out the door and then turned back to the pretty nurse. "I'll come by on my way out, and maybe we can have a cup of coffee."

She looked up and smiled. "That would be nice."

He took the elevator down to the basement, passed through the laboratory and finally wound up facing the secretary of Dr. Perry Rothman, the hospital pathologist and county coroner. After a short wait, the secretary allowed him through to the pathologist's office. Rothman was sitting at his desk lost in thought over his microscope. He was a short, fat, unkempt individual with long, curly, black hair, slightly graying. He could have been a relative of Einstein's. His personality matched the way he looked. Blain considered him more or less a slob and relatively lazy.

"Well, look who the cat drug in," Rothman said, looking up from his scope. "What brings an esteemed young surgeon down into these parts of the hospital? I thought we were only good for dead bodies, chopped up livers, excised gallbladders and such."

The man's pompous attitude irked Blain, as usual.

"Cut the shit, Rothman. I'm just down here trying to give you a little work so you can earn that inflated salary of yours and get off your big fat ass." Rothman sometimes seemed to respond better to invective and sarcasm than to normal decent conversation.

"Ahh, smart-mouth mood today," he said smiling. "Well, I've got one for you. The blood bank called me this morning and said they're out of components, so you're going to have to give up trying to save that piece of dead tissue you've had in the ICU for the last couple of days and quit wasting our blood resources."

"Save your breath, Rothman. Elkins just died."

"Just as well," the pathologist replied. "The man's bone marrow was empty—devoid, kaput, shot. He had aplastic anemia. He had no living cells anywhere in the marrow at all that I could see. He didn't have a chance in hell. It was a waste of blood to transfuse him in the first place. You know, some of you guys up there are going to have to be a little more practical about who we're spending all this money on. I don't think you know how hard the blood bank had to work to keep that blood and platelets coming. The ridiculous part is that it was obvious he was going to die. I could have told you that two days ago."

"Is that right?" Blain answered. "Why didn't you come up there and write that down in the chart and give those of us who were struggling to do something for the man a little advice?"

"Hah," Rothman laughed out loud. "You surgical boys would split a gut if a pathologist ever came up there and told you how to run your business. You don't listen."

"I'll listen now," Blain said. "I want an autopsy."

143

"Nothing doing."

"Why not?" Blain's voice lost its sarcasm.

"No cause."

"What do you mean, no cause? The guy comes in here in a coma and dies. That's cause enough, isn't it?"

"Cause enough, if the family approves," Rothman answered smugly. "Does the family approve?"

"Come on, Perry. I told you there was no family."

"No family, no autopsy."

"What about you ordering one, as a coroner—a medical-legal investigation."

"No, can't do it," the pathologist replied. "There's no legal question being raised here."

"What are you talking about? We don't even know why the man died."

"Yes we do. He died of aplastic anemia, and he was injured by a lightning accident on the oil well."

"Jesus Christ!"

Rothman pulled out some fingernail clippers and began, laboriously, to trim his nails. "Listen Blain, you're going to have to come out of the ivory tower. I know you just came here out of a big hot-shot academic institution, but that's not the kind of place we are. I don't have the time, nor the inclination, honestly, to start running around here doing autopsies on everyone who dies. We've got to have a very good reason for me to get in there and work that hard. It's not a matter of me just running in there and zipping out that tissue, you know."

"I just think it would be valuable information to see what's inside the man."

"I'm sure it would be valuable to you, valuable to the nurses. I'm sure it would be very interesting, but that's not the point. There's no legal questions being asked

144

here, and there's no family requesting an autopsy. So, as far as I'm concerned, it's a closed issue."

Blain could see that he was getting nowhere. To Rothman, the issue was indeed a closed one. He didn't care about anything except keeping from doing the bloody autopsy if he didn't feel like it. "All right," he said, glancing around Rothman's office, "at least let me look at the bone marrow slides."

"You won't see anything. There's nothing there. I've already told you that."

"Look, Perry, you don't have to do the autopsy if you don't want to, but you can't stop me from looking at the slides on my own patients. So how about letting me see them?"

"Aw hell!" Rothman said and put down his clippers. "You know I've got better things to do than fart around here showing you crap you won't even understand." He rose and turned to a box of slides against the far wall. He hunted through them for several minutes and finally pulled out several and spread them out on his desk. He was starting to place one under the microscope when the beeper attached to Blain's belt went off. "Dr. Robson to Emergency Room—stat. Dr. Robson—Emergency Room—stat."

"Ah, yes," Rothman said turning to him in delightful glee. "It's time for young Dr. Kildare to go dashing off to the emergency room to save another life, no doubt. You'd best be gone, my lad." He stood up and quickly opened the door.

"I still want to see those slides when I get back."

"I'm sure you do," Rothman answered. "And I can tell you where they'll be for now and forever, and that is, stored away safely in my office. You're welcome any

145

time, I'm sure." Blain walked through the door into the outer office as Rothman turned to his secretary, "Show Dr. Robson the way out, my dear, and when you finish that, please bring me another cup of coffee. Two cubes this time, please." He smiled sardonically at Blain and then disappeared into his office.

When Blain reached the emergency room, the place was almost empty except for one patient, but that was enough. The big man was raising hell and causing havoc. He was strapped onto a stretcher, which had been put in Treatment Room #2—the one that was sometimes used for patients who had undergone extreme trauma. The man was belligerently roaring defiance of his unwanted restraints.

"Get this goddamned shit off of me or I'm going to break your neck!" he yelled at the two rather large orderlies who were helping to keep him from throwing himself off the stretcher.

"Mr. Lockhardt, calm down! You're in the hospital," the little nurse beside him cried as he worked one foot loose and began flinging it wildly around, kicking over the dressing table that had been placed near by. The minor surgical instruments, carefully arranged on the tray, scattered noisily across the floor.

"You sonofabitch!" one of the orderlies cursed. "Calm down!"

"Fuck you!" the man answered, continuing to kick his foot wildly, dangerously near extracting his other foot from the straps. One of the orderlies jumped for the swinging foot only to be rewarded by a knee into the chest which sent him sprawling onto the floor.

The other orderly attempted to control the leg, but it was too late. The second foot came loose, and the patient, swinging his hips back and forth, turned himself sideways to the point where he slid out from underneath the chest straps and scooted to the floor. His hands, however, were still tied to the sides of the stretcher which he began to yank violently about from side to side within the small cubicle. The two nurses screamed, terrified, and ran from the now completely out of control man.

Dr. Jim Harper, the ER physician in charge, jumped up from the counter where he had been writing, sprinted across the room and put his arms around the man's chest. "Help me! Come on!" he yelled to the others. "We've got to get this man under control before he hurts himself." He glanced toward Blain. "Do something, Robson! Don't just stand there!"

The two orderlies grabbed the man by the legs and attempted to lift him back onto the stretcher, but he was so strong that his thrashing about pulled them off balance, and they all fell into a tangled pile on the floor.

Blain had never seen a wilder scene in an emergency room. He quickly moved around behind the patient, and while the others continued to try to restrain his body and arms, he put his fingers down behind the angle of the man's jaw bone, and pressed with all his strength. "Hold still!" Blain yelled, but the man continued to thrash. He pulled his thumbs harder into the soft tissue of the man's neck and yelled again. "Stop fighting and hold still!" The man grimaced in severe pain and then suddenly quit moving. He arched his neck backwards and turned a hateful stare toward Blain.

"Get the straps on him," Dr. Harper said. Within a few moments, the man was again subdued, strapped down more securely to the hospital stretcher. The two nurses were attempting to clean up the mess while the orderlies hovered over the patient, threatening expressions on their faces.

"Good grief!" Blain said to Harper as they finished and stepped back from the man's bed. "What was that all about?"

Harper smiled and continued tucking his shirt back into his pants and straightening his tie. "Beats the life out of me. They brought him in about forty-five minutes ago. His name is Ben Lockhardt. He works for Florexco, apparently got in a fight out on that rig of theirs."

"Is that where he got so black and blue?" Blain asked, glancing back at the man, whose face and chest were covered with blue blotches and bruises.

"I guess so," Harper answered. "Looks like somebody just beat the crap out of him."

Blain smiled. "It must have been somebody awfully tough. This guy's a mean son of a bitch."

"I guess so!" Harper said. "Anyway, the story is that this morning he was in this bad fight. They took him over to the first aid station at the Florexco headquarters where the company doctor was supposed to see him. He's been there for the last couple of hours until finally someone got around to taking a look at him and sending him over here. The puzzle is that he was very calm when he got here and the men who brought him in didn't say anything about this sort of belligerence."

"What's wrong with him?"

"Two things," Harper answered. "Apparently he had some sort of seizure and he's got an acute belly, I think. He's tender as hell and his abdomen is very rigid. He might be bleeding."

"What got him so upset?"

Harper smiled again. "I told him you were coming to see him. That's when he said he didn't want any bloodthirsty surgeon cutting on him." Harper glanced back at the now surprisingly subdued man. "Anyway, when they got him here, he seemed reasonably calm, neurologically speaking. The only thing about him was these really bad bruises. They're continuing to enlarge. He's getting big hematomas all over the place." Harper turned around to the counter and picked up the clip board. "And here's the other thing. We got a CBC on him and the hematocrit's a little on the low side, which indicates that he may be doing some internal bleeding."

Blain picked up the clipboard and looked at the laboratory data. The hematocrit was 32 per cent, almost a third lower than normal. "It's a cinch he's lost some blood somewhere," he said, glancing up at Harper and then back down to the chart. "Wait a minute. Look at this white count, Jim. He's only got 1600 WBC's."

"Yes, I saw that," Harper responded. "I'm getting them to repeat it. It's probably an error."

"You better get a platelet count and some clotting studies at the same time," Blain said. "With all the bleeding he's doing, he may have a clotting problem. I'll bet you a coagulation profile on him is abnormal. Does he have a history of hematologic abnormalities?"

"No. The paper work they sent with him from Florexco said he was perfectly healthy. They won't let these guys work on those rigs unless they are in good shape."

Blain looked up from the chart. "There's been more than a dozen people in the last few days with these low white counts from Florexco. I don't care what the doctor out there says, some of their people are having hematological problems."

"That's news to me," Harper said, and the two of them walked over to the patient's bedside. "Except for that story about the seizure after the fight, there was no evidence he had any other problems. Apparently, he was a pretty nice guy."

Blain shook his head. "That sounds bad, you know. He might be having a bleed in his head somewhere. First the seizure activity and then this inappropriate aggressiveness. We may have a real problem here. Look at him now. He's as calm as a kitten. Something's wrong."

Harper nodded. "But, if he's bleeding as bad as I think he is in his belly, we're not going to have time to worry about his head."

"Mr. Lockhardt," Blain said, looking down at the patient. "I'm Dr. Robson. I need to examine your abdomen. We're very much afraid that you have internal injuries."

Ben Lockhardt appeared confused, but subdued—almost passive. "Okay, Doc," he said. "Whatever you say, just take care of me. I'll do whatever you say."

Harper's mouth fell open. He looked shocked. Blain turned to him and grinned. "It's all a matter of bedside manner, Doctor."

Harper smiled, chagrined, as Blain proceeded with the examination. The man's belly was distended and swollen, and with even the lightest pressure from Blain's hand he winced. It was easily apparent that the muscles of the abdominal wall were in severe spasm.

Blain turned to Harper. "There's no question. He's got an acute abdomen, all right, and I'll bet there's plenty of blood in there." He picked up the chart that the nurses were maintaining and looked at the record of the blood pressure. "Looks like his pressure is starting to drop some, too. Let's tap him."

Blain stepped closer to the patient. "Mr. Lockhardt, we're afraid that you're doing some internal bleeding. I think your spleen or your liver could be injured, and you're bleeding inside your abdomen. If you are, the only thing we can do for you is to operate and see where the bleeding is coming from so I can stop it."

Lockhardt's eyes grew larger and he looked more confused.

Blain continued. "I have to do one more test first. I'm going to give you some local anesthetic to numb you up, and then I'll put a needle into your belly to see if there's blood in there. If there is, we'll have to operate immediately. If not, we'll get a few more tests. Do you understand?"

Lockhardt nodded and grabbed the sides of the stretcher. He shut his eyes, waiting.

Blain glanced toward the nurse who quickly pulled the new minor surgical tray she had just opened to the bedside and handed him a pair of sterile surgical gloves. He put these on and, while she washed the skin with an antiseptic solution, he drew up the xylocaine in a large syringe and arranged his equipment. He turned back to the patient and, after again probing gently at several areas of the abdomen, carefully injected some of the local and then withdrew the needle and put on a longer one. He then went through the now numb area and anesthesized the deeper layers of tissue.

Next he set aside the syringe and picked up an even larger needle, which he pushed through the man's thick abdominal wall until he felt a pop. He then turned to pick up a plastic tube, which he planned to thread into the abdominal cavity in order to apply suction to see if any free blood could be obtained. However, even before he could insert the tube, dark red blood gushed forth through the needle in a steady stream.

"Damn!" Blain muttered and glanced at Harper. "I guess that proves it." Harper sighed gloomily and Blain put his hand into that of the patient. "Mr. Lockhardt, your abdomen is full of blood. We've got to operate right away. We don't have any choice. You might die if we don't do something for you soon."

Lockhardt opened his eyes for a moment and looked pleadingly into Blain's face. He started to speak, but then stopped and merely nodded, clinching his eyes shut again. Blain stepped away from the bed and walked with Harper to the center of the room. They spoke quietly.

"Better get a big-bore IV going and start some blood into him immediately," Blain said.

"Right," Harper responded. "I'll get that started right away. I've already typed and cross-matched him for six units of blood. Think that will be enough?"

"Usually, yes," Blain answered, "but in this case, maybe not. I have a funny hunch this man is going to be doing an awful lot of bleeding over the next few hours. There's more wrong here than just being beat up. I'll have the OR send for him right away." He went across the emergency room and toward the elevators which he rode to the second floor.

The operating room was in a special wing just off the main corridor of the second floor. He pushed through the swinging double doors and walked under a blinking red "No Visitors" sign, through a second set of automatic doors, and was then directly in front of the nursing station for the operating room. The cute, but very smart-mouth secretary looked up from her work.

"Where's Patsy?" he asked, referring to the chief nurse of the OR. The secretary pointed down the hall.

"Miss Howell is in the lounge," she said. "Where else do the boss types hang out except with all the doctors around the coffee pot?"

Ignoring her sarcasm, he found Patsy leaning in the doorway of the lounge, chatting amiably with Stanford Wilcott. In her mid-thirties, a washed-out blond and a little too hefty, she was a typical supervisor—relatively pleasant, but mean and tough as nails when she wanted to be.

He interrupted their conversation. "I've got an emergency we need to do right away. It's a guy going into shock with probably a ruptured spleen or liver."

"You're in luck," she said. "We just came out of the room with Dr. Wilcott's case, so we can bump his next gallbladder and do yours."

He glanced at Wilcott, who closed his eyes and put his hand to his forehead in disgust. "Fine," Blain said. "Why don't you send for the patient right now? Where is Dr. Mason?"

"Right here," the anesthesiologist's voice said from behind him. "What have you got cooking, Blain?"

"I've got a man in the ER who got beat up this morning. His belly's loaded with blood. We're going to have to open him up real quick. I'm afraid he's going to bleed out."

Mason's expression turned serious. "What's he like otherwise? Any heart or lung disease?"

"I don't know," Blain answered. "We really can't get a decent history on him. He had some kind of seizure and he's been acting strange."

"Do you think he's got some intracranial injuries?"

"I don't know, but we don't have time to wait and see. There's one more thing you may want to know about, Richard. This guy may have some bleeding tendencies. He's bruised awful bad, and his white count's only 1600. I have a feeling he may have some kind of hematologic problem."

"You don't think we have to time to wait for the studies on that? It'd be nice to know what kind of clotting problem he's got."

"No," Blain answered. "We don't have time. This guy's going out if I don't get into his belly pretty soon."

"I'll send somebody down to get him right now," Patsy Howell interrupted and walked hurriedly down the hall.

"Good," Mason answered. "Blain, go get dressed. When he gets here, I'll get him set up in the OR. Who's going to assist you?"

"I don't know. Who's available?"

"Only Wilcott," Mason said in a low voice. "You just bumped his case so I know he's available."

Blain frowned, then turned back into the lounge and approached the chief of surgery, who was standing at the coffee pot with his back toward him. "Dr. Wilcott, I'm going to need some help on this exploratory lap," he said. "Can you give me a hand?"

Wilcott turned around and looked at him. "I guess so; you just knocked the hell out of my morning schedule. I don't have any choice, do I?"

"A physician always has a choice not to take on a case," Blain answered curtly.

"Not when it comes to human life," Wilcott said pompously, glancing at the two OR nurses who were silently watching. "I'll help you, Dr. Robson. I'll do what

154

I can."

Blain nodded and left the room trying to control his irritation. He would have chosen almost anyone to assist him other than Wilcott. He couldn't stand the old fart, but it looked as if he were stuck. A few minutes later, he emerged from the dressing room dressed in surgical greens, stopped at the nurses station to put a cap on, selected a mask and adjusted it to fit his nose. He walked back in the direction of Operating Room 6 where Mason was already supervising the movement of Ben Lockhardt onto the operating table. Blood in a plastic container was hanging above the man's head and was running rapidly down the tube into his arm. Blain stuck his head in the door. "How's it look, Richard?"

The anesthesiologist glanced back toward him and shook his head. "You'd better get your hands washed quick. I'm not kidding you." The urgent tone in his voice was unmistakable.

Blain stepped back into the scrub area, watching the developments in the OR through the window above the sink. Dr. Mason, with a nurse anesthetist assisting him, quickly attached the EKG machine and put on a blood pressure cuff. After a moment he turned back to Blain, shaking his head back and forth, as he pointed his thumb down toward the floor. Blain knew what he meant. Lockhardt was obviously going downhill fast.

He cut short his scrub and, holding his hands in front of him, pushed his back against the door and stepped into the room. Mason picked up his laryngoscope, pulled open Lockhardt's mouth and intubated the trachea. He then connected the tube to the anesthetic machine and turned on the flow of oxygen. He looked up at Blain. "I can barely get a blood pressure. He's practically unconscious without any anesthetic. I'm afraid if I give him much it would kill him. I'll give him just a little Valium and hope that we can make him amnesic." Mason took a large needle which one of the nurses handed him, stuck it into the side of the man's neck and drew out a large syringeful of blood, which he handed to the nurse. He then inserted a thin intravenous plastic catheter through the needle into which he plugged another unit of blood. Another nurse was changing the empty bottle going into the man's arm and hanging yet another unit.

Blain turned to the surgical scrub nurse who handed him a green towel with which he quickly dried his hands. She then assisted him as he donned a dark green surgical gown. It was tied quickly around him and the surgical nurse assisted him with his gloves while a second nurse quickly scrubbed Lockhardt's abdomen with antiseptic. The scrub nurse and Blain then rapidly covered the body with sterile sheets leaving his abdomen exposed. He picked up a scalpel, as she helped gown Dr. Wilcott who had just come into the room.

Blain glanced at Mason silently asking if he might proceed. Mason nodded. "Get moving, Blain. I don't know if I can keep up with the blood loss. He has had four units of blood already and his pressure is still going downhill." Mason adjusted the anesthetic machine and studied the EKG monitor.

Blain looked down at the man's abdomen, took a deep breath and plunged his knife into the center upper area beneath the ribs and quickly brought it down, carefully avoiding the navel, in a skilled slashing movement all the way to just above the pubic hair. The wound was at once filled with the two raw edges of skin and yellow greasy fat. Blain handed the knife to the scrub nurse and

156

received a new, cleaner scalpel. He now, more slowly dissected down to the muscle layer surrounding the abdominal cavity and made a gentle nick through the peritoneal lining—from which blood immediately poured. He took the small pickups the nurse offered him, and the scissors, which he inserted through the small nick and then cut rapidly upward toward the top of the incisions and then downward toward the bottom of the incision. Finally, less than 30 seconds after the initiation of surgery, the man's abdomen was opened wide from just below his chest to just above his pubis. The gastrointestinal tract lay exposed in big bloody coils. Bright red blood spilled over the sides of the open wound which Blain opened even further with his hands.

"Holy smoke!" Mason yelled. "It's no wonder he's in shock. He must have half his blood volume right there in his belly."

The blood continued to roll out of the man's abdomen while Dr. Mason hung two more units of blood. The sound of the suction filled the room in big slurping gasps as Blain held the device into Lockhardt's abdomen attempting to suck away the loose blood so he could get a visual grip on what was happening.

"Tell them to send us all the blood they've got for this man!" Mason yelled to the circulating nurse. "And get us some help in here. We're going to need lots of hands to pump it in."

Wilcott, finally gowned and gloved, stepped in at the other side of the table and helped retract the edges of the wound so that Blain could more effectively clear out the blood, looking for the source of the bleeding.

"You better find something fast," Mason said. "I'm losing his pressure."

The suction device was beginning to clear away the red liquid. Blain and Wilcott both watched the large container on the floor.

"Incredible," Blain said. "There are almost 3000 cc's of blood in that bottle now." Wilcott merely shrugged and looked back into the wound as Blain began a methodical examination of the interabdominal contents. "Look at this," he said pointing at large purplish bruises that seemed to be present all over the small intestine. They were evidence of bleeding from tiny vessels just beneath the outer covering of the multilayered organ. "It looks like this intestine has just been beat to pieces."

Wilcott gazed down silently as Blain, inch by inch, looked at the small intestine and rubbed his finger over the enlarging hematomas, the collections of blood beneath the serosal layer. "I don't know what to do about all these," Blain said. Wilcott didn't respond as Blain lifted up several coils of the small intestine and examined the mesentary, the supporting ligament that held the organ in place. There were many similar purple blotches dotting the mesentary also. Many of these were oozing blood slowly. He worked his way up toward the stomach which also seemed to be bleeding freely.

"Pull up a little harder, Stan," he said. "I'm going to examine the spleen." He reached far into the left upper quadrant of the abdominal cavity and ran his hand carefully over the pear-sized organ there. "Adjust that light for me," he said to the circulating nurse. "I can't see a goddamn thing up in there."

The light was quickly pulled down and turned to an appropriate angle, and he peered at the inferior half of the spleen. "It looks fine," he said and ran his fingers again up over the top pole. "I don't see a thing." He paused momentarily to see if a stream of blood could be seen running down from the organ. There was nothing. "I think the spleen's okay. Let's check the liver."

"You better look twice at the spleen," Wilcott said. "If he's had this much trauma to his abdomen, he's going to have a ruptured spleen, I can assure you."

Blain basically ignored him. "I think it's okay," he said and began to carefully examine the liver. He found a small laceration on the lower edge of the large fragile organ. A steady stream of blood continued to come from it. "Here's part of it."

Wilcott didn't respond, but moved his retractors into an area where he could pull back the sides of the wound in order to help expose the injury.

"Give me a couple of No. 1-0 chromic stitches," Blain said and quickly put them into place, pulling the edges of the injured liver gently together. "We still don't have an explanation for this much blood," he said, looking back at Wilcott. "Let's look into the retroperitoneal space." He began to pull the entire GI tract to one side, lifting it partially out of the abdomen as he moved toward the back of the large cavity. "Everything I pick up is bleeding," he said, indicating the multiple little oozing areas over the GI tract and the mesentary. The guy's bleeding out from everywhere. I don't think we're going to find any specific injury."

"Holy smoke!" Mason interrupted. "Look at this." The two surgeons turned toward him. "The results from the platelet count just got here. He practically doesn't have any. It's no wonder he's not clotting. The man doesn't have any platelets to speak of. He could bleed to death even from a razor nick."

"I knew it!" Blain said. "He has some kind of

hematologic depression just like those others. There's something that's happened to these people from Florexco. They're getting their bone marrow wiped out. They're bleeding to death."

"I don't know about the others," Mason said. "But that's what's happening to this guy. He's bleeding everywhere. I'll bet he's bled into his brain. That's why he had that seizure."

Blain nodded. "You better pump as much blood into him as you can get, and get some platelets, too."

"I'm two steps ahead of you, Blain," Mason commented. "They're all on their way. But you better do something to stop the bleeding. I don't think I can keep up with him any longer. His pressure's almost gone."

Blain looked back into the abdomen. "I don't know what I can do," he said. "There's just too many raw surfaces in here, all just oozing. I can't cauterize everything." He continued clearing out the GI tract and examined the back of the patient's abdomen. "This doesn't look so bad back here; there's just a few hematomas. Kidneys look fine. The vessels are okay." He quickly flipped the large and small intestines back into the large cavity. "I don't know what else I can do," he said. "This is not surgical bleeding. It's medical. It's this goddamn Florexco. I've seen too many of their patients in the last few days with aplastic anemia, bone marrow depression and bleeding problems. Something's wrong out there. I don't know what it could be. This man shouldn't be bleeding this much from just a fist fight. He looks more like he's been hit by a bus. I guess we better close him up."

"I think you're being negligent if you do," Wilcott interrupted, his voice stern and critical. "You better quit mouthing off about Florexco and bone marrow depression and get back to your surgical basics, Doctor. I told you once and you ignored me, but I'm going to tell you again that the major source of this man's bleeding has got to be his spleen. You better go back in there and look at it again."

"His spleen was okay," Blain said.

"Listen, Robson," Wilcott responded. "If you've some kind of axe to grind against oil companies that's your business, but don't start doing it in the OR. This is not the time to start screaming about problems with pollution or the environment or whatever bugs you. This is the time to act like a surgeon and attack surgical problems. I don't know what's up your ass about this oil company, but I don't think it has a goddamn thing to do with this man's bleeding. He was beat up and now he's dying from his injuries and you're his last chance. You better get your head out of it and get up there where that spleen is and see what's going on."

"Pressure's worse," Mason said. "We're going to lose him."

Blain flipped the GI tract aside again and placed a retractor in the left upper quadrant and handed it to Wilcott who pulled hard. The circulating nurse again adjusted the light and he reexamined the spleen. "There's nothing on the inferior surface," he said. "I can see it clearly." He ran his hand up the side of the abdomen and up on top of the spleen. "There's nothing here either . . . wait a minute!" He paused and had a puzzled expression on his face. "I might be feeling a little something." He pulled his hand back and with it came a small clump of partially clotted blood. Suddenly, running down the inside of the abdomen from the spleen was a large steady stream of bright red blood.

"God!" Blain said. "There was a laceration right on top. It had partially clotted. That's why it wasn't bleeding, but now I've knocked it loose. Let's take it out. Give me a large clamp." He quickly took the instruments offered him and clamped off the blood vessels leading to the spleen. He followed this with a large suture which he tied firmly around the vascular pedicle and then, with scissors cut the organ loose and pulled it down and out of the abdomen. There was a deep, two-inch, jagged tear in the top of it.

"There's your bleeding," Dr. Wilcott said. "There's nothing weird about this case. Trauma, simple trauma. We see it every day."

"Bullshit," Blain responded. "He was bleeding from this, but that's not the source of all his bleeding. That doesn't explain these hematomas all over his goddamn GI tract. That doesn't explain 3000 cc's of blood in his belly."

"If you're trying to build a case that there's something unusual happening here, I'm sure you can do it," Wilcott answered. "But it's not going to be very convincing to an impartial observer. The man had a liver laceration and a spleen laceration and he nearly bled to death." He paused for a moment. "The lesson you ought to learn is to quit trying to jump to conclusions that support your particular political or ecological viewpoint. Draw surgical conclusions, Doctor. The OR is no place to mouth your protest movements. Do you need me any more?" He stood back from the table, ripped off his gloves and removed his sterile gown.

"The trouble with guys like you," Blain responded, anger in his voice, "is that you don't consider anything but the obvious. There's more to this man's problem than merely getting hit in the belly a few times."

"That's inexperience talking, Robson. Inexperience. I've seen men injured worse with less trauma. There's no way to predict what's going to happen inside the abdomen. It's a delicate region. Some day you'll understand that."

"What about his platelet count and his low white count? How do you explain that?"

"I don't give a damn about those things. None of those had anything to do with punching a hole in his spleen and ripping up his liver. If you had had your head where it belonged, you wouldn't have missed it. You were about to close this guy, leaving a ruptured spleen in. That's malpractice, as far as I'm concerned."

"He's arrested!" Mason yelled. "Let's pump his heart."

"Oh, no!" Blain said, dismayed. "How much blood have you gotten into him?"

"We've given him almost ten units now," the anesthesiologist replied. "And a couple of packs of platelets. I've got six more I'm getting ready to start."

"Damn," Blain muttered. "I don't want to lose him. I think he'll be all right if we just get his clotting functions back to normal."

"I don't think so Blain. I think he's bled into his head. His pupils have been dilated since the moment I got here. I think he's a dead man despite whatever you do."

"Let's give him a chance," Robson said, continuing to compress the man's chest rhythmically while Mason pumped in various combinations of drugs attempting to get the man's flabby, almost empty heart to pumping better. "He's still got a fairly good electrical rhythm,"

Blain said.

"Right, but he just doesn't have enough blood in him to pump around. I just can't keep up with all the loss that's occurred."

The resuscitation attempt went on for almost thirty minutes before it was halted. "It's hopeless," Mason said. "His pupils have dilated wide open. We don't have a chance of getting him back."

Blain was still standing over the man's chest pumping methodically. He was dripping with sweat from the hard work. "I can't believe it," he said. "He changed so dramatically from the way I first saw him in the ER to the way he was by the time we got him here."

"He just ran out of blood."

"He must have intracranial injuries," Blain responded. "He must be bleeding everywhere." He kept pumping for another minute as he stared at the now flat-line EKG. "All right," he finally said. "Let's quit. He's dead."

Mason immediately stopped ventilating the man's lungs, and the tension in the room eased dramatically. Blain stepped back from the table, took off his gloves and gown. "I'm sorry," he said to no one in particular. "We didn't have a chance." No one spoke as they stood around the dead man.

The door to the OR suddenly opened and the chief nurse reentered the room. "Dr. Robson," she said, "this case may have just turned into murder. There's some Coast Guard officers waiting outside to talk about it. Do you want to see them now or should I tell them to wait a while?"

"No," he responded, the fatigue and exhaustion evident in his voice. "I might as well get it over with. They're going to want to know what happened." He followed her out of the room, glancing through the long window over the scrub sink into the OR where the nurses were beginning the arduous process of preparing the body to be sent directly to the morgue.

"They arrived about a half hour ago," Patsy said. "I didn't want to bother you at the time. Apparently they're investigating the fight. It took place out on the well." She paused. "I don't understand how men can do this to each other."

"I've seen so much of it, it makes me sick," he responded. "When I was a resident in New Orleans, we used to see this stuff every night, and when the weekend came, we'd have ten or twenty a day just like it. Line them up in the halls waiting to operate on them. We saved most of them, but not all."

"Go on in," she said when they reached her office. "They're waiting for you. I'll be in the lounge."

Sitting with the two Coast Guard officers was Aaron Fischer, the chief administrator of the hospital. He was a small man, dapper, in his late middle-age, with an irritating, high-pitched voice. He was subservient to the old guard of the medical staff and quick to be critical of the new members. "Dr. Robson," he said, "this is Capt. Kemper Daniels of the Coast Guard."

The taller of the two men held out his hand. He was a handsome, well-groomed military man with a serious look about him. He had a small, well-trimmed mustache and lots of brass on his uniform.

"How do you do, Doctor," he said. "And I would like for you to meet Ensign Overby. He is a member of the Security Police."

Blain shook Daniels's hand and then turned to Overby who was a younger, much stockier, blond-headed man who looked like a college football player. His uniform contrasted with that of the captain, who was wearing a more formal uniform with a jacket, while the policeman was wearing boots, spats, and had a big .45 strapped to his hip. Each man was holding his hat under his left arm. He shook Overby's hand. The man did not speak but smiled politely.

"Dr. Robson," Daniels began. "We're very interested in what's happening to your patient, Mr. Ben Lockhardt. The incident in which he was injured took place outside the waters that are controlled by the laws of this state, so it therefore became a federal matter. The Coast Guard will act as the police agency in this case, and any prosecution that is necessary will be undertaken by the FBI."

"I see," Blain responded. "Well, I guess Patsy told you what happened."

"No," the captain replied. "She didn't. She just said that you had found a lot of internal bleeding."

"We found a tremendous amount of internal injuries. He literally bled to death from thousands of bleeders in his abdomen."

"He died?" Aaron Fischer sat forward in his chair, looking quite surprised.

"Patsy didn't tell you?" Blain said.

"No," Daniels answered. "She said you were having trouble, but she didn't tell us he had died."

"Well, he did. He absolutely bled to death. It was an impossible situation. He was bleeding from everywhere. It was like someone had been in there with a hammer beating him to death. There was nothing I could do. We did everything possible." He paused for a moment. "I think he had some intracranial injuries, too. He must have bled into his brain."

Captain Daniels put one hand to his face and smoothed

out his mustache. "That changes things a lot. We're not talking about simple assault any more. It's now become a homicide. You're going to list the cause of death as internal bleeding, I assume."

"That's right." Blain turned to Aaron Fischer. "We need an autopsy on this case for sure. Will you take care of getting that authorized?"

"I don't think there'll be any problem on that. I'm sure that Captain Daniels will verify that we need one for legal purposes now."

The captain nodded. "No question about it, we'll have to have one. This is going to be a messy problem now. I'm not familiar with a case involving homicide on an offshore oil rig. I'm sure the lawyers are going to go crazy on this one. You know, Doctor, I'm surprised that he was injured this severely. The report from the scene was that he didn't look that bad after the fight."

"His abdomen was a mess, and the intracranial injuries didn't help any either. But there is another unusual aspect to this case you might need to know. I don't understand it entirely myself."

Kemper Daniels looked puzzled.

"This patient had something wrong with his blood that kept him from clotting properly. That's probably why he died from his injuries. If he had been normal he might not have bled so much."

"You mean he had hemophilia or something?"

"Well, it's a little more complicated than that. He didn't have the disease of hemophilia, but he bled like one. He didn't have enough platelets, the little blood cells that help to form clots and stop bleeding when injuries occur."

The captain and the ensign both looked surprised and Fischer sat forward in his chair. "You see, Captain,"

Blain continued, "there's a very complicated chemical reaction in the blood that leads to a normal clotting process. It also involves a tiny blood cell that circulates in large numbers, called platelets. Now, in a normal person, these platelets react very quickly to form a clot and plug any holes that occur in blood vessels or any tears; so when we get a minor injury, after a few minutes the bleeding stops. But without enough platelets it doesn't happen. The bleeding can go on indefinitely. That seems to be what happened to this man. After he got beat up, the bruises and abrasions that took place inside his abdomen continued to bleed and ooze abnormally. In other words, he was predisposed to bleeding to death from this kind of a beating."

"But it was still the beating that caused him to bleed to death, not his blood problem?" the captain asked.

"The blood problem didn't start his bleeding per se, but it made it impossible for him to stop even the smallest bleeding, once it started."

"What would a man like that be doing working on an oil rig?" Aaron Fischer asked.

Blain took a deep breath and sat back in his chair. "That's the hard part," he said. "I don't know why. He shouldn't have been."

No one spoke for a moment or two. "That is certainly going to complicate this case," the captain said. "They shouldn't have allowed a man this susceptible to injuries to work at this kind of job."

"I'm afraid it goes even beyond that," Blain said and glanced at Aaron Fischer, who was watching him suspiciously. "I don't exactly know how to say this because I don't have all the facts, but there's something about a lot of the Florexco employees that is wrong. I have personal knowledge that a number of them in the last few days have displayed evidence of this kind of blood problem. I feel like the men are being exposed to something in the work environment there, that is damaging their bone marrow. It's causing blood problems in the people. It may be predisposing them to this sort of injuries."

"Dr. Robson!" Fischer interrupted loudly. "You have no basis for making statements like that. As the administrator of this hospital, I have to caution you that making generalizations like that about a reputable company like Florexco is highly inflammatory and unnecessary." He turned to the Coast Guard officer. "Captain Daniels, Dr. Robson is speaking absolutely on his own and not as a representative of the hospital. It is my personal opinion that he is not in a position to be evaluating the working conditions of Florexco."

"I'm only stating what I believe to be the truth, and I have a lot of evidence," Blain said quietly.

"I doubt that," Fischer responded and looked back to the captain. "We will be happy to cooperate in any way with the investigation, but the hospital has no information as to the validity of what Dr. Robson has just said. He is speaking only for himself."

"I accept that," Daniels replied, "and I will regard his statements in exactly that light. So, you think there's something wrong at Florexco?" he said to Blain.

"I don't know for sure. There have been a lot of patients lately with abnormal blood counts that work for them. I think it bears looking into."

"Okay," the captain responded. "That's not an area of my expertise, but I appreciate your telling me. I'll pass it on to the persons who will be conducting this investigation. Thank you for your help, gentlemen. We'll be in touch." They shook hands and the two officers left.

"That was a mistake," Fischer said, after they were gone. "I don't care what you do on the outside, but when you're representing us as a member of our medical staff, I don't think you should make loose comments like that—statements that you're going to have a hard time substantiating."

"I get the picture. You want to PYA it, right?"

"What?"

"PYA. Protect Your Ass," Blain said and chuckled.

"Oh Christ!" Fischer looked at him disgustedly and then left the room.

Blain poured himself a cup of coffee from the pot at the side of Patsy Howell's desk and then stepped out of the door into the central area of the operating suite and took a long, slow sip. They were just now bringing the body of Ben Lockhardt out of the OR. He watched as they proceeded down the hallway toward the elevator which would take them to the morgue below.

It was late afternoon by the time Blain finished with his ward rounds and went down to the morgue to check on the autopsy of Ben Lockhardt. On his way through the lab toward Perry Rothman's office, he bumped into Elaine Adams, the pretty hematology technician. She was one of the many good-looking young females around the hospital that he had dated over the past half year. He found her coming out of the pathologist's office carrying a large tray of slides. "What's going on down in these parts?" he said pleasantly.

She gave him a wry smile. "Work. That fat cat Rothman's running my tail off," she said. "I'll bet you I've made a hundred slides on this autopsy case in the last half hour."

170

He smiled. "That's my case, so I'm making you do the work."

"Somebody should have told me that," she said. "Then I wouldn't have felt so bad about it."

He grinned. "Let me to talk to Rothman and then let's pick up a cup of coffee."

"Okay," she responded. "I'll be in my lab." He watched her walk down the hall. She had short, curly black hair and a tremendously well-built although slim body. He quickly decided that he should start taking her out again and then turned and entered Rothman's office. The fat, fuzzy-headed pathologist was sitting behind his desk as usual when the secretary let him in.

"Well, well," Rothman said. "If it isn't our young surgeon with the high mortality rate."

Blain smiled sarcastically. "What can I do? I'm the only one around here who can handle these tough cases."

"The way I hear it is that, if you don't watch your tongue, you're not going to be around here to handle any cases."

"What do you mean?"

"Fischer was down here just a little while ago asking about this Lockhardt case. He said you shot off your mouth to the Coast Guard about bleeding problems."

"That's right. This guy had them and I don't know why."

"Well, I do," Rothman said. "He didn't have any bone marrow, that's why. He was on his way to having aplastic anemia. His bone marrow was almost empty. We took a lot of sections and made a lot of slides, and I could count on the fingers of one hand the number of blood-producing cells we found. I'm surprised that he was still able to work."

"That's what I thought you'd find. What do you think

it means?"

"I don't think it means anything. It just means the guy was getting sick. It's a disease. People get it you know."

"Cut the crap, Perry. We've had too many people from Florexco come in here with blood problems. Don't you think there's kind of a striking coincidence occurring here?"

"I don't think there's a striking anything occurring here, Blain. I think we have a few people who have had aplastic anemia, a little higher incidence than normal, but that's the way things go. As far as I'm concerned, there's nothing more to it than that. I see no evidence of anything exotic, just a bad luck case."

Blain shook his head. "I don't understand you guys around here. Everybody in this whole damn place just wants to ignore a problem that's as bizarre as they come. I don't know what you guys are all afraid of."

Rothman's expression turned more serious. "Robson, I think you're making a mistake to go around talking like that. I don't have anything against you or your protest activities or any of those things you like to get involved in, but don't try to suck this whole hospital into it, okay? If you go out and carry placards and throw eggs at nuclear plants or oil rigs or whatever the hell you want to do, that's fine with me. But don't get my ass involved."

"This has nothing to do with protesting. This is people getting sick, getting serious diseases that they shouldn't have."

"Don't tell me about diseases that people shouldn't have," Rothman responded. "I see things down here everyday that people shouldn't have. Nobody should have cancer either. But what the hell can I do about it? I'm not going to go out and start blaming the local telephone company because two of their women came in with breast cancer in one week. I think you ought to get off your high horse, cut the bullshit, and just do your work. Nobody's blaming you for the deaths of these people, so just let it go."

Blain started to leave. "You know," he said exhaustedly. "Nobody around here cares about anything except what's right in front of their noses, do they? This whole place could go up in smoke and, until you guys actually felt the flames burning your butts, I don't think you'd do a thing about it."

"Screw you!" Rothman said. "And close the door on your way out."

Blain let go of the door that he was just about to close and purposely left it open and walked through the secretary's area out into the main hall of the lab. He turned into the hematology section but didn't see Elaine. "Where's Elaine Adams?" he asked one of the other techs.

"She had to go up on the floor to draw some blood. She'll be back in a little while," the man responded.

After he left the lab, Blain took the elevator to the second floor, went into the surgical dressing room and changed clothes. He grabbed one more cup of coffee and headed down the back stairs toward the doctors' parking lot. On his way out, he watched as the workers from Finley's Funeral Home brought out a shroud-covered body from the small back entrance to the morgue and loaded it into the back of their van. Another one of my patients, he thought. Third one in four days. He wondered if the owner of the mortuary would send him some green stamps or something for being one of their best referring physicians.

NINE

By mid-morning of the next day Blain was turning off the road running south along the beach into the Florexco headquarters compound. He had finished his morning rounds on the few patients he still had remaining in the hospital and was now intent on discussing with the company doctor the unusual circumstances of Ben Lockhardt's death as well as the other evidence of hematologic problems shown in other employees of Florexco.

He had never met Dr. Adam Thompson, but he had seen a little of the man's slipshod work already. It always disgusted him to see physicians demonstrating less than competent skills. He tried not to prejudge the man, but after all, one had to consider the crummy circumstances of his employment with Florexco. Blain had heard that he was a retired military man who had a little problem with booze, and who had taken the rather insulting job of company doctor because he had no other opportunities. The paltry salary paid by companies to men like Thompson, and the lack of professional respect accorded them, made almost certain that any physician taking the job was going to be from the bottom of the barrel. They were prostitutes in a way, taking money to rubber-stamp the company's health policies as well as provide an emergency service that could just as well be handled by a nurse. Few self-respecting physicians were willing to be company employees.

He was directed by the receptionist to the doctor's office at the far end of a large building near the docks. Following the instructions stenciled on the door to enter, he did and found himself in a dingy waiting room almost half-filled by a desk behind which sat one of the fattest nurses he had ever seen. She looked up from the movie magazine she was reading and surveyed him with annoyance.

"What can I do for you?" she said breathing out a huge lungful of smoke as she talked. "You don't work for Florexco, do you?" She looked down and put her cigarette out in the butt-filled ashtray in front of her.

"I'm Dr. Robson," he answered, "from Community General Hospital. I came to see Dr. Thompson."

"Oh," she said. "Well, wait just a minute. Let me check on him. He don't usually see people before 10:30. But he'll probably see you—being a doctor and all." She disappeared through a door behind her and returned a few moments later. "He said to come on in." She held the door open for him.

"Thanks," he said and walked around the desk. "Doesn't look like you're too busy here this morning."

She let out a snort. "Ha! This is our busiest time of the day. You ought to see it around here when it really slacks off."

He went through the door and glanced back at her as she pulled out another cigarette, picked up her magazine and waddled across the room to the short, ragged couch sitting in front of the desk.

"Close that door if you will, and come on in," a voice

175

said from behind him.

At the end of the narrow room a tall, gangly man was sitting behind a small desk. He had thin, brown, ill-kept hair above a narrow face and deep-set dark eyes. There were circles of loose, baggy tissue beneath the eyes and a bulbous, acne-scarred rum nose. The man's cheeks were blotched with dilated small veins and arterioles. The general appearance of his face and body was one of sad neglect. He couldn't have weighed more than 120 pounds and his clothes hung on him like a rag doll. He had a distinctly unhealthy appearance. He was obviously a rummy, probably had cirrhosis.

"Dr. Thompson?" Blain said questioningly. "I am Dr. Robson. I'm a general surgeon."

"That's what I heard," the man answered in a raspy voice. "So you're the one that took care of old George Elkins and that other guy. What's his name? The other one who got killed by the lightning."

"Yes. That's right," Blain answered. "And also Ben Lockhardt yesterday."

"Yes," Thompson responded. "Old Ben Lockhardt. Troublemaker that one was. It's too bad about the fight, though."

"That's what I'm here for, really. I wanted to ask you a few questions about that and some other things."

Thompson stood up, walked from behind his desk and held out his hand, which Blain shook, and the two men stood facing each other. "I'll tell you what I can, Dr. Robson," he said. "I don't think I have much for you. We don't run a very big operation here you know." He gestured around the room. "It's a hell of a place to try to practice medicine, isn't it?"

He walked across the room and laid his hand on top of

an ancient instrument sterilizer. He looked at it for a moment and then back toward Blain. "You know, they told me when I hired on with this company, almost ten years ago, that they were going to give me excellent and well-equipped facilities in which to practice my art." He grinned sadly. "This is what I got. This is what they call excellent and well-equipped facilities. A beat-up old sterilizer, a few syringes and needles, a couple of blood pressure cuffs, and a stethoscope. And I've been hauling this crap around with me from place to place for almost a decade now. None of it's worth a damn."

"Why won't they give you better stuff?"

"They don't want to waste the money. They don't really want me to practice medicine. All they want me here for is merely to decrease the liability risk. They figure that having a doctor on the premises makes it less likely for a lawsuit, should someone get injured."

"I doubt if you could do any good for anyone with what I see here, even if you had the chance," Blain said.

"You're right. I knew that. I knew that from the first day I signed on, but what can I do?" He turned and walked back toward the desk. "Have a seat," he said, pointing to an old chair. Blain did as he was asked while the old man reclaimed his chair behind the desk. "The irony of it all, Dr. Robson, is that I couldn't do anything worth a damn even if I had all the equipment. I don't know what I'm doing any more."

Blain responded only with a puzzled expression and Thompson continued. "That's what the military does to you. I practiced medicine in the army for twelve years, good years. Did a good job, too. Then they promoted me, made me chief, made me an administrator. That's what did me in. You see, I stopped practicing medicine then

177

and started making decisions. Decisions about how to allocate the money the hospital had, decisions about what to do with the nursing staff. Decisions about how to punish a stubborn medic who wasn't meeting his obligations. Pretty soon all I knew how to be was an old rundown doctor giving a few commands to the young men who were doing all the medicine. By then they had me trapped 'cause I had to stay until retirement time. I knew I couldn't make a living on my own." He stopped speaking and studied Blain for a moment. "But that's another story," he finally said. "You didn't come here to hear me bellyache and groan. There must be something I can help you with. But first, how 'bout a cup of coffee?"

Blain nodded and the man poured two cups from a pot beside his desk. He handed one to Blain and then rose with his, and walked to the end of the room, and entered a small lab area, off to the side and out of sight. Blain heard the sound of a cabinet being opened, the top of a bottle being unscrewed, and then the cabinet closing again. Thompson reentered the room, stirring his coffee. "I guess there's going to be some kind of inquiry about the beating death of Lockhardt," he said as he walked back to his desk. "Could even be a homicide, huh?"

Blain frowned. "Did you know the man had bone marrow depression on his autopsy? The day they brought him to the emergency room he had an extremely low platelet count." He paused for a moment waiting for the significance to sink in to Thompson. "His white count was only 1600 when I first saw him."

Thompson's eyes blinked several times. "Well, ain't that a hell of a note," he responded. "I wonder if that had something to do with him bleeding to death?"

"Damn right it did," Blain answered. "I don't think he

would have died from the type of injuries he received if he had been normal, hematologically speaking. He just couldn't clot."

"Well that is one hell of a coincidence." Thompson rose and pulled the top drawer of a large file cabinet open and lifted out a folder. Blain could see the name "Lockhardt" written across the top. "When he came to work here I did a physical on him, and he looked pretty healthy then. I didn't get a white count on him, though." He closed the folder and returned it to the file. "Well, disease is a funny thing isn't it? You never know what's going to happen to people." He paused thoughtfully for a moment. "That sure is going to complicate the legal aspects of this problem."

"That's part of what I wanted to ask you about," Blain responded. "Have you had any other workers out there having hematologic problems?"

"What do you mean?"

"I mean has anybody else had any blood problems, anything strange happening here?"

Adam's eyes narrowed. "What do you mean, strange, Dr. Robson? I don't think we have anything strange going on here. This is just an offshore oil drilling company. We have accidents and fights just like any other industrial organization. There's nothing unusual going on that I feel inclined to tell you about."

Blain sensed that the man was becoming hostile. "But what about all those low white counts that you got on that group of men in the emergency room last week, after the accident?"

"What low white counts?"

"You saw about a dozen patients in the emergency room a week ago. One of them even got admitted. But

179

they all seemed to be having nausea and vomiting type problems and the CBC's showed low white counts all across the board. And Jori Ashe's white count was low at the same time I had to take care of her for another problem. That's what I'm talking about. What about those results?"

"I don't think we have any problem there. Those men are all doing okay. I'm not sure it's any business of yours anyway. How did you find out about those lab results?"

"I just happened to come across them. But don't you think that's kind of strange? That more than a dozen people working on that rig have abnormal blood counts, and then I get a patient who's been all beaten up and who bleeds to death because of early aplastic anemia all within the span of a few days?"

"It's not entirely clear to me what you're after," Thompson responded. "But I'm beginning not to like the nature of some of your implications. If you have anything to say, why don't you spit it out."

"All right, I will. Something's going on here at Florexco. You have too many people with signs of bone marrow depression. I think you've got a problem here that you don't know about." He paused for a moment. "Or maybe you do know about it and are choosing to ignore it, or maybe cover it up."

Thompson stared at him for a moment, his face not quite concealing the hostility Blain knew was growing. "You're doing some awful strong talking, you know that, buddy?" he said. "I think I've got somebody else who better listen to you." He picked up the phone and dialed three numbers. "This is Thompson. You better tell Mr. Loggins to come over here right away." He paused. "No. I said right away." He replaced the receiver. "I think you better tell Mr. Loggins what you've been saying to me. He's chief of operations. I think he'd be interested in listening to you, but I'll bet you he ain't going to like what you're saying any more than I do."

"Yes. I know all about Loggins," Blain said quickly, but then checked his tongue. The two sat quietly for a few minutes more as the old man finished his coffee. Blain looked around the room. The outside door beyond the office opened and then closed, and a moment later Winston Loggins entered the room. Blain recognized him immediately and felt a sudden rekindling of the anger he had felt the night he had watched him knock Jori to the floor.

"What's going on, Adam?" Loggins said.

"I have here," Dr. Thompson said, "one Dr. Blain Robson, surgeon, from Community General Hospital. He's made a few comments about Florexco that I think you ought to hear. Dr. Robson, meet Mr. Winston Loggins, chief of operations for the St. Lucie One project."

Loggins stuck out his hand and the two shook quickly. His expression was one of suspicious curiosity. "Blain Robson," he said. "That name sounds familiar. Where do I know you from?"

Before Blain could speak, Dr. Thompson spoke for him. "You should know Dr. Robson well, Winston. He's on the Florexco enemies list. He took part in the protest movement to try to stop the well from going in. He's an environmentalist and ecology protector." He dragged the last word out slowly for emphasis. "He doesn't like oil companies or nuclear energy. He's a man who thinks we're dangerous."

Blain glanced quickly at Thompson, surprised at the

man's knowledge about his earlier activities. He began to think that the old doctor wasn't the rundown old rumbelly he had assumed him to be. He looked back at Loggins.

"Oh yes," the chief of operations said, "now I remember. You and your buddies gave us quite a run on this one." He curled his lower lip into his mouth and bit gently on it for a moment, staring at Blain. "But I've seen you since then, you look familiar to me. I can't place it, but I know I've seen you."

Blain let him think for a while and then answered him. "Yes. You've seen me, Mr. Loggins, and not too long ago. You bumped into me at Harpoon Harry's." Loggins's face turned more intent and Blain couldn't hide his own hostile expression.

"When were you at Harpoon Harry's?" Loggins scowled.

"The night of the well accident," Blain said slowly. "I believe you went there to meet Jori Ashe."

Blain felt his neck muscles tighten and one hand reflexively curled into a fist which he forced to relax. Loggins's expression changed to one of sudden recognition and he nodded slowly. His right hand went up and he rubbed his temple.

The two men stared at each other for a moment, and then the tension broke slightly at the sound of a match being struck by Adam Thompson. Blain glanced at him in time to see him lighting a thin black cigar. The old doctor took in a long drag and let out the smoke slowly. "Dr. Robson here thinks we're having too many men with blood problems. He thinks there must be something we're doing here at Florexco that's causing it."

"Oh yeah?" Loggins said. "What kind of problems do

you think we're having?"

"Look," Blain said, "I didn't some out here to make accusations or to cause you trouble. I merely wanted to ask a few questions about some strange laboratory results that I've seen from some of the workers here. I'm the one who operated on Ben Lockhardt. He died from more than just the results of that fight. He had aplastic anemia and there have been about a dozen other people who've had abnormal blood counts. Dr. Thompson knows about them. And the two old men who died from the accident had bone marrow problems. All I'm saying is that it's too much of a coincidence to be ignored."

"I still don't understand what you're saying," Loggins interrupted.

"You're having too many workers with blood problems. Don't you think it'd be reasonable to look into this and see if there's a cause?"

"We appreciate your concern," Loggins responded. "But as you can see, we have a full-time physician of our own here looking after our men. I'm quite sure if we had any kind of health problems, Dr. Thompson could handle it."

"Up until this moment, I don't think Dr. Thompson was even aware of the problem," Blain retorted.

"What problem, Robson?" Thompson interjected. "We have two men who get involved in a lightning accident who have all kinds of complications and die. Surely you don't relate that to the others. Then, we have one man who by bad luck gets into a fight and also has aplastic anemia. And we have a few men who've had slightly low white blood counts, probably because of a viral disease. Now don't walk in here and try to link all of those things together and say that we have a problem. I

183

think you're mixing fact and fantasy. I don't think there is a problem—those men are all fine now."

Blain looked at Thompson for a moment and then turned back to Loggins. "I don't think he's right," he said.

"What you think is not of any great interest to me or Dr. Thompson or Florexco," Loggins said caustically. "We can take care of our own situation here, and we don't need you butting in to help us out."

"I think you're ignoring a potentially serious situation. You could have men here that are getting exposed to something toxic. There could be more of the same."

"There it is," Loggins said. "I knew it would come out. You environmentalists are always the same. There's not a damn thing that industry can do without you guys complaining. Now we're exposing these men to something toxic, right?"

Blain made an exasperated expression. "I'm only suggesting that something may be wrong and you ought to look into it."

"We have looked into it," Thompson said. "I look into it all the time. That's my job, to preserve the health of these men. You know as well as I do that aplastic anemia can just occur spontaneously without cause. Sure, it can be caused by drugs or chemicals or radiation," he paused. "What about radiation? You hadn't thought about that. What do you think? Is it the nuclear power plant that's doing this to these men? Why don't you go jump on their asses instead of ours? I know why you don't, because it's not radiation, that's why. And it's not chemicals either. What it is, is just an unlucky coincidence, and you're trying to put that together with a bunch of other crap to come up with something that makes us look bad. It's just the kind of illogical nonsense that you protestors are good at."

"Look," Blain said. "I'm not saying it is caused by chemicals. And I'm not saying it isn't being caused by radiation. Lord knows it could be. But the main thing is, I'm not saying it's being caused by anything in particular. I'm just coming out here to help point out the fact that you have a statistically unlikely situation that's developed. To try to blame it on coincidence is being a little too casual about it. And I think you owe it to the health of your employees to at least check on it and make sure they're okay. I think you should get blood counts on everyone out there on that rig right now and see what's going on. What are you going to think if you find a whole bunch of them with early bone marrow depression? Then what are you going to do, yell at me for protesting too much?"

"Dr. Robson," Loggins said. "You can take your chemical theories or your radiation theories and blow them right out your ass as far as I'm concerned. We're not interested in your opinions or your ideas, and, as a matter of fact, your welcome here has been used up. I'd appreciate it if you'd turn right around and get the hell out. We don't want you on Florexco property. And in addition to that, we don't want you talking to Florexco people. And in addition to that, I can promise you right now that if you make any unsubstantiated accusations or charges against this company, our attorneys will eat you alive. We absolutely are not going to tolerate any cheap slander from you on this matter. If you come up with some solid data, you come to me and we'll do something about it. Otherwise, keep your fantasies to yourself or you'll wish that you did." He turned to his left, opened the door and signaled to the fat nurse sitting beyond. "Show Dr. Robson the way out, will you please?" She rose and opened the outside door.

Blain took one last look at the two men, shook his head and left Thompson's office and went through the outside door into the midday sun. It was quickly pulled shut behind him, and he stood alone looking out over the docks reaching into the St. Lucie River. A large crew boat loaded with men was coming toward him from the inlet.

Disgusted, he went to his car and left the Florexco compound. As he sped north up the beach road, he felt ridiculous for being unable to calmly communicate his concerns to Thompson. It was obvious that he must have challenged the old man too much, invoking his defensiveness and anger instead of appreciation. As for Loggins, it was clear that the man was an irrational bastard. The image of his fist coming up, slamming into Jori, knocking her across the floor at Harpoon Harry's kept crossing his mind.

He wondered how Jori was doing. He had not seen nor had he been able to reach her in several days, and he was very curious as to her white blood cell count. Perhaps, he thought, that's the way to get through to them at Florexco, through Jori. She seemed more reasonable than all the others combined and would be particularly so if her own bone marrow was being affected by whatever was causing the trouble. His next step, he decided, would be to contact her and explain the situation.

TEN

It was less than a day and a half after his meeting with Loggins and Dr. Thompson that Blain came face to face with the fact that his intervention into Florexco affairs was jeopardizing his career. The letter was hand-delivered by Aaron Fischer's secretary to him around noon the next day. It stated briefly that an emergency meeting of the board and executive council of the hospital had been called to consider his staff privileges and future status at Community General Hospital. It requested him to present himself to the administrator's office at 4 P.M. that afternoon for a review of the situation. The unnerving part of the letter was the statement near the end that Blain's attorney would be welcome at the meeting if he chose to bring one.

At first furious, and then nervous, Blain found himself performing very poorly through the afternoon. It was ironic that, in his attempt to function as a concerned physician, he had inadvertently provided an excuse for Wilcott and the others to go after him.

Still apprehensive, he arrived at the administrator's office a few minutes early to be told by the secretary that a meeting was still going on, but that it should be over shortly, and that they were expecting him.

"Who all's in there?" he asked.

"Well, let's see," the middle-aged, slightly pretty, but very dumb secretary pondered. "That's the executive council of the board so it would be Mr. Fischer, of course. It'd be the hospital attorney, that's Trudy Reed. She's in there. And there's several doctors. The chief of staff, Dr. Fieldman's in there. The chief of surgery, Dr. Wilcott." She paused for a moment. "I guess that's about it except for Mr. Stone, the board member."

"Who's he?"

She looked at him puzzled. "Jeff Stone. You don't know who he is? He's the chairman of the board of the hospital. He's also a very important stockholder of Florida Electric. He's given the hospital lots of money." She opened her eyes in mock admiration.

"How long have they been in there?"

"More than an hour now."

"Maybe you'd better buzz in there and tell them that I'm here. I believe I'm the purpose for the meeting."

"Oh no," she shook her head. "I don't think I should interrupt them."

He found himself getting annoyed. "Listen Miss Tilmore, I've got some patients to see. They asked me to be here at four o'clock and I'm here. Now, why don't you call in there and ask them if they want to see me? If not, I'll be on my way."

She frowned and hesitated, but turned on her intercom. Blain looked out the window over the residential section that lay to the west of the building. A moment later, she called to him. "They're ready for you now, Dr. Robson. Please go in."

When he entered the room, they were all sitting at the conference table at one end of Fischer's large office. Hoyt Fieldman was at the head of the table and seemed to be in charge. The little, sometimes cantankerous GP rose from his chair and extended his hand to Blain. "Thank you for coming," he said. "I apologize to you for the short notice. But it's a matter of some great concern to this hospital and the board." He seemed incongruously small considering the power he wielded with the staff. He was nearly bald, with a round face and a faintly detectible double chin. When he smiled, he appeared very fatherly. His frown had the same effect—one was afraid to dispute him when he seemed angry. He was, nevertheless, eminently well-established and loved by his patients.

He turned to the others at the table. "Of course you know Mr. Fischer and Dr. Wilcott. I think you have met Miss Reed, the hospital attorney."

The fiftyish, graying, but handsome woman rose and smiled perfunctorily. "No," she said. "Dr. Robson and I have not had the pleasure of meeting. How do you do?"

He looked toward her but said nothing as Fieldman continued the introductions. "This is Mr. Jeff Stone, chairman of the board of directors of the hospital." The large, silver-haired man rose and extended his hand without comment. Blain shook it and sat down in the chair indicated by Fieldman, who then walked back around to the other end of the table and resumed his position.

Blain glanced toward Wilcott, who was totally ignoring his presence, concerning himself mostly with the status and shape of his own fingernails. Aaron Fischer continued to leaf through a stack of papers lying in front of him.

"Now, Dr. Robson," Fieldman began. "We have a very serious matter before us this afternoon. I would like to keep this meeting short, but unfortunately, I cannot

189

keep it sweet. I want you to understand that we have no personal prejudice against you. We are merely functioning in our roles as officers of the medical staff and of the hospital administration." He paused for a moment and then continued as several of the others in the group shifted uneasily. "Although we find it an unpleasant task, this committee has been forced to examine several very serious charges which have been brought against you. These charges are relevant in two areas. One, pertaining to your professional competence and technical skills as a surgeon, as well as your judgment medically. And two, certain unprofessional activities outside of the hospital, which have tended to throw discredit upon this institution and the medical staff. You need to know that this is not a trial. It is merely a review of these matters and an administrative action that we are going to take. You are, of course, entitled to a more formal decision-making process should you so choose, and you may also be represented by counsel at those proceedings."

Blain said nothing, but continued to stare coldly at the man, a sickening ache in his belly beginning to grow. He glanced at Wilcott, who had still not looked up at him, and then toward Aaron Fischer, who avoided any eye contact, and then back to Dr. Fieldman. Jeff Stone, the chief of the board, was studying him carefully, an almost vindictive expression on his face. The lawyer, Trudy Reed, was watching everyone in the group very nervously and also seemed intent on chewing her lower lip into shreds.

"First let me address the medical incompetence charges," Fieldman continued. "Perhaps we should more properly address them as errors in judgment. It has been pointed out by Dr. Wilcott, in his role as chief of surgery, that his assessment of you has indicated deficiencies in several areas. First, you seem to lack adequate judgment as to what your area of expertise is, and you fail to call for appropriate consultations when necessary. These problems are typified by the Pendleton case, which has now, unfortunately, involved the hospital as well as several other staff members in what could potentially become a very messy malpractice suit. The cases involving the two injured men from the well accident are other examples. It is the feeling of certain members of the surgical staff that you attempted to take care of problems beyond your ability, and, as a consequence, the care given to the patients was substandard. Would you like to make any comment at this time, Dr. Robson?"

"No," Blain responded. "I'd rather just listen to the whole case you guys have built against me, and then I'll tell you what I think about it all." He was seething inside. This was obviously going to be a kangaroo court, run by Wilcott and his good friend, Fieldman.

The chief of staff continued. "The second area involves lack of technical skill, exemplified by the unfortunate death of Mr. Ben Lockhardt on the operating room table two days ago, a man who died from a ruptured spleen that went undiagnosed by you for an extended period of time during surgery."

"Wait a goddamned minute," Blain interrupted. "Wilcott, you know that man died from multiple injuries, not just that little thing in his spleen."

Wilcott did not respond, but looked up to stare contemptuously at him.

"Now hold on just a moment," Fieldman said calmly.

"No! I won't wait. Wilcott, you'd better tell them the

whole story!" Blain interrupted again. "You know that little tear in his spleen wasn't enough to kill him. That few minutes delay that I made before we found that tear didn't have anything to do with his death."

Wilcott raised his hand and pointed it straight at Blain. "Listen, Doctor, I don't know any such thing. All I know is that you were about to close the patient up leaving a ruptured spleen in. Any surgeon knows the most common area of bleeding in acute trauma to the abdomen is the spleen. It should have been the first place you looked. Face it, Robson, you missed it. If you had found it quicker, it might have made a difference."

"You money-loving, lying son of a bitch!" Blain said, rising to a standing position and leaning over the table down toward Wilcott, his face contorted with rage.

"Sit down, Robson!" Fieldman's booming, authoritative voice shocked him back into his senses, and Blain quickly returned to his chair, glaring at the chief of surgery.

"That's enough of that," Fieldman said more calmly. "I won't allow that in this meeting."

"Nor will I," Jeff Stone cut in. "It's absurd to see a member of this staff screaming hysterically like that." He stared angrily at Blain. "Who the hell do you think you are, anyway?" he said. "You don't own this hospital, and you don't run it. It's a privilege we give you to work here. Where do you get off coming into this place, thinking you're some sort of big shot who can change the way we've been doing things and act as if we have to cater to you. Since the month you arrived, we haven't had a board meeting where your name hasn't come up, Robson. You're going to have to realize that we've got more to do around here than keep a watch on you and some of your

192

ridiculous activities." He paused for a moment, and his voice softened. "You don't know how hard we've worked to get industries like Florexco into this community. If you did, you wouldn't be so anxious to cause trouble. There's lots of people in this county whose jobs and income depend upon big business like this, whether you like it or not." He turned to Fieldman, "I'm sorry, Hoyt. I didn't mean to blurt out. Go ahead with the meeting."

"Thank you, Jeff," Dr. Fieldman responded. "Now, Dr. Robson, that brings us to these extraordinary extracurricular political activities that you have engaged in. I'm speaking of the various protest movements you choose to align yourself with." His voice grew quieter. "Now, there is no one on this staff or in this room who would seek to deny you the right to engage in political activities on your own time. We have tolerated, and God knows we have been patient with, the various things you've done, particularly in the first couple of months you were here. I'm sure you know that it has been an embarrassment to this hospital to have your name in the paper linking us to certain protest activities that you have engaged in, particularly in regard to Florexco and to the nuclear power plant."

He looked at the others and then continued. "But that's your right, and we have not in any way interfered with that right. However, yesterday you exceeded all tolerable limits. Acting as a staff member of this hospital and as a responsible surgeon allowed to conduct his practice within this hospital, you went beyond all reasonable judgments and made some statements to the Coast Guard which are absolutely unsubstantiated about the Florexco Oil Company. You were in no way entitled to make those statements. You talked about things regarding patients who have had no contact with you. You may have revealed, technically speaking, privileged information about patients' lab work which the hospital was bound to keep confidential. Just in general, you were out of line to make statements above and beyond your actual medical knowledge about the case involved. Your statements that something was wrong with Florexco were totally inappropriate and intolerable."

Blain took in a deep breath and let it out noisily and slowly in exasperation.

"And now, even more shocking," Fieldman continued, "we have discovered that you actually went to the oil company yourself, representing yourself as a staff member of this hospital, and accused them of creating unsafe and dangerous working conditions. Based entirely upon your own speculation, you accused them of negligently contributing to the death of one or more of their employees and then attempting to cover it up. Blain, this is absolutely not right." He held up his hands, and waved his finger at him to emphasize his point.

"Dr. Robson," Jeff Stone interrupted, his voice calm and deep. "Do you realize that last evening, in my position as chairman of the board of this hospital, I got a call from Mr. Craig Strombeck, who is a member of the board of Florexco and also a very successful practicing attorney, telling me that the company was going to take action against you and the hospital if your harassment continued? He said you came to the company, uninvited, making harassing statements and ranting and raving about patients and laboratory results of which you should have no knowledge. He accused this hospital of creating a breach of faith with the company and these particular employees by allowing privileged information about their health care to be obtained by you." He paused for a moment. "Do you realize what kind of position that puts us in if they should make those charges in court?" He shook his head back and forth. "We couldn't defend them." He pointed to the hospital attorney, "Isn't that right, Trudy?"

"That's correct," she said. "Information on patients is privileged to the staff and physicians taking care of those patients. The records are not open books for any physician to use in any random manner he wishes."

Stone continued. "And what's worse is that you're not using this information for some medically related matter; you're using it to further your own political objectives. You're using this hospital and our patients to continue an unreasonable harassment and protest movement against this oil company. We will not allow it. We cannot be sucked into this kind of dispute. I can promise you that the board absolutely will not tolerate such behavior on your part." His face had an angry scowl. His voice grew quieter. "You're going to have to stop this unfortunate involvement with these protest movements and calm down if you're going to remain a member of our staff."

"What Mr. Stone says is true, Blain," Dr. Fieldman said. "There are several things you need to know. One of them is that Florexco has done a great deal for this hospital. They have contributed a lot of money. We are all appreciative of it. The board is appreciative of it. We have to recognize that the company is a friend of this hospital. We can't turn our backs on them now, based upon such ill-founded speculation as you have come up with." He grew quiet for a moment. "Now let's get to the final line here. It is my opinion and the opinion of this committee that you are going to have to make some changes in both your professional practice and your attitude if you are going to stay on the staff of this hospital. We feel that you have let your political activities interfere with your practice of medicine. You have used bad judgment on several occasions. You have demonstrated technical incompetence on at least one occasion, and you have created a great deal of adverse reaction because of political maneuvers, misrepresenting yourself as an agent of this hospital. Just in general, you are not performing up to the standard we expect here at Community General. Do you have anything to say about this?"

The eyes of everyone turned toward Blain. He thought for a moment, looked around at the others and then finally at Fieldman. "As a physician, Doctor, what do you think about two, possibly three, cases of aplastic anemia and a dozen people with very low white blood cell counts all from the same company, all happening within a week of each other?"

Fieldman answered him quietly. "I think it's all very interesting, and I think it's all very sad. But I don't think it's all related. There's an easy explanation for all of these cases, which does not involve some bizarre strange cause. The one man who died definitely had aplastic anemia. The two injured by the lightning—who knows what injuries lightning causes? They died from complications of the many effects of severe trauma. The patients with the low white blood cell counts—there are many causes for that, including common viral diseases, and you know it. It's not necessary to invoke exciting exotic reasons for these rather ordinary medical problems."

"But what if I'm right? All these individuals have been

at the same place at the same time. How can you overlook the possibility that this could be a single cause, perhaps still dangerous?"

Wilcott slammed his hand on the table and stood up, pointing his hand and waving dramatically at Blain. "Speculation! Damn it, Robson! That's what we're trying to say. You've got to stop this bizarre speculation. If you want to write science fiction stories, go ahead. But keep us and this hospital out of it."

Just as quickly as he had risen, he sat back down, but continued to stare coldly at Blain. "I hope you can see," Jeff Stone said, "that we're very upset about this. We all realize that, unfortunately, you have an ax to grind against this oil company. But, your judgment is skewed. I don't trust it. The board doesn't trust it, and neither does the oil company. You are going to have to absolutely cease and desist these activities or face extremely severe consequences. If it were up to me, you'd be gone this afternoon. But, fortunately for you, some of the others don't see it quite that way. However, be warned. You're close to termination."

Blain looked back to Hoyt Fieldman. "I don't think there's much else to say," the chief of staff said, "so let me conclude this by giving you the final opinion of this committee. Blain, we are placing you on Class II suspension. That means several things. Number one, any additional activities, either medical or political, which cause the hospital or the medical staff any concern about either your competence or about the public image of the hospital will result in your immediate suspension from the staff. In addition to this, all admissions and surgical procedures for as long as this suspension is in effect will have to be approved by the chief of surgery, Dr. Wilcott.

You will do nothing unless he knows in advance and gives his approval. Do I make myself clear?"

Blain nodded.

Fieldman continued. "This ruling will stay in effect for sixty days, at which time you will be reviewed unless, of course, you challenge it legally."

There was a pause and then the attorney, Ms. Reed spoke up. "You should be aware that you do have legal alternatives. According to the bylaws of this hospital, you can request a more formal inquiry into these matters and also be represented by counsel at that time. You also have redress to this grievance via the civil courts of this state. However, as a practical matter, I must advise you that either of those steps would involve publicity which, undoubtedly, would be adverse. It is my recommendation that you accept the ruling of this committee quietly and let this matter be done with."

"Very good advice, Trudy," Fieldman said. "Now unless someone has something else to say, I suggest that we call it quits. It's been a long afternoon."

The others agreed and rose from their chairs. Blain quickly started for the door. He felt sick. He had never before in his professional career come under such criticism. The accusations of incompetence were extremely demoralizing, and the criticism of his political activities he felt unfair. He wanted to run from the room, grab his possessions and leave, never to return, but he knew that he couldn't. He was halfway down the hall toward the outside door when he heard the voice of the chief of staff behind him.

"Blain, let me talk with you for a moment." He turned to face Hoyt Fieldman. "Let me tell you something, if I may," the old GP said, his voice much more gentle than in the meeting. The two walked slowly toward the exit, where they stopped just inside the door to continue their conversation. "I know this is hard on you," the older man said, "it's got to be. I know you're very hostile to me right now, but I want you to know that I'm very sympathetic about this matter. I have no vendetta against you. I know we've had some disagreements in the past, but believe me, as far as all those things are concerned, it's a dead issue. I'm only concerned about these particular problems now. I want to see you straighten out. I think you have fine potential as a young surgeon, and I think you can fit in here. I believe you've just got to work a little harder at it." He paused.

"There are a few things you must understand when you come to a small community hospital like this one," he continued. "I know we're not fancy. I know we don't do the things that you're used to. But remember, we're all this community's got. We're out here working. We're doing a good job. We're taking care of most of the sick folk. The ones we can't handle, we ship off to the big centers. But, in general, we do a good job, and we dish out a pretty fair brand of medicine. We're as good as any place can be away from a modern medical center. You should realize that and not be so skeptical about some of the things that you see here. Some of the members of this staff may not be up on the hottest and latest stuff, but they've taken care of lots of people, and they've learned by experience. We have a nice quiet little hospital here, and it works well." Blain listened patiently.

"There's something else to be considered. This hospital survives because of donations from important individuals and from big companies. We cut ourselves off from those donations, and this place will sink. And if that happens, the community's going to be hurt. It's a long way from here to the next hospital. It won't affect most of the doctors here because we live off our office practices anyway. But we need to have a place where we can take care of these patients, get them well, and solve their simple problems. We want to help them. And the main thing you must remember is that we owe it to this community to survive. We can't go around cutting our throats by upsetting some of the big companies that donate money to this place.

"Now I'm telling you Jeff Stone was in a rage when I saw him this afternoon. He wanted to kick you off the staff right now. Apparently, this board member from Florexco that called him was absolutely hot about the fact that you went out there. Those guys are sensitive, you know that. You've been involved in this protest movement. They don't want to look bad publicly. They're too vulnerable. So naturally when you go out there ranting and raving about people dying and blood counts being abnormal, they're going to react. And if necessary, they're going to react hard. They're bigger than you, they're bigger than me, and they're bigger than this hospital."

He paused and looked into Blain's eyes. "If you cause them too much trouble, they can hurt us all, believe me. Now, I can understand your concerns, but it's just speculation, Blain. You don't have any proof. You don't have any hard evidence of anything. You're just speculating. So let well enough alone; it's not your problem and it's not this hospital's problem. Our problem is to take care of our patients in this community and not to go out there attacking industry. If you can just accept that, then everything's going to be okay. Take some advice from an old man who's been in medicine a long time. Try to keep a low profile and work quietly, and things are going to be okay. You don't need any more trouble. If you get kicked off the staff of this hospital, it will be a scar you'll carry for a long time. You don't want that, Blain. Now please, for your own best interest, quit being so hardheaded and recognize that you could just possibly be totally wrong. What do you think?" He patted Blain on the shoulder.

Blain thought for a moment, looking out the window through the door into the parking lot. He took several deep breaths, letting them out slowly. "It doesn't look like I have much choice," he said. "I think I'm going to have to knuckle under and do it your way. I don't want to get kicked off the staff, that's for sure." He glanced at Fieldman.

"That's a boy," Fieldman said and again slapped him on the shoulder. "I knew you'd respond. I think everything's going to be okay. You can fit in. All you've got to do is play ball." He smiled. "Now look. Just to show you that there's no hard feelings, I've got a patient of mine I want to refer to you. A young woman who's got a small lump in her left breast. I'm pretty sure it's not malignant, but she's going to need a breast biopsy anyway. She's getting admitted sometime this evening. Her last name is Baily. I'll have the nurses call you when she gets to the floor and I'd like you to see her, and see if you think we ought to take that lump out. What do you say?"

Blain felt embarrassed at the almost blatant attempt to bribe him with a referral. He didn't know how to respond. He wanted to tell Fieldman to take his breast lump and shove it, but reason kept him from doing it.

"If you'd like me to see her, I'd be happy to," he responded coolly.

"Good man," Fieldman said and again slapped him on the shoulder and turned to go down the hall. "Just remember, take it easy and don't worry about all this. Concentrate on practicing good medicine and everything's going to be okay." He gave Blain a pretentious smile and then went down the hall.

"Dr. Fieldman," Blain said before he had gone many steps. The chief of staff turned and looked toward him expectantly.

"What happened to that patient, Tony Torres, the one from the oil company that Dr. Thompson admitted to you?"

Fieldman's expression grew dim. "Transferred him out two days after he was admitted. He went to Gainesville. I figured I'd let the big boys take care of him."

"Is he doing all right?"

"No. I heard yesterday he died."

"Did they give you a diagnosis?"

"Yes, they did," Dr. Fieldman said, coming back toward him a step or two. "It was aplastic anemia." He paused. "Anything else you need to know?" He eyed Blain suspiciously.

"No. I was just curious. It has nothing to do with me, does it?"

"That's right," Fieldman answered. "It doesn't. It's none of your business, and you'll be wise to keep it that way."

"I think I've learned that now," Blain answered, and without further comment, turned and pushed his way out into the early evening air. It was going to be a beautiful night, but he was not well. He felt a combination of dizziness and nausea. It was like a fog was over his head, and he was spinning. He walked slowly out to his car, oblivious of the persons passing him. It didn't matter that Tony Torres had died of aplastic anemia, or that Ben Lockhardt had had it, or George, or the others. It didn't matter at all. The main thing was that it was none of his business. That was perfectly clear now. Who gives a shit if four men from the same work place die of the same thing with a dozen others also affected? It wasn't that goddamned important, and he was just going to have to recognize it.

The important thing now was to find a place where he could have a nice quiet drink. To hell with everyone else. He was going to have to learn to work with blinders on. One man can't fight the system. That was clear to him now.

ELEVEN

The morning of the fourth day of drilling was cool and windy but the sky was a clear, deep blue and the sun was shining. It was slightly after seven when Jori emerged from the crowded dining room carrying her full cup of black coffee, and after shivering in the chilly wind, she pulled up the collar of her coveralls around her neck and started up the stairs toward the control booth. It had been the strangest four days of her professional career. It had started with the fight that killed poor Ben Lockhardt and ended with the readout from the computer last night, verifying what she already knew about the astounding progress of the drilling.

She reached the top of the stairs and stood for a moment looking at the surging green sea far below, reflecting upon what had happened. She was going ashore today for the first time since before the drilling began, and she was glad. It had been a strain, and it had taken its toll on her. She was mentally exhausted. She felt she had good reason to be. Although from the standpoint of getting the job done the drilling was going spectacularly well, she knew that something was wrong. What was happening just didn't make sense. It seemed geologically impossible. By midnight last night, they had crossed through 8000 feet; more than tripling the previous record as far as she knew of high-speed drilling.

Caught up in the hectic pace of the start up, she had not had a lot of time to dwell on her own anxieties about what was occurring. But she was uneasy about it, just short of being a little scared, actually. And so were some of the others. The overpowering memory of the accident and its horror was a definite factor. By unspoken agreement it was never discussed. But it was always there, lurking just out of view, constantly reminding them of the unexpected nature of sudden death. The cleaned-out lockers of old George and the others remained as haunting monuments to the frailty of flesh.

When the improved safety features were mentioned, all voices gave support and indications of confidence. Relaxed smiles and expressions of bored unconcern were worn like masks to a Halloween ball. But in their hearts festered a fear that something was amiss—a fear that each man knew the others shared. But it was never discussed. What would be the point? They were all stuck here for one reason or another: money or ambition. The main thing was to get on with it, put the concerns behind them. For that reason she wished Dr. Sumter would hurry and come home. She was anxious to hear his analysis of this unfamiliar situation.

The door behind her opened and Eric Duval stepped out of the control booth and stood beside her. He looked tired and sleepy. "Long night," he said and took a sip of the coffee he was holding.

She looked at him knowingly. "How far have we gone?"

"We're down to 8,750," he responded with a shrug. "I think it gets easier and easier the deeper we go."

"Any change in anything else?"

He shook his head. "Sand, just loose sand. There's not a damned thing beneath us but sand." He thought for a moment. "Maybe the pipe's just crumpling up on the sea bottom down there and we're not getting anywhere at all. Maybe we're using up more pipe, making a big pile of junk."

She smiled. "That'd be easier to understand than what's happening."

"It's a cinch I don't understand it. I've never seen anything to even compare with this before. Neither have the men. I think it's starting to get to some of them. They're getting a little edgy."

"We don't need that," she said.

"I think we're all right. The men would just like to feel a little rock underneath them for a change. We better watch the Latinos, though. They're a little more hyper than the rest. They sometimes tend to put religious implications on things."

"I don't see how they could make anything religious out of this."

"Well, there's several of them down there whipping those prayer beads around pretty good, asking for the Virgin Mary to watch over them." He grinned, showing his dirty mouth and missing bottom teeth.

"I guess that doesn't hurt anything," she said.

He continued grinning. "I'll tell you one thing. If I was religious and all, and needed something to bolster my courage a little, I'd sure as hell want something more substantial to rely on than the Virgin Mary."

She didn't return his smile. "What's the matter, Eric? You don't believe in the Immaculate Conception?" His condescending attitude was irritating.

"Hell no," he replied. "Not any more than I believe in

flying saucers and crap like that. It just don't ring true. It don't make sense, that's all."

"You only believe things that make sense, huh?"

"Damned right. And religion to me doesn't make sense. I think it's the fourth greatest lie in the world. You know the others."

"What are you talking about?" Her face showed mild curiosity.

He grinned delightedly, and she wished she hadn't asked him, as vague memories of an old, dirty joke stirred in the back of her mind. She started to stop him, but it was too late.

"Well," he said, "I'm sure you've heard them all. Money isn't everything, black is beautiful, and I won't come in your mouth." With the last remark he began to laugh hysterically, slapping his hand repeatedly on the rail in front of them.

She stood motionless beside him, her face registering none of the disgust within her. She waited until his hysteria had subsided into a broad, quiet grin. "You know, Eric," she finally said, "some of the things that come out of your mouth convince me that your brain is made of crap. And your manners are just about as offensive. I think you could probably benefit from a D & C of the mouth." Her expression mirrored her disdain.

"A what?" His smile was gone.

"*D and C,* you dumb ass. You think you're such an expert on women. Don't you know what a D & C is?" She turned before he could respond and stepped into the control booth. She heard him shuffle his feet a few times, but he didn't start down the stairs. She leaned over the main control panel. A moment later, as she felt his eyes burning into her backside, she turned around to face him through the open door. "What do you think you're doing?" she said.

"Just standing here taking in the sights," he answered.

"Why don't you go take in the sights some place else. I'm tired of looking at you right now," she responded.

He smiled. "Don't you want to hear the rest of my report?" he said provocatively.

"The rest of what report?"

"The report about what the men are saying you'd be good at."

"Get the hell out of here, Duval."

"It's one of the responsibilities of my job to report to you what the men are saying about you, isn't it?"

"You're not going to have a job or have responsibility if you're not out of here in ten seconds," she said. Her tone grew more threatening. "I'm serious, Eric. You've gotten on my nerves just now and I think you should disappear real quick." She reached forward and slammed the door shut and a few moments later she heard him going down the stairs.

She stood motionless in front of the window watching him descend and then put one hand up and ran it through her hair several times. She felt absolutely enraged. It was impossible to combat that sort of insulting behavior from men like Duval. Attempting to fire the man or protesting his behavior to Loggins would be fruitless. She felt guilty for allowing it to happen. She was always so careful to avoid this sort of thing. It had been a priority for her to control her relationships with men aboard the rig and never to allow a conversation to deteriorate to the point of flagrant sexual overtones. If there was ever any trouble, she knew that she would be blamed, not the men. It was one of the risks of her job, and she knew it would be pointed out to her if any controversy arose. She had already been told by enough people, women included, that an oil rig was no place for her. She had long ago realized she might very well fail at this job—but if she did, it was not going to be because of her sex.

In their own way, men like Duval were more of a risk to her than sexually motivated peers or higher-ups in the administrative command. Duval was crude by nature and to complain about him was to complain about the normal personality of many of the men who worked these tough jobs. If he, or others like him, were causing a problem for her, it was for her to solve because no one above her, or below her, or even other women who didn't face the same problem, would have much in the way of sympathy. It was something to be handled with strength and judgment, and she knew her judgment had failed her as the conversation had deteriorated.

She ran her hands through her hair again. This job's getting to me, she thought. I need a break. I'm beginning to hate too many people. She let out a big sigh and then continued examining the instruments. It's the tension of waiting, she thought. Waiting for whatever is going to happen. They had been expecting oil at 15,000 feet, but now, almost two-thirds of the way there, they hadn't even reached bedrock. And because of it, everyone was uptight, trying to stay relaxed, but getting on each other's nerves.

Finally, she sat down at the desk at the end of the room and wrote her 24-hour report in the log of the well's activities. She was just finishing a half hour later when she heard the helicopter approaching. It would be carrying Loggins, who was going to stay on the well for a couple of days while she was off. It was the first time in a long while that she was going to be glad to see the man. She watched as the craft landed and Loggins got out, followed, surprisingly, by Wally Jenkins. She had thought he left yesterday to spend a couple of days in Palm Beach in discussions with Matthew Downing, the Florexco president, and a few of the board members in preparation for next week's board meeting.

As they started across the platform, she quickly gathered up her papers and put them into her briefcase. Her clothes were already packed and waiting in the crew lounge. By the time she finished getting her things together, they should have reached the booth, so she was surprised when she turned around to look out the window and saw them still on the working deck below. Both Jenkins and Loggins were huddled closely with Eric Duval in some kind of discussion. Wally looked very angry and spoke rapidly to Duval, who shook his head back and forth and pointed up at the control booth.

Jenkins finally held up his hands in exasperation, made one more comment to the two of them and then started up the stairs. Loggins spoke for another few moments with Duval, who then finally left and went into the crew quarters. Loggins glanced up at the control booth and then started up toward her.

As she waited for them to arrive, she tried to control the growing irritation within her. Despite his new exterior, Loggins was still a blatant manipulator, and being the ambitious man he was, he would use any tool to destroy her. For Duval she felt more disgust, almost pity. He was a small and shallow man. His perception of life was insensitive and narrow. He obviously viewed women as merely an instrument of sex. He was, however, apparently titillated by the power of Jori's position, and she knew he was moved sexually by her. In the past few days she had frequently been the victim of his stares. He, more than the other members of the crew, seemed threatened by her. His own masculinity must have somehow become an issue. She despised him. He was repulsive. It was evident now that she was going to have to place more barriers between them.

The door opened behind her. "Good morning, Jori," said the gruff voice of Wally Jenkins, the pleasant tone blatantly artificial.

She turned to face him, unsmiling. "I suppose it could be," she answered. "But I'm not sure it is. I'll have to wait a little longer to see." She paused for a moment as he looked at her unhappily. "What did Duval have to say?"

"I don't think you would really want to hear it," he answered stiffly and turned to study the instrument panel.

"I have a right to know, don't I?"

"Then ask Loggins about it," he answered her crossly. "I don't give a damn what Duval or the men are saying about you. All I care about is this well." He stared down at the instruments again and then, after a short pause, looked up. His voice grew softer. "Jori, I can't protect you out here. You're on your own. If you're not going to be able to make it, if you can't control this crew, then I— I—" he stuttered. "I don't know what to do."

"Then if you won't tell me, I'll ask Winston," she responded. "I have a right to know what's being said if one of my crewmen goes over my head."

"Ask me what?" Loggins said, stepping into the doorway.

The bright sun behind his back made it impossible for her to see anything but the outline of his muscular body.

"I said, what was Duval complaining about?" she said forcefully.

"The usual thing," Loggins replied as he stepped through the doorway and closed the door. His face wore its usual calm, smug expression. It was one with which she was very familiar.

"What? You mean the fact that I'm female? He can't stand having a woman as boss?"

He smiled condescendingly. "You still don't undertand, do you, Jori? You can't get it through that thick head of yours." He glanced at Jenkins. "Can't you do something with her, Wally. I don't want to talk about it with her any more. I'm sick of it."

Jenkins was disgusted. He put one hand behind his neck and rubbed it as he rolled his head around. "Jori," he said in a quiet voice, "just let it go. Drop it. It won't do any good to go over the same stuff again and again. The man's hard to deal with. You're a woman. That makes it tough. You've got a lot of special problems out here, and you're just going to have to learn to handle them."

"No, I won't drop it," she said. "Because I don't think there is any problem here. That is, except the one created by you." She pointed at Loggins. "And by that creep crew chief of yours. I don't think there's any other problem. I get along well with the men. They respect me, and we're doing a good job."

Loggins smiled again. "I know you'd like to believe that was true, Jori, but it's not. You're just going to have to face it. Things aren't going well. As a matter of fact, the whole place is about to come apart. The men are not responding well to your leadership. There's bad feeling about it. They're suspicious of you. Many of the men think it's bad luck to have you out here. Valid or not, a lot of them are blaming you for the troublesome things that have happened."

"That's absurd," she said bitterly.

"Call it what you want, but you've been around every time something goes wrong. It was your idea that led to the excessive work load put on the engines the night of the accident. If it hadn't been for the overload caused by the—"

"Jesus Christ, Winston!" she yelled. "You're not going to try to blame the lightning on me, are you?"

"Oh yes," he sneered, "the lightning or whatever else you and some of the others prefer to call the accident."

"I told you to keep your mouth shut about that," Jenkins interrupted.

"Right," he said, an exasperated expression crossing his face. "We're not supposed to talk about it; I understand." He looked back at Jori. "So you were here in charge when the accident occurred, whatever it was. You were here in charge when the fight broke out."

"Wait a minute," Jori interrupted looking back and forth at the two men. "What are you talking about, 'the accident or whatever it was.' It was lightning, period. Right? Or is there something I don't know?"

Loggins pointed at Jenkins with his open hand as if to say, "You tell her."

Jenkins stood motionless as she stared at him, waiting. "Winston got a call from Adrian Sumter last night. As you know, we've kept him informed about everything from word one. He's due home from Europe the end of the week. Anyway, Adrian says there's no way that lightning could have done that."

Astonishment came to her face. "Why not?"

"He says, and I suppose his calculations are correct, he

knows more about this than me, that if lightning had hit this rig with enough force and energy to kill these men and blow all the breakers, that it would have done more damage."

"That's what the breakers were for. To protect from electrical damage," she said.

"That's right," Winston interjected. "They're designed to protect against electrical overload, but not electrical overload from lightning. That's what the lightning rods are for. Sumter said that if a big enough jolt of electricity hit this place and overrode the lightning rods enough to kill those men, that the overload would have come so quickly that the breakers couldn't have reacted in time to protect the rig and that severe damage would have been done before they tripped. He said the breakers can only respond to a slower buildup of power than what would come out of this kind of overwhelming hit by lightning."

"What does he think caused it?" she asked, with a puzzled, skeptical expression.

Loggins didn't respond, and after a moment Jenkins did. "He didn't say. I don't think he knows."

"The only thing we know," Loggins said, "is that it occurred during a time period when we were overloading our own power systems."

"Winston," she said, "if you don't stop trying to blame me, I'm going to—"

"You're gonna what?" He looked up, surprised at the threatening tone in her voice.

"Hold it, you two," Jenkins said forcefully. "This isn't the time or the place. Adrian will be home in a few days and you can all go over it. Until then let's just shut up about it. There's nothing that we can say."

"Fair enough," she responded. "I'll be happy to see what Dr. Sumter thinks about the possibility of me causing this by overdriving the engines." She looked back at Loggins disdainfully. "Now, what else is it that I've been doing so wrong out here?"

"It's your whole cocky attitude," Loggins answered. "If we'd had someone out here who could really take command, who was in charge, that unfortunate fight never would have happened."

"You're wrong!" she responded.

"No. That's fact," he retorted. "If I'd been out here that fight never would have happened."

"What was I supposed to do, jump right on top of the two of them and break it up myself?" she asked angrily.

"That would have been a hell of a lot better than strutting all around the goddamned place wiggling those tits of yours in everybody's face," he said.

Her face registered shock. "You son of a bitch," she said more quietly. "You sorry goddamned son of a bitch. So that's what it comes down to finally, huh? You think I'm causing trouble because I'm wiggling my tits. You goddamned cock-sucking son of a bitch!"

They stood glowering at each other until Jenkins spoke up. "That's enough! If I had my choice, I'd get rid of both of you right now." There was a bitter, angry tone to his voice as he looked at one and then the other. "I mean it," he said, raising his fist up in front of him to emphasize his point. "I'd get rid of both of you right this second if it was my decision alone to make." He moved to the window and stared pensively out over the rig. Jori and Loggins stood silently. Finally, he turned back toward them. "The bitterness between you two is the worst I've ever seen in forty years of working, and I don't know how to

215

deal with it. But I'm going to do something, I guarantee you." He looked at Jori. "You'd better solve your problems or you're not going to be out here much longer. I don't care how great Adrian Sumter or Gulf or anyone else thinks you are!" He glared at Loggins. "And don't think you're going to get entirely away with these kinds of cheap shots, either. I won't put up with it. I'm sick of you, too!" Still frowning, he studied the data being recorded on the instrument panel. He shook his head, "I would never have believed it," he said quietly. "Almost 9000 feet and no rock. I don't understand any of this."

"What does the all-knowing Dr. Sumter think about that?" she asked.

Jenkins shook his head slowly. "He doesn't know. He thinks we've got problems. He thinks something serious could be wrong."

"Like what?" she asked.

Jenkins shook his head again. "He couldn't say, or maybe he wouldn't say. In any event, he'll be here soon. You ask him what he thinks."

"No doubt it's something I'm doing wrong," she said sarcastically.

He turned to her, wearily. "Ease off, Jori. Just ease off." He waited for a moment and then his voice took a lighter tone. "The helicopter's waiting to take you ashore. I won't see you when you get back. I've got to get on with taking care of the rest of the company. It's going to be up to you and Winston to hold this thing together until Sumter gets here next week." He appeared discouraged. "You two, make it work. Okay?" There was almost a pleading tone to his voice.

"It takes two to tango, Wally," she replied. "But no one here seems to know that."

216

"Yeah . . ." Jenkins seemed to drift off for a moment. "You guys are just going to have to work this one out. I don't have time for it any more." She looked into his tired eyes. He seemed less enthusiastic, less fired up than usual—almost depressed. "From now on Adrian can do the thinking here, as far as I'm concerned," he continued. "I don't understand any of it any more—not the accident nor why we can't find bedrock—and I don't understand you two. I just wish things were simpler, like the old days. Sometimes I just want to quit. It's not fun any more."

As she watched him, she realized he was caving in, almost running away. He wanted to retreat to the simple, more traditional work, the kind he had grown up with. Surprised at what he was saying, she couldn't understand why he wasn't defending her more. Slowly, it dawned on her. She began to realize what was happening. Wally wasn't the solidly entrenched commander she had thought he was. He really hadn't been for a long time. He was slipping, like Matthew Downing. He couldn't handle the new technology, but Loggins could. That was why he had avoided the well until the accident. She understood it all now. That was why Wally had gone along with Sumter in hiring her—to try to cut off Winston's dash to the top. But she was failing, and now Jenkins was giving up. In self-defense he was all but abandoning the project, seeking refuge in other less complex areas of the company's endeavors. He was going to align himself with Loggins—he had to for survival. She knew now that Wally was not going to be Florexco's next president. Very passively, he was conceding the battle. He was out of style—a tough old tool pusher who had worked his way to the top, but was no longer good enough to stay there.

As she stood watching she felt a sudden sorrow for his defeat—and her loss. She no longer had a powerful ally. She resented having been made a pawn in a struggle for control. She picked up her briefcase and started for the door. "Good-bye, Wally," she said. "Keep in touch." He didn't look up.

Everyone in the room sensed what had just happened, and they each understood that the others also knew. The power had been shifted. She felt sick and wanted only to get out of there as quickly as she could.

"Jori," Loggins said before she could leave. "There is one more thing I'd like to mention. This Dr. Blain Robson, he's been trying to cause trouble for the company. I think you know him."

"So what?"

"He's a known ecologist and general hell-raiser. He tried to keep this project from getting off the ground, and now he's gone even further than that, accusing us of creating a health hazard of some sort. He's trying to cause trouble. I think he's a dangerous man. Craig Strombeck had to go to the hospital board to get him off our back."

"What's he saying?"

"I don't know, it's all junk. But we need to be careful around him."

"Why are you telling me all this?" she asked.

"It's been said that you know him socially. You've been seen with him."

"Oh, yes? I've been seen with him. Do you recall by whom?"

"It doesn't matter," he answered. "The point is, he's a dangerous man for this company, and all of us should regard him as someone to stay away from. If he asks any questions, refer him to the public relations section. You agree with that, Wally?" he said glancing at Jenkins, who slowly nodded.

She looked back and forth at the two of them, her face sullen. "Just like that, the two of you have decided that none of us should talk to the man who took care of Old George, the man who struggled to keep him alive. He helped me once. He also operated on Ben Lockhardt, didn't he?"

"The man's dangerous, Jori," Loggins repeated.

"I don't think so; I think he's a good doctor."

"I'm just telling you that you'll have to answer for it if you have dealings with him," Loggins said.

"Who do I answer to, you?" she asked.

Before Loggins could speak, Jenkins replied. "You answer to Florexco if you make a mistake like that, Jori."

"I see," she said slowly, then opened the door and stepped out into the cold wind. She felt her lower lip trembling and her eyes filled with tears. She had an overwhelming sense of defeat. She seemed to be at battle with everyone around her. It was almost as if everything was closing in on her—the accident, the deaths, the fight, Loggins's hatred, and now even Wally Jenkins seemed hostile. She struggled to regain her composure as she started down the stairs. She didn't want anyone to see her crying. She had only gone a few steps when she heard someone walk out onto the platform behind her, and then Wally spoke her name. She turned slightly and looked over her shoulder toward him.

"I'm sorry all this is happening to you," he said. She nodded. "Maybe it'll be better when you come back in a few days." Again, she didn't respond. "I've just got a job to do, you know. The company needs this well." She knew if she spoke she would cry, so again she merely

219

nodded and help up one hand in a submissive wave of good-bye and then turned and continued down the stairs.

The two black foremen, Skip Majors and Jimmy Jones, were standing outside the crew office when she reached the lower platform. "Have a nice weekend, Miss Ashe," Skip said, smiling warmly.

"I'll try," she said, managing a small grin.

"Don't spend all your money in one place," Jones said.

"Yeah, and don't take any wooden nickels either," Skip added as the two men chuckled.

She walked a few steps past them and then turned to look back. "I'll be back in a couple of days. You guys hold the fort down until then, okay?" She smiled genuinely, through teary eyes.

"Good enough," Skip replied. "We'll save your place for you. We're sort of getting used to having a lady boss."

She turned and continued to walk toward the helicopter at the far end of the platform. Loggins and Duval were wrong and Jenkins was being misled. She knew he was. The men thought better of her than it was being portrayed. It was a power struggle, that's all. A struggle which now she appeared to have lost. It was a bitter blow to have Wally seemingly coming down on Loggins's side of the fence, but it was something that she could live with. She had to. She wanted to hang on.

At first, as she had left the control booth and walked down the stairs, she had almost wanted to quit, to dump it all, get out. Why put up with this? she had thought. But now, as she stood at the doorway of the helicopter, she looked back at the rig. The tool pushers were swinging a new pipe into position over the drill table. The sound of the engines was like soothing music. She couldn't quit.

Offshore rigs were in her blood. She was just like her old man. She'd be back. She knew it. Whatever troubles she had to face, she would face them. Her daddy hadn't quit when the going got tough, and she sure as hell wasn't going to, especially not now with so many questions unanswered.

She climbed through the door and took the seat beside the pilot, who smiled at her. "How have you been doing, Miss Ashe?" he asked.

"Daryl," she said, "I'm hanging in there, buddy. I'm hanging in there."

He said nothing, but gave her a big smile and a thumbs up sign as he waited for the giant propeller above them to come up to full speed. The helicopter gently rose from the pad, swung out over the ocean and made a wide sweep to the west as he gained altitude heading for shore.

She looked back behind her and watched as the rig grew smaller in the distance. The sun in the eastern sky was already high above the horizon, and the well was becoming a gleaming steel reflection on the deep blue sea below. The view from here gave no hint of the awesome progress the drilling had made, but it did nothing to abate her disquieting dread of what lay ahead for the big project.

To the west, she could see the sparkling beaches of the Florida shore. It was a beautiful day and she was feeling better. She was glad she had a few days off.

TWELVE

The Personal Journal
of Adrian Sumter, Ph.D.

NOVEMBER 5, Hamburg, Germany. *Received the good news yesterday that the drilling has been resumed without problem. It is such a relief to know that the rig was not seriously damaged. The meetings here will be over soon, and I can return home and personally investigate the source of my problem. It is still such a distressing thing to me, and such a loss of life. I cannot believe, however, the explanations being put forth for the accident. I will obviously have to see for myself exactly what happened. I cannot allow anything to destroy this magnificent accomplishment. It was such an enormous task, bringing this apparatus from its early concepts into its final form. The technology we have incorporated into it will soon be recognized by the industrial and scientific world as being a major step forward in the commercial exploitation of the world's offshore petroleum reserves. As I have written before, it has great potential for certain scientific contributions also. In any event, it should* salvage Florexco from the abyss of financial disaster, which the company has approached.

How strange it is that the drilling should be going so easy. I have no idea why they have not hit bedrock yet. It must be a good sign, although surely it can't continue for much longer. If it does, then we most certainly will have stumbled on something quite remarkable.

Hex St. Claire continues to have a fine time. He certainly loves to visit the Continent. He seems, however, still to have strange feelings about the rig. He is worried and has been playing with those damned cards again. How a man as intelligent and educated as he is can pay attention to things like the Tarot, I'll never know. I guess, despite everything, you can never totally educate the black out of a man.

THIRTEEN

During the season, when the town was filled with tourists and winter residents, Harpoon Harry's would ordinarily have been crowded on a Wednesday night. But the snowbirds not having yet arrived, the summer visitors gone, and the winter tourism not having begun, there was just a handful of customers, most of them sitting at the bar when Jori went in. Old Joe, perpetually wiping the bar with his white towel, looked up with surprise and cheer when he saw her. "Why, Miss Ashe," he said animatedly wagging his head back and forth. "I didn't think you'd be back. I thought we'd seen you for the last time that crazy night."

She smiled. "I don't want that to happen again. That's for sure."

Joe yelled through a window into the other half of the club. "Harry, you better come over here and see who just came in!" He looked back smiling at her and a moment later Harpoon Harry himself came through the door at the far end of the bar. He was a large, rotund man, his body bloated by the thousands of beers he had consumed over the years, but he had a warm, friendly face surrounded by a scruffy gray beard and an almost totally bald, shiny head. His voice was rough and gravelly and he had an emphysematous cough. But everyone who knew him liked him—that is, except for those unlucky individuals whom he decided didn't belong in his establishment. The surprising fate he dished out to them was being tossed out the front door by Harry's big, burly and strong arms. Jori guessed that he must be in his mid-sixties. He practically trotted toward her, holding his hands up in the air in mock exasperation.

"Oh, my God! I didn't think I'd ever see you in here again," he said. "They told me you were okay, but I just couldn't believe it. I would have killed the son of a bitch myself if I could have found him. He just disappeared!" He looked at her seeming to show great concern. "You look just fine. Were you hurt bad?"

"I'm okay now," she said. "A few stitches on my cheek and tongue and maybe a loose tooth—but I'm okay."

"You don't know how relieved I am to hear that," he said. "I just can't believe a thing like that could happen." He turned to the bartender. "Joe, an extra large Margarita for Miss Ashe and make it just right." Harry guided Jori to her usual table on the deck. He held the stool out as she sat down and then pulled one up beside her and sat down with her. "Did you press charges against that creep?"

"No. I didn't want to get involved in a big hassle."

"I see," he answered. "Well, if he ever comes back in here, he's going to get a little of the same from me, I'll tell you. I don't put up with that sort of thing in here. I mean, if a couple of guys throw a few punches at each other that's one thing, but to have some jackass walk in here and hit a lady is a totally different matter." He frowned.

A smile crossed her face. "What's the matter Harry? You don't think I can defend myself?"

"You weren't doing too good that particular night," he

225

said. "I think perhaps you might have needed a little help. If it hadn't been for the explosion I think you would've got it."

"Well, I'll let bygones be bygones," she said. "I don't think that'll happen again. What's been going on here in the last week or so anyway?"

"Oh, nothing much—a few tourists here and there. Mostly busy only on the weekends. Another month though, and the season'll pick up. Say," he said, seeming to remember something. "That guy you were talking to when you had the fight was in here the other night looking for you. Blain something."

"Oh yeah? Dr. Robson? When was he here?"

"He's a doctor? He doesn't look like it," Harry said. "I guess it must have been two nights ago. Said he'd been trying to reach you at home, but you'd been gone."

"Yes. I've been on the well for the last four days. We're busy working out there."

"Well good—good. Now, what can I get you for supper? It's on me tonight with the house compliments. Whatever you want. I'm going to fill you up." He smiled.

"I might just accept that offer," she said. "Then I won't have to sue you for letting in such unruly and dangerous men. Let's see now. Since you're paying, I'll take a whole dozen oysters on the half shell and after that a big bowl of conch chowder and some conch fritters to go with it. And I'm probably going to need another Margarita to follow this one." She held up the glass which Joe had just placed on the table and took a long sip.

He smiled. "Whatever you want, it's yours. You just relax and I'll get things going for you." He stood and headed into the kitchen.

The band on the other side, having finished warming

up and tuning their instruments, broke into their first song of the night. It was a pleasant gentle-sounding melody with lots of lead guitar and rhythmic bass. The group had a good sound. There was one thing Harry always provided in his establishment and that was live music. During the season some of the bands would be really good. Occasionally even a name group would play the place. Summertime however, the pickings got a little thin and the quality deteriorated. This particular group, however, was pretty good, especially for this time of year.

She loved music and she loved to dance. She looked forward to getting just a little bit drunk and doing some serious dancing tonight. Harry's was good for that sort of thing, and experience had taught her that the place would be crowded with singles in just a few hours.

She glanced out over the ocean and in the distance could barely see the lights of the well. It was a pleasant evening and Harry's was a pleasant place. All in all she felt good.

Harry's remark about Blain Robson looking for her came to mind. She wondered what he wanted to talk to her about. She pulled from her purse the note she had found under her door and read it again. It said he'd been trying to reach her and would she please call. She had, but he had been in surgery. She had left the message that if he needed to see her she'd be here tonight. She wondered if what Loggins and Wally had said was true. It didn't seem reasonable that a charming young doctor like Blain could be a serious threat to Florexco, but she wondered and she was curious. She halfway wanted to see him just to spite the others. She did not want to submit and adjust her social life in any manner to please Loggins.

Her oysters on the half shell arrived as did another Margarita. A few minutes later came the conch chowder and another Margarita. By the time she had finished eating—stuffing herself rather—with Harry's delicious fare, she also had begun to feel rather nicely mellowed by the tequila. She moved from the restaurant half over to the bar half of the club and assumed her favorite seat on a high-backed stool at the end of the bar which extended out onto the deck and gave her a panoramic view of the band and the dance floor. From the boxful of cigarettes on the bar she took one, lit it, and took a few short puffs. She never inhaled and she was not a regular smoker, but when she was drinking and nightclubbing she enjoyed playing with them.

As time passed, the music seemed to get better and better. She danced once with a middle-aged man who appeared to be a traveling salesman. She refused him when he came around a second time. He was a little too much like the married type, and she didn't play that game. It was almost ten o'clock and the crowd had started to drift in when Blain showed up.

She saw him as he came through the front door. He seemed to be looking for her, or for someone, anyway. He surveyed the room quickly, glanced toward the dance floor and then finally stopped at the far end of the bar and ordered a drink. He stood there for a few minutes after he had been served, looking around intermittently and listening to the band. Finally he looked out toward the open deck and began to meander slowly in her direction. He didn't actually recognize her until he was almost next to her.

"Hey!" he said, surprised. "I almost didn't see you. You look different with your hair pulled back. How's your tongue?"

She smiled, opened her mouth and stuck out her tongue, wiggling it back and forth. "Back to normal. Feels great," she said. "How's it look?"

"Looks good to me," he said smiling. "But then I'm no expert on tongues."

"Well," she said, "there's a lot to know about tongues. There's beef tongue. There's the tongue of a shoe. There's tongue-in-cheek. And then there's the famous song about tongues."

"Oh yeah?" he raised his eyebrows quizzically. "What's that?"

"Oh you know," she said. "The one by Tennessee Ernie. You load sixteen tongues and what do you get? Another day older and deeper in debt." She grinned broadly at her own joke.

He stood looking at her silently in mock amazement. Finally, he picked up her drink, looked down into it, and then turned to the bartender who had just approached. "I don't know what she's been drinking," Blain said, "but bring her another one and a couple for me."

She laughed. "I'm not as drunk as I sound, really. But I am feeling no pain. You're going to have to hustle to catch up with me."

"Just give me a few minutes. I'm ready to hang one on."

"Rough day?"

"Rough week," he said. "But you look like you're doing great. I love that shirt." He glanced down at the dark green pullover blouse through which could easily be appreciated the round shape of her breasts and the outline of her nipples. Emblazened in sequins across the front was the word "Yes!"

"I think it's been a hard week for all of us," she said growing more serious. "But we can't dwell on it. You have to cheer up sometime you know."

He nodded and took a sip of the Margarita offered by the barman. "Have you been doing okay, really?"

"So-so," she answered. "It's a busy time getting a well started."

"I guess so, particularly with all the damn things that've happened out there."

"Yes. We've sure kept you busy, haven't we?"

"Up until a couple of days ago you did. It's all quieted down now. My practice kind of comes in spurts. I'll work my head off for a few days or a few weeks and then have nothing to do for the next month. I haven't had a case to do for the last couple or three days until I finally picked up a little appendectomy to do tonight. Just finished it."

"A little appendectomy," she said curiously. "You make it sound easy. Almost fun."

"They usually are, but not this one. It was ruptured. Her husband was a kook."

"What does his being a kook have to do with her appendix being ruptured?"

"It's kind of sad, really. They were migrant workers, and her husband wouldn't let her come to the doctor. She said her belly had been hurting for almost a week. He kept stuffing her full of Alka-Seltzer. She worked in the fields this morning, poor thing. And she had a damn ruptured appendix."

"Jiminy," she said. "He didn't have the money, right? He didn't think he could afford the doctor."

"That's it. But the sad thing is they could have come to the emergency room any time. They don't turn anyone away, especially if they're really sick."

"That may be true," she said, "but the problem is, why should poor people have to wait until they get really sick to get the attention of a doctor? We need to have a way of giving them some kind of medical care to keep them from getting so sick."

"It's true," he said. "But what do you do? You can't expect doctors to work for nothing."

"I don't think anybody expects that. But why is it that all doctors are so damn rich?"

"All doctors aren't rich. I'm not."

"You will be though," she said smiling and pointing her finger in his face. "I'll come to see you in five years, and you'll be living in a big house on the river or at the country club—swimming pool, yachts, the whole bit."

He laughed. "It doesn't sound too bad now that you mention it. Sounds quite a bit better than my little two bedroom condo."

"There'll probably be a lot more doctors selling their fancy places and living in two-bedroom condos when national health insurance comes in," she said, smiling victoriously.

"Maybe so," he responded. "And we might even be able to keep the cost of the program down by using some of the excessive profits the oil companies are ringing up." He broke into a broad grin.

She laughed with him. "Score one for you." The band began to play a louder, more raucous song. She pointed at the other side of the deck. "Let's go over there where we can talk," she yelled.

He followed her through the tables out into the open air and the relative quiet of the restaurant side. She selected the table nearest the rail overlooking the sea. He sat down beside her. "They tell me that you're trying to stir up a little trouble for the company," she said.

He shook his head and let out a long sigh. "I suppose it could be interpreted that way, but not any more. I've given up on that."

"What did you think was wrong?"

"That was the whole point I never could get across to anybody. I didn't necessarily think that anything definite was wrong. It's just that I wanted to make sure. It seemed that there was a possibility that there might be."

"What kind of things?" she asked.

"Blood problems." He went on to describe the four cases of aplastic anemia including the bleeding death on the operating room table of Ben Lockhardt. He told her about his discovery of the Florexco workers with the low white blood cell counts, including her own.

"What can cause that sort of thing?" she asked.

"It's hard to say. Several things. Toxic chemicals, radiation, I guess even certain viral diseases. That's what everyone wants to blame it on."

"Is that what you think?"

"I don't know what to think any more," he answered. "At first I was certain that there must be some explanation. But after everyone seemed to be against me on the matter, I began to wonder whether maybe they were right and I was just an alarmist."

"You don't think there's anything going on now that's hurting people, do you?"

"I guess not. You seem okay. We ought to check your white count, though," he said. "What about the other men on the well? Is anybody sick? Are they having any funny problems?"

"No," she replied. "I don't think so. Everyone seems well. There's been no sick leave."

232

"We'll probably never know the answer. It's just one of those things that happen for some reason, and now it's done. I've learned a bit of a lesson though. I think I must have been a little too trigger happy on this one. I approached it wrong somehow. I got everybody stirred up." He took a sip of his drink and then glanced back at her. "You know they've put me on probation at the hospital."

"For what?"

"Your friend Loggins pulled it off somehow. I had a little argument with him the morning after Lockhardt died on the table, and he apparently got some bigshot board member named Strombeck to call the chairman of the board of the hospital. They said that I was trying to disrupt the company's work and was saying slanderous things about the company. They told me, in no uncertain terms, that I had to either cool it or get out."

"God!" she said. "I can't believe they'd do that. You'd think they would need something a little more dramatic to justify putting you on probation, for Christ's sake."

"Well, truthfully, it goes a little deeper than that," he responded. "I've made a few enemies here. I haven't exactly handled myself very diplomatically with some of the other surgical staff. The problem is, I came out of an academic institution where I had done my training and the big emphasis was on modern approaches, doing the right thing, taking care of the patient come hell or high water. And I get out here in the outside world, and I guess in a sense I haven't adopted a more realistic outlook on things. I felt from the very beginning that the way surgery was being practiced here it was more like a business. The things that made good money were being done the most. Anything that was too complicated or too much trouble was shipped out. I even think that there's some things done that aren't exactly necessary, and I hate to say it, but I think that some of the motivation is money. It's a hard thing."

He paused and took another sip of his drink. She waited. "It would have been all right if I had kept my opinions to myself. But, unfortunately, I spoke out, made a few comments. Some of the old guard surgeons got offended and their cronies got involved, and pretty soon I had a large segment of the medical staff that thought I was some kind of radical. That kind of thing frightens all of them because nobody wants the apple cart overturned. It's a big business, medicine, and these guys have all built a lifestyle based upon the high income it generates. Even the threat of a little trouble or something panics them all, even the good guys. So, as a consequence, they don't do anything to try and get rid of the rotten apples that exist. They're too afraid that the whole thing could snowball and mess it all up."

"It must be hard for you," she said softly.

"Yes," he answered. "It's discouraging. I really came here with good intentions. I wanted to practice medicine. I wanted to fit in. I just made a few political mistakes. Unfortunately, when this kind of thing happens, then people tend to turn on you and any other little mistakes you make, they blow out of proportion and use against you. And that's what's happened to me now, it looks like. The chief of surgery, Stan Wilcott, led the tirade against me. He didn't want me here in the first place. He and his buddies sort of had a monopoly here, and when I came along I threatened that. It probably would have been okay except something that happened less than a month or two after I got here. It inflamed the whole thing and got him super pissed off at me along with the chief of staff, a GP named Fieldman."

"What happened?" she asked and then signaled the waiter to bring two more drinks.

"It was a fluke. I was sitting in my office late one afternoon with not much to do. I had already seen the couple of patients that I had at that time. This lady walks in, about sixty years old, very pleasant, and asks to see me. So they brought her back into the office and she told me that she had a lump in her breast. Well, I examined her and sure enough she did. It was a possible cancer, too. And when you have this kind of a situation, the way I was trained, you have two options. If the lump is real superficial, close to the surface, you can, just with local anesthetic right there in the office, take a little biopsy of it, send it to the pathologist and have an answer within 45 minutes as to whether this thing is malignant or not. That's what the patient's worried about, of course. Or if it's located more deeply in the breast, you have to admit them to the hospital and give them an anesthetic and do the biopsy in the OR before you can find out. The problem is, most older surgeons haven't been trained to do the biopsy in the office. So they admit almost all breast lumps straight into the hospital, do the biopsy under general anesthetic and if it turns out to be cancer, go ahead and do the radical mastectomy right then. It's all very horribly traumatic psychologically for the woman and I'd prefer not to do it that way if I can. That's why I like to do that little quickie biopsy in my office whenever it's practical. It answers the questions immediately and avoids a lot of unnecessary psychological trauma."

"That sounds reasonable to me," she said. "I think if it was my breast, I'd like it done that way. How could anybody criticize you for that?"

"Well, the problem was that this lady didn't tell me she had just left Dr. Wilcott's office, where he had examined her and told her that there was no question in his mind but that she had to go straight into the hospital that night. He was going to give her an anesthetic the next day and do the biopsy and then possibly do the cancer surgery if it was necessary. It scared her half to death and she didn't know what to do, and she just happened to see my office. Saw the sign 'General Surgeon,' so she came in to get a second opinion. But she didn't tell me all this. So when I proposed doing the biopsy right then under just local anesthetic, she thought the idea was great. We did it. Sent the specimen out. Less than an hour later, the report came back from the pathologist—benign. So I told her the whole deal was off. She had a little tiny incision on her breast, sent her home with a little codeine and we could forget about it. It was all done—signed, sealed, and delivered. Well, I sent her home, but unknown to me, she didn't go home. She went straight over to the office of Hoyt Fieldman, the GP, and started raising hell with him because he was her regular doctor. She was real upset that he had sent her to Wilcott, who had wanted to put her in the hospital and make a big deal out of this, when all she really had to do was come see me and get it all done in a flash. Needless to say, both Fieldman and Wilcott were sort of caught with their pants down, and it was a very embarrassing situation for them."

"So what? That wasn't your fault."

"They didn't see it that way. Wilcott started screaming first of all that I had stolen his patient. He didn't believe that the patient had not told me she was just coming in for a second opinion. He claims that I talked her into

236

letting me do the surgery instead of letting it be his case. Well, Fieldman seemed to agree with him and was just in general pissed off at the whole embarrassing mess. The final upshot was that nothing really could be done or was done because I was right and the problem was taken care of. But I made two very important enemies: the chief of surgery and the chief of staff. Those two guys have been around here a long time, and they carry a lot of weight. If I'd wanted to pick any two people to make sure I stayed on their good side, it would've been those two."

"Screw 'em. You can't help that sort of thing," she said. "You've got to do your best and if they don't like it they can lump it."

"That's been my attitude about it. The only problem is a surgeon lives off his referrals and the referrals are coming pretty slim right at the moment."

"It's hard for me to believe that other doctors would hold that kind of ridiculous thing against you."

"It goes deeper than that. About a month later I accepted a transfer from a little hospital out west of here, near the lake, a patient named Pendleton. A real jarhead surgeon out there had done some abdominal vascular surgery on him and he had developed all kinds of complications and was sick as a dog. They wanted to know if I would take him. Well, it was the sort of thing I was used to. We took care of them as residents. I was geared up for high-risk surgical patients, intensive care problems. So I accepted the transfer. They shipped the guy over to the hospital, and it just turned into a big hell of a mess. He really was a little too sick for the girls in the ICU to handle. One problem after another developed. He got better for awhile, then worse, then better and he finally survived. But only after I had amputated both of his legs, which had developed gangrene, none of which was my fault, none of which I could control. And I don't think even in the most hot-shot of medical centers he would have done any better. He was too sick when he got here. He was lucky to have made it. Unfortunately, the family didn't see it that way and they got a lawyer out of Miami and he's suing everybody; suing the original doctor, the original hospital, suing me, suing Community General Hospital and a lot of the staff. It's just a big mess. It's one of the typical flagrant abuses of the malpractice legal system. It sucked me and everybody else into it and has irritated a lot of people who think that I should've done just like everybody around here does, and that is stay away from the high risk tough stuff. Send it all into Gainesville or to Miami where the medical schools are. Let them take the risks, not us."

"I see what you mean," said Jori. "First one thing and then another. Then everybody starts adding them all up and it makes you look bad."

"Exactly. First I come in here and supposedly steal a case from the chief of surgery. Then the next thing I do is get involved with a big malpractice suit that involves a lot of the other doctors on staff, through no fault of my own. And on top of that the word gets out that I have a funny attitude about medical ethics and all the money changing hands. All in all, it paints a dark picture of me. So then, along comes this little problem. I start looking into what I thought were some very unusual medical occurrences in relation to the well and I wind up getting the chief of the board of the hospital down on my ass, raising a lot of hell. So they finally all just decided I wasn't worth the trouble, and they put me on probation."

"They can't stop you from practicing medicine,

though, can they?"

"No, of course not. But if they take away my staff privileges at the hospital, what can I do? What good is a surgeon without a hospital to operate in?"

"I see," she said. "It looks like they've got you right where it hurts."

"They do, and I don't want to leave here. So, the only answer is for me to shape up. So you're looking at the new Blain Robson. From now on I keep my mouth shut, I do things in the conventional way, and I ship the high-risk stuff out. And also, I'm keeping my nose out of other people's business. If you guys at Florexco want to bump off everybody that's fine with me. Just as long as I don't get involved." He grinned.

"Well, you can quit worrying about that because everybody's okay on the well. I don't know what caused all those problems you were talking about, but it certainly doesn't seem to be doing anything now. We're having some trouble on the well, but none of it seems to be medical, at least not now."

"I guess anything's an improvement after the lightning."

"They're not even sure now that it was lightning."

He looked puzzled. "What do you mean? What could it have been?"

"I don't know. But the chief geophysicist who works for the company, a brainchild named Adrian Sumter, has calculated it out, and he says it'd be impossible for lightning to do that without completely destroying the rig."

"Do you believe that?"

"I don't know what to believe. Dr. Sumter is not one to be taken lightly. He's a brilliant man, well-recognized for

239

his work in the area of geophysics."

"What does a geophysicist know about lightning?"

"A hell of a lot, Blain. The man is brilliant when it comes to geology and the earth's environment. If he says lightning couldn't do that, then it probably damn well couldn't."

"There has to be some explanation, Jori. What else could it have been besides lightning? It must have been some other type of electrical malfunction."

"No evidence of it. That ass Loggins still wants to blame me for it somehow. But he doesn't have a leg to stand on. You see, I had ordered the drilling and the engines that run it pushed to maximum levels. We had come across a very resistant spot and I wanted to break through it. He claims that somehow I must have overloaded everything."

"Is that possible? Could it have been something like that?"

"No," she laughed, "it's ridiculous. The very worst it could have done would have been to overload the engine, but that wouldn't have killed everybody."

"What were you drilling through?"

"That's the big question," she said and took another drink. "We don't have any idea. It's confusing. Something very peculiar has happened. Normally, when you drill a well offshore, you go through sand for awhile, then pretty soon you hit bedrock and then it's hard going. Every foot comes tough at that point. But for us, we've gone almost ten thousand feet now and there's nothing there but sand. It's almost like we're in a predrilled hole."

She paused, took another drink and sat thinking about what she had just said. "That's exactly what it's like," she finally said more forcefully. "It just like we're drilling right down through an area that's already been drilled before, as if the hole was already there—a big opening in the bedrock."

"That doesn't sound very plausible."

"No, it doesn't," she answered. "It's impossible, absolutely impossible. First of all, no one's ever drilled there before. Second of all, for us to drill right down through the same area would be an absolute statistical impossibility. Even if we were trying to find someone else's hole."

"Maybe it's just a soft spot. Don't those kinds of things exist?"

"No," she answered slowly. "It's not a soft spot. There's no such thing as a soft spot. When you get below a few hundred feet, the earth's covered by a rocky crust. It's solid rock everywhere."

"How thick is the crust?"

"It varies. In most places it's fifteen to twenty miles thick. Sometimes even deeper. Under the ocean it gets a little thinner in a few spots. It may be as shallow as five or six miles in certain places."

"What then? The mantle?"

"Right," she said smiling. "You're not so dumb. First there's the outer crust and underneath that the mantle, which is almost 1800 miles thick. And finally you get to the core of the earth, which would extend maybe 2000 miles to the very center of the earth."

"So what's it all made of? Green cheese?"

She grinned. "Who knows? We're all just guessing about what's beneath the crust. Nobody's ever really drilled through the crust."

"I thought I read about a scientific project to do

241

something like that a few years ago," he said.

She nodded. "The Moho."

"Yes, that sounds like it."

"The Moho, or the Mohole Project as it was called, was an attempt to try to drill through the crust and get down to the mantle. It comes from the word Mohorovic Discontinuity. That's a technical term used to describe a change in the way that sound waves are transmitted through the earth from one point to the other. There's a lot of evidence that as sound waves or seismic waves pass through the crust and go into the mantle, it changes their speed of conduction somewhat. One of the most famous geologists of all, Dr. Mohorovic, described that as a discontinuity in sound conduction."

"Jesus. Why couldn't he have had a nice simple name like Robson?"

"Yes. Or maybe Ashe," she said.

"No, that wouldn't work," he responded.

"Why not?"

"Well we wouldn't want all these geologists walking around telling everybody what a deep Ashe hole they were going to dig, would we?" She laughed. "And then you know what comes next, don't you?" he said. "Everybody would start talking about geologists, and saying they don't know the difference between their Ashe hole or a hole in the ground."

When she finally stopped laughing, she looked him straight in the eye. "You turkey."

"That's no worse than your song about sixteen tongues," he replied.

"It must be the Margaritas."

"You're probably right. Let me get us a couple more." He waved at the waiter and then turned back toward her.

"Now tell me a little bit more about that big Ashe hole Loggins."

She smiled again. "Cut that out, damn it. That's a very nice family name you're insulting."

He grinned. "What's with that guy anyway?"

"He hates me because I'm a threat to him. I hate him now because he's hated me so much."

"Is he really a homosexual like you implied the night he busted your mouth?"

"I think so," she answered. "Maybe AC-DC. I know he takes out women every now and then."

"What makes you think he's gay?"

She smiled. "Oh, it was dumb. It was purely by accident. It was right after we had put this project together, and he was raising all kinds of hell with me, obviously very irritated that he and I were having to share some authority. So one night I went over to the apartment he was supposed to be living in. I was going to talk to him about it. Try to break the ice, let bygones be bygones. I wanted to be conciliatory, straighten this whole mess out. Well, I knocked on his door. He didn't answer it, but I heard his voice. He said, 'Come on in.' So I went in. But there was nobody there. So then I hear his voice again from the back of the apartment. He said, 'Come on through. We're back here.' So what the hell, I did it. Then the next thing I know he's standing there just wearing a jock strap and a Nazi cap. He's got some guy, naked as the day he was born, all tied down and moaning in ecstasy. Loggins was just as shocked as I was. But before he could say anything, I ran down the hall, and just then the outside door opens and in walks this big muscular, very gay-looking guy with peroxide blond hair, wearing a little tiny bathing suit you could practically see

243

through. He was carrying a tray with two drinks on it. The guy didn't see me. He just takes a look at Loggins standing there and says, 'I got the drinks, good-looking.'"

"What did you do?" Blain said, smiling in amazement.

"I couldn't do a thing," she said. "All I could do was laugh. Loggins got hysterical and ran back down the hall. The big blond boy just stood there looking at me until I finally got myself together and cleared out."

"What did Loggins say about it later?"

"Nothing. We've never discussed it. We've never said a word about it. I think it may be one of the reasons he hates me even more."

"Jesus Christ. I don't blame him. What an embarrassing situation it must have been for him. It sounds hysterical."

"It was," she answered. "I can't keep from laughing now, when I think about it."

"Why don't you blackmail him with it. Get him to get off your case?"

"I thought about it once," she said. "But it might not work. There might be somebody else in the company who's gay. It could backfire in my face."

He nodded. "You may be right. I wonder why he doesn't just go open. Most people accept gays. I don't have any particular objection to it."

"Yes, but you're not an oil rig worker. How easy do you think it'd be to control thirty or forty tough offshore oil drillers if you were an open homosexual?"

"I see what you mean," he said. "It might tend to dampen some of your authority."

"Darn right it would," she said. "But anyway, I've always got it stored away as my big gun. If I ever had to use it against him, I guess I could."

"From the way he reacted to your comment, I don't think he would take it very well."

"No. He wouldn't take it well at all. He hates me, absolutely hates me. I may not be working around here much longer anyway, the way things are going."

"What do you mean?"

"He's winning the battle out there. Turning some of the men against me, turning my boss against me, sort of. They're all beginning to feel that a woman in command of an offshore rig just doesn't work well."

"It does seem like a tough spot for you out there."

"It shouldn't be, not really, but they're making it tough. It's hard to fight that kind of sexism stuff."

"It must be."

"You've never had to deal with it, Blain, not like I have. You don't know what it's like to have everything you do questioned and doubted. All of it just because I don't have testicles. It's depressing."

She stirred her drink slowly, as he watched her. He found her very attractive.

"It's funny," she continued, "so many of the men I work with want to lay me, not just for the sex and not because they want to be with me. They want to screw me to show their superiority. Getting into my pants would be a victory. They all want to see me defeated, if not intellectually, then flat on my back. They want to be like some wild stallion, with me beneath them, obedient and passive, but definitely beaten and maybe begging for more. I don't know why they have to view my sex in such ego-challenging ways."

He could see how deeply felt her comments were and, for the first time in his life, he understood what women were complaining about. "It's got to be hard, I can see that," he said. "You must have to fight for every inch you gain. Don't give up, though. I think you've got what it takes. I know you do. You're a lot like some women doctors I've known, tough as nails, pioneers really."

She sighed. "Yes, somebody's got to break down the barrier. Might as well be me," she smiled. "I don't want to get depressed again. Let's talk about something else."

"What're you going to do about the drilling? Tell me more about this big hole you have found."

"That I don't know," she said. "I guess it could be some kind of fluke, some kind of defect in the tectonic plate that we've just stumbled onto." She looked up from her drink at him. "You know what the tectonic plate theory is, don't you? The theory that the whole earth's crust is really made up of a series of large land masses sitting on top of these so-called plates, some as big as half a continent—they're shifting slowly over the centuries, changing the geography of the world."

"I've heard a little about it. It has something to do with earthquakes and things doesn't it?"

"Yes," she answered. "Earthquakes occur at the edge between one plate and another. That's what a fault is. As one plate pushes against the other, or scoots under it, it creates kind of a strained place as they rub against each other. That leads to turbulence and tension—and earthquakes."

"Is that what you've done, maybe? Drilled right between two of the plates?"

"No, no. That's not it at all. We're drilling right in the middle of a plate. There's one whole plate that supposedly includes the Caribbean and the eastern United States. We're right in the middle of it, or at least well away from the edge. So it couldn't be that. But I guess it's possible that we've stumbled onto a defect in the plate and we're just going to go straight down without ever hitting anything solid."

"You mean go all the way through the crust into the mantle?"

She smiled. "I guess so. I don't know. Maybe we'll be the first ones to drill a Moho."

He grinned with her. "Then I guess they really will have to call it an Ashe hole if you're the one that does it, won't they?"

"Yes. I guess that I'd have the most famous Ashe hole in the world, wouldn't I?"

They both laughed hysterically.

As the humor finally subsided, they sat quietly for a few moments, both looking out to the ocean and listening to the music in the background.

For whatever reason the music grew softer and the band began the first of several slow numbers. He put his hand on hers and she turned to look into his eyes. "Do you want to dance?" he asked. She nodded.

On the dance floor he put both arms around her and pulled her in close and she held him tight. As they moved around the floor cheek to cheek, the congenial feeling growing in each of them about the other became even warmer with their physical closeness.

They didn't speak much, and they didn't leave the dance floor for almost an hour. They both realized and enjoyed what was happening. They found themselves holding on to each other, even between the songs. Once she pulled her head back away from him slightly and stared into his eyes for a few moments. In silence, they communicated something that was good. She hadn't felt this way in a long time and neither had he.

When the band finished the set and started another break, he didn't immediately release her, but stood motionless with his arms still around her, holding her tightly, enjoying the feeling of her breasts against his chest. Finally, he relinquished his grip and stood back looking into her pretty eyes. "I didn't want to let go of you there for a minute," he said, smiling.

"I know," she replied, squeezing his hand. She ran her fingers along the side of his soft beard. "I've never danced so close to a man with one of these. It feels good. It's like snuggling up to a warm puppy."

He laughed as they walked out on the open deck. They stood with their arms around each other, leaning against the rail, gazing into the dark night. "Life's so unpredict-able," he said. "Things come along just when you least expect it. I'm very glad we're getting to know each other, Jori."

"Me, too, Blain. I really feel good about you. I didn't think they were making men like you any more."

He chuckled, "Thank God, eh?"

She poked him in the ribs. "Goose. I meant that in a nice way."

"I know," he replied. "And I like you, too, very much." He leaned toward her and kissed her sweetly.

The rest of the evening seemed to pass quickly. It was mostly touching, holding hands, dancing and enjoying the surprising exhilaration the new feelings were bringing. Her slender but voluptuous body moved him, and she could feel his arousal against her pelvis. Finally, some time in the early-morning hours, when Harry's was about to close, they quietly left the place and went the two miles down the beach to her house.

She showed him around the small cottage, and then they opened a bottle of wine, which she had been keeping for just such an occasion. After pouring a large glass for each of them, they stepped out on the back porch. The dark night was very pretty with a half moon faintly lighting the deserted beaches and gently rolling surf.

"Do you want to go for a swim," he said, with a challenging smile.

She looked at him, mockingly suspicious. "Haven't you ever heard of the 'jaws theory'?"

He chuckled. "They don't have those big sharks around here," he said. "That's New England stuff. Our sharks are all little and friendly."

"Sure," she said, grinning delightedly.

"Besides that," he added, "what better person to be around if you get bit than a surgeon. I could have you fixed up in no time."

"Uh-huh," she replied, "and I'll bet you didn't even bring a swim suit either."

He smiled again. "Do you have one that'll fit me?"

She shook her head in feigned exasperation. "Let me at least get you a damned robe." She disappeared quickly into the house.

In her absence, he rapidly undressed and ran down the beach to dive into the surf. By the time she came back onto the porch, he was yelling to her, standing chest deep in the water.

"Come on in! The water's great."

She was wearing a blue terrycloth robe. "You nut," she yelled, as she went down the steps and walked slowly down to the ocean's edge and stuck her foot carefully into the cold water. "What's it feel like?"

"It's as cold as a witch's tit, but other than that, it's

great," he replied, as a breaking wave slapped him in the back, almost knocking him down.

She laughed. "All right. But I'm not staying in long. I'll be damned if I'm going to become shark bait." She dropped her robe and scampered into the water, screaming in discomfort at the icy shock.

They met, wrapped their arms around each other, and huddled together, skin to skin, for warmth. After a short while of being knocked around by the big rollers and becoming miserable because of the coldness, despite enjoying the physical closeness of the two of them, they had had enough.

"How about a warm shower?" she said through chattering teeth.

It was an offer he could not refuse.

They came out of the water, arm in arm. He could see how beautiful she was, her smooth, wet skin glistening in the moonlight. As they shivered, he pulled her close once again and kissed her, holding her even more tightly than before. She picked up her robe, and they pulled it around their shoulders and, with arms around each other, went up the beach and into the house.

In the shower, with the warm water soothing their chilled bodies, they embraced and kissed. He moved his hands slowly around her sides until he cupped each of her breasts, as she rubbed her hands across his shoulders and chest.

Then, finally, they were warm and dry, lying nude side by side in her bed, stroking, caressing, and enjoying each other. In the faint moonlight coming from the window, she was beautiful—her curly auburn hair splayed out over the pillow, her beautiful round breasts with erect nipples. They did not speak but communicated with their eyes, their touch. She rubbed her hand over the strong muscles of his back and arms and felt secure in his strength as he held her. His soft beard caressed her gently, as he kissed her breasts and then, finally, he loved her in a way that she had never been loved before.

As she exploded with passion and joy, she felt more like a woman than she ever remembered.

Lying over her, guiding her gently rocking hips with his hands, he was driven to please her and take pleasure from her as he had never had with other women.

In the end, they both lay consumed and exhausted by passion. Filled with feelings of tenderness and bliss, sleep came quickly and easily upon them.

FOURTEEN

On Thursday Jori chose to ride the crew boat to the rig instead of the helicopter. The sea was smooth and the day clear and pretty. The 25-minute ride passed quickly and, after the gentle docking, she dropped her case by the crew office and went straight to the control booth.

The drilling seemed to be progressing normally as she climbed the stairs. She noted a new shipment of pipe stacked neatly in the far corner of the rig. It looked like about ten thousand feet worth. That would be the third full 10,000-foot load they had received since the initiation of the drilling, and she was anxious to find out the present depth.

Duval was watching the controls when she entered the booth. He glanced up and nodded perfunctorily.

"How deep are we?" she asked immediately.

"Coming up on 15,000," he answered.

She let out a surprised whistle and stepped forward to look at the incoming data. "Any other changes?"

"Like what?" he said, somewhat sarcastically.

"You know like what. What are we drilling through?"

"Come on!" he replied, irritated. "We've gone almost six thousand feet since you left two days ago, and you still want to know what we're drilling through?"

"You're being a little testy this morning, aren't

you, Eric?"

"That's right. I'm irritable," he snapped. "It's easy enough for you to say. You go shack up for a couple of days, leaving the rest of us stuck on this overgrown monster and then come back all refreshed. Don't act surprised that the rest of us are a little uptight."

Her eyes narrowed in anger and dismay. "What did you say I did?"

His expression changed from hostility to guilt. "Nothing. I didn't mean anything."

"Duval! Who said I was shacked up?"

He looked embarrassed and exasperated. He let out a long sigh. "I can't keep up with who's supposed to say what around here . . . Loggins told me I wasn't supposed to say anything about it." He looked down at the instruments. "He said you were hanging around that doctor they don't like. They're all mad at you. I think they're going to put Winston totally in charge. They don't trust you being around that guy or something." He looked up at her. "I shouldn't have told you. It's not my goddamned fault."

Caught by surprise, she did not immediately respond to Duval, who rose a moment later and started for the door. "I'm going down to the crew office," he said.

Dismayed, she sat down. Loggins and Wally were going to do it to her. She was sure of it. Duval wouldn't lie about that. Things had changed overnight. Loggins was obviously now pulling the strings. They were after her. They weren't concerned about Blain. What had he done anyway, other than inquire about some illnesses? Her first thought was to call Jenkins immediately and confront him with the idiocy of this action. It seemed so incredible that a normal relationship, very benign, with a

253

man like Blain could be used against her this way, while an S & M artist like Loggins went untouched and, as a matter of fact, became even more powerful.

She stood up and went to the control desk and glanced at the readouts. There was nothing spectacularly unusual, only the steady, inexorable, mystifying rapid progress of the drilling. But she was barely aware of the dials in front of her. Her mind was still whirling with shock at Loggins's victory. How could they even know, she thought, but then realized that with Loggins after her like he was, it wouldn't have been hard to have someone keep an eye on her, hoping to catch her in something. Because she was a female, she was more vulnerable. She felt anger and a tremendous desire for revenge against the man. But she was powerless to gain it for the moment. She didn't really care, anyway, she told herself. She was tired of fighting. She just wanted to get on with the work. That was the important thing, she kept thinking . . . to find out what the hell was wrong with the crust below them. And what had really killed the men.

About an hour later, having had time for the bad news to sink in, she decided to make the rounds over the rig for the daily inspection that was part of her routine. When she reached the main platform, she stopped Duval, who was just coming out of the crew office.

"Eric, get me a 48-hour service report on the engines and drill equipment, will you?"

"Sure," he replied. "But I've already given that to Mr. Loggins."

"Mr. Loggins isn't responsible for the drilling operations," she said. "Those reports are supposed to come to me." She felt anger again, not just at Duval, but at the whole damned organization. How was it possible that a subordinate like him could know about the change in administrative structure even before she did? "He is still not in charge of day-to-day drill operations, Eric, I am. Routine decisions are still mine."

He looked at her, annoyed for a moment. "You don't have to be so sensitive about it, Miss Ashe," he said. "There's nothing wrong with the fact that he's been put in charge. It's not a good job for a woman anyway."

"Oh God, Eric," she said disgustedly. "You ought to know by now that I'm not interested in your concepts of what's good for a woman."

"Maybe you ought to be more interested in what other people think," he replied. "A good-looking woman like yourself doesn't belong out on an oil rig. You belong in a nice clean office some place. Or maybe even at home having kids. You're too much woman to be out here in a place like this."

She wanted to scream at him, to tell him to mind his own damn business, but he seemed so pitiful, and for once almost sincere. As she looked at him, she saw him as the weak, insecure man he was. She had a small rush of sympathy for him as she realized how hard it must be for a man like him to take commands from her. But still, she didn't like him. He made her nervous. She hated the way he was always looking at her. "I won't even reply to that, Eric," she said and walked away.

She felt him watching her for awhile and then heard footsteps on the stairs, and she knew he was headed up. She continued to cross the platform over to the drill deck where she watched the tool pushers work for a few minutes, and then spent the next two hours thoroughly inspecting every aspect of the rig.

*   *   *

It was almost 10 P.M. when the unexpected helicopter appeared out of the darkness to the west and slowly settled down onto the heliport. Jori was sitting in the control booth reading, thinking about going to bed just as it landed.

She stepped out of the booth and stood at the top of the stairs watching to see who the craft had brought. The first to exit was a large Negro. He wore a black suit. Following him was a tall, slender man dressed totally in white. It was Dr. Adrian Sumter and Hex. She started immediately down the stairs.

The unexpected arrival of the two was comforting. She felt almost like a small child whose father had just come to the rescue. It had been two months since she had seen them. Hex looked his usual somber and mysterious self: dark and powerful. The appearance of Sumter was warm and friendly in contrast. Taller than Hex, but much thinner, he walked gracefully toward her, using his cane in a lordly manner, alternately touching the deck and pointing out things of interest, speaking quietly to Hex. He seemed very interested in his surroundings and looked this way and that, as he indicated various features of the well.

When finally he approached her as she reached the bottom of the stairs, he held out his arm and smiled. "My, my, Jori Ashe," he said. "You look more like a tool pusher, decked out in those clothes than the expert geologist I know you to be."

She returned his smile. "Hello, Dr. Sumter. Welcome back. We've been needing you."

"Yes, that's what I'm told," he said and glanced

toward his companion. "She looks in good spirits, wouldn't you say, Hex?"

The black man gave her a very small smile. "I think so, considering everything."

Sumter stood in front of her, both hands resting on his cane. "Well, how does it go? Is the drilling at last proceeding as it should?"

"Depending upon one's viewpoint, much better than it should," she answered.

The smile left his face. "Yes. I understand what you mean." He nodded knowingly. "What do you say we go up and look at the data. Give me an idea what's been happening here."

"Certainly. I think you'll find it all very interesting."

"I'm quite sure you're right," he responded and glanced around the rig again. "How's the equipment functioning? Does the design seem to be appropriate?"

"It's beautiful. Operationally speaking, this is by far the finest drilling platform I've ever seen."

He smiled. "Well, we put in a lot of thought on this matter, and a great many people with experience contributed to the layout of things, even the simple points like the design of the handrails," he said, holding his cane out and tapping on the rail.

"It's all laid out nicely," she said. "Even the crew quarters are roomy and comfortable."

"You know, believe it or not, I stayed on one of these things for almost a month once, and it let me appreciate how terrible it is to have to live in cramped quarters. I made up my mind then that if ever I built one it was going to be more comfortable for the men."

"This one is," she replied, "right down to the projection room for showing those old movies." He smiled, but then, as he entered the control booth, became more serious. He hung his cane on the doorknob, took off his coat and laid it across the desk. Occasionally putting his hands in his pockets, he walked back and forth in front of the control panel studying every detail, every printout, every switch position. He frequently stopped to study an individual piece of information, and on several occasions, made slight adjustments in control knobs, watching the dials to see what effect it had.

Hex St. Claire, standing in the doorway with his arms crossed, said nothing and seemed uninterested, except once when Sumter turned to him and pointed at the drill-depth indicator, which at that point was reading 15,640 feet. Sumter had a concerned look on his face as he tapped the face of the dial several times. St. Claire nodded, but said nothing. Jori stood back by the desk, allowing the scientist to study the results of his own design.

After about twenty minutes, he turned to her. "Now let me see the printouts that I have been told occurred just before this accident." He stood in front of her, his teeth clenched and the corners of his lips turned down slightly, a mild frown upon his face, his chin held high as he waited.

"I have them right here," she said and opened the drawer, withdrew them. "I'm anxious to hear what you think."

He put his hands on the desk, leaned over the sheets of paper that she unrolled, and carefully studied them all. He put his finger down on the chart of magnetic field forces and thoughtfully traced the line with his finger which showed the abrupt shift of forces during the ten or fifteen seconds just prior to the well shutdown. He also looked at the temperature indicator, noting the dramatic rise which occurred prior to the accident. He mumbled to himself several times as he looked back and forth from one sheet to the next and then finally leaned back from the desk and sat down in one of the chairs, his arms folded in front of him.

"How many men died, Jori?" he asked.

"Twenty-four before it was all done. George Elkins was the last. He died in the hospital."

He nodded, then frowned more intensely. "What do you think about it, my dear? What did this?"

"I've been told lightning," she answered. "I had just assumed that was what it must be."

"No! Absolutely not!" he said sharply, shaking his head. "There is no way lightning could have caused this problem. This rig was too well designed for that. The amount of electrical energy that could override the protection system of this structure would have done far greater damage to the electrical components here than I am told happened."

He stood up and walked back to the control panel. He paused, deeply buried in thought, looking out the big window at the work going on below. He paced back and forth, glancing alternately at the control panel and at the rig outside. At length he stopped and turned toward her. "Jori Ashe," he announced, "the secret to that disaster is right here." He pointed to the depth indicator. "Almost 16,000 feet in little more than a week of drilling. That's our problem, my dear, our real problem. Somehow this geological fluke," he continued to point at the dial, "is related to the accident and the deaths of those men. We have had something very bizarre and very unusual happen." He paused and stood staring at her. He seemed to be thinking hard. "It doesn't seem possible that all these things could have happened. What do you think?" he said.

"Dr. Sumter, I don't know," she answered. "I'm totally bewildered by what's happening. I feel very uneasy about it, quite frankly."

"Yes," he said. "I think you have good reason to feel uneasy, wouldn't you, Hex?" He glanced at the black man.

"It all sounds very strange indeed, sir," the man answered. "I would have thought that you would have surely reached something solid by now."

"Yes. Yes I know," Sumter replied. He turned and looked again out the window. "So what we have here is a problem in two parts, or three really. First of all, we hit something very solid very early in the beginning. Almost too early in the beginning of the drilling. Second, after a very intensive effort, we punch through this barrier and almost instantaneously have an electrical accident of some sort that leaves twenty-four men dead and the rig shut down—only temporarily, mind you. Then we follow that extraordinary circumstance with the most unbelievable rate of drilling ever achieved—advancing almost three miles in a week's time. I don't know which of those points is the most amazing. Any one of them would have been a fascinating enough adventure, but to have all three together staggers the mind." He looked again at Jori. "What do you think, dear? Why is it that we have found no resistance to our drilling?"

"Maybe we've stumbled across some sort of defect in the tectonic plate," she said without much confidence.

"Oh come now, Jori," he responded. "Surely you can say more than that. By definition what we have here is a defect of the tectonic plate, the question is why—and in what manner was the defect created? But you made an even more important error. You said 'stumbled across.' No." He shook his head. "We didn't stumble across this place Jori, we came here purposefully."

A puzzled expression crossed her face. "You mean you knew?"

"No," he interrupted smiling. "Of course I didn't know the defect was here. The point is the data that we gathered, gathered very carefully, gave some readings right over this spot that looked very attractive for drilling. Now obviously there are things that we do not yet know about geology and the measurements that we are able to take. What I mistook for good indications of possible petroleum deposits must have been, at least in some way, a manifestation of the strange nature of the tectonic plate beneath where we are standing."

"I see," she said slowly. "You mean to say that this defect in the plate in some way affected the readings that you got. Readings which we misinterpreted, not realizing that a defect like this could exist."

"Exactly. We were led by our own ignorance to this very spot, not by blind luck."

"That explains a lot of things."

"That explains nothing!" he said loudly, turning to look at her, raising one finger into the air dramatically. "I mean nothing. It merely raises more questions." His voice grew more soft. "The real question now is why. Why is this opening here? You understand that less than 500 feet from this spot such an opening through the crust of the earth does not exist. During test drilling, right over there," he pointed to the north, "just 500 feet away, we hit stone at 700 feet. And the same thing in that

261

direction." He pointed south. "There was stone beneath the sea floor 600 or 700 feet from here. I think we have an opportunity to learn something here. We're lucky in the broadest sense. Unfortunately, I don't know what this development does to our chances of finding oil. I need to study this matter and look at the figures again." He stood regarding her quietly. "I tell you Jori, when I figure out what this hole is, through which we are drilling, then I will know what killed those men." He turned slowly to stare at her silently.

His use of the word hole fascinated her. She recalled her own astonishment at having herself describe the drilling process as being akin to drilling through a predrilled hole. "It's almost like it's predrilled, isn't it?" she said after a pause.

He looked away from her out the front window. "Therein lies the real question doesn't it, dear? What caused it . . . or who?"

She took a deep breath and let it out slowly. "You don't really think that someone has drilled here before, do you?"

"I am implying nothing," he said. "I am aware of no information that any present or past civilization would have been able to create a perforation through the crust like this one. All I am saying is that we have found something which is not supposed to be here. And, in the process of breaking into it, forces which we do not understand have taken twenty-four lives. There is obviously much more to this problem than meets the eye. Simplistic notions like a little lightning bolt and an accidental fifteen thousand-foot perforation into the crust of the earth are two theories upon which I put very little weight. What we have here is a much more awesome problem, the solution of which may alter our thinking about a great many things." He glanced at Jori and then back down at the control panel. "Something very important may be happening here, Jori. More important than you, or perhaps even I realize." He turned toward her and smiled. "But enough of this serious talk; whatever it is, we shall see. Right?"

"Yes, sir," she replied. "We're not quitting."

"That's a very good point," he said as the smile faded away. "No matter what happens out here, we're not quitting now. Who knows, we may be making discoveries that will change the world." He glanced out the window again and seemed to study the sky intently for a moment. "Someone's coming," he said. Jori and Hex stepped beside him. In the distance they could see the blinking lights of a second helicopter approaching the platform.

"I don't know who," she said. "No one's expected, but then again, I didn't expect you."

"One never knows who's going to drop in, does one?"

"No," she answered as they watched the helicopter slowly lower to the deck. A moment later Loggins and Craig Strombeck emerged from the craft and walked to the center of the platform looking around as if hunting for someone or something. Loggins finally pointed up toward the control booth and they started toward the stairs.

Strombeck was a very influential member of the board. He was fat and slovenly appearing, although always well-dressed. She found him physically very unattractive and, on the few occasions that she had met him, he had seemed even rude.

"I think I've been discovered," Sumter said as he watched them coming up.

"They don't know you're here?" she asked.

He glanced at her and smiled sheepishly. "I really didn't want to see anyone until I had surveyed the situation here at the well. They didn't know I was arriving tonight."

"You may find out that they didn't want you to talk to me," she said. "Right now they're all a little peeved at me."

"Why?" he said, watching her inquisitively.

"It's a long story, but basically it's because they perceive me as being too weak for this job."

"Too weak? What does that mean? That's a strange way of putting it. As far as I'm concerned, you're the best geologist in the company. You've got a big future, my dear."

"That remains to be seen."

"I suppose so. But in any event, I don't care about all these interpersonal squabbles. My major concern is that we keep this well drilling, no matter what. And I want to make that clear to everyone that no matter what, we cannot stop now. We must go on, if for nothing else, for science."

"The stockholders and the accountants may not be interested in science, Dr. Sumter," she said.

"This is too important to be left to stockholders. We can tell them whatever it is they want to hear, but we cannot jeopardize the project. Not until we see what this is." He looked at her, smiling strangely as the door burst open.

Loggins was the first one in. "Dr. Sumter, welcome aboard. We didn't expect you this soon."

"Hello, Winston," the scientist said coolly as he shook the man's hand unenthusiastically and then turned to greet Craig Strombeck.

264

"Adrian, you old son of a bitch! You should have let us know you were here," the fat man said, and then greeted Hex as did Loggins.

Sumter smiled tolerantly. "I wanted to get the unadulterated truth about what was really happening out here before you gentlemen had a chance to fill my mind up with facts, fantasies, and misconceptions."

"You couldn't have gotten any of that from me," Strombeck said. "I don't know a damn thing about what's going on out here except it's costing too much money."

Sumter chuckled. "As a responsible member of the board that's what I would expect you to say. But of course the cost is not always the bottom line, is it Craig?"

Strombeck smiled. "Winston can fill you in on all the technical data. He's got a lot of things to tell you."

"That's why I wanted to find out for myself before anybody told me anything," Sumter responded. "And I think Miss Ashe has done a pretty fine job of filling me in on the events and the facts." He turned and smiled at her. "I think she and I see eye to eye on a few matters about this problem."

Loggins frowned. "Maybe we should go over it again to make sure you've got the story straight."

"I think I've got what I need to know, Winston. Is there some information you have that Jori doesn't?"

"No. I just wanted to make sure—"

"The truth is," Strombeck interrupted, "Jenkins has made a few changes in our organizational structure since you were last in touch with us. Winston's in total charge out here now. He may ultimately have some information for you above and beyond that which Jori has supplied." He glanced at Jori and then back to Sumter.

"I see," the scientist replied, annoyed. "Perhaps someone should have informed me before any changes were made." He gazed silently at the others before continuing. "Well, we'll have plenty of time to discuss these matters. I have nothing else on my agenda now, except seeing that this project gets completed successfully. Why don't we all ride back to the mainland together and if there's anything you want to fill me in on, you can do so. It's rather late and I'm a little tired and hungry."

Hex St. Claire stepped through the door out onto the open deck and the others began to follow. Sumter turned to Jori and held out his hand. "I'll be in touch with you tomorrow. Think about the things we've talked about. There are some very interesting possibilities here."

She smiled as she put her hand in his. "I certainly will. Welcome back, Dr. Sumter." She glanced behind him at Loggins who was glaring at her fiercely. Sumter stepped quickly out of the room followed by the others. As he left, Craig Strombeck turned toward her, started to speak and then thought better about it and turned away.

She watched from her window as the four men crossed the platform below and reentered the helicopter. A few moments later it was gone into the night, followed quickly by the second empty one, and then she was alone on the rig with the crew once more.

She sat there awhile, staring into the darkness and watching the work below, pondering the things that Sumter had said. Some of his implications seemed crazy, but no more so, really, than the things that had already happened on the well. Most puzzling were his comments about what or who had caused the defect through which they were now drilling. She felt hard pressed to keep her imagination in check as she considered the possibilities he had raised.

She rose and stepped outside into the open air and

looked out toward the east over the moonlit ocean and the black star-filled sky above. She finally laughed to herself at the wild things which raced through her mind. She was not yet willing to consider the "who" part of the question. Whatever was happening, it was strictly natural phenomena as far as she was concerned. She looked up at the sky once again. If Sumter wanted to boggle his own mind with ancient astronaut theories, that was his business. But she was surprised at his lack of an adequate explanation for the accident. If he was right and the answer lay ahead of them, somehow related to the unexplained opening in the crust, then it could certainly happen again. And very likely would. Unnerved, she examined again the recordings from the minutes surrounding the accident.

The changes in the magnetic field still appeared bizarre and impossible. And what about the hard layer itself? What could it have been? It certainly wasn't anything she had ever heard of. As she pondered again over Sumter's remarks, she realized that he didn't seem to understand the situation any more than anyone else. But he had, without a doubt, linked everything. The dense layer, the accident and the defect were each different aspects of the same phenomenon . . . a phenomenon which was just as unexplained now as it was the instant it killed twenty-four men. And perhaps just as dangerous. In her mind she could still see Sumter tapping the depth indicator and looking around strangely at Hex St. Claire.

"The secret to that disaster is right here," he had said.

She shivered as a chill ran through her body. Sumter knew more than he was saying. He had to. He seemed so anxious to keep going. What had he been thinking? As she stood in front of the big window and watched the crew at work, vivid images of the totally destroyed bit came to mind. And she could still picture the distorted, destroyed faces of the dead men. Slowly, she put it all together. They had discovered something. She didn't know what, and she doubted that Sumter did either, but it was definitely unprecedented. And dangerous. They were obviously dealing with forces far more powerful than they had realized. Forces with a potential for death and destruction. She had already seen that.

For the first time since the project had been restarted, she felt fear. True, disconcerting, painful fear. The well and the men were in danger. She was certain of it. The work needed to be slowed. They were rushing too fast into the unknown. More time was needed. Time to think and analyze what was occurring. Time to control what they were discovering, before . . . before whatever was going to happen, happened.

She wanted to talk to Sumter and Jenkins and all of them. They needed to understand what she feared, but it was going to be hard to explain. She had to get her thoughts together so she could give them a logical explanation. Otherwise, her credibility would be lost. She needed to relax and calm down. She didn't want to overreact. They would only use that against her like they did everything else. What she needed now was to think about it all, carefully. Then she could decide what to do.

Thinking that a hot shower would relax her, she went quickly down the stairs, into her small room behind the crew office, picked up her shower kit and a robe, and walked back around to the shower room. As she was taking the "No Men Allowed" sign from the box beside the door and hanging it carefully on the handle, a funny feeling made her turn and look up toward the engine deck.

It was Duval. He was standing there watching her,

leaning against the rail. He didn't turn away as she looked up. She watched him for a second or two and then went into the shower. The man made her nervous, but he was quickly forgotten as she undressed and spent the next twenty minutes standing under the soothing waters. Finally, feeling wonderfully clean and relaxed, she stepped out and stood in front of the wall of mirrors above the sinks and dried her hair carefully with the towel. She folded it up into a big turban on top of her head and then stood in front of the mirror looking at herself for a moment. She felt good about her body. She looked at her breasts and nipples and flat abdomen, and she reflected back over the pleasures that Blain had given her.

It was only when she turned to get her robe that she saw Duval. He was standing just outside the entrance to the shower area in the dimly lit locker room. He had a strange look on his face. She froze as their eyes met. "Get out of here," she said angrily and then reached for her robe.

His eyes flickered up and down over her body, and then he stepped forward into the room with her. "You've been wanting this for a long time, haven't you, Jori? I can tell."

"No, you son of a bitch, get out of here!" she yelled as a deep fear gripped her. She covered her breasts with her hands and, as he stepped forward to grab her, reflexively brought her knee up with all of her strength between his legs. She felt his scrotum being crushed between her leg and his pubic bone. He emitted an anguished cry and bent forward, gasping. In a flash her other knee came up catching him squarely in the middle of the face. He reeled backwards and slumped to the floor. His eyes glazed over, and he looked disoriented. He rolled over onto his back and lay moaning and gasping, both hands clutching his groin. She ran past him and stood by the door to the outside and quickly pulled on her overalls. As she was leaving, she glanced at him once again and he was writhing about on the floor beneath the sinks. Blood was all over his face and dripping in big drops onto the white tile.

"I'll kill you for this, you little whore," he groaned and started trying to get to his feet.

She stepped hurriedly into the outside air, frightened, wanting to run, but not knowing what to do. He would be after her now, she knew that. She had hurt him more than she had intended. It looked like his nose might be broken, and God knows what else. She needed the protection of the other men and she turned and started into the crew office, but the sudden rumble and vibration of the rig stopped her.

For a moment there was silence and then it came again, only this time worse. The whole rig seemed to tremble slightly and there was a distant sound as if thunder. But there was also a more intent vibration and then a shrieking metal-on-metal sound from the drill turntable. It only lasted an instant and then stopped again. She ran across the deck to join the two tool pushers who were staring down at the turning platform. As she jumped up on the drill deck, Leo Silverchief was backing away from the still spinning pipe. Jimmy Jones had a puzzled look on his face. "What the hell was that?" he yelled.

She didn't have time to answer as a high-pitched shriek filled the air. The whole deck vibrated and trembled and deep rumbles seemed to come from below them. The drill pipe abruptly stopped spinning and for an instant seemed bathed in an eerie glow. An almost green iridescence flickered up and down the steel pipe. The smell of ozone filled the air. An instant later the weird glow arched across and seemed to bathe Jones in a shimmering green layer. He screamed once and fell backwards, and she started to run. But something happened to her.

She felt as if her hair were standing on end. All of her muscles seemed to jerk and become useless. The breath was knocked out of her. She looked at her hand and for an instant it seemed to glow a faint green. There was a crackling noise in her ears and then a moment later it was all over. She stumbled forward, completely disoriented, confused. Her mind was swirling; she felt lost. She didn't know which way to go, but she wanted to run. She felt as if she couldn't breathe and that her heart had stopped. She fell down the stairs to the deck a few feet below and rolled over onto her back for a moment and looked up at the rig above her. Her eyes wouldn't focus. The lights seemed to be swirling in circles, and suddenly they all went out. All was silent and dark. The sound of the engine was gone. Her head began to clear.

She sat up and looked around. Men were screaming and yelling. There was the sound of people running across the deck. She looked toward the turntable. Jimmy Jones was slumped motionless on the floor. The rig seemed to have shut down completely.

The control booth, she thought. The readings. It's happening again. She jumped to her feet and pushed away from several men who tried to grab her, ran across the deck and up the stairs two at a time. She heard the sound of people and feet on the stairs behind her. As she reached the top, she began to feel dizzy again and nauseated. She threw open the door and stepped into total darkness. The power was completely off. She floundered about looking for the flashlight and finally found it, but it was useless. She flipped the switch several times and nothing, total darkness prevailed.

She stood for a moment looking out through the window and could see the men scurrying about in the moonlight on the platform below and then, to her amazement, the flashlight—very weakly at first—began to come on. At the same time, the emergency lights outside on the rig flickered several times and then lit up. She looked down at the dials. They all read "zero." The electrical power was totally off. She turned to the printouts. The depth reading was 16,108 feet. She looked at the magnetic field indicator. It was now back to normal, but the printout showed that, in the previous minute, it had swung wildly around and, after gyrating back and forth, had ended up 180 degrees opposite the normal direction just prior to the shutdown. The temperature recording showed that, for the ten seconds before the shutdown, the temperature at the drill bit had accelerated upward astronomically. It was a familiar pattern. It looked just like the tapes she had shown Sumter earlier.

She heard voices behind her and turned to see Skip Majors and several others come into the room. "Jori," he said, "are you okay?" His face went out of focus and the room started to spin. She felt nauseated, leaned forward and vomited. She stood up and then her legs went limp. She started to collapse, but Skip and the others caught her. The room was spinning. She could see Skip's face above her. "Are you all right?" he seemed to be saying, the words echoing back and forth. The room moved faster and faster and became dimmer and dimmer. The lights went out and the sound went away and then, a moment later, came back shimmering and spinning. "Jori!" someone seemed to be yelling in the distance. She tried to speak, to warn them. They had to stop. She felt nauseated and her throat filled with vomitus. She couldn't breathe. The lights flickered again. She felt herself being moved, being spun, lifted, tossed, and dropped. She heard voices in the distance, much talking. Suddenly lights were blinking above her and she saw faces looking down at her.

Everything seemed to go away for a long time and then the lights came again. She opened her eyes and saw something whirling above her. There was the sound of an engine. She felt herself being lifted again. Her name was called in the distance, over and over. "Jori. Jori." Things grew quiet. Everything went dark and then she was aware of a throbbing pulsating sound and a blinking light just above her. She realized she was in a helicopter. A face hovered above her, but she couldn't recognize it. It began to spin and the sound of her name echoed again through her ears. "Jori . . . Jori . . . Jori . . ."

A few moments later there was a bump. She felt herself being moved. Then she heard many excited voices. There were lights, blue and red. She was being moved out and turned and lifted. She opened her eyes and there were people in white standing around her. She listened to excited voices and felt the lights, and then slowly they began to fade away. The voices were becoming dimmer and dimmer and the lights growing darker and darker, and finally they were all gone. At last, peace and tranquility. At last she could relax. All became dark and her thoughts faded away. She felt empty and alone. She was isolated and lost. She felt nothing, heard nothing, saw nothing. She was peaceful and quiet. She could get rest at last. All became nothingness and she went away into the darkness—alone.

273

FIFTEEN

Blain Robson's day was running long. It was almost midnight by the time he finished his evening rounds, and, after stopping by for a last cup of coffee in the doctors' lounge on the second floor, he took the elevator down and started toward the exit. The announcement from the speakers lining the hallway forced a change in his plans. "Code Blue, emergency room. Code Blue, emergency room."

Slightly irked at having his evening delayed even further, he did an abrupt about-face and headed down the hall to the ER. The place looked like a disaster. Two patients had apparently been brought in at the same time, and the room seemed confused and crowded. There must have been almost a dozen nurses, several Coast Guard personnel and Jim Harper, the ER physician. He was standing over a black man's body frantically administering closed chest cardiac massage. He looked up as Blain entered.

"Help me with this one," he said. "It's some kind of electrical accident. He's had a cardiac arrest. See if you can intubate him, would you?"

A respiratory technician was attempting to inflate the man's lungs with oxygen using an Ambu Bag and mask. With each attempted breath, the patient's abdomen seemed to swell and grow larger.

"Jesus!" Blain said. "I think all the ventilation's going into his stomach, not his lungs. Look at that abdomen."

"I know. I tried to intubate him myself and couldn't do it," Harper replied. "He's going to vomit if you don't get him intubated soon."

Blain took the laryngoscope, pried open the man's mouth, and pushed the instrument into the back of his throat, lifting the tongue out of the way, hoping to get a view of the larynx in order to pass the plastic endotracheal tube into the trachea.

"I can't see a thing," he said. "Give me that suction. His mouth is filling up with vomitus." He stuck the suction tube into the back of the man's throat, sucking out copious quantities of saliva, gastric fluid, and partially disgested food. He then took another try with the laryngoscope. "Damn!" he said. "I can't do it." He took the bag and mask from the technician and attempted to ventilate the man's lungs himself. The swelling in the abdomen grew even larger. "I'm not doing anything but blowing air into his stomach. Maybe I ought to do a tracheotomy."

"Wait a minute," Dr. Harper said. "Here's Mason. Let him take a crack at it." Blain gladly handed the laryngoscope and endotracheal tube to the anesthesiologist, a man far more experienced at intubations than he was.

Mason frowned, but said nothing as he slid the laryngoscope smoothly back into the patient's mouth and then, using extraordinary strength, forced the man's mouth open, practically suspending his head from the bed by the instrument. "Give me that tube," he said, and then quickly passed it into the trachea. He then took the oxygen bag, applied it quickly to the end of the tube and, squeezing gently, inflated the man's lungs with oxygen.

"Good job," Blain said, and then turned to study the electrical tracing of the EKG displayed on the monitor above the patient's bed. "He's in fibrillation. Let's shock him."

"Let's give him some bicarb first and let me ventilate him for just a second here," Mason interjected. "It won't do any good to shock a heart as hypoxic as his."

The requested drugs were administered while the cardiac massage continued and Mason intermittently filled the man's lungs with oxygen.

"What happened to him?" asked the anesthesiologist.

"Some sort of electrical accident," Harper responded. "Do you think we can shock him now?"

Mason nodded, and Harper took the paddles from the nurse and placed them carefully across the man's chest. "Stand back, everyone," he said and hit the button.

Every muscle in the man's body jerked and then instantly went limp again. They studied the EKG. "He's still in fibrillation," Harper muttered, and the others agreed. "How about some more bicarb and let's give him some adrenalin and then shock him again." Harper looked at Mason, waiting for his approval.

"The people who brought him in said they thought they could feel a pulse right up until the time they reached the emergency room," Harper answered.

Mason shook his head doubtfully. "I'll bet not. Electrical accidents usually fibrillate at the time of injury if they're going to. It's not likely that he fibrillated just as he got here. Let's shock him once more."

The patient was shocked again with no results. More drugs were given. Cardiac massage was continued and the shock reapplied and then again, still with no results. Finally, the EKG began to grow less irregular and became a straight line, totally unresponsive to the electrical shocks. Mason and Blain grew pessimistic, but Harper persevered in the massage. A moment later Dr. Adam Thompson rushed into the room.

"What in the world is going on?" he said.

Harper looked at him. "I'm afraid this one's dead, Dr. Thompson. Your other patient's in the next room."

"How is she?" the older, gaunt-appearing man asked.

"She's alive. That's all I can say. I didn't even get time to examine her; this one looked so bad."

Thompson looked exasperated. "Did anyone call Dr. Fieldman?"

"He's on his way. He should be here any minute."

Thompson glanced at Blain and then disappeared. Harper looked down at the patient whose chest he was continuing to compress and then suddenly stopped. "I guess you guys are right. It looks hopeless." They stared at the flat line on the EKG, and then Harper turned around to wash his hands.

"What's Thompson doing here?" Blain asked. "Are these patients from Florexco?"

"Yep. The other one's a female, pretty young, too. Something happened out on that well of theirs. That place has been keeping this ER pretty damned busy the last couple of weeks."

Blain didn't hear Harper's last comment. He had already started toward the room next door to Trauma Room Two—his heart and mind filled with anxiety about the identity of the young woman from the well. A moment later his fear was confirmed.

Jori looked as if she were near death. Her pupils were

dilated, her face ashen, her respirations labored. Her pulse was feeble and erratic. She was moaning softly, completely unresponsive to any external stimulation. He felt sick and didn't want to believe it was her. He had to help.

Dr. Adam Thompson was listening to her heart and chest as Blain entered, but said nothing until Hoyt Fieldman arrived. "Electrical accident," he said to the chief of staff. "She seems stable, but she's almost in a coma."

"For crying out loud," the general practitioner said irritably. "You guys have had your share of these accidents, haven't you?"

Thompson didn't respond but looked at him strangely and then back at Jori.

"How'd this happen?" Blain asked.

"I don't know," Thompson answered. "Wells are dangerous places."

"It looks like this one is a little too goddamned dangerous," Blain retorted angrily.

"It's not exactly your problem, now is it?" Dr. Thompson said.

"Damned right it's my problem. This woman is a close friend of mine," Blain answered. "If my experience with your company and the injuries it produces is of any significance, she's going to get a lot sicker before she gets better. She's going to need a lot of care." He looked down at her. "We'd better start an IV right now." He turned to the nurse. "Get me some dextrose and saline solution, please."

Fieldman glanced at Thompson and then back to Blain. "Don't you think you'd better defer those kinds of decisions and therapeutic plans to the physician in

278

charge of her care, Dr. Robson?" he said.

"What're you talking about?" Blain said.

"I mean, you're not the patient's doctor," Fieldman responded. "And I think you'd better let her physician do the decision making."

"Wait a minute, you guys," Blain replied. "Let's cut the crap. I'm just trying to help. This girl's one sick lady. We better do everything we can to get her stabilized. We can't just stand here and watch her die like the others. I won't do it!"

"We appreciate your help. We really do," Fieldman said. "But it may be inappropriate right at this moment. I'm not sure that anyone's even formally consulted you about her care."

Blain looked at Adam Thompson and then at Jim Harper, who had just walked into the room with them. Richard Mason stood in the doorway, listening to the discussion. "All right," Blain said abruptly. "Who's supposed to take care of this patient?" he asked the ER physician.

"Well, technically she's Dr. Thompson's patient," Harper answered.

"But Dr. Thompson doesn't have admitting privileges," Blain said.

"In that case, he'll have to decide who to refer her to."

Blain looked at Thompson.

"I've already asked Dr. Fieldman to take care of her," the man said. "I see no reason to change my mind now. He takes care of all the Florexco patients that need admission to the hospital."

"But this is a patient of mine," Blain protested. "I've taken care of her before. I've been following her for the last couple of weeks because of some injuries to her tongue and a problem with her white count."

"I'm afraid that doesn't count here. This looks like it's a totally different problem," Thompson said. "I'm her regular doctor and I'm referring her to Dr. Fieldman."

"Bullshit!" Blain responded. "You're not her regular doctor any more than Hoyt is. I'm the only one in this county who's given her any medical care at all. She's never seen you."

"That's not true," Thompson said. "I gave her a physical before the well drilling started, and I keep her medical records on file in my office."

"I don't care about that," Blain said. "She's my patient, and I'm going to take care of her."

"I don't think so," Fieldman interjected. "Protocol dictates that this patient will be referred to the physician of Dr. Thompson's choice. You're getting ready to dig yourself into a hole with this argument, Blain. I think you'd better cut this out and get out of here and stop interfering with the care we're trying to give this girl." He paused as Blain put his hand across his forehead. "I understand your concern," he continued. "But don't jeopardize her health or your privileges here by continuing to obstruct what we're trying to do."

Blain was about to speak again, but was interrupted by Mason, still standing in the doorway. "Blain, don't do it. Come on out here. Let me talk to you a minute."

Blain stared at the other doctors in the room, obviously exasperated and angry, and then stormed out of the room.

Mason put his hand on his shoulder. "You're treading on thin ice now," the anesthesiologist warned him. "You better remember what you're up against. They're going to win this no matter what you do. You'll only jeopardize your status here if you keep it up. So take some good advice and cool it for a few minutes. Let this situation settle down, and then you can talk about it with a cooler head."

Blain put both his hands on his face and rubbed his eyes and let out a deep sigh. "I know you're right. I was just about to explode in there. Those sorry bastards. I don't want to let them kill her. She means something to me."

"They won't," Mason responded. "Fieldman knows what he's doing, and if there's anything that can be done for her he'll do it. I don't know anything about this Thompson character, but Fieldman's sharp, and you know it. One more thing. Don't get any crazy self-defeating ideas about helping to take care of her whether they like it or not. You'd better stay totally out of her room and keep away from her chart unless they ask you to look at her. If you have to go see her, go only as a visitor and during visiting hours—and don't do anything medical. They'll have good grounds to can you if you do."

"You're right. I'll only cause trouble if I interfere."

"I'm glad you see it that way." Mason patted him on the back and then turned to leave the ER.

Blain was standing in the middle of the emergency room, feeling frustrated, wondering what to do when a student nurse, unaware of the dispute, tapped him on the shoulder. "Doctor, can you talk to one of the people who brought these patients in? He wants to know how they're doing." Blain looked around to see a very unhappy and frightened young black man standing in the doorway between the emergency area and the waiting room. He walked toward the man.

"I'm Dr. Robson. Did you come with Jori Ashe and the other man?"

"Yes, sir," the man replied. "I'm Skip Majors. I'm chief mechanic on the well. Are they going to be okay?"

"No, I'm afraid not," Blain answered. "She seems to be in very critical condition and the other man just died."

"Oh no! That can't be . . . Jimmy Jones is dead?"

Blain nodded. "I'm very sorry. Everything that could be done was done."

"What about Jori? Is she going to be all right?" Skip Majors was almost ready to cry.

"I don't know. She's very ill. We don't know much about her yet, so I can't tell you much. How did they get shocked?"

"Shocked?" Majors said surprised. Anger filled his face. "Did they tell you they got shocked? That was no electrical shock, man! That was something else. I don't know what it was, but it wasn't any electrical shock."

"What do you mean?" Blain asked.

"I mean I've seen lots of things, working on a well, but I ain't never seen anything like that. It wasn't no electricity. I'm sure of that. It wasn't natural what happened to them. Old Jimmy looked like something just ate him up. He was almost glowing for a minute there, and the way Miss Ashe jumped up when it left her and went running around the well, climbing up to the control booth and talking real crazy like, that weren't no electricity. Lord knows it weren't no electricity." Big tears were running down his face. "I can't talk about it any more. I gotta get out of here." He turned and walked through the waiting room to the outside exit.

Blain started to follow him, but then turned back as they rolled Jori's stretcher out of the trauma room and pushed her in the direction of the elevators. Her skin was pale and her lips unmoving. There was a gentle expression on her face as if she were asleep. Watching her leave and seeing Thompson and Fieldman engaged in intense conversation, Blain felt his anger rising again. He resented bitterly their callousness about yet another victim of the Florexco operation. He was determined to make sure that everything possible was done for Jori whatever jeopardy it put him in. He started to follow her upstairs and then on a sudden inspiration he went to the hematology lab instead. As he was hoping, his friend Elaine Adams, the lab tech was on duty.

She smiled as he came in. "What's going on?" she asked.

"I'm not sure," he answered. "Did you get some blood on a Jori Ashe from the ER a few minutes ago?"

"Yes. I'm getting ready to run it now."

"Did they request a platelet count?"

"No, just a CBC," she answered.

"Do a platelet count for me, would you?"

"Sure," she replied. "Are you going to be taking care of her?"

"No, so don't write my name down. I just want to see what the result is."

She looked at him inquisitively. "If she's not your patient, why are you so interested?"

"She's a friend of mine and she works for Florexco. I'll bet you she's going to be developing some bone marrow depression just like all those other accident victims of theirs."

She picked up the specimen, twirling the small tube in her hand. "I'll run it right now."

"Thanks Elaine. It's important to me."

"What do you think's happening out there?" she said as she carefully withdrew a small portion of the blood, inserted it into the giant blood counting machine against the far wall and then smeared a drop onto a slide, drying it briefly over a Bunsen burner.

He shook his head. "I don't have any idea, but I've been told by the powers that be to keep my nose strictly out of it."

"Well, there's big money involved with an oil company like that. When they drill for oil they do it in a big way. So what if a few poor workers get radiation poisoning?"

"Radiation poisoning?" he said. "What're you talking about? I don't think this is radiation. I think it's more likely some kind of chemical."

"What kind of chemicals would they use on an oil well?" she asked.

"How the heck should I know," he said. "But for sure, they don't use radioactive materials. What made you think that anyway?"

"I didn't really think that," she answered glancing back as the machine started to print out a result. "It just sort of slipped out. I didn't think they used chemicals for anything on an oil well. So I figured the only thing that could be doing it would be radiation of some sort. The blood counts from all these Florexco patients have been looking just like the ones I used to see when I worked in the lab at the big cancer hospital in Detroit. Radiation therapy'll do it every time."

"There's no radiation on this oil well, that I know of," he said. "It's bound to be some sort of chemical, maybe something they clean the pipe with or some benzene or something."

284

"Don't get so touchy about it," she said smiling. "It was just a suggestion. I don't want to argue about it."

He frowned and shook his head. "I know. I'm just a little uptight. I don't want to see this girl die like the others have."

"She's not going to die with that white count. Look at those results."

He glanced at the printout. Total white blood cell count: 6100. Total platelets: 102,000; slightly lower than normal, but not enough to cause any problems. He felt relieved. Maybe he had been wrong. Maybe she was just the victim of an electrical shock. "I guess that eliminates my theory of chronic exposure to some sort of marrow-damaging chemical." He thought for a moment. "Elaine, have they ordered another CBC for in the morning?"

She looked through the stack of orders for blood work in the A.M. "No, not yet."

"Get one anyway, for me. Would you?"

"I can't get one without an order, Blain. I might get in trouble."

"Just a minute," he said and opened the drawer, pulling out the blank order forms for blood counts. He wrote in Jori's name at the top right-hand corner and checked off what he wanted to see and dropped it into the pile after scribbling an illegible signature on the bottom line. "That should cover you. Just tell them you have no idea where it came from if it ever comes up."

She shook her head back and forth grinning. "Some people have nerve. I wish you were as concerned about me as you seem to be about her."

"I really want to see her get well. She's more than a patient to me."

"I'll do what I can," Elaine replied. "I was just kidding."

"I know. I appreciate your giving me a hand. She's in bad shape, I'm afraid. Who's going to draw that blood in the morning?"

"I am. I'm working a double shift."

"Okay. Get it early, would you? I'll be by around seven. I'd like to see it. And thanks a lot, really."

As he left the lab and went out into the hall, he looked at his watch. It was a little after eleven. The nurses upstairs would all be in their meeting room exchanging the necessary information prior to the change of shifts. It would be a good opportunity to sneak a quick look in on Jori.

He took the elevator to three, the medical floor, and went slowly down the darkened hall. The noise from the nursing station was louder than usual. He could hear a few people laughing. They were obviously all in good spirits, probably through with the busiest part of their meeting and now exchanging pleasantries. He knew he wouldn't have long in her room.

He moved quietly along the hall, looking at the names posted on the door, hoping he would reach hers before he reached the nursing station. She was in Room 316. He carefully opened the door and then closed it behind him after he entered. All the lights were on, and her chart was spread open on a table beside her bed. He glanced quickly to see the vital signs that the nurses had recorded—nothing abnormal. Blood pressures and respirations were fine. He looked at Jori, and she seemed unchanged from when he had last seen her being wheeled out of the ER. There was almost a smile on her face as if she were dreaming, but then her face became more tense—and then almost frightened or angry. A moment later her face went blank, totally neutral. Her eyes were partially open, and he could see her pupils roaming back and forth over the room.

He spoke to her but got no response. He dug his fingers in behind the angle of her jawbone, attempting to create pain. She winced slightly but said nothing. He took her hand in his and dug his fingernail into one of her fingers. She withdrew the hand slightly—a good sign. He removed his reflex hammer from his pocket and tapped gently below her knee and in her elbow region. The reflexes were quick and strong and normal. There was definitely no localizing neurological sign, but she was just totally unresponsive to visual or auditory stimulation. Overall, she didn't look too bad. Her breathing was quiet and easy. Her pulse felt much better than it had in the emergency room. He wondered what was going on inside her pretty head, but he knew, at least for the moment, he had no way of reaching her. Gently, he kissed her.

Realizing he was running out of time, he was just going to leave when he heard one of the nurses coming down the hall, still talking to someone back at the nursing station. He jumped back from the door and started to hide in the bathroom, but her footsteps trailed past the room and on down the hall. He cracked the door just a bit and looked up and down before easing out and then hurriedly made his way to the emergency stairs, which he took upward to the fifth floor to the on-call doctors' sleeping area. He hoped desperately she was not going to be like George Elkins.

*   *   *

It had been a fitful night of tossing and turning, but Blain had finally drifted off to sleep when the phone beside him rang loudly. "You asked me to wake you up," the operator said. "It's 6:30."

"Thanks," he grumbled and replaced the receiver. He looked around him, partially disoriented, but then suddenly remembered the repeat CBC on Jori. By the time he dressed and made it to the lab, it was almost seven.

Elaine Adams looked like hell. Her eyes were blood-shot and her face puffy. "Honey, you look tired," he said. "Been up all night?"

She nodded. "I hate these double shifts."

"Why do you do it?"

"One reason only, money."

"Did you get that white count on Jori Ashe?"

She pushed a clipboard in his direction. "Just finished."

He glanced down the list of about twelve names and found hers. The white count had dropped drastically to 1700. Platelet count was less than 20,000. In addition to that, her hemoglobin level had dropped to the extent now that it was evident that she was doing some bleeding. "Jesus Christ, would you look at this," he said.

"I've never seen changes like that happen overnight; she's sick," Elaine said. "What do you think is wrong with her?"

"The same thing that's been wrong with every son of a bitch they've brought in from that well."

"What's that?"

"I don't have a name for it," he responded, "but it's deadly."

He remembered what Skip Majors had told him in the

emergency room about the way Jori and the dead man had looked just after the accident, and he thought about Elaine's off-hand comment last evening about the possible cause. He looked down again at the numbers on the sheet indicating a broad-spectrum depression of all the cellular elements of Jori's blood.

Blain looked up at Elaine. "You're right!" he said suddenly. "The only thing it could be is radiation!"

She seemed surprised. "Why do you say that?"

"It's the only thing it can be," he responded. "There are only four things that can really cause bone marrow depression like this, and none of them can happen this quickly. Infection can do it, but not in a few hours. Chemicals can do it or primary diseases of the blood, but none of them can do it fast. The only thing that can wipe out the bone marrow overnight and affect the cells already circulating is intense radiation. That's the key—it all happened so fast. The blood we got last night was just beginning to show the early effects of what must have happened to her. Now it's had time for the effects to become apparent." He stood up and walked across the room, staring through the big glass window at one side looking over the rest of the laboratory. He turned back to her. "That would explain all the GI tract damage, too. Somehow they're getting exposed to radiation out on that rig."

His voice was full of conviction and authority. "I don't have any idea how, but that's the only thing it could be. They might not even know it's happening." Elaine looked puzzled. "I can't talk to you about it now," he said, "but I'll be back. I've got to get hold of Dr. Fieldman and tell him what's wrong with her."

He took the elevator straight to the third floor and

sweeping past the nurses station, signaled one of the nurses to follow him. "I've got to examine Jori Ashe," he said. "She's developing a coagulopathy; I'm afraid she's been irradiated. Get me an examining glove and a hemoccult slide. I want to see if she is starting to bleed internally."

The bewildered nurse quickly did as she was told and scurried behind him into Jori's room. She looked almost unchanged. Blain gently examined the areas of her body which might have been subject to mild trauma in the process of moving her from the emergency room and then taking care of her during the night. As he suspected, there were several tiny, very faint bruises over her elbows and along her buttocks. The needle stick in front of her elbow where blood had been drawn was still oozing blood from the puncture almost 45 minutes ago. The one on the other arm from last night was surrounded by a large bruise—all evidence of impaired clotting ability. The first signs of disaster were evident.

He took the glove from the nurse and put it on his left hand and pulled the sheet back from her body. He inserted one finger into her rectum and retrieved a small amount of stool which he smeared on the tiny white paper slide the nurse was carrying.

"Go test this for blood right now," he ordered the nurse, who immediately scurried out. He looked down at Jori and noticed for the first time that her eyes seemed to be focusing on him. When he moved his hands back and forth in front of her face, her eyes followed them briefly and then returned to look at him. He pinched her finger and she moaned softly and pulled the arm away with great strength. He said her name loudly, and her facial expression changed. She was obviously making some neurological improvement despite the ominous findings about her blood clotting. He felt better. He felt almost optimistic. He pulled the sheet back over her and went out into the hall to find the nurse with the stool-blood test. She came out of the small lab just behind the nurses station.

"It's positive," she said.

"Just as I suspected. Her platelet count has fallen way off, she's got bruising, and now she's getting GI bleeding. I'm going to call Dr. Fieldman." She followed him into the nurses station where he sat down at the phone and, after locating the chief of staff's number on the roster posted there, called him at home. Fieldman himself answered the phone. Blain immediately launched into a full analysis of Jori's condition as he saw it. He carefully outlined the facts which led him to the conclusion that she'd been exposed to radiation, as had probably the other injured workers from the rig. Finally, he explained what he had found on his examination and outlined what therapeutic measures he thought were necessary.

"She's going to need all the platelets we can get, some white cell concentrates and probably some fresh whole blood. It's going to take an extremely vigorous effort to keep her in shape, hematologically," he said. "The only chance she's got is that we keep her platelets and white counts normal until her bone marrow recovers from the injury—if it does. It's that damned oil well. I knew something was wrong out there. This is what killed the others. But I think we can still save Jori."

Fieldman had only one question. "You examined her yourself?"

"Yes, as soon as I saw the CBC results."

There was silence at the other end of the line. After a

long pause, during which he could hear Fieldman breathing, the chief of staff spoke again in a soft, almost emotionless voice. "Blain, I think this case now has implications above and beyond a change in the white count of my patient. I suggest that you and I meet in the medical library in about half an hour to discuss this."

"Fine," Blain responded, although disappointed by the lack of a more definite response from Fieldman. "I'll go ahead and order the necessary blood work, so that can be cooking."

"I think you'd better wait until I can examine my patient myself before you jump off the deep end."

Blain clenched his teeth and held back the remark that he wanted to make. "All right, I'll see you in the medical library. Thirty minutes won't make much difference."

He put down the phone, and sat in disbelief at the other physician's reaction to the deteriorating state of Jori. Finally, he left the floor, stopped by Medical Records, and picked up the chart which he had made out the night he repaired the laceration in Jori's tongue in the emergency room. He then left the hospital and drove to his office and brought back the additional medical records on her he was keeping there. When he returned, he just had time to stop in the cafeteria for a quick cup of coffee and some toast before he went to the scheduled meeting with Fieldman.

The gathering in the medical library was brief and unexpectedly volatile. When Blain arrived, he was surprised to find not just Fieldman, but also Aaron Fischer, Trudy Reed, Stan Wilcott, and Adam Thompson. The meeting was obviously geared for more than a professional discussion of Jori Ashe's problems, but Blain had come prepared.

"This looks like a familiar group," he said, smiling uneasily as he entered. The humor seemed lost on them. Wilcott sat smugly in a large chair to the right of the room. His expression was one of stern victory. Fieldman looked upset and the others merely irritated.

Aaron Fischer spoke first. "Dr. Robson, I'm very sorry that we have to meet with you under these circumstances, but you have given us no choice. Dr. Fieldman called me this morning and told me that you, without authorization, have examined a patient of his in the hospital. I have verified this with the ward nurse, and I have also verified with the primary referring physician, Dr. Thompson, that you were not requested to see the patient in consultation. Because of previous problems we have had with you, which you know you've been warned about, I'm going to have to take action. This is a gross violation of the hospital rules. As of this moment, you are suspended from the staff. I recommend that you leave as soon as you can. Dr. Wilcott, as chief of surgery, will assume care for all patients presently admitted under your name. Depending upon your choice, you may or may not explain this situation to your patients, but, in any event, Dr. Wilcott will take care of them until they have named another physician to replace you."

Blain stood staring intently at the administrator. "Do you know that there is a girl dying up there, probably from radiation injuries, while we're sitting down here going over this cheap bullshit that you guys have concocted? I don't think you have the right to suspend me from this staff. You should be concentrating on getting that well shut down, not on trying to screw me."

Fischer's face flushed with anger, but Stan Wilcott spoke first. "Cut the crap, Robson. You've been acting bizarrely for days around here. What you have done is clearly and unequivocally unethical, and we won't tolerate it. You had your chance to shape up, but you wouldn't do it, so now you're going to have to get out. You can't just go around here trying to take over your colleague's patients. I think it's an outrage that you went in there to examine her this morning. You ought to be charged with assault."

"Jori Ashe is my patient," Blain said quietly, "and I've got the records to prove it. She should have been assigned to me when she came through the ER. I have been treating her recently for some injuries."

"Don't give us that," Adam Thompson interrupted. "Just because you've been sleeping with her doesn't make her your patient."

Blain turned to glare at the Florexco doctor, but before he could speak Fieldman interrupted. "Blain, no matter what arguments you make, the patient was assigned to me. I'm responsible for her. There's no excuse for what you've done. It's unquestionably unethical for you to go into her room and start examining her like that." His voice grew calmer. "I suggest to you that what you should do right now is calm down, take our advice and leave the hospital immediately. There is going to be more trouble for you if you don't."

Before Fieldman could go on, the attorney spoke up, "Dr. Robson, I feel that I must warn you that you are in a very precarious situation right now. Technically, you could be accused of assault and battery, performing an unauthorized examination like that. A quiet suspension from the staff would be much preferable to the public hearing that could come from this." She paused. "Mr. Fischer has told me—and I have indicated to him that it is perfectly appropriate—that if you return to the hospital, he will seek a court injunction against you and perhaps call in the assistant state attorney to press charges against you for your unauthorized involvement with this patient."

"Blain, I think you're sick, you need a psychiatrist," Wilcott said gruffly.

Robson paused for a moment, looked around the room slowly and finally stared at Aaron Fischer. "I'll tell you, Mr. Fischer, you can call in all your attorneys and you can call in your chiefs of staff and you can call in anybody else you goddamn want to, but you're not going to win this one without a big goddamn struggle. Jori Ashe is my patient and here is the documentation to prove it." He placed the copy of the emergency room and his own office record on the table. "The hospital bylaws clearly state that a patient entering the ER is to be considered the patient of the last physician treating her. These records will clearly show that I am the last physician treating her. So she is *my* patient, and my attorneys will argue that in court as loudly as they need to. As for the other crap you guys have been drumming up against me, go ahead and pursue it if you want to, but let me tell you now, and I want you to hear it clearly, there's something rotten going on here and you guys are trying to suppress it. We've had too many problems with men coming off that well—far too many injuries—and the information about this has been covered up. I think I am beginning to get a glimmer of what's happening out there, and I'm going to do something about it if I have to call in the Coast Guard or the Department of Health. And if you guys try to stop me, I'll have the press in on this thing within an hour. It will be the biggest scandal ever to hit this little hospital.

As for my suspension, I'm going to completely ignore it and if you want to go into court go right ahead.

"As for your remarks"—he turned to Wilcott—"you make one more comment like that, and I'll have your ass in court for slander. You're a featherbedder and a self-protecting asshole as far as I'm concerned, and I'd like nothing better than to blow you wide open." He looked at Thompson. "I couldn't give less of a shit what *you* think about this. As far as I'm concerned, you're bought and paid for by Florexco, so keep your comments to yourself regarding me or my patients." Lastly, he turned to the stunned, white-faced Fieldman. "I don't know what your problem is, Dr. Fieldman. I don't understand why you're doing this. Your patients think you're the best. They trust you. Listen to me, please. Something's wrong, and I need your help. What you do counts. Help me take care of Jori. I'm also calling in Bill Hallam. I'm not going to let her die."

Aaron Fischer's face filled with rage, but he said nothing as the others sat in shocked silence at Blain's outburst.

Blain picked up the phone in front of him, asked the operator for the blood bank, and a moment later gave the following orders as the others looked on, "This is Dr. Robson. My patient, Jori Ashe, in 316 is going to need some emergency blood components. As soon as you can, I would like for you to get a dozen packs of fresh platelets, six white blood cell concentrates, and also start trying to locate a compatible donor and some fresh whole blood. I want to start those platelets within half an hour."

Stan Wilcott rose and started toward him. His expression was menacing and his hands curled into fists. "You can't get away with this," he said, moving closer.

Blain slowly stood up and looked him straight in the eye as they stood face to face. "You touch me and I'll kill you," he said to the older man.

There was a moment of tenseness, and then Wilcott turned to Fischer. "Are you going to let him get away with this?" he said angrily.

Fischer looked frustrated. "Look, I don't know what I can do to keep this thing quiet. It's about to blow up in our faces."

Trudy Reed put her hand on his shoulder, "Aaron, let's go to your office and call an emergency meeting of the executive board, that's all we can do now. We've got to step very carefully." She glared at Blain, "You're a cocky bastard," she said, "but we're going to crush you."

She picked up her papers and started out of the room followed by Fischer, who turned to make one last comment before he left. "You better leave this hospital if you know what's good for you, Robson."

Blain looked at him coolly. "I'm not leaving; I'm going to take care of my patient." Fischer disappeared beyond the door. Blain picked up the charts in front of him. "Well, gentlemen, this has been a lot of fun but I've got work to do."

Fieldman stared at him, a look of almost hopeless despair on his face. "Blain, I think you're making a big mistake; it's going to be very hard for your career."

"No, I'm not, Hoyt. It's what I should have done last night. Something's very wrong here, and I'm going to find out what it is." He paused for a moment and then looked at the chief of staff with less anger in his eyes. "I don't understand you guys," he said softly. "I'm trying to be a good doctor and I'm trying to fit in. All I want to do is help my patient. I don't know why everyone here thinks that's so wrong." He turned to leave. "I don't mind telling you that I'm scared. I'm scared for Jori, and I'm scared for you guys and myself. I don't understand this cover-up, but it could bring us all down." A moment later he was gone.

"I'm not going to let that pimp get away with this," Wilcott said as soon as Blain had left. He glared at Fieldman. "What are you going to do about this—you're the chief of staff?"

Fieldman returned his stare for a moment and then looked at Thompson, "Adam, what the hell is going on on that well of yours? Something's got to be wrong out there."

Thompson nodded slowly, "I don't know what it is. We're having a meeting this afternoon to get the thing straightened out."

"Is there any chance that Robson's right?" Fieldman said. "Could these really be some kind of radiation injuries?"

Thompson shook his head. "No, that's impossible; they're not using any equipment out there that could emit radiation. It's got to be something else, some kind of short circuit or something."

"That's a little hard to believe, don't you think? These patients don't look like they've had electrical injuries," Fieldman said.

"I know," Thompson said reluctantly. "But they'll get it figured out. It's up to Dr. Sumter—he's the geophysicist who designed the whole thing. He's been looking into this."

Fieldman looked impatient. "Whatever is wrong, you better do more than look into it. You'd better fix it or you'd better shut that place down. This is getting to be just a little too goddamned much to put up with. I don't know how many people you're willing to kill before you figure out what's wrong."

"Wait a minute, Hoyt," Thompson said. "Nobody's willing to kill anybody. We're just as concerned as you are about getting this problem resolved."

"Yeah? Well it's gone too far this time. You'd better do something quick."

"Is that so?" Thompson replied. "Maybe you'd just better mind your own business and take care of the patients, and let Florexco take care of the well."

"Look, jerk," Fieldman said. "I'm not just going to stand by while you kill people. You've pushed me to the limit on this thing already."

"You haven't had such a hard time standing by so far—getting those fat checks the company keeps sending you," Thompson retorted.

"Those were just retainers for my standby availability, and you know it."

"Is that right? I want you to tell that to the press when they ask you why you waited so long to come forward, if this affair turns into a big scandal. That'll look real good, won't it? The chief of staff of the local hospital getting money from the oil company while his patients die."

Fieldman's face slowly filled with hostility. "I'm telling you one thing, Adam, and you'd better get it back to the people in charge out there—if this girl dies, I'm blowing the whistle on you. I'm calling in the public health authorities and everybody else and open this thing right up."

Adam Thompson smiled sarcastically, "You can't afford the loss of income, you snake. You've been bought off just like the rest of us. You're not going to do anything except cover your own ass." He stood up and started to leave and then glanced back at Fieldman. "If Florexco has troubles, so do you. You're in this thing right up to your ears." He turned and opened the door.

"I'm not in anything, you son of a bitch!" Fieldman yelled. "The money Florexco has paid me has been for my medical services only, and I'll tell that to anyone. I'm not ashamed of what I've been doing, but I'm giving you a warning: you bastards better stop it, whatever it is. Shut that thing down until it's fixed. This is serious."

Thompson smiled sarcastically again and then left.

"Dumb ass," Fieldman muttered under his breath when the door was shut.

Wilcott walked across the room to look out the window. "What about it, Hoyt? What are we going to do about this Robson thing? I can block his surgical privileges, but it's going to take your action to keep him off this staff, and I want him off."

Fieldman looked at him with disdain. "Why exactly do you want him off, Stan?" he said after a few moments.

"He's an incompetent surgeon, that's why."

"That's garbage and you know it. You want him off because you don't want any competition. Besides that, he doesn't charge as much as you. I know that irritates the hell out of you. He's the only one here who's not thinking about his pocketbook."

"Wait a minute."

"He only does surgery when it's absolutely necessary, doesn't he, Stan? That makes you nervous, doesn't it? It's not a typical surgeon's attitude, is it?"

"What the hell are you implying?" Wilcott responded angrily.

"You know what I'm implying. You've been doing it

for years. You do so much knife-happy surgery on paying patients that it's incredible. Think about it a minute. When was the last time you did something elective on a charity case? The only time you ever touch them is in an emergency when there's no choice but to operate."

Wilcott's voice softened. "Something sure put a cob up your ass, Hoyt. You're being a little harsh on me, aren't you?"

It was obvious to Fieldman that Wilcott didn't want to fight. The GP referred him too many patients. The chief of surgery had made hundreds of thousands of dollars over the years off the lucrative referrals sent him from Fieldman's office. In a way it made the surgeon prisoner to Fieldman and the other primary practitioners who fed him. The GP stared at him for a moment. "No, I don't think I'm being too harsh. We're both shits, we ought to admit it."

"That's not true," Wilcott answered. "I think you're being unfair."

Fieldman looked at him disgustedly. "I've got to go, Stan. I've got an office full of patients waiting to be seen. Most of them little old ladies with nothing else to do and very little wrong, so they spend their money coming to see me. It's a sad way to make a living. We'll have to talk about this later. I know you've got some gallbladders to take out, some of them might even need the surgery."

Wilcott's mouth dropped open and his face paled. "Well, fuck you, you son of a bitch," he said, and then abruptly went out the door.

Fieldman sat alone in the room for a few moments. He reached into his coat pocket, pulled out a package of antacids and quickly swallowed several. He put his hand on his abdomen and rubbed at the gnawing deep pain he felt there. I don't know how long I can keep this up, he thought.

He felt disgusted and disappointed with himself. He had too many patients to see in the office, and he hated his arrangement with Florexco, but he needed the money. He needed it badly. Being their on-call hospital doctor had been fine before all this trouble. But now he was afraid they were going to try to use his association with them to cover up their problems. He couldn't do that. He wouldn't let them try to blackmail him into helping them, especially with this young woman near death.

He wondered if there was any possibility that Blain was right. What if something strange was going on out there? The last thing he wanted to do was to help that goddamned oil company cover up their sloppy safety record. It was a bitter pill to swallow, but maybe he had been wrong about the whole thing. He picked up the phone. Maybe he'd better call the administration and tell them to cool it, at least for the moment until the smoke cleared about this Ashe girl. If she died, he didn't want to take any chance on being blamed for her death, whatever the hell caused it.

SIXTEEN

Hex St. Claire knocked softly and then opened the door leading into the gloomy study of Dr. Adrian Sumter. He was carrying a tray of food and coffee. The scientist looked up from the desk where he was sitting, a huge fluorescent lamp lighting up the stacks of textbooks, articles, scientific papers, charts, and graphs which seemed to cover every available surface on the floor around him as well as the top of the desk. "Ah, yes, food," he said. "I was starting to get a little hungry."

"You ought to be," Hex replied. "You haven't eaten or slept for twelve hours now. It's not a healthy way to work, you know."

The doctor smiled and picked a sandwich off the tray and a cup of coffee. "Someone has to do this," he said, "and if I didn't, who would?"

"It's not a matter of who would, but who could," replied Hex. "Have you figured anything out?"

"I'm not sure yet, but I have a strong suspicion. Do you remember back in the '40s when the big panic went around the scientific circles here in the States about the possibility that the Germans were close to the development of nuclear weapons?"

"Yes, but it turned out to be a false alarm as I recall. The Germans had taken the wrong lead. They weren't working to develop a fission reaction type bomb, but were investigating some other sort of thing, possibly involving some unusual heavy elements."

"Exactly," Sumter said. "They had taken Einstein's work and that of a few other brilliant Germans, and come up with a theoretical proof of the existence of a super element. They called it Balthorium. Theoretically, it would have had an atomic weight of 450, which is considerably heavier than anything known to exist."

"Right, Uranium is 235. Hahnium is supposed to be the heaviest known element, isn't it? It checks in somewhere around 260."

Sumter smiled. "Don't give me that false modesty of yours, Hex, you know better than I that Hahnium is exactly 260. You needn't attempt to be so humble around me."

Hex St. Claire chuckled. "And I know a few things about the super element Balthorium, too, although I have never known that you took its existence very seriously."

"I haven't, up until now, but the Germans claimed to have recovered a very tiny amount of it just before the end of the war. Unfortunately, it was never found."

"You mean never found by the Allies. We don't know what the Russians found," Hex said.

"You're right again, Hex. We don't have any idea what the Russians found, but surely, if they had gotten some of the Balthorium, we would have heard about it by now. They would have put such an element to good use, I can assure you."

Hex nodded. "Some say that Hitler and von Tullinger, his chief nuclear physicist, may have taken it with them when they escaped to South America."

"Hogwash. I'm sure they never had any, and besides that, von Tullinger's body was clearly identified in the ruins of Berlin."

"Do you think Balthorium has something to do with the well?"

"It very well could," Sumter replied. "What's occurring definitely fits with some of the concepts the Germans had developed about the element."

"I don't follow you."

"Well, for one thing, the sudden bursts of energy release we seem to be encountering after drilling through these very hard layers. Balthorium was supposed to be very heavy and super-hard—one of the hardest substances known—when cold. The calculations indicate that only when Balthorium is heated up to around a thousand degrees does it begin to undergo fission and emit bursts of radiation and heat. The interesting thing is the breakdown products of the reaction: iron, nickel, and a little cobalt, exactly what we think the core and mantle are made up of. That's why the Germans thought it might have been one of the original elements. It could have been the fuel for the internal fires of this planet."

"What kind of radiation would it emit?" Hex asked.

"That's the puzzling point. No one seems quite sure. It was probably some kind of cross between electrical energy and x rays, mainly composed of electrons and a few protons—as opposed to the type of radiation from uranium. It's possible that the radiation would be more destructive than other forms, but also more short-lived."

"Very interesting," Hex commented, "but there's no concrete evidence at all that the element even exists. It's all just theoretical, or should I say mythical?"

"True, but if it does exist, it would be right where

we're heading."

"What do you mean?"

"Well," Sumter said, "from the beginning, it would have been in the core of the earth, where the extreme heat and pressures would have raised it beyond its critical temperature, so it would have been involved in an ongoing fission reaction over the eons of time that have passed since the beginning of this planet. As a consequence, by now almost all of it would have been consumed, leaving a residue of cobalt, nickel, and iron. It's been a puzzle for a long time as to why these three elements were in such predominance there. The Balthorium theory explains that."

"Yes, but if that were true," said Hex, "then the resulting nuclear reaction going on would certainly lead to a great deal of radioactivity which we could surely detect from the surface. We have no evidence of any radioactivity in the core."

"True, but since the beginning of this planet enough time would have passed that almost all of the Balthorium would have been consumed. So, as a consequence, there would be no fission reaction going on and no consequent radiation. Only the base elements would remain, and, as I have mentioned, there is no residual radiation after Balthorium has broken down. So it all fits very well with the theory."

"So," replied Hex, "if all the Balthorium is consumed then there would be none left to find so the element will remain forever only theoretical."

"Not so, my friend. The theory goes that Balthorium breaks down only under extreme heat, so those portions of Balthorium that were just above the core and the mantle, lying slightly beneath the crust of the earth would probably not have been heated enough to undergo fission. Theoretically, there could be deposits of the element in the area just between the crust and the mantle. They, of course, would not show any radio-activity because, as I have already said, Balthorium is only radioactive when it heats up. It would be as hard as diamond, or maybe even harder in its inert state."

Hex St. Claire nodded thoughtfully. "It's a fascinating concept, Adrian. If it existed, Balthorium could be the near-perfect energy substance—a nuclear furnace fueled by a steady stream of Balthorium fed into it, with no residual radioactivity, and no chain reaction that could get out of control. You just cut off the supply of fuel entering the furnace and the heat stops. A beautiful idea."

"Exactly," Sumter smiled. "It's too nice to believe."

"I still don't see how it fits with the problems we're having," Hex said. "We are not even close to drilling deep enough to be through the crust and approaching the area where you can say Balthorium could theoretically exist. No one ever has."

"Ah, you could be wrong there, Hex. In the first place, where we're digging now the crust may be reasonably thin. There are a number of areas, particularly along the edges of the continental shelf where the crust is only nine or ten miles deep as opposed to the twenty miles over the great land masses of the world. No one knows for sure, but in the Atlantic trench between here and Europe where the sea floor is seven to eight miles down, the crust may be only three or four miles thick."

"Okay. Even if you're right, you're still talking about 50,000 feet where we're drilling right now, and we're less than a third that far. And, in addition to that, one of the

307

accidents occurred at 300 feet."

"You're right," Sumter replied. "It's hard to make any sense out of it. There's just one thing that keeps making me think that Balthorium is a possibility."

"What's that?"

"This defect that seems to exist in the tectonic plate where we're drilling. Somehow, some of the Balthorium must have worked its way up through this soft spot in the crust."

"Now that's an interesting thought."

"I don't know where the defect came from, though. It's probably a natural phenomenon, but what if it's not? Perhaps someone drilled here before, and somehow a small amount of Balthorium found its way to the surface. And then we come along and drill right into these two small deposits on the way down and, in the process, the friction from the drilling heats it beyond its critical temperatures. So, there you have it—a burst of radiation."

Hex smiled. "You think this may be what happened to the Russians, don't you? They found one of these defects and went for the Balthorium—only it was more than they could handle."

Sumter returned Hex's grin and rose from his chair, walked around to the window and pulled back the drapes to let in the late morning sunshine. "Well, it's certainly an entertaining thought, I suppose. Balthorium might not even exist, but I'll bet it does. The idea just keeps coming around as I try to understand what's happening out there. Think of the significance if it were true, Hex. Can you imagine what it would mean? The world would be changed. A new era could begin."

Hex leaned over the desk, examining the geological

charts spread out there. "It's the only logical explanation, isn't it? I think you're on to something, Adrian. I really do. It could explain everything."

"Perhaps. We shall see. We certainly shall see."

"And what about this defect in the tectonic plate? If it's unnatural, you're not talking about past civilizations of man creating it, are you?"

"Who knows, Hex? Who knows?"

"The shadow knows," the black man quickly replied.

Sumter whirled around instantly, incredulous, to gaze into the face of his friend. Then they were both engulfed in laughter at the humor. "Your mind works just like mine, you know that, Hex?"

"Some say we're both insane."

They chuckled as Sumter rolled up the charts and carefully put them away. "Let's get dressed," he said. "We've only an hour until that meeting."

"What are you going to tell the Florexco board?" Hex asked. "They're going to want to know some good reasons why their billion-dollar investment isn't working right."

"I haven't decided yet, Hex. But one thing's for sure. That rig is working right. We're just finding some things we didn't expect to."

"Yes, but a lot of people have died."

"I know. It's a tragedy. What happened to the Russians was even worse. But the important thing is that we keep the drilling going now. This could be very important."

"I'm not so sure they'd be ready to hear the Balthorium theory just yet. I think you need more evidence."

"Whatever I tell them, I'll have to convince them to go

on a while longer. Maybe by then we can get enough mud collections and do some spectrographic analysis and see if there is anything at all unusual in the specimens we're bringing up. If we can find even a shred of evidence, then we'll have enough to jump in with both feet. I'm sure I can evolve a method to do this safely."

"Balthorium," Hex said slowly. "The super element. Sounds like a Nobel Prize winner to me."

Sumter smiled broadly. "Hex St. Claire, I swear we do have a similar mind."

The report to the board went well. Sumter's charm and wit was received in good humor as it usually was by the largely unscientific members of the directing body. His comments, laced with anecdotes from his recent European visit, brought smiles and expressions of delight from his appreciative and somewhat captive audience. He stood before them speaking in a broad and sweeping style about the adventures and challenges ahead with the use of the newly developed platform. Making analogies to the hesitant beginnings of the space program, he characterized the early problems of St. Lucie One and the tragedies that had occurred as being the unavoidable hesitant new steps of a developing infant. An infant which would soon bring glory and financial success to the company.

He spoke in glowing terms about the tremendous rate of progress in the drilling and he went into some detail about a presumed cause of the electrical accidents. "Static electricity," he told the uncritical group, "was the culprit."

Because of the high rate of drilling, an unanticipated charge had begun to develop along the rapidly spinning pipe line due to the friction created in its spin through the sand. Because the casing, from the platform floor all the way to the sea bottom below, completely enclosed the drill pipe itself, the static charge was not being dissipated into the sea water, but was being allowed to build up—until finally it discharged when just the right circumstances developed on the drill platform itself. He assured them that this problem would be solved by better grounding of the drill apparatus.

His audience listened approvingly, their uninformed heads filled with the notion that they had a perfect grasp on the problem as elucidated by the great scientist.

"Just to be on the safe side," he assured them, he personally was going to spend more time at the well site, instructing the crew in safer operating procedures and making sure that no additional accidents would happen. He even planned to dress the work crew in safety uniforms that would resist the conduction of static electricity.

Finally, to the great joy of his audience, he gave them a glimpse of some ideas he had recently developed for new and profitable energy sources for the company. Details, he promised them, would be forthcoming in the next few months. He concluded his portion of the meeting by putting them on notice to expect news of dramatic success with St. Lucie One in the next few weeks.

As usual, the board, particularly the several female members, was absolutely charmed and flattered by his presence. His grace and style and manner of presentation were such great entertainment to them that they would have done whatever he requested, and he knew it. With a smile and a wave he had left the meeting early in order to finish some last-minute work in his laboratory before going to the well in the morning to renew the drilling.

He stayed long enough, however, to hear the expected announcement by President Matthew Downing, that he was going to retire as soon as St. Lucie One hit paydirt. The time had come, the old gentleman had said, to step back and allow younger minds and more nimble feet to take command of Florexco, as the company prepared to become one of the giants in the energy business. He challenged the board to come prepared at their next meeting to consider the executive reorganization of the company.

It was that potential reorganization of management that occupied Sumter's thoughts as he and Hex approached the well the morning after the meeting. In the past it had seemed reasonable to promote Wally Jenkins to executive president. The man was knowledgeable and tough and cooperative. He recognized the economic necessity of taking risks at times, but in recent months it hadn't seemed so clear. Wally was slipping. He didn't seem to have a full grasp of the implications of the new technology. Having the right man in charge had become ever more important now, especially with the new development. Sumter turned to Hex, "What do you think about Loggins?"

"In what context?" Hex replied.

"Just in general, Hex. As a man—as a leader—how trustworthy is he?"

"I think he's one to be watched. At times he has seemed strange to me. I think he knows his business, though. But I am not sure about his sense of loyalty. I doubt if he would make personal sacrifices for anything

312

other than his own gain."

Sumter smiled, "Isn't that the way we all are?"

"No," Hex replied emphatically. "I think there is something still to be said for personal loyalty and integrity. I think perhaps the man is too ambitious. I feel he has a certain capability for—" He paused. "For *evil*, for lack of a better word."

"A man like that can be useful sometimes in a crisis."

"Yes, but only if you are absolutely secure in the man's loyalty. Evil influences must be carefully controlled if one does not want to suddenly find himself confronted by those very same forces."

"An interesting observation, Hex. Loggins might be in line for promotion. Let's watch him closely. He may be useful to us in the days ahead. We need someone who will take a few chances."

"Test his loyalty first, Adrian. I feel there are things about the man that we don't know."

The conversation ended as the helicopter touched down on the landing pad. A hundred yards north of the rig sat the mother ship, the *Florexco Lady*. She was just in the process of retrieving from the water the small deep-diving sub. Everything seemed to be in order. It looked as if Loggins had the drilling ready to restart, just as Sumter had ordered him to do yesterday morning.

The two passengers exited the helicopter and, glancing around, noting the apparent readiness of the rig and crew, went straight to the control booth. As they reached the top, Eric Duval came out of the booth and passed them on the stairs.

"Good Lord! What happened to your face, man?" Hex said, surveying his grotesquely swollen and bent nose and his lacerated lip.

313

Duval glared at the black man and kept going down the stairs. "It's nothing I can't take care of myself," he said sullenly.

Hex watched him descend and then turned to Sumter. "I'd like a look at the other fellow." Sumter grinned and they entered the control room.

Winston Loggins was waiting for them. "Where do we stand?" Sumter asked, looking at the control dials. Fresh, blank paper rested under all of the now-stilled needles on the recording graphs, all the previous tapes having been removed to Sumter's lab. He had been studying them intently along with the graphs and readings that occurred just prior to the bigger accident.

"Everything's all set," Loggins replied. "The submersible just reported that the casing's intact. Electrically, we're ready to fire up. All we have to do is give the signal. Skip will start the engines and then we can go."

"Then do it," Sumter said.

Loggins went to the door, pulled it shut securely and locked it from the inside. "I think we've got to do a little talking first," he said. "Why don't the two of you sit down?" He pulled a chair up for himself and, sitting in it backwards, he faced the two men, who glanced at each other and then sat down. It was obvious from the tone of his voice and his expression that something serious was on his mind.

Sumter was annoyed at the authoritative attitude Loggins was taking, but nevertheless was interested in what was bothering him. "What's on your mind, Winston?"

"I talked with Dr. Thompson last night," Loggins began. "He said that Jori Ashe is still very critical and may die. She hasn't really come out of a coma yet."

"Yes, it's a tragedy," Sumter said. "She had such a promising career. I had been told that it was going to be touch and go for her."

"Right," Loggins said, slightly sarcastically. "And did they tell you what they have diagnosed her problem as?"

"No. I assumed just the effects of her shock."

Loggins shook his head. "Nope. Radiation exposure. Can you believe that?" He looked at Sumer questioningly.

"Where did they get that idea?"

"Thompson said it seemed pretty clear cut. He told me privately he agrees with what her doctors are saying, although he hasn't told them that. He doesn't think there's a chance in hell that a simple electrical injury could do that to anyone."

"I'll be damned," Sumter said, looking around cautiously at Hex and then back at Loggins.

"Yes," Loggins responded, "radiation exposure. And you know what else?" His tone was very sarcastic. "We've had a whole bunch of men working on this well, back right after the first accident, who showed mild symptoms of radiation exposure. Dr. Thompson said it didn't make sense at the time, but putting it all in perspective now, that's exactly what happened. They had changes in their blood. They had nausea and vomiting. We even had one guy whose blood got so screwed up that it didn't clot right. He's the one who got in a fight here on the well and then bled to death. Thompson said it's very likely that he died simply because he couldn't clot well enough to stop the bleeding that he got from his fight."

"No one told me all of this," Sumter said defensively.

Loggins stared at him silently. "It's true though," he said finally, a strange smile on his face. "We've had a whole lot of people show evidence of exposure to radiation. In addition to the men who died in the original accident, we had one guy get so sick they had to ship him out. They told us later he died of anemia. No one knew why. Thompson said it all fits into a pattern. He's scared. He says we got something real bad out here. Isn't that strange, Dr. Sumter?"

The geophysicist didn't respond as Loggins continued. "Thompson says we're killing people right and left out here. He also says the doctors over at the hospital are starting to get upset about it. Even the ones the company's been paying off to take care of our patients. They're ready to start talking." He shook his head back and forth, mockingly sad. "Thompson said that this whole thing is getting ready to explode right in our faces, and we're going to have more attention and scandal and trouble than we know how to deal with."

Sumter sat quietly, astonished at some of the revelations and surprised at the defiant, sarcastic attitude Loggins seemed to be taking with him. He was taunting them; it was very offensive.

"You know," Loggins continued, "I told Dr. Thompson what you said caused this accident, Dr. Sumter. I told him all about the static electricity and everything. And you know what he did? He laughed. He laughed out loud. He said you must be one of the world's great bullshit artists." Loggins glanced out the window. "That's exactly what he said. One of the world's great bullshit artists. What do you think about all that?" He turned to look condescendingly at the two. He obviously thought he had them where he wanted them.

Hex St. Claire's face clearly showed the anger he was feeling, and Adrian Sumter felt his irritation rising at both the situation and Loggins's accusing attitude. "What the hell does Adam Thompson know about all this?" Sumter said. "That drunk hasn't seen a medical textbook in years."

"Never underestimate people," Loggins replied. "The man seems to have come alive on this issue. So far, I'm the only one he's talked to. The three of us here and Thompson are the only ones in the company who know the real extent of our problem." Loggins stood up and walked to the window. "The men out there don't have any idea what's going on, but they're scared. Almost rebellious. I think there's a chance they might walk off the job."

"They can't do that," Sumter replied. "We'll pay them more money. We'll do whatever they want, but we've got to keep them working."

Loggins nodded. "We probably can, but there are a few things you're going to have to do." He smiled mockingly sweet. "I have to be very frank with you, Dr. Sumter. I don't think you're being very honest with me. Now that's not very nice, is it?" He smirked. "I can understand all the reasons why you would tell the board that cock-and-bull story about static electricity, don't misunderstand me. It was the proper thing to do. But let me tell you one other thing." His face turned into a menacing frown and his voice grew suddenly very angry and powerful. "Don't bullshit me!" He became quiet again. "You know what bullshit is, don't you Doctor? The excrement from a male cow?"

His tone grew angry again. "I don't want any of it." He smiled. "I think you have some idea of what's going on, and I'm sure you want to share it with me, don't you?" He glared at the two of them. "Because otherwise I'm going to destroy this whole stinking project!" He sat down suddenly. "I'm all ears. What have you got to tell me?" He looked back and forth at the two of them, smiling expectantly.

Sumter and Hex both sat in silence, studying the man in front of them. Sumter's initial irritation at the challenge by Loggins gradually changed into recognition that he would have to be informed. He needn't know everything, but just enough to gain his cooperation. "Very well," he finally said and walked to the far end of the room where he fixed himself a cup of coffee. "I'll tell you what I think is happening, Winston." He took a few sips of the brew and sat the cup down and leaned against the wall with his arms folded in front of him. "Have you ever heard of the theoretical element Balthorium?"

"I've heard the name, that's all. I know nothing about it except that it's not supposed to exist."

"Well, I think it does. It could be the explanation for what's happening to us." He reviewed the history of the element and described some of the theoretical properties it would manifest as Loggins sat nearly spellbound, skeptically listening to the tale and afterwards was filled with questions.

"But you said the radiation would be very short-ranged. Why does it affect the platform when what's happening is taking place thousands of feet below us? And the second thing is why doesn't the drill bit melt in the heat of the reaction?"

"Good questions," Sumter responded. "The one about the drill bit is simple. I think that it's such a thin layer of the Balthorium that we're drilling through that the reaction is relatively brief and the energy is released as a peculiar form of radiation more than heat. I think the energy is conducted along metal, much like electricity.

318

The steel pipe right in the middle of the reaction may conduct the heat and energy away from the drill bit and dissipate it so quickly that the temperature of the bit and pipe doesn't rise high enough to melt down. That's the key to the injuries up here. The radiation comes right up the pipe just like an electrical shock would."

He hesitated, watching Loggins's reaction carefully. "It's the only explanation that makes sense. The radiation released by Balthorium, in its very nature, is going to be atypical. We have a lot to learn about it. I think the first accident was proof that what happened during the reaction is unusual in that more radiation is released than heat itself. That's the only way the well could have survived with as little damage as it had."

"How do you plan to recover the Balthorium even if we find it? It seems obvious that we just can't drill pell-mell into it," Loggins said.

"Yes," Sumter answered. "That would be very dangerous, in fact, potentially cataclysmic if the deposit were rich enough, and we set off a reaction that was self-perpetuating. I think we can use an acid wash technique similar to the manner in which some soluble minerals are recovered in traditional drilling. We could pump sulfuric acid down the main shaft under pressure. It would then presumably dissolve some of the Balthorium and bring it up with the washings alongside the pipe. We recover those washings, neutralize the acid and precipitate out the Balthorium. It'll be a difficult and expensive commercial process, but I think the yield could be well worth it."

"That could work," Loggins replied. "As a matter of fact, you might start testing the mud washings now and see if there's any residue at all of Balthorium there."

"I plan to start that today. There's a chance that the washings we get from the area of the bit right now might have some trace of the element."

"One more question. How do you plan to recognize that we're right on top of a Balthorium deposit without accidentally drilling into it and setting it off?"

"That's going to be a delicate problem, but I think I've got the solution," Sumter replied. "The German calculations as well as my own indicate that the very nature of Balthorium distorts the magnetic field around it. As you no doubt know, our own readings here have shown dramatic changes in the electromagnetic field just a few seconds before we made contact. The calculations indicate that very tiny amounts of the element create abrupt changes in the electromagnetic field, but only extremely close by. Logically enough, larger deposits should cause changes in the field from great distances, changes which will gradually increase in intensity as the element is approached. At a point very nearly upon it, the magnetic field will be totally obliterated."

He paused and took another sip of his coffee. "Fortunately, St. Lucie One is almost perfectly adapted to this type of drilling. We can watch the magnetic field readings at the drill bit, and as we get closer they should begin to change. When abruptly the readings become totally erratic and meaningless, I think we'll know that we're right on top of it. At that point, we'll slow down to a snail's pace until we finally take the drill bit right up next to it. Then, we'll continue the washings, but just add acid to it and analyze what we get back. I think we can do it safely."

Loggins stood up and smiled. Once again he stood in front of the large window and looked out over his rig, thinking. "That must be it," he said. "That explains everything, if it's true." He looked over at Sumter. His tone was skeptical. "How sure are you about all this?"

"It's the only thing that makes sense," the scientist replied. "I am convinced that we can find it. Luckily, fate has given us the chance. We would be fools not to take it. Think how many great scientific accomplishments have hinged on a bit of luck. And how many more have been lost because some idiot didn't recognize opportunity when it came?"

Loggins paced back and forth without responding. Clearly, he was considering the implications of Sumter's revelations. He walked to the geological map on the far wall. "What you're proposing essentially is that we drill the Mohole. Now, if everything we've learned is correct, at this spot along the edge of the continental shelf the crust should be reasonably thin. That means we could hit it in the neighborhood of 50,000 feet. At the rate we're going, that won't take long. That's assuming that this defect in the tectonic plate persists."

"If my theory that Balthorium caused our first two accidents is correct, then the defect must go all the way through in order to explain the superficial presence of the Balthorium," Sumter replied.

"That's true," Loggins said. "But don't make it sound too easy. We've still got 35,000 feet of unexplored crust to go through." He looked at Sumter and Hex, who stirred uneasily, but neither spoke. He continued, "Balthorium would be commercially very valuable, wouldn't it?"

When he said that, Sumter knew he had him. Loggins was a greedy, selfish man and the potential wealth was more than he could resist. "What do you think?" he answered.

Loggins smiled. His sly and almost wicked expression instantly annoyed the two others. "All right. I'll do it," he said. "But let me tell you something. Don't you ever cross me, or you'll be sorry you did, I promise you." For a moment he hesitated. "You're no better than me, neither one of you. We're three birds of a feather. For different reasons, maybe, but we're all the same."

Hex looked displeased. "Speak for yourself."

Loggins laughed condescendingly. "It doesn't matter. In any event, we've got the equipment to give it a good shot. On a practical level, we've got to do several things. First of all, Adrian, you've got to get over to the hospital and call off those doctors. You'd better convince them that everything's safe out here. Otherwise, they're liable to cause trouble. I think we're all in agreement that this kind of project absolutely has to be kept top secret. We don't want any of the other oil companies or the federal government or any goddamned environmentalists breathing down our backs on this one."

Sumter agreed. "I'll go visit Jori this afternoon. I can talk to the doctors at that time. I'm sure I can make them see it my way."

"I'm not totally convinced of that. One of them—that Dr. Robson—is an arrogant meddler. He's the one to work on. Now the other thing we have to do is convince this crew that what we're doing here is safe."

"I've got some plans for that," Sumter said. "I think they'll buy the static electricity explanation, but what I want to do is equip every man out here with some radiation protection suits, just in case we come across another small deposit. I think we can construct a good enough cover story about the problem to convince them of the necessity."

"You're going to have to sweeten that with money also," Loggins said. "Which brings me to my third point. We will have to inform some key members of the upper management, including the board, about the truth."

"No," Sumter said firmly. "This has absolutely got to be kept secret. I'm too afraid they might go soft on us and want to stop."

"No, they won't," Loggins retorted. "There are tremendous economic incentives at work here. You're not inclined to think about things like that as much as the rest of us, but if this company can produce a significant amount of Balthorium, even the smallest stockholder is likely to become a millionaire. Persons with significant holdings in this company could find that they're worth billions. Why do you think I'm so interested in this? For science?" He shook his head. "Don't be naive. I've got everything I own tied up in Florexco stock. That's motive enough for most of us to take a risk. I won't mind being so filthy rich I never have to get my hands greasy again.

"There's no need to let Wally Jenkins know what we're up to. But I think we should inform Craig Strombeck. He can decide who else should be given the word and he can guarantee that the board takes whatever action in terms of finances or economic decisions that need to be made in order to sustain our drilling effort. If we don't, something's liable to happen—some kind of trouble—and the board could pull the rug out from underneath us. If they think we're just out here farting around, they're liable to shut us down. We need them behind us."

Sumter frowned. "I don't like having so many people

323

know what we're up to. It's too risky. What do you think, Hex?"

"I don't think you have any choice. He's right. With the special equipment and supplies that you may be needing and some of the things that you're going to have to do here, I don't think you can keep from arousing suspicion among the more knowledgeable persons on the board."

"All right," Sumter said reluctantly. "But tell Strombeck to keep it at a minimum as to who's informed."

"Okay," Loggins said. "Let's go talk to the men. I'd like for you to say a few words. Tell them about our new safety plans. We'll get everything into place before we start drilling. It may delay us a day or two, but it'll be worth it if we can keep their confidence. I think we need to promise them a bonus when we hit paydirt, and I think we need to up their wages considerably right now."

"I agree, but they are not to have any idea as to what we're really planning. As far as they're concerned, we're going for oil."

Loggins grinned. "Except for the few people that we're going to inform, everyone else has to believe that. It will be your job to keep those doctors off our back. And if Jori lives, you're going to have to convince her that everything's okay out here. She can be very hard to deal with."

"Part of that may be the personal antagonism between the two of you," Hex said.

"Perhaps," Loggins said, frowning slightly. "But she's a very tough bitch. I doubt if she will be easily conned, and now that she's been hurt—hurt bad by this rig— she's going to be very paranoid and suspicious about the whole thing. You may disagree, but I personally perceive her as a real threat to what we are doing. But that's a threat I can deal with if I have to," he added. "This is too big a project to have a little jackass like her screw it up. If she survives, she'll have to be watched. I wouldn't put it past her to try and stop us."

"Well," Sumter said, "one girl can't do much."

"Don't you believe that for one minute. Get it into your head right now that she is our enemy. Just remember why you hired her. She's smart and tough. If she lives, she will hate this rig. I know her, believe me, and she's the type who will stop at nothing to get things her way. She's fearless."

"Then improve the security. That should be a simple matter."

"I'm going to, Doctor. I've got a few things in mind already. Nobody is going to be able to get to us. I'll guarantee it. In the meantime, I'll contact Strombeck and we can plan a meeting." He stepped to the door. "You know, if you're wrong, Adrian, we're all going to look like stupid shits. But, if you're right . . ." he said, "if you're right, we may change the history of the world." He looked thoughtfully at the two of them and then stepped out of the room, pulling the door shut behind him. They watched him going down the stairs in front of them.

Sumter studied the uneasy expression on his black friend's face. "You look unhappy, Hex."

"I don't like that man," he replied. "He frightens me. He seems too eager to accept this risk and almost happy to lie to his own men. He doesn't do it with regret and for a higher purpose. He does it to exert his control. He wants to buy them for a few dollars more. I have the feeling he doesn't care if anything happens to them."

"Weren't we willing to do the same thing?" Sumter said, solemnly.

"For science, for discovery, for the achievement, yes we were. But somehow that seems like a higher motivation than the greed that drives Mr. Loggins. I think he is a selfish, dangerous man. We should watch him closely."

Sumter agreed. "The important thing, though, is that we go on with the project. It's unfortunate that we have to do some of the things we must and deal with men like Loggins."

"I wonder if we should," Hex said moodily. "I see a great risk here. I wish we knew what had befallen those who might have drilled here before. Did they reap sorrow or treasures? And what about the Russians?" He reached into his coat pocket and pulled out a small deck of old, well-worn cards. He shuffled them slowly in his hands.

"Hex, don't start that again. Put those bloody things away."

The black man ignored him. His eyes were aglow with anticipation. He seemed isolated and withdrawn into himself as his big hands shuffled the cards back and forth methodically. Finally, to the chagrin of Dr. Adrian Sumter, Hex St. Claire produced two cards from the middle of the deck, flipped them over and placed them on top of the control booth.

They showed the symbols of fire and damnation.

SEVENTEEN

Jori Ashe was far, far away in the dark. Then there were lights above her in the sky, moving back and forth, up and down. Colors, all colors. Then black lights blinking off and on, off and on, invisible against the black sky. But she knew they were there because she could feel them. And the drums, loud drums beating slowly. No, not drums, an engine. An engine turning, the steady throb of a giant diesel turning and in the distance was the well.

There was water between her and the well. She was in a boat fighting against the waves to get to the well. Overhead the lights continued to blink off and on. The waves were big, some bigger than the boat. The boat tossed and rolled. Sometimes she could see the well and sometimes not. The well was big—bigger than she had ever seen. The throbbing was louder. It was the engine of the drill.

There was a man on the well. He was shirtless, but he wore riding pants with big black boots. He had a hat, a military hat and dark glasses. He was laughing and swinging a whip. He called to her and she was afraid. He laughed again and signalled for her to come. She ran to the back of the boat. Overhead the lights were blinking. The sea became rougher.

She looked back to the beach. There were people there

waving and shouting at her. She saw George, old George. He waved to her. "Come back!" he shouted. "Come back." There were tears in his eyes.

In the darkness along the beach she could see the bodies stacked neatly, rows and rows of bodies stacked one on top of the other. They all wore hats. They all were oil workers. George was walking up and down gesturing frantically and shouting, "Come back, Jori. Don't go!"

She looked at the well. It was closer. Red lights on either side of it pulsated alternately. She heard a ringing as at a railway crossing, and up on the derrick stood the giant man, shirtless, laughing again and swinging his whip. Its cracking sound echoed across the sea toward her. She looked back and there were more bodies on the beach. They were unloading them from trucks. The sea was rough. The lights overhead continued to blink. The people along the beach were yelling at her, "Jori, come home. Jori, come home." The well looked frightening; it was large and dark and the red lights were blinking. The sound of the engine's roar was deafening, and the shirtless man at the top was laughing. She was frightened and scared.

"Boatman, turn back," she said, and looked up at the pilot standing on the bridge above her. He ignored her. The sky grew angry, lightning flashed. The boat was tossed and turned by the heaving sea. The laughing of the man on the well grew louder and more frightening. Soon there were others beside him, laughing and shouting to one another. They were waving at her to come. The lightning flashed through the sky. Old George's voice grew fainter, but in the distance she could still see him along with the stacked bodies.

"Boatman," she said again, "turn back, turn back!"

Nothing, no response.

There was more lightning. The air was filled with sounds of thunder and roaring laughter. She climbed up the ladder to grab the pilot. He fell away to the floor at her touch and lay motionless. His face was bloody and his nose bent and broken. With the roll of the boat, he slid off the side and disappeared into the sea. She turned and looked down into the cockpit from which she had come. A tall gangly man was dancing. He was covered in an eerie glow of green. She could only see his back. When he finally turned, he was all bones and a picture of death. His glowing, shimmering presence jumped at her in small strands of glimmering brilliance. He finally faded away and was gone.

The man on the well was laughing. The engine was roaring. The light in the sky blinked off and on. She turned the boat and looked toward the beach. There was a light. She aimed for it. The voices chanted her name, "Jori . . . Jori . . ." The light grew brighter. She could see old George. He was smiling and waving. The dead bodies were stacked beside him. The light grew brighter and brighter. The sky overhead disappeared. The boat was gone. There was no sea, only the light ahead. The light moved back and forth and became brighter and brighter. It was all she could see. The chanting faded away. One voice called to her. "Jori, Jori!"

The light moved from side to side. She felt hands on her wrists. A familiar voice called to her. "Jori, wake up. Jori." Suddenly the light grew dim and in its place came a face, blurred and distorted, but a familiar voice, "Jori." She tried hard. She looked at the face. Slowly she could recognize. She felt hands on her wrists. She heard the sound of nurses talking. She heard Blain's voice. "Jori.

Are you awake?"

The face in front of her gradually focused from its blur into the bearded friendly gaze of Blain, dear Blain. He was smiling.

"Jori, you're okay," he said.

Someone patted her arm. She looked, a nurse. She was in a small room. Blain was smiling. She was confused, but she felt better. The blackness was gone and Blain was here, and nurses and doctors.

"Can you hear me?" Blain said. His face was in perfect focus now. She felt his hand in hers. She squeezed it. He smiled.

"Am I okay?" she said.

"Yes, you are," he responded. "You most certainly are."

She looked at the nurse. "Welcome back, Jori Ashe," the lady in white said, and Jori smiled.

Dr. Blain Robson stepped out of Room 316 and spoke to the nurse accompanying him. "I think she just turned the corner, Hazel. I believe she's going to be okay."

The middle-aged matron smiled. "That's the first time she's said anything rational since she came in. I think she may be talking to us by tomorrow."

Blain examined the chart he was holding. "Let's give her some more platelets today and maybe another unit of packed red blood cells. Hopefully, in a few more days her bone marrow will be back at work and we can wean her off these things."

"Fine," Hazel responded. "And will you write some routine IV orders for us, too, please?"

"Sure. If at all possible, let's try to get her sitting up,

maybe in a chair, this afternoon. She's going to get pneumonia if we leave her lying around in that bed too much longer."

"Will do," Hazel said and disappeared into the nursing station, while he continued making notes in the chart.

It had been more than four days since Jori had been brought into the emergency room, and now, finally, she seemed to be making some improvement. She was still a long way from recovery, but at least she had made an intelligent response to their presence. Blain was almost positive now that she was going to be all right.

Phil Hallam, the internist, as well as Dr. Barker, a neurological consultant, had predicted that she would eventually recover. Her big problem now was hematological. Her bone marrow was still suppressed and doing very poorly at manufacturing the various components of the blood: red and white cells, as well as platelets. She had been receiving daily transfusions, and, by following her extremely closely, Blain and her other physicians had been able to keep her clotting ability near normal. She was demonstrating no evidence of bleeding susceptibility at present. This was only, of course, because of the massive amount of transfusions and blood components she had been receiving. Without them she would most certainly have died, probably bleeding into her GI tract or perhaps from infection. As he finished with the chart and started down the hall to see his other patients, Dr. Fieldman arrived on the floor.

"Hello, Blain," the GP said as they met each other in the hallway. "How's the star patient?"

"Looking great. She spoke to us a few minutes ago. I think she is starting to come out of it."

Fieldman broke into a sincere smile. "Thank God. Any

changes in her blood work?"

"No, nothing significant, but Phil feels that if we keep giving her the components, eventually her bone marrow will bounce back."

"Great," Fieldman said. "I'll look in on her later. I've got a patient I'm admitting now with abdominal pain. It could be an acute cholecystitis. Would you be willing to see her in consultation after awhile?"

"Sure," Blain replied. "Just have the nurse let me know when she gets in."

"Right," the GP said. "I'll talk to you later."

Blain continued down the hall and took the stairs to the fourth floor. A lot of things had changed since his confrontation with Fieldman and the administrator. For reasons not entirely clear to Blain, the chief of staff had made a complete about-face in his attitude toward him and the things he had done. With that change had come the obligatory approval of the hospital administrator and many of the others, because of the influence wielded by Fieldman. Stan Wilcott was, of course, still hostile as expected, and Blain doubted if anything would ever win the man over. Perhaps, because of the change in Fieldman, Wilcott was even more angry and bitter. The GP, one of Wilcott's busiest referral physicians, had sent Blain two, and now today a third referral.

Almost everyone, finally, seemed to be working together to save Jori and stop the carnage on the well. It was encouraging to Blain that it was no longer just himself who was suspicious of what was going on. He believed that whatever had happened out there was going to be rectified.

Dr. Adrian Sumter, the chief of research and development for the oil company had had a long conversation two days ago with all three of the physicians intimately concerned with Jori's care. It was obvious to them that Sumter was an intelligent, articulate, and concerned scientist who was shocked and disheartened about the accidents. Blain felt convinced that the man was going to do everything possible to avoid any repetition of the problem, although he was not entirely convinced by the geophysicist's explanation of the accidents. But the man seemed honest and possessed by a strong sense of integrity. Whatever had caused the problem, steps were being taken to rectify it.

Blain would have his secretary call Sumter's office that afternoon to inform him that Jori was making good progress. He knew the man was interested, and he had promised Sumter the earliest possible notice when she would be able to receive visitors.

On the fourth floor, he stood for a moment outside the nurses station, looking through a window out over the St. Lucie River. It was a beautiful fall morning and the waters below glimmered in the sunshine. Blain felt better than he had in a number of days. Jori was improving. His position at the hospital seemed to have turned around overnight, and the screwball accidents at Florexco were, hopefully, now going to be brought under control.

He turned quickly back to the station and began going through the charts of his postsurgical patients. He was anxious to finish up his morning's work so he could make a more extended visit in Jori's room before lunch. He had high hopes that by the time he returned to her room she would have grown even more lucid.

During the next two weeks, Jori made slow—almost

333

painstaking—progress toward her normal mental status. She seemed to wax between a relatively oriented state and a bizarre, semi-hysterical neurological state. She seemed almost like a child. Large gaps existed in her memory, scattered widely over a number of areas. She expressed no interest in current affairs and never mentioned the well or the accident. She spoke occasionally of her childhood and happy memories with her father. Although she had a warm and friendly attitude toward Blain and seemed to feel close to him, she appeared puzzled when he once mentioned the night they had spent together. She asked a lot of curious questions about the hospital, the town and the past, but was satisfied with very simple and superficial explanations.

Her mind was like a child's, accepting and uncritical. She developed an apparently very contented and occasionally happy attitude during her lucid periods and was, for all intents and purposes, completely unaware of the emotional turmoil she displayed when she slipped back into her disordered state of mind.

At the suggestion of Dr. Hallam, Blain had kept her isolated from all except hospital personnel. They had not pushed or stimulated her with questions, nor had they volunteered information. They merely waited for her to lead the way back toward reality. All in all, she gave good reason to believe she would eventually regain complete mental competence.

The decision to protect her from any emotional crisis was a joint one. Hallam, Dr. Fieldman and Blain met over coffee in the hospital cafeteria.

"It's just so puzzling how she jumps back and forth from those frightened, almost nightmarish moods she has and then to the sweet, gentle, almost happy times she seems to be experiencing," Blain said. "And when she feels good, she is absolutely unaware of the bad times she has had. It's like some sort of selective amnesia."

"It probably is," Hallam responded. "She may be reliving the accident and the whole horrible mess during those times, and then her psychological defense mechanisms completely block it out when she calms down. Fortunately, they seem to be more infrequent."

"Yes, but she's going to have to face those memories eventually," Fieldman said. "And in my experience that's a rough time. I've seen a lot of patients over the years who have blocked out one thing or another and then when, at last, it becomes impossible to deny and they're confronted with the true facts, they just decompensate. I think we'll gradually have to help her work through this and face up to what's happened to her."

"Eventually, yes," Hallam agreed, "but not now. She's not ready. We need to sit tight and let her alone. She'll find her way back."

"What should we do if she starts asking questions about the accident, or the well for that matter?" Blain asked.

"Tell her what you think she wants to hear. Tell her anything. Just don't let her get upset. Later on, when she's stronger, we can straighten out any distortions we may have made," Hallam said.

"There's risk in that," Fieldman interjected. "It's like putting a bandage over a sore, then when later it gets uncovered, it may be more horrible than ever." He took a sip of his coffee. "We will have to be prepared to face a crisis, and maybe even her hostility, if she suddenly becomes aware of the truth."

"Let's do it that way then," Blain said. "I'll keep visitors out, and we'll see how she is doing in another week or so."

"Good," Hallam said. "By then her bone marrow may start to regenerate and, hopefully, we'll have her out of the woods. I feel fairly optimistic about the whole situation at this point." Blain and Fieldman were in accord and Hallam stood up to leave. "She's certainly been an interesting case so far," he said. "God knows if we'll ever figure out what really happened to her. See you guys later." He picked up his small black bag and left.

"I had a call from Adam Thompson this morning," Fieldman said. "They've certainly changed their attitude about everything out there. He said the blood work they drew on all the workers on the rig day before yesterday all came back completely normal."

"That's what I heard," Blain replied. "One of the techs in the lab who knows I am interested told me about it last night. I don't think it would hurt if they would monitor the blood counts on those guys once a week, just to make sure there are no other problems."

"I couldn't agree more. I mentioned it to Adam and he didn't have any objection. So I imagine they'll be doing it." He absentmindedly put his spoon back into his cup of coffee and stirred it again. "I wonder what really happened out there."

"Hallam's right. We may never know." Blain gazed off into the distance through the windows overlooking the tropically landscaped hospital grounds. "The Coast Guard sent me a copy of the accident investigation report. As far as they're concerned the well is no different from any other, just a little more sophisticated."

Fieldman studied the younger man intently. "You still think it was radiation, Blain?"

Blain remained silent, buried in thought as he watched several small children playing outside. "I don't know," he finally said, and then turned back to look at Fieldman. "I was so convinced that first night, but now the way things have gone, I'm not so sure." He sipped his coffee. "There's a lot of things we don't know about medicine, that's a certainty. These cases have been so strange. They don't really fit any pattern I'm familiar with. I may have been shooting from the hip—a little too quick with my snap diagnosis. Hallam's a lot smarter than I am and he doesn't seem convinced of anything. Maybe Sumter was right. He certainly seems to know his stuff."

"He's a well-respected scientist, I know that."

"He knew a lot more about medicine than I expected him to. That caught me by surprise," Blain said. "I wonder where he picked all that up?"

"Men like him absorb knowledge like a sponge, Blain. They're in a category totally by themselves. None of the rest of us have any idea what it's like to have the intellectual abilities they have. He may have picked it up anywhere. He could have read a medical textbook once just for a break. You know, a little light reading."

Blain smiled. "He's an impressive guy, I'll grant you that. I didn't understand everything he was saying about electromotive forces and static electricity, but he sure seemed convinced that was the source of the trouble."

"Thompson told me they have made some significant changes out there. He said Sumter's convinced they won't have any more trouble."

Blain frowned. "I'll be honest with you, Hoyt. I wouldn't trust Adam Thompson as far as I could throw him. I think he's an ass, second only to that jerk who runs the well out there—Loggins." He stood up, preparing to leave.

"Oh, I don't know. Adam's not too bad, really. I've seen worse. You never really know about people, do you?"

"You never do, that's true." Blain shrugged. "I'll see you later, Hoyt. I've got some work to do." Without further conversation, he walked across the cafeteria and, from the wall phone, dialed his office to check in. The afternoon's schedule was full and he found out that Dr. Sumter had called again. No other messages of any importance. He pulled a small notebook from his coat pocket and examined it briefly, mentally arranging the order in which he would see his patients, leaving a little extra time to visit with Jori at the end.

It's curious, he mused, how interested Sumter seemed to be in Jori. For two weeks now, he had called almost every day for a status report. He asked repeatedly for the opportunity to visit her, but seemed to understand when he was denied. He had made Blain promise, though, that when the time came, the scientist would be among the first allowed to say hello to her.

Blain concluded Sumter felt guilty because the giant platform he had designed had in some way caused so many deaths. He probably needed Jori's survival to help absolve his guilt. No harm in that, Blain thought, especially since he seemed so concerned to prevent anything else from happening out there.

If what Sumter had said yesterday meant anything, the drilling was going great without even a hint of trouble. He had assured Blain again that the changes he had implemented had solved whatever problem existed. That was fine with him. They could drill all the way to China as far as Blain was concerned as long as they didn't kill anybody in the process.

It was on the twenty-third day of her hospitalization that Jori began to put it all together. She had been feeling good all morning. After breakfast, she had a cheery conversation with her nurse and then arranged the several vases of flowers, putting them closer to the window so they could get more sunshine. A beautician employed by the hospital came up to wash and fix her hair. She spent the next hour idly brushing it herself and studying her face in the bedside mirror. She even put on her lipstick and some eyeshadow. It was in doing this that she first noticed the funny-looking, rather recent scar on her tongue. She studied it carefully, wondering where it had come from. For some reason which she did not understand, her bright mood seemed to slip away, and she felt herself becoming tense and blue.

Jori ate as much as she could stand at lunch, following the instructions of the nursing staff, who were encouraging her to begin regaining the weight she had lost, and then, after an hour or so of daytime TV, she turned off the set and pulled the drapes closed.

She felt strange and angry, but she didn't understand it. She felt as if there was something she was trying to remember, and it was irritating to her. She studied her tongue again, and it seemed like she could almost recall what happened, but not quite. Finally, in the subdued light, feeling frustrated and isolated, she drifted into a troubled sleep. Again, she dreamed of the well and the voices. The stacked bodies on the beach and old George calling to her, but this time the boat, fighting the heaving seas, reached the platform. As she tried to climb from the craft, a giant wave crashed across her and knocked her screaming and spinning into the foaming waters. The shirtless man standing above on the derrick continued to laugh and shout. The lightning flashed, but suddenly there was a rope around her and she was jerked roughly from the water and dumped abruptly at the base of the spinning turntable.

"No!" she shouted, as men with no faces tied her to the turning shaft. Her ears filled with the screaming rage of the dead. The tall man above her, the one with no shirt, cracked the whip and laughed on. She looked up into his face and it was a familiar one. She knew him. The others seemed subservient. He was boss. He was king.

"Stop the well," she pleaded. The noise of the engine was thunderous. Everyone laughed in a haunting, taunting way. She stumbled and fell as she struggled to get away. She lay beside the body of a dead black man. She screamed and pulled, but she was bound too tightly. "Stop the drilling," she pleaded and looked back toward the spinning pipe, but it was too late. A tiny finger of green fire leaped out toward her and consumed her. Her body was aglow. "Stop! Stop! Stop the drill!" she screamed as she jerked and danced at the end of her tether. "Stop the drill!"

"We can't get her to stop screaming, Dr. Robson," the nurse said as Blain came rushing into the room. The other nurses and an orderly were restraining Jori as she struggled in her bed. Her face was terrified.

"Stop the drilling!" she screamed. "We can't go on!"

"How about some Thorazine?" one of the nurses suggested.

"No, I want to try talking to her first," Blain answered. He put his hand in hers. She continued to yell. "Okay!" he said loudly. "We'll stop the drilling. The drilling is stopped."

The intensity of her struggling suddenly diminished. "Please, she begged, "stop the drilling."

"The drilling has stopped. The well has been shut down," he said. She lay very still continuing to breathe rapidly and heavily. He repeated what he had said. "The drilling has stopped."

She opened her eyes and looked around wildly and confused. "We can't go on this way. It's not safe. It's too dangerous. We've got to stop." She looked from person to person.

"It's over," Blain said. "Jori, it's over. The drilling has stopped. You're okay. You're in the hospital."

She looked at him and her face seemed to relax. The intense grip with which she had held his hand eased. She looked around at the others and took a deep breath, exhaling slowly. "I was daydreaming again," she said suddenly.

"Yes, you were," Blain said. "But it's over now. You're okay." He signaled to the others to leave.

"God, that was terrible," she said and then smiled. "I feel better now."

"You're all right," he responded. "It was just a bad dream."

Suddenly her face became more intent. "What's happening on the well? They've stopped the drilling, haven't they?"

He studied her for a moment, remembering Phil

341

Hallam's advice. "Yes, they have. It's been shut down."

"Oh, thank God." She sank back into the bed. "Something's desperately wrong out there. I know it is. They've got to quit before they kill someone."

"How are you feeling?" he asked. "Do you know where you are?"

"Of course I do, Blain. I'm in the hospital. I've been here since the accident. How long has it been?"

"More than three weeks."

"Holy smoke, I didn't realize it was that long. I've been having some memory loss, haven't I?" She looked at him earnestly.

"Yes, but I think you're getting over that."

"I know I am," she responded and turned to look in the mirror at her tongue. "I know where that came from and I know how I got here. I'm going to be okay now, though, aren't I?"

"Yes, you are. I'll see to that."

"Was anyone else hurt in the accident?"

He paused for a moment. "No, you were the only one."

"Good," she replied. "And the drilling's been stopped? Are you sure? The well has been completely shut down?"

He nodded. "How much do you remember?"

She looked into his eyes for a moment. "I remember everything," she said. "I remember the well, you . . . you and me. I remember it all." She held out her hand. "You've been taking good care of me, haven't you, Blain?"

"We've been trying. You've been very sick, Jori."

"I have all the confidence in the world. I know I'm in good hands. But tell me, what are they doing about the well and what happened to me? I was so frightened."

"We'll have plenty of time to talk about that. The main thing is, you're going to be just fine. But you're going to need rest. You're still sick and you're going to be in the hospital awhile."

"That's okay. It feels so good to be back. I feel like a fog just cleared out of my head. You're sure that the well has stopped? I guess they had to. There's something too strange out there, Blain. I don't know what it is, and I doubt if anyone else does. What I saw happen was not normal."

He nodded again. "The drilling has been completely shut down. You don't have a thing to worry about, pretty girl." He hated backing himself into a corner of lies like this, but from the way he had just seen her reacting, he was convinced that Hallam was right. They would have to ease her back to the truth. Give her a chance to get reoriented. The best thing to do would be to keep the conversation away from the well and the accident to minimize the degee that he would have to distort the facts. That way it would be easier to set her straight later. The main thing now was to keep her isolated for a few more days so that they could help her face the exact truth before her visitors could confront her with it. "The first thing I want to do is talk to you about what's been happening to you. We've had to give you a lot of blood."

"Speak," she said. "But first, bend over here just a little bit."

"What?"

"Come a little closer just for a minute."

He bent forward and she kissed him long and sweetly. "I know you saved my life, Blain. I trust you completely."

He sat back in his chair and smiled, but he felt guilty and distinctly uneasy at the lies he was telling. It was going to be hard to keep the truth from her for long.

EIGHTEEN

Captain Kemper Daniels waited patiently as Winston Loggins and Craig Strombeck slowly read through the set of official papers he had just delivered to them. He was anxious to get this matter settled. It was almost six o'clock, and he had had to wait for more than an hour before Loggins had returned from the well to this office in the Florexco compound. Even Dennis Overby, who had accompanied him—normally a very patient individual—was beginning to show signs of edginess.

It was apparent that the president of the board did not like the Coast Guard directives any more than did Loggins, who, when he finished reading, handed the last page to Strombeck and looked up at Daniels. "So it appears, Captain, that the Coast Guard wants us to turn over all of our drilling data and testing information."

Kemper nodded. "It's a routine request. From time to time the department likes to gather this information on the offshore drilling operations in progress."

Loggins eyed him suspiciously. "In all my experience, I must say this is the first time I've ever been faced with such a request."

"That's interesting," Daniels responded.

Loggins glanced toward Strombeck who was now finished reading the document. "I sort of feel like this is some kind of harassment, don't you, Craig?"

The senior man looked intently at the Coast Guard official. "Exactly why is it that you want this information? It seems very unusual to me."

"It's not unusual at all, Mr. Strombeck. The federal government has the right and the obligation to monitor drilling operations in the offshore territories. It is, as I have tried to explain, a relatively routine matter."

"Unfortunately, we don't look at it that way," Loggins replied. "We are doing some extremely innovative and highly experimental drilling on this rig, as you well know. The last thing we are interested in doing is turning over our information to persons not under our control. Florexco has an extensive amount of money invested in this project, and we cannot afford to risk the possibility of the premature release of our technical developments. There are many companies who would love to reap the benefit of our research without going through the cost of the development themselves or leasing arrangements from us."

"I can assure you that any information turned over to the Coast Guard is strictly confidential and will be treated as such," Daniels replied.

Loggins laughed sarcastically. "That's absurd, Captain, and you know it. The U.S. government can't keep a thing secret. If we release our technical data to you, the other oil companies would have it within a week. I guarantee it. No, I'm afraid we can not comply with the request. I'm very sorry, but our answer is no. I believe we're standing on firm legal ground."

The captain's face grew more stern. "I think you don't understand, sir. This is not really a request per se. This is an order. We are empowered under the offshore leasing agreements Florexco has with the federal government to demand this information."

"Yes, we know," interjected Strombeck. "However, if you will examine the contracts a little more closely, you will see that we have up to forty-five days to deliver the data."

"Only for due cause," Daniels replied.

"We have due cause," answered Loggins. "We are an experimental rig. Our data is difficult to obtain. We don't have it organized properly and we have concerns over security."

"Is that your final answer then? You're refusing to comply?"

"Yes, I'm afraid so," Loggins said, rising and holding out his hand. "I can assure you, Captain, that we want to cooperate in every way possible with the Coast Guard. But we have had enough troubles and delays with this project now, and we have to devote our full attention to getting the job done."

"I can understand your problems, Mr. Loggins. Unfortunately, I believe you're going to wind up wasting more time trying to resist this legal process than if you would very simply comply. I'll relay this response to the commander, and I'm sure you will be hearing from us soon."

"Let me say one more thing," Strombeck said. "Our legal position here is very sound, and I caution the Coast Guard against attempting to harass us. We are involved in a significant search for petroleum. It is a major undertaking supported by the Congress and the people, especially considering the energy needs of this country. It would be very poor judgment of the Coast Guard, indeed, were they to obstruct our efforts with petty legal or harassing maneuvers. You can depend upon me to guarantee that we will use every legal defense necessary should you or anyone else in the Coast Guard seek to hamper the work we are doing."

"I understand your position," Daniels said. "I hope you understand the Coast Guard's."

"We do," replied Loggins. "Good day, Captain."

The two Coast Guard officials left the room and Loggins closed the door behind them. "Damn it," he said as soon as he was sure they were out of earshot. "Those sons of bitches are getting suspicious."

"It's no frigging wonder," Strombeck replied. "As much attention as we've called to ourselves out there."

Loggins grimaced. "It probably doesn't matter anyway. I think we're going to have this issue resolved within the next week or ten days anyway. We're bound to be getting close."

"That's what's got me worried. You'd better make sure there's no more trouble out there," Strombeck replied. "I mean not even so much as a cut finger. We can't afford any publicity at this stage."

"My sentiments exactly. I've got that place locked up tight as a drum. Nobody comes or goes without my knowledge. And we're doing everything Sumter has recommended to avoid any further accidents."

Strombeck frowned. "Yeah, that's what I worry about. I wonder if he knows for sure what he's doing."

"That he does, Craig. And besides, he's too hungry for a Nobel Prize to make a mistake this big. If he came off looking like a fool, he'd never get it. He wants more fame. In the process, I think he's going to make us all millionaires."

"He'd better," Strombeck replied and rose to leave.

"What's going on with this Jori Ashe thing anyway? How's she doing?"

"I don't know. Sumter is going over to see her at the hospital this afternoon. Apparently she's doing better."

"Good. We don't need any more deaths than we've already had. How's her attitude about this?"

"I don't know."

"You better find out when she gets well. Make sure it's appropriate to our needs."

Loggins frowned. "She's a difficult one to deal with, but I'll take care of her."

"Good," Strombeck replied. "We don't need her as a thorn in our side." He started out the door and then looked back at Loggins. "Listen now, be prepared for some harassment on the well. The Coast Guard may start trying to come aboard for all kinds of bullshit safety checks. Don't let them on. We have every right to refuse their entry without a court ordered search. Just make them stay off. I don't know what they're up to, but whatever it is, it couldn't possibly be any good to us."

"I'll be ready," Loggins replied and then closed the door as Strombeck left.

He went back to his desk and reread the Coast Guard directive. They couldn't possibly have any basis for suspecting the real truth, he thought, unless someone had gotten to them. But there was no one. Even Jori and that goddamned doctor friend of hers didn't know what was really going on. He wondered what Sumter would find out at the hospital. Hopefully, he could fill her head with enough things to keep her satisfied and quiet, no matter how pissed off she was about the accident. In a way, he thought, everything would have been better off if she had just died. As he thought about that he smiled. He was very glad to have her off the project and off his back. If he did anything he was going to make sure that she caused him and the company no more trouble.

He wondered what Sumter was telling her. The old man was brilliant, that was for sure. But the strain of the project seemed to have been wearing on him the past few days. He wondered if the scientist was tough enough to hang in there if things got rough. He was glad he had taken the time to warn Sumter about the volatile nature of Jori before he had gone to the hospital. Before he had spoken with him, the physicist did not seem to clearly recognize the potential risk she was. The old coot loved to hear himself talk, and Loggins hoped that somehow he wouldn't slip up and tell her too much. He had better start keeping a close eye on the scientist, he decided, just to make sure, and also that nigger lackey, Hex St. Claire. There was a dangerous man if he had ever seen one.

Capt. Kemper Daniels dropped Ensign Overby off at the headquarters complex and then turned into the officers residential section of the base. The commander's home was at the far eastern point of the Coast Guard property along the beach. Rear Adm. Reggie "Bulldog" MacMahon had been in charge of the Fort Pierce station more than two years, having previously been a district commander along the New England coast. He was a tough, no nonsense sort of commander, typical of New Hampshire, from which he came. Daniels thought at times that he was a bit too conservative, however. Too careful, perhaps. But then again, MacMahon never seemed to screw up, and there were plenty of opportunities for Coast Guard commanders to make mistakes with the new responsibilities of blocking the drug trade as well as monitoring shipping and nautical activities in coastal waters. A more brash, devil-may-care attitude might lead to embarrassing incidents with the Coast Guard storming aboard a ship expecting to find drugs only to find grain instead. It was the sort of thing that was humiliating to the Guard as well as potentially troublesome because of charges of harassment by industry.

The commander's house was a rambling old wooden structure built during World War II, but well taken care of. It resembled a New England house more than a typical Florida dwelling. Daniels was shown to the back porch where Admiral MacMahon was taking his supper alone, as usual, having been widowed some years earlier.

"Ah, come in, Kemper," the commander said to him and rose immediately from his chair.

"Don't let me interrupt you," Daniels said instinctively and the older man returned to his seat.

"Wilma," MacMahon yelled to the maid. "Bring Captain Daniels some coffee. Well, what did you find out? How did they take it?"

"Not well," Daniels responded. "As a matter of fact they absolutely refused. I don't think they're going to cooperate at all. They're hiding something."

"Just as I thought. They wouldn't have any objection to us coming aboard if they weren't doing something out of the ordinary."

"Loggins claims that because it's an experimental rig they have too many technical secrets to allow us to come around. He says they're afraid the other oil companies will steal their ideas."

MacMahon took another bite of his steak, talking while he chewed, using his fork to punctuate his speech. "That may be true, Kemper. I don't blame them on that score. But I'm sure there's more to it than that. There's too many strange things going on out there."

"I want to get aboard it . . . get a look at it. I don't care what they want."

"That's two of us. I can't understand what they'd be wanting to hide. And those photographs we have—strangest looking things I've ever seen on an oil rig. I'm sure there's a purpose to it all, but it looks more like science fiction to me." He continued to eat his meal.

"I put a call in today to Dr. Robson, the one over at Community General. He's the one who told me awhile back that he thought something was wrong out there. Something about some blood problems. Maybe he'll have some thoughts on the matter. He's taking care of the Ashe woman, you know."

"How's she doing, anyway? Maybe we ought to go talk to her."

"Won't do any good from what I've heard. They say that since the accident she's been a little crazy."

"What we need, Kemp, is some solid evidence that there's something peculiar going on over there, and then we can go aboard and find out what it is. Until we get that, our hands are tied."

"You don't think the photos are strange enough? It may be all we're going to get."

"They wouldn't hold up in court, Kemper. I've been there before. I don't want to look like a fool on this."

"Okay," Daniels responded and stood to leave. "I'll keep working on it. Maybe we can come up with something."

The commander stood up with him. "Good. Thanks for coming by. I was wondering how that meeting would go."

Together they walked to the front door. "Now, Kemp, I'm putting it on your back to make sure that we don't have any trouble with this thing. I don't want any harassment of that rig. I don't want any of our vessels hanging around, and I don't want anybody attempting to board it. Let's leave them completely alone until we are ready to move on it."

Daniels frowned. "I'll certainly follow your orders, sir. But if I might, I'd like to say that you're making it very tough on me to gather information on them. I'd like to put an observation boat right next to the rig and keep a much closer watch on them. See exactly what it is that they're doing. I don't see how that'd be illegal."

"That's not the point, Kemper. It's not that it would be illegal to do that. It's just that it's not our responsibility to do that. We're not an investigative agency. We're merely supposed to enforce the law as we see it. But I don't want to push the authority that we do have and take a chance on getting our hands slapped by the courts. Florexco is a big company with lots of financial resources, and a project as big as this one might make them pull out their big guns and go for us if they think we're bugging them. We're just going to have to lay low and hope we come up with something—if there is anything."

"There's no doubt in my mind that there is something," Daniels responded. "There have been too many bizarre accidents out there, too many deaths. Maybe I'm just paranoid, but I'm convinced that there's something happening that Florexco doesn't want to talk about."

The commander nodded. "Maybe you're right. We'll get to the bottom of it. It's just going to take some time. I want to make sure that we do it absolutely by the book."

"I understand, sir. See you in the morning."

Daniels walked down the sidewalk toward his car. He felt frustrated. He respected MacMahon, but he wished the man weren't quite so conservative. Going precisely by the book wasn't going to get the information the Coast Guard needed about this well, and waiting for something to change might take too long. Somehow he felt that time was running out, although he didn't know why. It was just a gut feeling—probably nonsense, he told himself.

NINETEEN

Blain finished with the last patient of the day and hurried to complete his notation in her chart. It was after six and he was anxious to get to the hospital. Tonight he would begin the enlightenment of Jori. He was very pleased with her progress and impatient to begin the process of gently correcting the lies he had been telling.

The previous week had gone exactly as planned. Jori returned rapidly to her old self. Her mind cleared and she became the articulate, perceptive young woman she had been before the accident. It was Blain's observation that she seemed to have sustained no damage to her intellectual capacity. The happy thing was that, combined with the frequent rest periods and the numerous conversations about her past life and present health, Blain and the others were able to keep her mind off the well.

Her hematologic problem had, luckily enough, been resolved. Her bone marrow was rapidly returning to normal function, and her WBC counts, platelet counts, and other parameters were approaching normal in the absence of the lifesaving transfusions. Because she was feeling so frisky, it was becoming difficult to keep her in isolation, and Blain and the others had decided that the time had come to start slowly introducing her to the truth about what had happened. The nightmares had ended and, hopefully, her hysteria regarding the well was over. Blain felt sure that his explanations, as well as talks with Dr. Sumter, would help her to relax and accept the fact that whatever had happened was finished. But he needed a few more days with her before Sumter could be allowed to see her.

As he was about to leave, the phone rang. It was the unlisted number—the one used by the hospital to reach him. He took the call himself. It was Hazel, the chief nurse on Jori's ward.

"Doctor, you'd better come over here quick. Jori's gone crazy. She's extremely angry and threatening to leave the hospital. She doesn't even have any clothes, but she says if we don't get her some, she's going to leave in her robe."

"Why for Pete's sake?" Blain asked excitedly.

"It's a long story," the nurse answered. "But apparently she had some kind of visitor and now she's just gone berserk. She's in there screaming and hollering about you lying to her. She says we're acting like this place is some kind of prison."

"Keep her there until I get there," Blain said angrily. "No matter what, don't let her leave. I'll be right over. Christ!" he said as he put down the phone. He opened the door of his office and yelled to his secretary, "I'm going to the hospital." Without waiting for a response, he exited through the back door.

Adrian Sumter was coming out of a phone booth in the lobby when Blain roared through. "What are you doing here?" he asked the scientist angrily.

"She called me," he said defensively. "Damn it, man! Someone should have told me you were deceiving her."

"What the heck did you say to her?"

"I told her the truth. She wanted to know if we were

355

going to restart the well. I told her we had never stopped, that all the problems had been solved, and that we were drilling like blazes. You should have told me you didn't want her to know that. She went berserk."

"Why the hell did you even come over here? I told you she couldn't have visitors."

"Now you listen for just a minute, Doctor. She called me herself early this afternoon. She said everything was fine, that she was going to be leaving the hospital soon, and she wanted to know what was going on. When I told her that everything was going fine, she sounded a little odd, but she asked me to come over here and tell her all about it. And that's exactly what I did. She met me by the elevators. I never even went into her room. It's certainly not my fault you can't keep your patients under control. It appears to me, it was a little stupid to misinform her like that, anyway."

Blain shook his head back and forth. "Didn't you realize that she'd be fragile at a time like this? We didn't want her to get upset. She's scared to death of that well, so we were telling her whatever was necessary to keep her calm. We planned to little by little bring her up to date about that killer monstrosity of yours."

"I'll tell you one thing," Sumter replied, "she's not just fragile, Robson. She's sick. The girl's gone insane, absolutely insane. She needs help. You had better get her sedated."

Blain was becoming extremely annoyed. "We can't keep the truth from her forever about all the goddamned things that have happened out there. You guys did it to her, not me."

Sumter's angry expression became more intent. "Now you listen to me. You have a very sick patient. She's lucky to be alive. I'm sorry about it. Everybody's sorry about it, but nobody can change the facts. And now the truth is, she's irrational. She's overreacting. She's throwing around some very strange and powerful accusations. For her good, as well as your own and this hospital's, you'd better get her under control and calm her down. She's saying some very dangerous things about me and the oil company. Her mind is not functioning right and I, for one, am not happy to see her this way. We must do something. I suggest that you get her some place where she can get more psychiatric help. Perhaps we should send her to the Mayo Clinic. The company will pay all the expenses, of course."

It suddenly occurred to Blain that Sumter was more than just irritated and angry. He seemed almost scared, worried, but not about Jori, more about things Jori was saying. "I can assure you we'll make the best decisions for her medically, Dr. Sumter, but that's not going to include shipping her out of here."

Sumter clenched his teeth. "We shall see, Robson. We shall see," he said stiffly, and then walked across the lobby and out the door.

Glad that he now knew what had upset Jori and anxious to get her calmed down, he didn't wait for the elevator, but ran up the stairs to the third floor and came onto the ward just down the hall from her room.

A nurse and security guard were standing just outside her door. The woman looked up as he approached. "Oh! Dr. Robson, I'm glad you're here. We're sorry this happened. I don't know where she made her phone call from, but apparently she had a meeting with an older man down in front of the elevators. It's made her extremely upset."

Blain knocked gently on her door, opened it and stepped into the room. She was standing with her back toward him, looking out over the river. "Jori, I'm sorry," he said. "We thought it was the best thing for you."

She turned to stare at him with a cold and defiant expression. "I don't understand how you could lie to me about something so important." Her tone was cool and accusing.

"Jori, we thought it was the best thing for you. You were too hysterical about it."

"I haven't been hysterical for the past few days. What's kept you from breaking the news to me? Are you working for Florexco now like everybody else?" she asked bitterly.

Blain was stunned. "That's unfair, honey. We've been trying to save your life."

"I believe you have, but perhaps you missed the larger point."

"What do you mean?"

"Didn't it occur to you that if Jimmy Jones was killed and I nearly died, that something ought to be done? Didn't it dawn on you that something was wrong out there and that other lives were at risk? Or was one dead nigger and one nearly dead woman not enough to worry about?" she said bitterly.

"Cut it out, Jori." He felt his anger rising. Sumter was right. She was talking irrationally. "We were worried about the problem, but we have every indication that it's been solved. The Coast Guard even checked into it."

"The Coast Guard? What for God's sake does the Coast Guard know about drilling operations? Did you hear Sumter's explanation? The most ludicrous idea I've ever heard. Static electricity! It's preposterous!"

"Look, Jori," he said softly. "You know how I feel about that oil company. I'm on your side, but whatever's caused this accident seems to be under control.

Apparently, there's been a big investigation and the company has done its best to straighten out the problem. Now you need to relax and calm down. You're getting yourself worked up. I know you're upset and frightened about the well, and that's natural because you got hurt real bad there. But in all honesty, there's no basis for shutting down a multi-million dollar operation now that the investigation has shown that the problem is solved."

She shook her head back and forth slowly. "You just don't have any idea what's going on out there, do you?" she said, almost sadly. She took a deep breath and let it out very slowly. "Something's deadly wrong, Blain . . . something unnatural. There are going to be more deaths if we don't stop it. This drilling operation has stumbled on something that we didn't know was there. It defies logical explanation. I know, because I've been out there. I was almost another one of the victims."

Her blue eyes were filled with conviction. "Something's happened to me. I'm not exactly the same person that I was. You may not realize it, but Sumter does. He's scared, Blain—real scared. He doesn't like the things I'm saying because he knows they're the truth. Everything he's been telling you is a lie. Whatever is happening out there—and Lord knows, I don't know what it is—it's not static electricity."

"Okay," he said. "Okay, Jori, maybe you're right. But whatever it is, there's nothing you can do about it now. We'll get in touch with the Coast Guard and anybody else you want to, and we'll have this whole thing looked into. But, you've got to calm down."

"I'll calm down, but I'm leaving the hospital."

"You can't. You're not well."

"I'm well enough. My blood count this morning was just fine. I can rest at home just as nicely as I can here."

Blain's voice grew stern. "It's absolutely out of the question. I will not release you."

"You don't have to release me. I can leave any time I wish."

"You mean you're just going to walk right out of here despite what I say?"

"I'm afraid so, Blain. This is just too important."

Blain's voice grew louder. "This is ridiculous, Jori. It's absurd. You can't do anything about that well, anyway. You've become obsessed."

"Call it what you wish," she said slowly, "but I'm going to do something about that well. I may be the only person who knows the danger. I'm closer to it than anyone. It nearly killed me."

Her mind was set and she was obviously determined. Blain studied her carefully for a moment. She seemed resolute in her decision to leave. It was hopeless to argue, but he really didn't want her to go. Physically, she was almost back to normal, her bone marrow was doing fine, and she was starting to gain back the weight she had lost, but he was afraid of what she might do. He didn't trust her judgment. She was rational enough, obviously not mentally deranged, but she seemed so obsessed—filled with vengeance. He was afraid she might do something irresponsible. No, he decided, he definitely didn't want her to go.

"All right," he said finally, gambling. "Do what the hell you want. Kill yourself if you want to. Go ahead and leave, but you'll be back, I guarantee you. They'll bring you back on a stretcher. You're not ready to leave and you know it. You won't make it out there, Jori."

He turned and started to leave. Her expression was unchanged. He looked back at her one last time. "Jori,

I'm asking you to stay. I've worked too hard to get you this far to have you screw it up by acting irresponsibly. If you leave now, I'm going to be extremely angry, and it'll be your own ignorant fault when they bring you back, if you last that long." He walked out the door.

It was a ploy he had pulled off successfully numerous times with surgical patients who had threatened to leave before they were ready—and even on patients in the emergency room who refused lifesaving surgery. It usually worked. Most of the patients wanted to argue and fight, and throwing the responsibility squarely on their backs for their own death usually knocked them back into reality. He strode briskly down the hall to the elevator, then to the doctors' lounge. He had no idea if the plan would work on Jori. He had a cup of coffee and watched the six o'clock news.

What was it that compelled her so dramatically to try to stop the well? Why was she, of all persons, so distrusting of Dr. Sumter? He hardly heard the news as he waited, pondered the fate of this charming young woman—a woman who had gotten to him a lot more than he had anticipated.

When the program was over, he wandered back to the third floor to her room. He knocked, received no answer, and entered—to be filled with a deep, brooding sense of despair. She was gone.

There was a small note carefully laid on the partially made bed. It read:

Dear Blain,
  Thank you for everything you have done. Good-bye.
                    Love,
                    Jori

TWENTY

It was after 10 o'clock when Blain finished up at the hospital and started for Jori's house. His original anger at her ridiculous stunt had diminished and he was now consumed with anxiety as to how she was doing. No matter how mad she was at him for the deceit, he didn't see how she could be upset if he just checked on her to make sure she was okay. He hoped she was doing as she had said, resting at home. He had a feeling she wasn't.

As he passed Harpoon Harry's, he was relieved to see that her car was not in the parking lot. A minute later he felt even better. Her pickup was sitting in front of her house. The lights were out, and at first he assumed she might be asleep, but he decided to knock anyway. To his dismay no one seemed to be at home. He waited a long while and then knocked again, more loudly than before, but still no response. He walked back and forth on the wooden porch and looked in the window into the living room. The house seemed empty. Finally, he walked around to the side of the house and to the back and looked up and down the beach. There was no one there.

"Damn," he muttered. "What's she trying to pull?" He walked back to the front of the house and stood frustrated beside his car trying to decide where to go to hunt for her.

As he was about to leave, the sound of a boat engine started filtering through the dense stand of seagrape and Australian pines across the road from her house. Beyond the trees lay the river and boat docks belonging to the property owners on the ocean side of the road. There was a small path leading beneath the trees disappearing into the darkness. At first he decided to dismiss the fleeting thought, but then he changed his mind. It was remotely possible she was over at the docks, perhaps even fooling with a boat, the stubborn idiot.

Exasperated, he quickly crossed the road and followed the path which led onto a sandy beach and to a long wooden dock extending more than 100 feet out into the river, at the end of which was tied a beautiful thirty-one-foot Bertram. One engine was running, and in the darkness he could see a lone figure doing something under one of the engine hatches. He started down the dock just as the hatch was closed, and the woman climbed quickly to the flying bridge of the fishing boat. By the time he reached the end of the dock, she had started the second engine. It was definitely Jori.

He stood beside the boat, watching her prepare the vessel to depart. The running lights were turned on and the bilge was pumped dry. It was only as she descended from the bridge into the cockpit, presumably to let the lines go, that she saw him.

She was startled at first, but quickly recovered. "What are you doing? This is private property," she said.

"Jori," he replied, his voice filled with exasperation. "What in the hell are you doing? You are supposed to be resting. You're not well."

"I don't have time to rest right now," she said. "Besides, I really feel good. I do. I'm going to be all right,

363

believe me. I won't hurt myself. I'm not that stupid."

"Where are you going?"

"Out to the rig. I just want to see for myself what's going on out there," she said.

"Jesus Christ! Jori, you're out of your mind. Do you realize how late it is? That's a ten-mile trip in open ocean. You're by yourself. Why don't you go in the damn company boat?"

"I don't think they'd take me. Besides, I don't want anyone to know I'm coming. I want to see what's really happening out there."

"Why don't you wait until in the morning? Give yourself at least a day. My God, checking out of the hospital was one thing, but this is near idiocy."

"Did you have any other reason for coming out here?" she said. "Or did you just want to get into another argument."

His voice softened. "No, I didn't want to get into another argument. I didn't come out here to give you any flack at all. I was worried about you. I wanted to check on you. I'm your doctor."

"Thanks, but no thanks," she said. "I'm okay now and you don't need to worry about me every minute. I'm a big girl. I'll keep checking in with you, but for now you've got to let me do what I need to."

"What do you think you'll find out by going out there tonight?"

"I don't have any idea. That's why I've got to go. I've got to start some place. I know there's something funny going on from the way Sumter acted."

"Is there any way I can talk you out of this?"

"No, Blain, but I appreciate your concern, I really do. You're a good doctor."

"I'm coming with you then," he responded.

"Why?" she asked. "What concern is it of yours? I think it'd be a waste of your time."

"You're my patient. That makes it my concern and I won't take no for an answer. If you're going, I'm going with you, if only to watch over you and make sure you're okay." He climbed into the boat and looked around. "Where's the beer?" he said. "I never ride in boats without drinking beer."

She smiled. "You're as crazy as I am." She looked up and down at him. "You're not even dressed for boating. You look like a city slicker to me." She pointed to the ropes attached to the back of the boat. "You get these lines and I'll get the ones forward."

He quickly took the rope loose from the cleats and tossed it onto the dock, while she let loose the bow line and went back up to the bridge and took the controls. She looked down into the cockpit where he was standing holding the boat off the pilings. "There's one more thing you need to know before we leave."

He glanced up at her. "What's that?"

"The beer is in the icebox down in the cabin." She smiled, turned back to the controls, pushed them into forward gear and the boat slipped away from the dock.

He quickly secured two beers, climbed up to the bridge, sat down beside her and popped the cans open. He held his up in a mock toast. "To lunacy," he said.

She clinked her can against his and smiled. "To lunacy."

"Are you sure you've got enough gas to make this trip out there and back?" he asked. "And besides, how are you going to find the well in the dark?"

"Just aim at it, dummy. The lights can be seen for

twenty miles."

"What about a radio and life jackets and things like that."

"They're all in the cabin below," she said, continuing to grin.

"Where are the seasick pills?"

"The Dramamine's in there," she said pointing to a small drawer to the side of the console. He opened it, got one out and immediately swallowed it with his beer. "Any other questions?" she asked as she turned the boat into the center of the river and headed south toward the inlet.

"Yeah. Have you ever driven one of these things before?"

"No. But I've read the manual."

"Wonderful," he said. "You'd better let me take over. This looks like a job for a man."

She laughed out loud. "Listen, buster, you better hold on. This machine can really fly and I'm going to put it in high gear. I don't have all night to wait getting out there."

"Is the sea rough tonight?" he asked.

"No, the weather report said less than three feet. It should be like riding on a lake."

"Good, because I don't want to lose my supper. I paid too much for it."

She smiled and the conversation ended as she turned past the last marker and headed into the inlet. As the weather station had reported, the sea was calm. There were a few large swells coming through the inlet, but after that it was a smooth ride. As soon as they passed the sea buoy half a mile out from the inlet, she put the compass on 95 degrees and headed into the darkness of the sea. In the distance were the faint lights of St. Lucie One.

They sat silently for a long while as the beach disappeared behind them. The lights of the large condominiums a little south of the inlet looked warm and comforting. But before long even they dimmed and fell back into the distance as they raced over the dark waters toward their target ahead. As the well began to loom up in front of them, the jolly mood they had been in earlier disappeared to be replaced by one of uneasy anticipation and intense curiosity.

"There's more light," she said as they got within a mile. "They must be pushing hard as they can go. I'm positive they've got the place better lit up." A few minutes later they were much closer. She stood up, squinting her eyes and staring intently up toward the working decks of the drill platform. "There's a lot more workers there than usual," she said. She paused for a moment as they went closer. "They look funny, Blain. They're wearing something strange."

He stood beside her trying to make out the distant outlines of the men working. His feeling of nervousness grew. He ignored it, but a strange sense of foreboding came over him. He didn't understand it. He glanced toward Jori. Her expression was cold and tense. She was staring intently at the giant structure ahead. Outlined against the dark night sky, it looked ominous and powerful. The working decks were brilliantly lit up, but the derrick above had alternating areas of darkness and light. At the very top a brilliant red flasher blinked intermittently.

As she pulled the engines back into idle speed, her expression changed into one of surprise. "Oh my God," she muttered and a moment later he realized why.

The workers on the rig looked distinctly abnormal. He had never seen anything like it before. They were wearing bulky, very heavy-appearing suits covered with a metallic outside lining. They seemed to glow in the reflection of the lights. They wore gloves and boots of the same bulky material, but the most startling was the head piece. It was a large silver helmet with a curved face plate of reflective mirrored glass. The face of the wearer was totally invisible. The men looked like something out of the future, more like astronauts than oil workers.

"I don't believe it," Jori said, glancing quickly at him. "Something's crazy out here." They looked up into the glowing face plates of several workers, leaning over the edge of the platform looking down at the small boat below as it eased its way around the bottom of the rig toward the landing platform.

A large sign, newly erected, had been placed on each of the legs illuminated by a bright light. It read: "Private Property. Do Not Approach Within 100 Yards."

"Those are new," Jori said. "I don't even think it's legal."

A loudspeaker underneath the main deck suddenly came to life booming its message at a tremendous volume. "Please leave this area. Private vessels are not allowed to approach within 100 yards. This is a dangerous area. Please leave this area immediately." The quality of the speaker was harsh and authoritarian. A spotlight was turned on them from above and the loudspeaker repeated its message.

Blain was nervous. "Are you sure we should be doing this?" he said quietly to Jori.

"I'm not so sure about anything, but we're going in. Something's wrong out here. I know it is. This is not normal for an oil well."

He grimaced and looked back up at the ominous structure and the austere, almost frightening appearance of the men above them.

They rounded the northern leg and turned in toward the landing platform. There was a guard booth located in the center of the deck and from it emerged a man dressed as the others in the silver suit and helmet. In his right hand he was carrying some sort of weapon. It looked like a semiautomatic rifle. In his left, he had a bullhorn loudspeaker.

The man put the speaker to his lips. "Keep clear of this area. This is private property. You must leave this area at once. Do not attempt to come any closer."

Jori headed the boat straight into the landing dock.

The man's voice became more threatening. "I repeat—keep clear of this area. You must leave at once. No vessels are allowed within 100 yards of this rig. This is private property. This is a dangerous zone."

Jori continued to head straight into the dock. When they were less than twenty yards away, the man put down the bullhorn and held his weapon with both hands. A moment later, a second guard came out of the booth similarly armed. Jori turned on the boat's spotlight and shined it into their faces. They lit up like mirrors. The highly polished silver helmets reflected the spotlight in eerie, jerking movements about the rest of the landing deck and onto the bottom of the platform above. The two stood at the edge of the platform, their weapons ready. There was sudden movement at the top of the stairs from the main deck above, and a third man similarly dressed, with a weapon slung over his shoulder, came quickly down to join the other two.

Jori glanced at Blain as the boat made a final approach into the dock. "Here goes nothing," she said. "We may have a little trouble."

For the first time he noted an element of anxiety in her voice and her expression was less confident than before. Blain wished desperately she would turn the boat around and leave. The rig seemed awesome and foreboding. There was obviously something here that someone wanted well protected. It seemed distinctly possible that harm could befall them if someone made a mistake.

There was suddenly a loud ringing clank and a group of spotlights came on, completely illuminating the boat and the landing area. He could hear a small bell ringing in the distance and the sound above them of more men moving about on the deck. Behind all of this and unchanging was the steady throbbing drone of the giant engines high on the derrick. Through the opening at the top of the stairs, he occasionally got a glimpse of the reflections of the red beacon high above the well. The brilliant lights and the latticework of the steel created a maze of light and darkness in eerie shadows across the base of the well and upon the waters below. St. Lucie One was definitely not a friendly place to be. It was of no comfort to Blain to recognize that Jori, who should have been completely familiar with these surroundings, seemed to be puzzled and nervous. She took the boat out of gear, then popped it into reverse just for an instant, and the vessel gently bumped against the railings of the dock.

Before she could speak, the largest of the guards stepped forward and swung his large booted foot with tremendous force into the side window of the boat's cabin. There was a shattering of glass. He slammed the butt of his gun onto the side of the flying bridge.

"Goddamn it, lady, I told you to stay away from here!" he yelled, his voice filled with anger. "Now get this goddamn boat out of here before I tear it up."

Jori stared at him, but saw only the distorted reflection of herself and the boat in the front of his helmet. "You're going to pay for that, mister," she responded and climbed down into the cockpit where she picked up a large gaff and swung it in the direction of the men, who stepped back quickly. "I'm Jori Ashe. I work here. I'm in charge of drilling. So take these lines and tie this boat up."

No one moved. "Lady," the man said again. "I'm telling you one more time to get this boat out of here, and if you swing that gaff at me again I'll break your neck."

Jori replaced the gaff and looked up at Blain. "Get the front line and I'll take the back." She picked up the rear line and stepped to the edge of the boat and started to climb out. The guard closest to her moved over and using the butt of his weapon pushed her gently back into the boat.

Jori grew furious. "You son of a bitch!" she said. One of the men lifted his weapon up and pointed it toward her. She turned instantly and disappeared into the cabin. A moment later she came back up carrying a snubnose .38. "This is normally for sharks, but I guess you guys'll do," she said pointing it at the taller of the three.

The other two guards slowly raised their weapons.

"Lady, you're looking for real trouble. You're trespassing on private property and under federal law we can blow you out of the water. If you don't get out of here we may have to do exactly that."

"No, you're not," she said. "I work for Florexco. I'm in charge of drilling."

"You're not on our list, so you'll have to leave. And if

371

you don't put that gun down someone's going to be hurt, and, whoever else it is, it's going to include you and your friend." He glanced toward Blain.

"Jori, I think they're serious," he said. "Maybe we better go."

"Not until I get aboard and see what's going on here," she said without taking her eyes off of the men.

"There's absolutely no chance of that, lady. The only way you're getting aboard here is to come on a crew boat with an I.D., and have your name on our list."

"Don't be so sure," she said. "Call Loggins or Dr. Sumter. Get one of them down here. Tell them it's Jori Ashe. They'll be glad to talk to me, and if they don't want to come, get Skip Majors or maybe Carl Young or how about Leo Silverchief." She called off several names of the other workers. "Ask one of them to come down and verify who I am. You guys aren't going to bluff me. I'm coming aboard."

The tall guard nodded to the man on his right who promptly went into the booth. A few minutes later he emerged and rejoined the others.

Blain climbed down from the bridge and spoke quietly to Jori. "Why don't we just leave. This has the potential for an accident. I think these guys mean business."

"Give me a few more minutes," she said quietly. "I don't want to have wasted this whole trip." The light coming through the opening at the top of the stairs was suddenly blocked by a tall figure. He stood surveying the scene for a few seconds and then came slowly and deliberately down toward them. The three guards stepped back deferentially as the man approached the edge of the dock and looked down into the boat.

Jori peered hard into the man's face plate, hoping to

get a glimpse at his face, but it was to no avail. He looked first at Jori, then at Blain, then walked up and down, looking at the boat. He stood motionless, staring at them for almost half a minute and then turned toward the taller of the guards and slowly and dramatically raised his hand with a clenched fist, thumb out, pointing toward the open ocean. He turned, walked across the deck and, never looking back, started up the stairs.

Jori watched him ascend to join another figure standing in the shadows just beneath the entranceway to the platform above. The two of them seemed to engage in a brief conversation, and then they both disappeared through the portal above.

"Lady," the tall guard said, "the man says no. You're going to have to leave." One of the other guards disappeared into the booth and came back out again carrying a large axe. "I'm going to tell this gentleman to begin disassembling the top of your boat if you're not out of here in thirty seconds," the guard continued. "It's your choice. Leave now with one broken window or leave in ten minutes with a chopped up cabin. It's up to you."

What had been a stalemate now became obviously a loss for Jori and she slowly put down the gun. Without another word she went to the bridge, put the engines into gear and slowly backed out of the docking area. A few minutes later she was clear of the platform. She slowly spun the boat around and accelerated the engines and turned the craft into the wind, headed toward the inlet.

Blain sat beside her feeling weak and mentally exhausted at the encounter. He looked up at the woman standing to his left. With the wind in her hair and the glow of the running lights illuminating her pretty face she looked extremely feminine. God knows she's more than that, he thought. He had seen a side of her tonight he hadn't known existed. For the first time he understood how she had survived in the rough and tough men's world of offshore drilling. Jori Ashe was one strong lady.

He looked behind them, watching the well grow smaller as they moved away from it. From a distance it did not seem so awesome or so frightening. From a distance it did not appear to be anything to be afraid of, but he knew better. Something was wrong out there. Someone was very intent on keeping the place secure from the eyes of strangers. He looked up again at Jori. She still had not spoken. "What do you think?" he said.

She glanced down at him. "It's trouble—bad trouble. I've never seen an offshore rig with that kind of security, and I don't know of any reason for oil workers to wear that kind of protective suit. There's a lot more to this thing than meets the eye. I don't have any idea what's going on, but I'm going to find out. My father gave his life to this business and working for this company has nearly taken mine. Whatever Florexco's doing out there, I have a right to know. If those bastards think they can stop me, they've got another think coming. They can't just brush me aside like a broken toy. This well has killed too many people. You've got to understand that I don't have any choice—not now—not after what they've done to me. I've just got to continue on this thing until I find out what it's all about and I'm not going to let them stop me." She looked down at Blain and then back toward the approaching inlet.

Blain nodded, but he didn't speak. If there was one thing he knew now, it was that Jori had the courage to do what she thought was right, whatever that was. It frightened him, because big money was involved, and big money wouldn't worry about the feelings or the safety of a pretty lady geologist who got in their way.

It was after midnight by the time Jori finally brought the boat through the inlet and turned north. She was still silent, introspective, and largely uncommunicative with Blain. It was obvious to him that her loss of round one in this battle in no way signaled the end of her willingness to fight. If anything, it had strengthened her commitment to uncover what was going on. This became very evident as she headed the boat toward the Florexco docks.

"What are you doing?" he asked. "Your docks are farther up the river."

"We're going to stop by my office at the company headquarters for a few minutes. I have an idea."

"What kind of idea?" he asked suspiciously.

"There may be a simpler way to find out what's going on than beating my head against the wall out at the rig," she responded. "It's probably all summarized very nicely. Sitting right here in this building just waiting to be read."

"But from what I've seen so far, you may not be that welcome."

"They won't stop me from going to my own office to get a few things."

"And I suppose the fact that the information you're looking for won't be sitting on your desk won't deter you from looking until you find where it is, will it?" he said, as he realized what she was thinking.

She grinned smugly and throttled back the engines as they approached the docks. Very quickly she brought the boat alongside and the two of them tied the lines. As they finished, the night watchman came hurrying out toward them.

"Miss Ashe," he said surprised. "What are you doing

here? I thought you were still in the hospital."

"No, Lynley," she said to the old man who was carrying a time clock. "I got out today. I'm doing a lot better."

"I'm mighty glad to hear that," he replied. "What are you doing here tonight?"

"We were just out for a moonlight cruise and one of the engines started acting up. I think I may leave the boat here tonight and have someone check on it in the morning."

"That shouldn't be any problem," he said. "Would you like me to call someone to take you home?"

"No, I think we can just walk. It's a pretty night and it's not more than a few miles up the road to my place. I think I'll stop by my office on the way out, though. I have a few things I want to get."

The man's expression changed. "I'll have to come with you in that case," he said. "Things have gotten real tight around here lately. We have strict orders that no one is to go in or out of the building without tight security. Things aren't like they used to be. I guess everybody's a little edgy what with all the accidents and all."

"When did all this start?" she asked.

"Right after you got hurt. I guess it was because they moved Dr. Sumter's office and lab into the building. They don't want to take any chances with all his stuff."

"I don't blame them. Which office is he using?"

"He took over the old conference room right next door to you."

"I see," she replied. "Well, why don't you take Dr. Robson and myself down to my office so we can get out of here. It's getting late and I'll admit I'm a little tired."

"Right," he said. "You got the boat tied down good?"

She nodded and then followed the old man down the dock and into the building. The extra security was noticeable. New locks seemed to have been placed on the doors and some of the lightweight interior doors had been replaced with heavy duty ones. Clearly, they did not want anyone snooping around the Florexco building.

He led them through the outer lobby and down a corridor to her office. The door was locked.

"Oh no," she said innocently. "I didn't expect it to be locked. I never worried about anyone going in or out. Do you have a key?"

He frowned. "I used to. That is until they changed all of these. My master doesn't work on any of the offices on this corridor any more."

"I really wanted to get in there. Are you sure there's not a master somewhere?"

"Well," he said hesitantly. "We have one in the security office."

"Oh great," she said. "That'll save me a lot of trouble. Could I possibly borrow it?"

The guard seemed uncomfortable. "I'm not supposed to," he said. "It's a master for this entire wing. We keep it in the security safe and they said under no circumstances to use it. But what the heck," he grinned. "I guess there's no harm done. Just keep it to yourself. Come on, let's go get it."

They followed him down the hall, across the main lobby and into the security office, where he carefully opened a small combination safe and pulled out a key ring with one key. "If this won't open it, nothing will," he said.

"Do you have any coffee here, Lynley?" Jori asked.

"Sure do," he responded. "If there's one thing a night watchman has to have plenty of, it's coffee. Let me make you a cup."

"Super," she said. "Make one for Dr. Robson, too. I really appreciate this." She turned to Blain. "By the way, I'm sorry I haven't introduced the two of you before. Lynley McCreary, I'd like you to meet Dr. Blain Robson. He took care of me while I was in the hospital."

The night watchman smiled broadly. "It's a pleasure to meet you, sir," he said. "Let me get that coffee."

"Good," Jori said. "Go ahead and do that. I'll take the key, run over and unlock my office. I'll bring it back, and you can have it in the safe before you even finish mixing up the first cup."

The man hesitated, seemed slightly embarrassed for a second, and then smiled again. "Go ahead. Let me get the coffee for you. Just hurry back with it."

She took the key and left the room quickly, while the old man carefully poured two cups of coffee, and, opening the cabinet beneath the pot, pulled out a small bowl of sugar and artificial creamer. "How do you like yours mixed, Doc?" he asked, and then poured a third cup for himself. As he was doing so, Jori returned.

"Now get this key locked up where it's supposed to be," she said and picked up her own cup of coffee and took a long sip. She was carrying a small folder of papers. "I got what I needed, Lynley," she said to the older man as he closed the safe. "We'll head back now. I appreciate your help a lot, I really do. Tell them in the morning that I'll be around to get the boat sometime."

"Will do," he answered and smiled again. "Let me show you out. I need to lock the door behind you. You locked your office up real good, didn't you?"

"Oh yes," she responded. "I wouldn't want anybody stealing my secrets."

Lynley chuckled. "You've got to watch this one every minute," he said, poking Blain in the ribs gently. "She's no lilting Jill by any means."

"That I'll agree with," Blain replied. "She doesn't take anything off of anybody."

They stepped out into the night air and the guard prepared to lock the door behind them. "Glad to see you out and about, Miss Ashe. Now you take care of yourself." He waved and pulled the door shut between them and conscientiously locked it.

Blain and Jori started slowly down the side of the building toward the entrance of the parking lot. In the distance they could see the guard booth out on the main road. The light was on. The guard was sitting inside. He had apparently not yet seen them.

"Come on, hurry," she said as soon as they were around the corner of the building in the shadows. "I left a window in my office unlocked. I want to get back in before he has time to check the doors up and down the hall."

"For Christ sake, why?" Blain responded hurrying to follow her. "You just left there."

She didn't answer but went quickly to the window outside her office. The screen was loose and the window was slightly ajar. She hurriedly removed the screen and laid it on the ground and pushed the window all the way open. "Give me a hand," she said, and with his assistance climbed into the building. "Come on in," she said turning back toward him. He lifted himself up to the sill and then swung his legs through the window and a moment later was inside. She quickly pulled down the window and went across her office and stood by the door listening carefully. There was no noise to be heard. She opened the door very carefully, peeked out, saw that there was no one in the hall and then, signaling to him, stepped out into the hallway with him right behind her. She locked her door from the inside and pulled it shut.

"What in the hell are you doing?" he whispered.

"Shh," she said quietly and tiptoed to the office next door and opened it and stepped in. The name printed on the outside was *Adrian Sumter*.

She quickly closed the door and locked it, and they stood alone in the darkness. "I unlocked it when I had the key, dope head," she said. "Why do you think I wanted to use it myself instead of letting him bring us down here? I wanted to get back in here before he had a chance to come down and check those doors. I'm sure he will. He's a compulsive watchman. Couldn't you see that he didn't want to let me use the key?"

"Holy Cow," he whispered. "You're unpredictable. You're going to get me killed, I know it."

She held a finger to her lips and, a moment later, they heard the sound of someone coming down the hall. There was the distant sound of a doorknob being checked and then one even closer and then, finally, the door behind which they were standing was tested. A few more doors were checked, and then they heard the sound of the man's gait moving away from them down the hall.

"Now," she whispered, "I think we're safe here. Let's see what we can find out." She went first to the window and pulled the drapes shut, carefully closing the Venetian blinds behind them. Then she bent the gooseneck fluorescent lamp down very close to the desk on which it was standing and turned the light on. She looked back at the drapes. "I doubt if this little light is very visible outside. What do you think?"

"I'm sure they won't notice it, but hurry. I don't want to spend a lot of time here. I'm not trained for this sort of thing."

She began to shuffle through the papers scattered on the desk and he looked around the room. It was a large office. On one wall, in the dim light, he could make out a large, meticulously drawn, very impressive geological chart. It was labeled: "Geological Structures at the Proposed Site—St. Lucie One." On the other wall was a series of eight small photographs, arranged in two rows. Each was the close-up of a different man, none of whom were recognizable to Blain. He looked more closely at the names beneath each picture and recognized three of them as Nobel Prize winners. He assumed the others were also.

Beside the pictures was a large calendar. With a red marker, a group of three days had been circled: the fourteenth, fifteenth and sixteenth of December. "Look at this," he said to Jori. "What do you suppose this means?"

She glanced up at the calendar. A puzzled expression crossed her face. "I don't know. That starts tomorrow. I wonder if it has anything to do with the well?" She shrugged and returned to the papers on the desk.

Finding nothing, she opened the large drawer on the right side and peered into it. She brought out a large, thick manila folder and a brown leather-covered note-book and set them on the desk in front of her.

The leather book was imprinted with rich, gold lettering: *Personal Journal of Adrian Sumter.* "If this doesn't tell us something, I don't know what will," she said and flipped through the pages to the latest entry. It was dated as of the previous evening. They read it together:

December 13, Palm Beach—The situation is deteriorating rapidly. Although the drilling is going faster than ever, I am beginning to wonder if I will be allowed to achieve the success that is rightfully mine. I am afraid that the people around me are going to bring me down.

I saw the Ashe girl this afternoon. How sad it is that I cannot share this great scientific adventure with her. She was nearly hysterical about the drilling and seems determined to stop it if she can. She could possibly become dangerous to us. I hope not. She seems like such a nice girl. Because of her illness, she probably will not be listened to. I know for a fact, she has no idea as to what we are doing. She is mainly suspicious about the easy drilling and the possible defects in the tectonic plate. If only she knew what we are about to accomplish. But we must hurry.

I am having some difficulty with Florexco itself. The fools are motivated only by money. Fortunately, Strombeck and Loggins have believed everything I have fed them about the economic windfall should we discover the Balthorium. How can they be so naive? It would take billions to develop a way to retrieve the element and use it successfully. The real reward is in the scientific achievement of having proven that the element exists; and being the first to reach the mantle itself would be a glorious honor.

I hope I can hold this uneasy alliance together for just a few more days, but I have told so many lies and half-truths, I am afraid of losing control.

Hex continues to be worried, God love him. He has been so loyal to me. I must reward him somehow. I have told him everything I know about the Soviet debacle. I believe I can avoid the tragedy that befell them. The men are probably safe enough with their new protective suits and I suspect that the well itself can withstand another short blast of radiation were it to occur.

I had hoped to make a slower, studied, and safer approach to the Balthorium, but now as we are within a day or two of reaching our goal, I am forced to speed up rather than slow down the advancement of the drill. I cannot take a chance on being stopped by the company or other, outside, forces. I know we are being watched closely. I realize that I am taking a risk, but I am being forced into it by the imbeciles who would choose to have me abandon this historic effort.

Nature and fate willing, by the time of my next entry into this journal, I will have accomplished what we have set out to do—what the Russians could not do. It should be a moment of glory for mankind.

I have prepared a press release and have begun work on the scientific papers for publication. It has been a long and strenuous effort, and I am nearly exhausted. The calculations and work have been immense, but I have double checked all the figures. With any luck, we should be safe.

I just wish Hex were happier about it. He can be so difficult sometimes.

I hope we lose no more lives, but I am ready to pay that price if we must. Whatever risks we are taking, the challenge is worth it. With each advancing yard of the drill, I know I am closer to my rightful destiny.

"My God," Blain said when he had finished reading. "The man's crazy. What's he talking about—the Russians?"

"I'm not sure," she answered. "There was something about it in his book, but it's all very sketchy." She put the journal aside and picked up the folder. A white label had been pasted on the front: BALTHORIUM. After a quick glance at Blain, she turned back the cover and for the next half hour silently studied the scientific summary accumulated by Dr. Sumter about the mythical element. There were a great many equations and computer printouts and several copies of other articles by geophysicists and mathematicians. There was even one that was an apparent translation from Russian.

Finally, there was a three-page summary bringing together the major scientific theories about the nature of Balthorium. It was written in basically nontechnical language, obviously designed to explain the new element to a layman. There were three copies. Jori removed one, folded it and pushed it into her pocket.

"I don't understand what this all means," Blain said again.

"I think I do." Her tense expression increased the anxiety that Blain was beginning to feel. For the first time, he began to sense that they might be in significant danger if discovered. What they had been looking at was obviously very sensitive, and perhaps dangerous, information.

"I don't know where to start explaining this," she said quietly. "But it's much bigger than I even imagined. I'm not enough of a geophysicist to understand everything

384

that I've read, but I believe the man may be on a suicide mission."

"What's Balthorium?" Blain asked. "And what's it all got to do with a Russian well?"

"He wants to drill through the crust into the mantle, and, if the information here is true at all, there's a risk it could turn into a disaster—maybe destroying more than just the well. Apparently, something happened to the Russians when they tried it. Sumter wrote about it in his book."

She looked around on the book shelves and found a copy of *Seek the Distant Shore*. She pulled it down, opened it to the section about the Russian accident and handed it to Blain. "Look at this," she said, and silently read it with him, glancing frequently to study his changing expressions.

"Incredible!" he said when he was finished. "What is it that everyone thinks destroyed the Russians?"

"I've never heard the theory, but by putting two and two together, I get the impression that Sumter thinks it was Balthorium they were after, and somehow it destroyed them all."

"And you think he's trying to do the same thing now?"

"He must be. According to his papers, the presence of something like Balthorium is the only thing that really explains the accidents we've had. Maybe that's what's put him onto it."

"And you think if he keeps going the same thing could happen here that happened to the Russians with the whole rig being destroyed, everyone killed?"

"Worse than that, Blain. It might not be just the rig that goes up. There's apparently some information that the Russians lost more than just their drilling operations.

385

It's rumored that they caused an earthquake."

"How?"

"I never understood it before, but if everything Sumter says about Balthorium is true and, if the element does exist, it's pretty simple to understand. The deposits of Balthorium that existed, if they did exist, would be located right in the upper regions of the mantle just beneath the crust."

"Right," he said. "I understood that part. The rest of the Balthorium would have been used up eons ago with just a tiny bit left in these cooler layers."

"Yes," she replied. "So now along comes a drill bit churning into it, and the friction drives the heat sky high. All of a sudden the temperature passes critical take-off point and the fission reaction starts. The heat created by the smaller reaction gets the surrounding Balthorium going and, before you know it, a huge chain reaction has been triggered, generating a tremendous amount of energy all along the thin layer of Balthorium. The energy has no way to dissipate so pressures build up and eventually they are great enough to cause a shifting of the tectonic plates in the crust above. And what do you have then? An earthquake, a movement of the tectonic plate. And what's even worse, there's no assurance that the reaction would be limited to the area of drilling. Once the reaction got started, it might run for hundreds of miles beneath the crust, creating stresses that would be relieved only by a massive movement of the crust above. The potential earthquake could be astronomical in scope. The potential damage done is unthinkable."

"You think that might have happened to the Russians?"

"Nobody knows. It all took place in the middle of

Siberia. The word is there were no survivors anywhere around to tell the tale."

"Surely Sumter's considered all these things and has a plan to prevent this kind of thing from happening."

"I'm afraid he's gone crazy with ambition, Blain. It looks like he thinks he can stop the drilling just as they reach the Balthorium, before enough friction had occurred to raise the temperature high enough to set it off. But I don't buy it. What if the Balthorium that he drills into is only a few degrees below its critical temperature already? After all, the temperature down there goes up 150 degrees centigrade for every mile you descend. Even leaving lots of room for error, that still means that the temperatures are going to be damn hot when you get close to the mantle, and it could be that the stuff's sitting there just a few degrees away from what it needs to take off. It might be that just punching the drill into it would be all it would need to raise the temperature enough to get it going." She paused, thinking for a moment. "Do you know what would happen along the Florida coast if he caused even a mild earthquake offshore?"

Blain stared at her intently.

"Tidal wave," she said quietly. "Any earthquake at all would probably generate a tidal wave that would wreak havoc upon everything near the beach. The land elevation around here is so low, anyway."

"Jori, let's get out of here. I think if we got caught we might be in serious trouble."

"I think Sumter's putting his whole career on the line here," she said quietly. "Even though he's well-known, he's never quite achieved the recognition from among his peers that he wants. This may be his one shot at it. I think he's going to go for this, come hell or high water. If he wins, great. And if he loses, who gives a damn—because to him it was well worth the shot. We've got to stop him. It could be a disaster if we don't."

"I don't see any question in that. We can't do it though. Let's get to the Coast Guard."

Before she could speak, they heard voices coming down the hall.

"But I told you that no unauthorized persons were to come down this hall." The voice was distinctly Loggins's.

"But I thought she was authorized. Her office is down here." It was Lynley, the guard. "She works here, doesn't she?"

"Not any more, goddamn it. What the hell did she say she wanted anyway?"

"She just needed some papers. I saw what she took. It wasn't much, just one folder."

"How'd she get in anyway? I thought this place was kept locked up."

"She had her own key," the guard lied. "I had to open the outside doors for her, of course, but she had her key to her office."

"And you stayed with her the whole time. She never got out of your sight?"

"Yes, sir, Mr. Loggins. I did exactly what I was supposed to do. I was with her every second. We didn't go anywhere but straight into this office and straight out."

She heard the knob being jiggled next door—her office. Thank God she had locked it. "If they left so quick, how come the guard out front didn't see them go out?" Loggins asked, his voice filled with vexation.

"That's something you'll have to ask him," Lynley replied. "That's his responsibility, not mine. Maybe he was goofing off."

"Yeah," Loggins responded sarcastically. "Get me the key. I want to see what's in here." The sound of Lynley's shoes disappeared down the hall, and they could hear Loggins muttering to himself. Suddenly he was just outside their door. They could sense his hand on the knob as it turned slowly, hit resistance and then wiggled back and forth quickly several times. His footsteps went down the hall. They could hear other knobs jiggling and doors being tested. Obviously satisfied, he went back down toward her old office, and a moment later Lynley returned. They heard the door being opened and her desk drawer being pushed back and forth. Through the wall, the conversation was mumbled, but within a short time her door was being closed.

"From now on, keep her out of here," Loggins said. "And tell that stupid turd at the gate to get his head out of his ass and pay attention to what's going on. If people can just walk out of here without being detected, you know damn well they could sneak in. I'm going to be in my office. If anybody calls for me, let me know."

One set of footsteps went down the hall, and a door opened and then closed as the other sounds disappeared in the direction of the lobby.

Jori's heart was racing. Thank God she had locked all the doors.

"We'll have to get out of here by the window," Blain said quietly as she replaced the folder and Sumter's journal into the drawer from which they had come. They turned off the light, opened the drapes and slowly lifted the Venetian blinds. They peered out over the deserted parking lot. It was empty. From their view they could not see the guard booth on the main road. Their exit from the window would undoubtedly go unobserved, but they would have to be very quiet. Loggins was less than fifty feet away. But, since no one suspected they were still in the compound, their escape would be easy. The only touchy part would be the guard. He had probably already been criticized by Lynley and would now be more alert than usual.

They opened the window very quietly. She went out first, and he came right behind. Once on the ground the window was carefully closed, and following his lead, they both removed their shoes. After glancing cautiously around the corner to make sure the guard was still in his booth, they ran silently across the parking lot, avoiding the lighted areas, and soon found themselves in the dark next to the tall fence surrounding the compound. Instead of turning toward the gate they went west toward the beach following the fence several hundred yards to where it went up over the dune and down across the beach below.

Fortunately it was low tide and the fence extended out into the water only a few yards. It was a simple matter to wade out beyond the end of it and then scramble back up onto the beach outside the Florexco borders. Smiling with relief, they ran a hundred yards or so down the soft sand and then slowed down to a walk.

Jori was exhausted and she looked it. "Are you all right?" Blain asked.

She nodded, too breathless to speak. "Yes, I'll be all right. Let's get out of here."

Carrying their shoes, walking high up on the beach where the sand was packed hard, they started the long trek toward her house. In the distance they could see the faint lights of St. Lucie One.

TWENTY-ONE

A little after eight the next morning they told the story to the Coast Guard. Admiral MacMahon and Captain Daniels listened gravely as Jori detailed her interpretation of the well, the accidents and the ultimate purpose of the drilling. They were very curious about the discussion of Balthorium and even had a copy made of the sheets she had removed from Sumter's office. Each of them studied with interest the section in Jori's copy of *Seek the Distant Shore* where Sumter gave his opinion about the Russian accident.

"There's one thing I still don't understand," Mac-Mahon said. "That is, how deep is the drilling at the present time?"

"I don't know," Jori answered. "I don't have any way to guess. It all depends upon whether the drilling was going as easy as it was before my accident."

"If what you say is true, and they are very close to having some sort of serious problem," MacMahon said, "then they would have to be 40,000 to 45,000 feet down by now. That's eight or nine miles. I don't see how they could possibly have gotten that far."

"Maybe I didn't explain that adequately," Jori answered, "but it's been one of the strange things about this whole project. We never hit anything solid, at least, not while I was there. We were drilling as much as 2000 feet a day at one point. It was just sand. The only limit in the day's progress was how fast we could insert the new piping."

MacMahon shook his head. "Frankly, that's just very hard for me to believe, Miss Ashe. I've been around a lot of offshore drilling, and I just don't see how anyone could go 40,000 feet in this short a period of time."

Jori let out a long, slow breath in exasperation. "I told you, I don't understand it either. Dr. Sumter didn't understand it. Nobody understood it. There was something wrong where we were drilling. There was some sort of opening or defect in the crust . . . or maybe something even stranger."

"Like what?" Daniels asked.

She glanced at Blain and then back at the two Coast Guard officers. She hesitated, doubtful that she should mention it, but finally blurted it out. "Sumter thought that it might be a previously undiscovered geological anomaly." She paused again. "There was even the remote possibility that the hole had been predrilled by another civilization—someone looking for energy."

MacMahon glanced at Daniels. "You mean some kind of advanced civilization from long ago or maybe even visitors from outer space—something like that?"

"Yes. That's what Sumter said." She looked embarrassed and uncomfortable. She glanced at Blain. "I know it sounds crazy, but that's what he said. I don't have any idea why the drilling went so easy."

"I see," MacMahon said, skeptically as he rubbed his chin. He seemed to have made up his mind. "We appreciate very much your coming to us with this information, Miss Ashe, and you too, Dr. Robson. You both have been very cooperative. Unfortunately, I'm not sure that there is any action that we can take right at the present. You see, we can't go aboard that well and do anything to stop them unless we've got some firm evidence that something is going wrong out there. What you've given us, as I'm sure you understand, is pure speculation. There's no proof at all that the rig is engaged in what you're talking about.

"I think that we're going to have to study this issue a little more and see if we can round up some hard data. If we knew, for example, exactly how deep they were drilling, and if it turned out to be 35,000 or 40,000 feet, then I think we would have grounds to act. That's the sort of information a court needs to give us reasonable cause. Anything less than that and I think we could justifiably be accused of harassment. You have suggested some pretty wild things. I'm sure that you will admit it would be hard to convince an unbiased outsider that what you are suggesting has a reasonable chance of being true."

"But, Admiral," Jori interrupted, "I'll testify. I can make a statement that the things I'm saying could very well be true. I know that rig like the back of my hand."

"Miss Ashe," MacMahon said, "there are a few things you need to understand. Florexco has every right to conduct its drilling operations in whatever manner it sees fit. I cannot, just on a whim, go out there and start raising cane about the way they're doing things. If I have cause to believe that they are, in some way, endangering the lives of those workers out there, then I do have the authority to intervene. But in order to do that, I need to have very good reasons. You have given me some very startling and interesting information that, quite frankly, stretches the limits of credibility. And you have said that you've gained most of this information by illegal entry, a crime in this state. And one other thing. How do you think it would look for the Coast Guard if we took action based solely on the advice of a worker who had just recently been seriously injured, and who has every reason in the world to be vindictive about the oil well? A person who also could be suffering misconceptions because of the psychological and physical trauma she has undergone?"

"You mean you think I'm crazy?"

"That's your word, not mine. You have been sick, and it's my understanding that you left the hospital against medical advice. Isn't that right, Doctor?" he asked, looking at Blain.

"Yes," Blain answered, "but I can certify that her mental processes right now are absolutely back to normal. She's perfectly rational. I think you're forgetting the fact that I'm a witness to some of these things, too. I saw that journal and the papers that were in Sumter's office."

"That doesn't change anything," the commander responded. "You have no proof that those writings are fact. Dr. Sumter has published one book—perhaps he's working on another. This time, maybe a novel. Most of the best science fiction is written by scientists. You've got to admit that you and Miss Ashe could easily have misinterpreted what you saw last night in the dark."

"Of course, that's possible," Blain snapped. "Anything anyone writes could be part of a potential novel, but you're overlooking some of the definitely strange things that have come out of the accidents on the well. The strong evidence that some of the people have been affected by radiation, for example. That may have been what almost killed Jori."

"We're aware of that possibility, Doctor. I know you've mentioned it before, but again, that's speculation. There are apparently other things that can cause the sort of changes in the blood that have been seen in these patients. I believe you have indicated as much to some of our investigators."

He turned back to Jori. "What I suggest you do now, Miss Ashe, is let the Coast Guard take this from here. We will continue to look into this situation. We'll monitor that well to the best of our ability, and if anything else substantial comes to light, we'll move on it. In the meantime, why don't you go home and rest and continue getting well. You had a very close call. You don't need to spend your time engaged in cloak and dagger stuff right now." He smiled benevolently.

"If you had indisputable evidence that they were drilling beyond 35,000 feet, would that be enough for you to act?" she asked.

"It would, yes—at least to initiate an onsite investigation."

"Admiral, they're never going to admit to that as long as they think there's a possibility you'd try to stop what they're doing. I think that if Dr. Sumter's notes are accurate, the only hard evidence you're ever going to get by sitting back and waiting is when the cataclysm occurs."

"Young lady," the commander replied, "I don't think that waiting a week or two to see what happens out there is really going to lead to the destruction of Florida. Do you, really?" He smiled again.

She rose and stood in front of his desk. Her face was taut and her eyes filled with anger. "I don't honestly think that you or the Coast Guard give a damn what I think, Admiral. I think you're going to sit on this and hope it just goes away."

MacMahon was clearly antagonized. "You're entitled to whatever opinion you wish, and now, if you and the doctor will excuse us, Captain Daniels and I have work to do." He stood and walked to the door.

Blain stood with Jori, not quite believing that they were going to ignore what she had discovered. "Wait just a minute!" he said. "This is not just some minor incident that you can brush off and forget. She's talking about a very dangerous situation—a situation that could cost a lot of lives, if she's right."

"That's the question, isn't it, Doctor? If she's right?"

Blain stared at him in disbelief. "If there's even a tiny chance she's onto something, it needs to be investigated. The potential harm is too great. And your theory about Sumter's papers being fiction is ridiculous. There's no fiction in the world that looks like what we just saw. That was scientific data, I'm sure of it."

"Hold on now," MacMahon said. "Let me—"

"No! You hold on. I've been suspicious of that well for weeks and everybody's tried to talk me out of it. Men have died from radiation out there. I know they have. I've taken care of them. If you don't get involved, there will be more deaths, too. You've got to do something."

MacMahon frowned. "I don't have to do anything. Now, as I said, we will look into this. In the meantime, I've got other matters to attend to."

Jori walked to the door and stopped. "There are a lot of lives that could be resting on the judgments you make. I hope you keep that in mind when you shrug off the things we have told you. I know it all sounds strange, but prophecies of disaster always do until they come true."

The admiral smiled, but said nothing. Blain followed her out the door and then turned back to the two officers. "Do something about this," he said. "If she's right, we don't have much time."

MacMahon sighed impatiently. "We'll take care of it, Doctor. Don't you worry." He closed the door and walked back to his desk.

Daniels was rereading the copy of Sumter's summary on Balthorium.

"She's crazy, Kemp," MacMahon said. "I've never heard a more bizarre story in all my life. Holes drilled by visitors from outer space, previously undiscovered radioactive elements that are going to explode when they drill into them. I think she's probably gone bananas."

"But what about the doctor—what's making him buy all this?"

"That's the puzzle," MacMahon responded, biting gently on his lower lip. "There's no reason for him to be saying these things unless he's just a rabble-rouser."

Daniels got up and went across the room to examine a map of the offshore Florida waters hanging there. "I'm not ready to swallow their story, but something is going crazy out there, there's no doubt about that." He looked at the commander. "What if they're even partially right? It could be trouble."

"Yep, it could. It puts us in a bad situation. If they're right and we do nothing, it's negligence. If they're wrong and we do something, it will make the Guard look like fools. I don't know what to do, but I don't suppose we can ignore it. The only reason I can consider it plausible is that the whole story hangs together so well, all the pieces fit. It's the one explanation that brings all the parts together."

Daniels agreed. "That it does. I wonder just how deep they are drilling out there?"

"Tell you what—if I knew for sure that that story about the Russian disaster was true, I'd be more inclined to act on this. At least find out how deep they're drilling. Why don't you get on the horn to Washington? Don't tell them too much about what we're doing, but give them enough so they can give you a reasonable answer. Find out if there ever was any accident in Siberia involving some kind of unusual drilling project. Also, see if they've got anything on this Dr. Adrian Sumter. There may be more to him than we know."

"All right. That should be easy enough. I can probably get all that together today."

"Good. In the meantime, I think I'll just grab the bull by the horns and I'll call this Dr. Sumter myself and just confront him with the whole damned story and see what he says. He will most likely have a very logical explanation for the whole thing. He might even invite us aboard the well to check it out for ourselves. That would be nice, wouldn't it? I'd sure as hell like to close the book on this one and get back to more important matters."

"It does seem to be dragging on, doesn't it?" Daniels replied. "But it's hard to dismiss totally."

Adrian Sumter put down the phone. He was furious. But thank God Admiral MacMahon had called! It was clear now that he was going to have to work very vigorously to discredit Jori Ashe. The woman's loose talk was threatening to bring down the whole project. He'd been able to convince the Coast Guard commander that her charges were insane and preposterous.

The officer had been pleased at his invitation to come aboard the rig some day next week and inspect things for himself. That gave them at least four or five days to work unhampered, but he would definitely have to keep Jori from doing any additional damage. Damn, he thought, how foolish to have allowed my notes to be so casually guarded that someone like her could have seen them. He opened the drawer and looked down at his journal. To know that someone else had, just a few hours earlier, been reading his innermost thoughts was infuriating. He would definitely have to be more careful.

But first he must make sure that the other uninformed members of the board were prepared to be confronted by Jori. He had to plant the seed of suspicion in their minds that the girl was insane. He had to be sure that no one would believe her. That was the most important thing at the moment. And if anything else seemed necessary— well, he could ask Loggins about that. And maybe Loggins could also help with the nuisance created by the intervention of Dr. Robson. Surely, there was a way to put pressure on this man to stay out of what did not concern him.

He pressed the button on his intercom and spoke to his secretary. "Please try to locate Mr. Loggins if you can. I would like to speak with him." He then lifted his journal and the Balthorium papers from the drawer and placed them in his briefcase, which he carefully locked. These must be kept away from prying eyes, he thought. He wanted no one, especially not Loggins, to be aware of what went into his personal journal. He would most certainly have to move them to a more secure spot, away from the many persons who seemed to come and go as they pleased around this place.

TWENTY-TWO

It had been a long day and a bitter one for Jori. She sat brooding on the back porch of her house, looking out over the ocean watching the eastern sky slowly fade into darkness. An unusually chilly northeastern wind had been blowing, and the surf was starting to pound as the sea began to build.

She stood up, pulled her sweater more tightly around her, and walked barefooted down onto the beach. It will soon be dark enough, she thought, and time to go. Time to begin her final act. She had been disappointed and angry at her failure to convince the Coast Guard that something was wrong. Even Blain seemed to have lost his initiative. There was no one left who really understood the consequences of such deep drilling or even cared what might be about to happen.

She walked along the water's edge, watching the distant lights of St. Lucie One. She glanced at her watch and then back into the sky. She was nervous and scared, but she had no choice. It had fallen to her to do something. It seemed certain now that no one else would. She reflected on the events of the day. First, the police had come around noon, just after they had returned from the Coast Guard station. They had asked a lot of questions about last night and she had, for the most part, told the truth. She had argued in her defense that as an employee of the company, she had a right to be in the building and those offices, and that she had not, in fact, done anything wrong. Blain called a little later and she discovered that the police had been interrogating him at the same time. Fortunately, they had agreed upon their stories before they had separated that morning, just in case.

As she watched the waves rush up to the beach and barely reach her feet, she thought about the other thing they had agreed on. They would not discuss with the police her ideas about the well. That had probably been a good idea. The officers had already been quite emphatic in their request that she return to the hospital and resume her medical treatment. Telling them the bizarre tale would have only increased their confidence that she was still sick.

And then she had taken the long shot. She had called Matthew Downing, the president, and also Sarah Brenner, one of the board members who lived in Stuart. But it was a lost cause. Sumter had reached them both first. From the way they had reacted, she was convinced that they did not know what was going on. But unfortunately, they had both been conned into believing that she had gone almost berserk running away from the hospital, breaking into the offices, and telling irrational stories to the Coast Guard. The two had been gentle and sympathetic with her, but they had hardly heard her case. They had spent most of their time trying to convince her to calm down and return to the hospital where she belonged. She felt a surge of bitterness as she remembered Sarah Brenner's last words, "All we want you to do is just get well, Jori honey. We want you to get over this and be all right."

Even Blain was discouraged. He was apparently getting some flack from the chief of surgery and an important board member at the hospital about his visit to Sumter's office. Undoubtedly, the company was pulling strings to get him suppressed. But, it didn't make any difference what anyone else did now. She was committed. Tonight, one way or the other, she was going to do whatever was necessary to get the well shut down, at least until a good hard look could be taken at what was going on. She glanced at her watch again. Time to get moving.

She followed her footsteps in the sand back up to the porch and went inside the house. In her bedroom she changed into her dark blue heavy-duty coveralls and put on her work boots. Carefully she clipped her Florexco I.D. to her pocket. She pinned her hair up into a tight knot behind her head, and then took from the closet her black baseball cap with the Florexco emblem on the front. She put it on and studied herself in the mirror. From a distance in the bulky clothes, she would easily be mistaken for a male worker. That was all she needed.

She left the room and started out the back door, but then paused in the short hallway between the kitchen and the porch. She needed some kind of weapon, just in case. God knows, she wouldn't use it, but it might be useful. A knife was not enough. She looked in the utility closet and brought out a small hatchet she used for chopping wood washed up on the shore. She studied it for a moment and then, thinking better of the idea, laid it on the kitchen table, and, with a last glance around, went out onto the porch. There was nothing in the house that would be helpful to her. Perhaps she could get the gun off the boat.

She opened the screen door and stepped down onto the

402

sand and started the walk south toward the edges of the Florexco compound, her mind consumed with one thought: She had to stop the drilling. Clearly she was the only one to prevent the horror she feared would soon occur. Sumter's notes had been precise about it. They were about to reach what they were after: the Balthorium. But why were they doing it at all? It didn't make sense. Didn't they care about human life? According to Sumter's notes, the answer was no. He was prepared to pay that price, if necessary. The bastard! And Loggins, too! They cared nothing about anyone but themselves. If another crew was killed, what the hell did they care as long as they had their way? And what about her? They hadn't blinked one eye after she had nearly died. They didn't care. Not about her or anyone. Not the crew, not the environment. Not one goddamned thing! Only their own glory. If what happened in Russia, happened here, then so be it, as far as they were concerned. To hell with everyone else. They were going to take their chance at the big time.

But she wasn't going to let them get away with it. It was just too much for her to take. She didn't feel like a hero, but she had no choice. It was up to her to stop them or no one would. Whatever the risk, she had to do it.

Fortunately, with the oncoming night, the beach was deserted. The chilly winds and the threat of rain had kept away the rare visitors to this isolated stretch of the coast. And besides that, it was practically inaccessible. The only road into here was the one that went in front of her house, and then traveled along the other side of the peninsula near the river all the way down to the Florexco headquarters. Once the road turned away from the beach, it became an increasingly distant walk over the

403

dunes to reach the sea. At the point where the Florexco property was bordered by the ocean, it was almost a three-mile walk from the road. Because of this, probably, no significant security measures had been undertaken to prevent trespassers from gaining access to the compound via the beach route. It had never been necessary before.

The fence around the compound was a reasonably secure one: twelve feet tall with multiple strands of barbed wire above that. It would have taken a super-human effort to go over it. The compound wasn't truly locked tight, but there was enough hindrance to keep out vagrants, wanderers, and busybodies. The real security was in the building itself. Fortunately, for her that would be no problem.

By the time she reached the fence, she noted with satisfaction that the evening had become totally dark. The overcast sky blocked even the moon's faint radiance.

It was about midtide, and the water was higher around the end of the fence than it had been last night. She took off her boots and waded into the sea, getting wet to about her waist, and then turned back up onto the beach, this time on Florexco property. She dried her feet with the arms of her overalls and then, after replacing her boots, continued down the beach again. She would stay behind the dune, completely out of sight until she'd gone around the sandy point in the distance near the entrance to the inlet. That way she would stay south of the building and the docks when she came up from the beach. It would be very unlikely that she would be spotted.

Twenty minutes later, she was there. She glanced at her watch. It was almost 8:15. She would have to hurry. The last crew boat would be going out at nine.

Crouching, she edged her way up the dune and then

glimpsed down into the compound. She had a view of the whole place. To the right was the parking lot and beyond that the main entrance. A car was just coming through the gate. She could see the guard standing outside his booth talking to the occupant. The lot itself was about one-third full, most of the cars belonging, of course, to the workmen. In a little while, twenty or thirty more cars would appear as new workers arrived to take the last boat out.

The building itself looked deserted except for a few windows which were lit up and, of course, the central part of the building which contained the check-in station and waiting area for the men. To her left was the dock area. She could see the 31 Bertram still tied at the far end of the pier. The two crew boats were tied about halfway down the docks.

The risky part would be from the time she reached the edge of the back parking lot until she got to the docks. Once out there she would be out of sight in between the boats and relatively safe. The question then would be to decide which of the vessels was going to be used.

She went over the top of the dune and slid down the other side. There were several smaller dunes between her and the building for about 100 yards, covered with scrub brush and an occasional palm tree. After she crossed that, there would be no cover, no protection. It would be at least a two- or three-minute walk across open ground to the docks. She would have to trust good luck once she committed herself into the open. She went over the smaller dunes and started quickly across the flatter sandy area and then paused behind the last clump of scrub brush to survey the situation.

Everything was absolutely quiet. A few more cars had

405

come into the parking lot, but there was no sign of life between her and the docks. Her pulse was pounding and her stomach in knots as she edged away from her last protection and walked the final fifteen feet across the sand and stepped onto the parking lot.

She had gone about fifty feet over the black asphalt when to her horror the back door of the building, not more than eighty feet to her right, started to open and she heard the voices of men talking. There was no time to run back into the sand. There was nothing around her to hide behind. Instinctively, she fell flat onto her abdomen and lay with her head against the ground, watching the three men come out of the building. They were mumbling, talking to themselves, but she couldn't understand what they were saying. As they came through the door she could see they were struggling with a large container. It was a wooden crate. She lay motionless, almost afraid to breathe. She felt totally exposed, but, thank God for the dark overcast skies, she hoped desperately they had not seen her.

Sixty seconds later she knew she was safe. The men carried their crate down the side of the building, out onto the docks and put it into the first of the two crew boats. A piece of luck—she now knew without a doubt which boat would be going. She waited patiently, her confidence beginning to grow, as the men loaded their cargo and finally came back down the walks and retraced their path along the side of the building, past her, and in through the back door. She stayed motionless for another twenty seconds and then was on her feet walking quickly but quietly toward the docks. A minute later she was almost onto the pier.

Unexpectedly and frighteningly, she was suddenly

bathed in spotlights coming from the parking area. She wanted to run, to scream, but she suppressed it, clinging precariously to calmness. She glanced in the direction of the lights as she heard a car engine being started. She felt as if she were on stage, but she continued to walk toward the boats. She expected any moment to hear alarm bells go off, but as quickly as they had come, the lights turned away and the car backed from its parking space and turned toward the gate. She felt almost faint from the shock. Her hands and face were wet with perspiration, but she was almost there.

A long fifteen seconds later she reached the first of the crew boats and stepped quickly down into the cockpit, glanced around, then disappeared into the cabin below.

Her heart was still pounding. She didn't know how she had survived the tension, but the first stage was over. She now knew that, at the very least, she was going to reach the well before she was detected. She went through the main cabin past the engine room, through the small forward cabin and then opened a tiny door and crawled forward into the rope locker at the bow of the boat. There was an opening above her through which the rope and chain could travel up to the top deck. Through it she had an obstructed, but adequate, view of the bridge of the boat and the dock beside them. She wiggled around to make herself comfortable. She would have to stay there awhile. She held her watch up to the light coming through the small opening: a quarter till nine.

Fifteen minutes later, right on time, the men— unusually somber and quiet—filed off the dock into the vessel. There was none of the usual banter. They were strangely reserved. For a moment she felt a deep sympathy for them. Oil workers, while not well-educated, are reasonably bright, and they are hard workers. They take the risks they take, for the money. It's a hard way to earn a buck. She had the feeling that these men were aware that something was wrong, and she also had the feeling that they were well-paid to continue working despite their anxieties. Even though reluctant to be going out, they probably all needed the extra money.

Fifteen minutes later they had left the docks, passed through the inlet and were on their way through the heaving seas toward the well. Jori was miserable and sick. With the rolling and bouncing of the boat, waves of nausea passed over her and then, finally, she vomited, lying face down between two piles of rope—too sick to worry about the noise she was making. Afterward, she began to feel a little better, and she tried to prepare herself mentally for the task ahead.

She sat up and peered through the opening. They were getting close. She could see the well looming ominously ahead. A light rain was falling, which seemed to form an even more frightening shroud across the great structure. A chill ran through her as she suddenly remembered her dreams in a heaving boat in a stormy sea and the well in front of her. She remembered the voices calling to her from the beach and the dead men, and she remembered the frightening specter of the man with whips standing on the platform above her. She realized now that the man had looked like Loggins, dressed as he was the night she had inadvertently stumbled into his apartment and witnessed his perversions.

She watched as the boat slowly made its approach to the landing platform. It was going to be more dangerous than usual, almost too rough to bring the boat safely into the loading dock. But slowly, carefully, and skillfully, the pilot worked the boat in and soon the lines were being tossed aboard and the vessel tied down.

Through her opening she could see one guard in the booth and one standing outside looking over the boat, his gun propped on his right hip. Several other workers that helped moor the boat had started back up the stairs. Everyone was in the silver metallic suits and the awesome helmets. It was a strange and mysterious spectacle.

The bow of the boat and the opening through which she was observing the scene were far forward along the loading platform. It was actually somewhat beyond the lighted area, partially in the shadows. All the activity was to the stern of the boat where the men were slowly unloading. She watched carefully as the men were checked in by another worker and then went across the landing deck into a recently constructed dressing area on the far side. A few minutes later the men emerged, fully suited up, looking exactly like the others as they started up the stairs.

It took some time for the activity to slow down. Finally all the men were off the boat. They were either in the dressing room or had already ascended to the platforms above. She waited awhile longer until she was absolutely certain that the last man had left the dressing area, and then she made her move. She slowly opened the door to the rope locker and looked out. The boat was dark, silent, and seemingly empty. She eased out and stood up in the small cabin, relieved to be able to stretch out. She stood up on one of the bunks and unlatched the small hatch above her and opened it carefully. Cautiously she raised her head through the opening and looked around.

The situation couldn't have been better. The front

portion of the boat where she was standing was totally in shadows. The loading platform was deserted except for the one guard sitting in the booth. He was apparently reading something on the desk in front of him.

It was time for another moment of risk. If the guard looked up and saw her, it would be all over. If he kept doing what he was doing, in thirty seconds she would be hidden again. She climbed carefully through the hatch and quietly pushed it shut. Moving cautiously, she crawled across the bow of the boat to the rail, and then, timing her movements very carefully with the rocking of the boat, stepped silently onto the platform.

Walking as quietly as she could, even though she realized that any noise she would make would be lost, mixed with the sounds of the sea, she went quickly around behind the guard booth, across the platform, and into the dressing room. As she had hoped, it was empty.

A few minutes later, just as she had finished pulling a helmet over her head and locking it down, the far door snapped open and a large, silver-suited man stared into the room. There was a moment of panic, of hesitation, and then she turned, walked straight toward him and, holding up one hand in a casual greeting, went through the door, past him, and started up the stairs.

About halfway up she glanced back down and the man had disappeared into the dressing room. So far, so good.

The big shock came when she finally emerged through the portal above and stepped out onto the main deck. Tremendous changes had taken place. First of all, the work force had been doubled, maybe tripled. There seemed to be men everywhere. A new crane had been added, working between the area of the new pipe storage and the turntable. It was obvious that the process of drilling had been made more efficient and speedy. In a situation where the only limit to drill depths reached was how quickly the pipe could be moved into position, the operations had been streamlined. It must be going as fast, or faster than ever, she said to herself. The other thing was a peculiar shielding which had been positioned around the turntable itself. There were several panels which rose and fell with the pipe as they were swung over the turntable. It seemed more awkward for the tool pushers to work alternately on the inside and outside of the barrier. It was obviously some kind of device to protect the men from the kind of accident that had happened to her.

The biggest change, however, was in the number of observers or perhaps guards, posted around the well. There were several even carrying weapons. The mood of the place had definitely changed. There was only the sound of the engines and pipes clanking. There were no voices to be heard. The wise-cracking and occasional angry shouting common to drilling rigs were gone. The well now had a distinctly mechanical feeling. There was the pounding roar of the engines and the dull vibration of the drill and the sound of metal on metal, but nothing else. The place seemed alien and cold.

She glanced up toward the control booth and could see several silver figures within. They seemed to be occupied with something over the control table. She would definitely have to get them out of there somehow. She turned to her left and walked past the crew office, past the shower room and into a small supply building. Once inside, she pulled the door shut behind her and turned on the light. There was a stairway going upward to a second level where many boxes of small instruments and tools

411

were kept. She went up the stairs and then opened a small emergency exit door, which led her out onto an unlit rampway in the shadows just below the control booth. From there she had a commanding view of the well, but was nearly invisible herself.

Just above her head ran a thick electrical cable which carried power into the control booth. It was a simple electrical circuit hooked to a main breaker down below on the main deck and to a smaller breaker and connection box within the booth. If the line were interrupted here, the problem would be easily corrected and rapidly diagnosed, but in the ensuing confusion most of the attention would be at the main breaker box down below. She would have a few moments to be in and out of the control booth and be gone before they realized what had happened.

She walked back into the supply room and picked up some of the bolt cutters she knew were stored there. She took one last look around the rig and then reached above her and snipped the wire. There was a flash of sparks and then the glow of lights from the booth above went dark. A second later, the lights in the upper half of the derrick beside her blinked off, and an alarm bell began ringing two decks below. She was surprised but delighted, something unexpected had happened. In cutting the cable, not only had she knocked out the control booth, but somehow, something had short-circuited, causing a breaker to trip shutting off the upper part of the derrick. More attention would now be devoted to the main breaker, giving her more time to get what she wanted out of the booth.

Down below, there seemed to be confusion. For the first time she heard men shouting, many of them were looking upwards toward the booth above and the derrick. It made her nervous, but she knew she couldn't be seen in the dark.

She heard the door above her open and then the sound of men's boots on the metal staircase. Two men descended and she waited for a third but he didn't come. Had she made a mistake? Had there been only two persons in the control booth? Perhaps one had left while she was coming up the stairs inside the supply storage building. She couldn't imagine anyone staying in the dark room above her while everyone else was hustling around to see what had gone wrong.

She listened carefully. There was no noise from above. All was clear, she decided, and walked to the outer edge of the small deck and looked into the dark waters below. She was standing next to one of the major supporting legs of the entire platform. On the outside of it was a narrow ladder which ran from the sea all the way past the top of the control booth up to the level beyond. She got a firm grip on one rung and carefully swung herself out over the water and started up the ladder. The rungs were wet and slippery in the drizzle.

She had reached the level of the control booth and was starting to climb over the rail when a sudden movement inside the open door startled her. She quickly retreated back down the ladder out of sight, but in the process slipped once and kicked the steel leg, before regaining her foothold. She was scared but unhurt. She pulled herself as closely as possible, held her grip firmly on the ladder and waited.

She heard footsteps above as the remaining person in the booth stepped out onto the deck. She could see his hands placed on the rail next to her, but he never leaned out or looked down, so she was sure she had not been seen. A moment later he turned and walked away from her and then down the stairs.

She quickly climbed up onto the deck and entered the room. It was almost totally dark, but she knew exactly what she wanted and where it was.

Aided by the faint light coming through the large window, she carefully tore lose all the printed graphs containing the recorded data about the drilling. Then she went to the desk at the far end and picked up the two sets of rolled up data sheets stored there. With any luck at all these would be the recordings from the moments just before the other two accidents. Combined with the most recent data, the tracings would present a complete picture of what had been happening, and what was happening on the well. It was everything she would need.

She quickly combined the rolls of paper and then stood looking out the big picture window at the scene below. The confusion seemed to have ended. There was a small group of men clustered around the breaker box. Suddenly the upper half of the derrick blossomed with light. She could see a flurry of interest around the breaker panels. After that, as they realized it was not a tripped breaker that had shut off power to the booth, several flashlights began to shine on the power cables leading upward from the breakers. The lights moved slowly up the steel girders toward her.

In a few more moments, they would find the cut. She had to move fast or risk being caught in the booth. As she started to turn away from the window, one of the figures began to point upward, and then he tapped one of the others and pointed toward the storage room. The man took off and quickly disappeared. She knew he would soon be emerging on the level below her. She could not leave the way she had come.

She stepped out onto the deck and, clinging to the roll of graph paper, swung herself back out onto the ladder and started to descend. She had to get past the next level before the workmen reached it, or else she would be seen.

She made it with not a second to spare. As her head dipped past the railing on the level where she had cut the wire, she heard the door from the storage room open and a worker burst out onto the deck. A moment later she heard him yelling to those below, and then there was a stampede of feet coming upward, obviously to inspect the damage she had done.

Shielded from view of those on the various platforms by the immensity of the support legs, she carefully made her way down two more levels to the main deck. Cautiously she peered around and noted with satisfaction that she was out of the line of sight from those still clustered around the breaker panel. No one else was in her general vicinity. After climbing over the rail, she walked slowly around some of the heavy equipment and then turned out toward the center of the platform from underneath the derrick itself. She walked past the group still standing at the panel box, passed in front of the main stairs leading upward, and headed toward the crew office.

She recognized Eric Duval's voice from the level where she had cut the cable, "Someone cut this goddamn power cable up here!"

The conversations of those on the main decks stopped. Loggins's voice was unmistakable. "What the hell are you talking about?" he yelled up toward Duval.

"I said, someone cut the goddamn cable. It's been done on purpose."

415

"What the hell for?" responded Loggins angrily as he stepped away from the breaker switch. He glanced around him and then up toward Duval. "Find out who did it and find out right now," he said. "And get it fixed!"

Suddenly Loggins was walking toward her accompanied by several of the others. "Goddamn son of a bitch," he was saying. As he reached her, he put out his hand and pushed her shoulder. "Get the shit out of the way!" he said and stepped into the crew office.

She moved well clear of the others and started toward the portal leading to the stairwell down to the landing deck. Inside the office she could hear him yelling. "What the hell are we paying all these security men for, if they're not going to prevent crap like this? I want every one of those guards out on the deck, and I want to figure out what the hell happened! I will not allow sabotage on this well. I won't tolerate it!"

Suddenly she felt eyes burning into her back. She turned to see one of the guards standing about thirty feet away studying her intently. The man took his weapon off his shoulder and held it in front of him. She felt her heart in her throat and panic screaming in her head. The man began to walk slowly toward her. She looked about, trying to decide which way to go, but there was no escape. She was going to be caught. She wished she had taken time to put the papers inside her suit. The man approached to within several feet of her and stopped squarely in front, staring intently at her.

"You want to tell me what you're doing?" he said. She recognized the voice as being the man who had kicked in the window of the boat the day before.

She felt speechless and scared. Before she could respond, Loggins came roaring out of the crew office and

416

saw the guard standing in front of her.

He walked straight to the man and grabbed him by the shoulder. "What the hell are you doing standing here?" Loggins yelled. "Don't you know somebody's been screwing around with the electrical work? If you guys can't keep shit like this from happening, I'm going to find me somebody who can. Get up there and find out who did it!" The man turned away as Loggins gave him a push in the direction of the stairs.

Jori was petrified as Loggins turned toward her. "Now get the hell back to work," he said and then started toward the stairs himself.

A moment later she passed through the portal and started down to the landing platform. She didn't understand how she had been so lucky as to escape detection, but she realized she had to move fast before they started a man-to-man search for the papers she was carrying. It would not be long until it was recognized that they were gone. She reached the dressing room and went through the door. She crossed through it and then quietly opened the entrance facing toward the boat.

The guard was in the booth. The way he was sitting he had a clear view of the boat in which she had come, but behind him on the other side of the dock, was a second vessel. That was the one she would use. Trying to stay in the shadows, she moved quietly along the edge of the platform and then stepped quickly into the cockpit of the boat. She knew she would have one chance to escape, and one chance only. Surprise was her only defense.

Working quickly, she released the lines from inside the boat. First the two aft lines, then the spring cleat in the middle, and then she returned to the cockpit, went through the main cabin into the forward cabin, opened

417

the hatch, leaned out and took the main forward lines loose from the cleats there. She slipped back into the boat and, using the inside stairs, climbed up to the bridge.

She unsnapped the locks of her helmet and lifted it off and placed it on the floor beside the crumpled graph papers she had been carrying. She glanced toward the guard booth, the man was sitting calmly inside. A quick look at the stairs verified that she was so far undetected.

Now came the most critical moment of all. If she had any luck left at all, she wished for it now. When she hit the start button she would have no more than ten to fifteen seconds to get the engine running and get away from the dock. Otherwise, the guard would be aboard with her and she had no way to resist him. She thought about the .38 left behind on the Bertram. She wished she had taken the time to bring it with her, but it was too late for that now. It was down to one last roll of the dice. If the engine didn't start immediately, her adventure was over. If it did, she would escape. She would have at least three to four minutes jump on them before they could get the other boat loose and the engine started and be after her.

She took a deep breath, turned the fuel switch to "on," and depressed the start button. The engine almost immediately came to life. She threw it into forward gear and pushed the accelerator control as far forward as it would go. The large boat lunged forward and began to pick up speed.

Almost simultaneously, with the reflexes of an animal, the guard was out of the control booth and running toward her. His speed was phenomenal. He crossed the thirty feet separating the booth and the boat in what seemed like a fraction of a second. An instant later he was airborne, heaving himself toward the vessel which was separating itself from the dock. As incredible as his speed was, it was no match for the thrust of the big diesel engine accelerating toward its top r.p.m. His outstretched arms reached the side of the boat, and he hung precariously for a second before slipping harmlessly into the water. A moment later she was speeding from the well, and he was swimming back toward the landing platform.

She shouted with ecstasy at the event, recognizing that it would give her extra time for her head start, as well as eliminating the extremely remote possibility that he might open fire.

She headed due east toward the inlet, knowing she was being watched from the main deck of the rig by now and wanting them to feel sure that that was where she was headed. Later, at the last minute she would change course in the dark. She kept the throttle pushed full forward and the diesel engine below her bellowed a roar of strength as the boat pounded into the sea ahead. Empty, it was surprisingly fast. As it flew through each wave, huge sheets of white water were thrown high into the air from each side. An occasional blast of salt spray was caught by the wind and swept across the windshield of the bridge.

Almost six minutes after her startling escape, she saw the bow lights of the other boat ease out from underneath the rig and then turn toward her. The race was on. By then she had become totally invisible, hidden by the darkness of the night. Behind her she could see the spotlight of the pursuing vessel being flashed around in different directions as they searched for her. But she knew it was impossible, with the head start she had—they could not possibly see her.

The question now was, which boat was faster?

Presumably hers. The two vessels were almost identical in construction, same engines, same hull, and surely she was carrying a lighter weight. No telling how many men were on board, in pursuit. The real question was probably one of maintenance. Should either boat be in better condition, it would be the definite winner. If one engine was running better, or if one hull had more recently been cleaned and scraped free of the speed-consuming barnacles, then that boat would be the victor. But with luck, it would be an even match. And that's all she needed. In a few more minutes she would be lost in the dark and home free.

She looked ahead. In the far distance she was just beginning to see the entrance lights to the inlet. In a little while she would make her turn. She glanced behind her again; the vessel was on a true course for the inlet. It seemed uncanny that as invisible as she was, they were staying dead on her trail, the spotlights still swinging back and forth in vain attempts to locate her. With unqualified accuracy, it stayed right there, neither gaining nor dropping back and not varying a degree from the course she was following. It was almost as if they could see her. She hoped they couldn't. In a few minutes she would know.

Ten minutes passed and nothing changed, except the tiny sensation she had that the gap between the two boats was diminishing; not much, but enough to be perceptible. She was still safely out of view. She looked ahead toward the inlet. She could clearly see the lighted buoys. She was probably only a mile off. Now was the time. Without reducing speed, she pulled the boat into a hard turn to dead north. This was the tricky part. If somehow they caught a glimpse of her and stayed in pursuit, she would eventually be caught, but if not she was safe.

She watched the lights of the oncoming boat. For the moment they were to the right of her and slightly behind. For the first time since the chase began, she could only see one bow light, the green one. The red one, being on the other side of the boat, was out of sight. If it should come back into view, she would know they were turning and that they must have spotted her. To the left was the beach and the lights of the Florexco compound. Ahead of her was just darkness. She watched and waited. Slowly the green bow light moved further beyond her and continued on toward the inlet. She was free. They had not seen her. They had not turned. There was no stopping her now. They would not realize she had eluded them until after they had gone through the inlet and into the river. Only then would it become apparent that she had slipped away. What they would do then she couldn't guess, but she wasn't waiting around to see.

She turned the boat slightly to the east and angled toward the beach. A few minutes later she pulled back the throttle to a fast idle and turned the boat even more east, directly at the beach.

The noise at first was very faint and then rapidly became louder—the surf beating on the beach. She carefully took the boat up to within a hundred yards of the sand, staying just outside the breakers. Finally she spotted what she was looking for, the back porch light of her house. Fortunately, she had left it on.

She quickly reached up into a cabinet above her and pulled down a long, black plastic tube. She unscrewed the water-tight cap and pulled out the navigation charts stored within it. She rolled up the graphs she had taken from the well, inserted them into the tube, and then securely replaced the cap. From the same cabinet she withdrew a bright orange life jacket. She unzipped the silver suit from the well which she was still wearing, let it drop to the floor, and then carefully pulled on the life jacket.

She now brought the boat down to full slow idle, swung the stern around toward the west and backed up another fifty feet to within thirty or forty feet of the breaking waves. She then pushed the gears into forward and, as the boat ever so slowly started to pull away from the beach, she jumped down the stairs, ran across the open cockpit, and clutching the valued graphs in their tube close to her chest, jumped into the water.

It was colder than expected, but she didn't have time to contemplate it. A few seconds later, she was swept up by a huge wave and, as it broke into a great sea of white foam, she was tossed toward the beach. A minute later she felt the sand beneath her feet. As she struggled upright, she was hit squarely in the back by another wave, which tumbled her forward again scraping her back across the sand. But she was okay. A few seconds later she was out of the water, running with the graphs up toward her back porch.

Standing there, she dropped the wet life jacket and brushed off some of the sand and looked out at the boat, which was still barely visible. It was headed slowly away from the beach. She smiled. She had done the impossible. She had escaped in a manner no one would believe, and she had with her everything she needed to prove the dangers of the well. It would be hours before they would find the boat and no telling how long before they realized what she had done. It was going to be a good story to tell.

She went into the house and turned on the kitchen

light. She opened the tube and spread out the papers on the table where the small hatchet was still lying. As she glanced at it, she was glad she had not been so foolish as to take a weapon. She might have been tempted to use it, and that would have been disaster for sure.

She took a good look at the charts and then knew for sure she had been right. The drill depth was almost 48,000 feet, more than nine miles. The temperature at the drill bit was 912 degrees, incredibly warm and getting hotter, but most significant of all was the electromagnetic force indications. For the previous forty-eight hours they had been gyrating wildly, but to a much greater extent in the last two or three hours. The changes were very similar to those seen prior to the first two accidents, but this time the magnitude was much greater. And even more importantly, the changes had been growing over a longer period of time. It was obvious that whatever was causing the unusual variations was not far from the advancing drill bit. It all fit with the notion recorded in Sumter's journal that whatever was going to happen was imminent.

Surely now the Coast Guard would listen. It was critical to get these papers to Admiral MacMahon immediately. Something could conceivably happen on the well within the next few hours. In any event, the drilling had to be stopped as soon as possible. It seemed incredible to her that Sumter was stubbornly pushing ahead. Ambition that great was insane.

She placed the charts back into the tube and carried them into the bedroom with her, laying them on her desk. She sat down on the bed and dialed Blain Robson's home phone. No one answered at first. She glanced at the clock—almost eleven. A moment later a woman's voice came over the phone and her heart sank. She felt better an instant later. "Dr. Robson's answering service."

"This is Jori Ashe. I'm trying to reach Dr. Robson on a personal matter. Do you know where I can find him?"

"I'm sorry, he's in emergency surgery right now. Can I take a message and have him call you back?"

She paused, trying to decide what to do. "Tell him I called and that it's extremely urgent for him to get back in touch with me as soon as possible. Tell him it's an emergency. I went to the well. I have some thing the Coast Guard needs, and it proves everything we've been talking about. Tell him if I don't hear from him soon, I'm taking them myself. So, if he can't reach me here, try me at the Coast Guard Station in Fort Pierce." She paused for a moment, then finally added, "Tell him that I think I am in danger."

"In danger?" the voice said.

"Right," Jori answered. "Tell him to hurry." She got up from the bed, took off the wet panties and bra she was wearing, and pulled on some shorts and a shirt.

Trying to decide how long to wait, she went back into the kitchen and, on intuition, locked the back door. She fixed a cup of instant coffee and then, beginning to feel nervous, went back into the bedroom and turned off the light. I shouldn't stay here, she thought. There might be a chance someone would come. She mulled over her options and finally decided that for the moment she should leave. She could even go by the hospital and find out how long Blain was going to be tied up, and then go on to Fort Pierce by herself if necessary.

In the distance she thought she heard a noise. She walked into the dark front room to check the lock on the front door. Through the window she looked out and

424

down the road toward Florexco. There it was. About 200 feet down the road parked on the side was a car, and a man was walking toward the house. The gnawing anxiety she had been feeling turned into true fear. There is no reason to get upset, she told herself. It's probably just a fluke. Maybe someone out of gas. If I just stay in the house and keep quiet, they'll figure no one's home and go on. They had no reason to suspect that she was here. They couldn't possibly have found the boat by now, and it would not dawn on them that she would have considered going overboard.

It's nothing, she told herself. There is no way anyone from the well could be here this quick. She crouched down in a chair next to the front window and peered out through a gap in the curtains. The man kept coming closer and closer. Her pulse was pounding. She considered for a moment going out the back way and running down the beach, but realized there was no time for that. She would give herself away. If there was any chance they were looking for her, the safest place was in the dark, seemingly empty house. She wished she had left sooner. It was foolish to stay around so long. She had only meant to come through, call Blain and then leave anyway, but now that option was gone.

The man came into the front yard, started up the steps toward the porch and then stopped, looking around at the door and the windows. As he stepped closer to the window, she got a clear look at his face and her heart nearly stopped. It was Eric Duval—his nose bent and ugly, but there was no question about his identity.

A helicopter, she suddenly thought. They must have come in the helicopter. She had forgotten entirely about it. They might even have watched her escape onto the beach. In her race, and with the roaring of the boat, she had never thought to look up. But now, not ten feet away, was a man she knew would be happy to kill her. It would be senseless to run now; the best bet was to hope he didn't know for sure she was in there. She wished desperately she had the gun.

Duval walked back and forth on the porch, pushed his face close into the windows and attempted to look into the house. Finally, he tried the door knob. It was locked. He rattled it harder and attempted to force it open. It didn't come. Again he pressed his face to the window and wrapped loudly against the glass.

"I know you're in there, Jori baby," he said loudly, and then rapped harder on the glass. "Come on out now before I get mad. I'm not going to hurt you."

She knew he was lying. She was afraid to move. He was just a few feet away. He went back to the door and yanked on the knob a few more times and finally kicked it with one foot. "Come on out now, goddamn it!" he yelled. "If I have to come in there, you're gonna be sorry."

She was sick with fear. He walked back to the window and this time banged on it harder than ever. She could see the anger in his face. "You little bitch!" he yelled. "If you don't open up, I'll tear this door down getting in there, and when I get you, you're gonna be sorry I did!" He stopped speaking for a moment and turned and placed his ear against the window pane, listening. She was afraid to breathe.

"Goddamn, you little whore, open up now. Last chance." She didn't move.

"That's it," he said and stepped back from the door, reached into his back pocket and pulled out a large screwdriver. He let out a peculiar laugh. It sounded almost like an animal. "You asked for it. I'm coming in now, and when I get you, you'll be sorrier than you've ever been. I'm gonna do some things to you you never even thought of. You're gonna pay for my nose now. I'll fix your bottom up real good. You'd been a lot better off to screw me the first time like you really wanted to, but now you're gonna get it my way. By the time I get through with you, you're gonna wish all you had was a broken nose." He laughed again and then pushed the screwdriver through the crack in the door and gave it a strong jerk.

There was the sound of metal parts breaking and the door sprung open. In a flash he was coming into the room, and she bolted for the kitchen, pulling down a dining room chair as she went by. A second later he tripped over it and tumbled into the wall. "You bitch!" he screamed. "I've got you now!"

Never in her life had she experienced such fear. She knew she was in a struggle for her life. As she reached the kitchen her eyes fell on the small hatchet and she grabbed it and raced for the back door. Her nervous, uncooperative fingers fumbled with the lock. She could hear him getting to his feet and then the sound of the chair being thrown across the room. Suddenly he appeared in the doorway. The lock in her hands came open, she darted out onto the porch, took the stairs in one jump and, as fast as she could go, ran down the beach into the darkness.

She could hear his feet on the sand right behind her. She gave it everything she had, but she was no match for him. She sensed him right behind her and turned just as he launched himself into a flying tackle. His head hit her squarely in the chest and they both rolled to the sand. He had lost his grip in the fall, but then suddenly he was on his knees above her, reaching for her throat.

He never saw the hatchet coming. Jori's hand tightened around the wooden handle and, with every bit of her strength, she brought it sailing around in one final desperate act of survival. The sharp blade slammed into him exactly in the middle of his face. The gaping wound it produced cut diagonally from his forehead, across the bridge of his nose, and down over the right cheek. His outstretched arms suddenly went limp, and he straightened up over her, still on his knees. An instant later, the instrument had been drawn back for a second blow. This time it dug into his left eye and came down around through the top of his mouth. Blood was spurting everywhere and he was making a grunting noise. But he stood upright, arms hanging limply at his sides. She swung the hatchet into him one last time. The sound of split bone and tissue was awesome. His nose and the center of his face practically disappeared as the hatchet buried itself between his eyes and his mouth. It sunk so deeply this time it could not be withdrawn. She let go of it and pulled herself away from him. A gush of blood was running down the handle, dripping to the sand and his face was totally unrecognizable.

He grunted and gurgled a few more times and then slowly leaned backwards and finally rolled over into the sand, his legs twisted awkwardly beneath him. He was no longer breathing. His open mouth and the crater where once his face had been became pools of thick red blood which ran into the sand. The destruction was so severe that he was not even recognizable. The hatchet seemed permanently fixed into the matted tangle of tissue, teeth, and bone.

Jori stood up slowly, gasping for breath. Her right hand was dripping with blood and her shirt was soaked in it. She felt it in large, sticky drops across her face. It was his blood—Eric Duval's—and he was dead.

She stood over him shaking with fear. She was breathing in large gasps. She had killed him. He had come to get her, and she had killed him. She looked again at her bloody hand and her dripping shirt and then glanced back up toward the house 200 feet away.

She would have to get the police and Blain. Oh God, why had this happened? She wanted to cry. She looked again at her bloody hands and walked down to the water's edge and rinsed them off, scrubbing them with sand to remove the sticky clots. Walking slowly, she started back up the beach toward the porch, but then stopped as she saw the lights of more cars coming from the south, from Florexco. A moment later they stopped in front of the house and she heard the sound of doors slamming and men's voices. Jori panicked. They wouldn't understand. She couldn't take a chance. She needed to be able to give her version to the police before the Florexco people could get hold of her.

Quickly she ran north, past Duval's body, staying alongside the dune in the darkness. After a few minutes, she stopped and crouched down in the sand, looking back toward the house and where Duval's body lay. In the distance she could hear the voices of the men shouting and talking, and finally one of them appeared on the beach. A few moments later he yelled for the others. He had found Duval. Two of them bent over the man's body and there was a great deal of angry, excited talk. Finally, one of them pointed north up the beach in her direction, and several of them broke away from the others and

429

started up the beach at a fast walk. The others went back toward the house.

She knew they couldn't see her yet, but she would have to run now. They were coming after her. She ran fast and hard, probably too hard. She stumbled over driftwood and rolled in the sand, but scrambled quickly to her feet and took off again. After several hundred yards, she was far enough ahead of them to pause a moment and decide what to do.

It seemed futile to keep running along the beach. It would probably be better to go up over the dune and get lost in the broad expanses of sand and dune brush there. Slowly she climbed to the top and then down the other side. There was a great plain of smaller dunes and sandy hills.

Jori walked along for a few minutes feeling desperate and frightened. To her left she could see the house. Suddenly the lights from two of the cars parked in front lit up, and they pulled onto the road. They came slowly past her. She ducked down and watched them go by. After another half mile, they pulled over and stopped. A small group of men got out and walked across the sand toward the beach. They were all carrying flashlights, but two of them didn't go all the way to the beach. They spread out and started slowly coming toward her over the broad expanses of open sand, shining their lights here and there.

Then, behind her there were more lights coming from the house, more men. She was trapped. A net had been formed and they were starting to close the ring—coming from both directions. She couldn't go north and she couldn't go south. Straight ahead of her was the road— too dangerous to cross—and behind her lay the water.

There was no escape. Bending over to be less visible, she ran back up to the main dune and climbed to the top.

From there Jori had a view of the whole area. It looked like there were ten or twelve men in all, coming from various directions. There was still several hundred yards between her and the nearest, but the noose would close soon. She was going to have to break through the ring if she was to have any chance of escape. She looked back toward the road. She would have to chance it. Across it lay another four or five hundred feet of sand and then the river. If she reached the river, she could try to swim across to safety. An engine started and she looked back to the house. Another car was moving. It came down the road and stopped right in front, just across from her and two men with lights got out.

It was too late. Her last escape route was cut off. But then she looked out at the ocean. It scared her to look at it. The surf was pounding hard, but she had no choice. She would have to evade them by sea. No, she thought, it's too dangerous. She couldn't do it. But then she looked again at the men coming closer. A moment later, she slid down the dune, trotted quickly across the sand and waded into the water. When it became too deep to walk, she ducked her head and swam through and under the big rolling breakers. For a few minutes she was tossed and bumped about and then she was beyond them, and the swimming was easier. Every now and then, bobbing to the top of a wave, she could see the lights moving down the beach. Swimming, and being carried rapidly north by the current, she progressed up the beach. Soon she was beyond the hunters to the north.

She stayed well out from the beach, being careful to avoid the breakers, and continued moving north, getting further and further away from the danger behind her. The swimming was going surprisingly well, although she was becoming fatigued. As she glanced behind her, she could see in the far distance, men with lights all huddled together on the beach. They wouldn't guess what she had done. It would seem too foolish.

Trying to swim at a relaxed pace, resting frequently, Jori slowly progressed north, and after a while, the bright lights of Harpoon Harry's became bigger and more inviting. She would be safe there, safe in a crowd, until she could get help. She swam a little longer, then finally turned, and using the last of her strength, body surfed in on the breakers and hit the beach about fifty yards south of Harry's. Crawling out of the water, she lay on the sand resting for a few minutes, catching her breath.

The heavy rhythmic music of a rock band drifted out as did the sounds of people laughing and talking. She felt safe. She climbed to her feet and walked across the sand, up next to the dune, in the direction of Harry's. The driving music was like a beacon calling her home. It all seemed like a nightmare, but now she knew she was going to be okay. She wished that she had never gone to the well, but she would be with the police soon and Blain, and it was all going to be over. It would be obvious that she had killed Duval in self-defense.

There was a sudden movement to her left from the dune above her, but before she could react she was knocked to the ground, and someone was lying across the top of her. She felt something sharp—a needle—being jabbed into her leg, and then a burning pain. A hand was clamped tightly across her mouth. She tried to scream, but nothing happened. She struggled, but he had her tightly in a grip. It was hopeless. When she stopped struggling, the man eased his grip on her a little bit and lifted some of the weight of his body off her. She could see his face.

It was Loggins. His eyes looked wild and his expression was of animal rage. "You killed Duval, you sorry bitch! Eric's dead. You mutilated him."

She jerked her head back and forth, trying to free her mouth. She wanted to scream.

He smiled evilly. "It won't do you any good," he said. "Try anything you want, but in a few minutes you won't care. You'll come quietly, believe me."

The empty syringe lay on the sand. She struggled a little more and then gave up. Whatever he had injected her with had started to work. She didn't care as much any more. Finally, after another minute, he slowly took his hand off her mouth. "Scream, and I'll break your neck," he said.

"Duval tried to kill me. I had to do it," she said quietly.

"You shouldn't have done what you did," he responded.

"He hated me. He tried to rape me once on the well."

"That's a lie. That's a dirty lie," he said and slapped her across the face.

She was feeling dizzy, and the slap didn't hurt. She looked at Loggins, and she hated him. He hadn't liked it when she had said Duval wanted to rape her. As groggy as she was, she realized she could still get Loggins. There must have been something between him and the dead man.

"Yes, Winston, it's true. Duval tried to rape me. He wanted me real bad. He said so." She didn't know why she was saying this, but she didn't care. Things were too fuzzy around her, but she wanted to hurt Loggins, no matter what. He was probably going to hurt her. "What's the matter?" she asked. "Did you think Eric was your lover?"

"Shut up," Loggins said and slapped her again, harder.

But this time it hurt even less. It was almost funny in its own way. Everything around her seemed to be spinning. She tasted blood, her lip was cut. Again. Every time she got around Loggins he was always hitting her and cutting her lip. He really liked that S&M. She let out a loud, peculiar laugh and didn't know why. She felt so strange.

Loggins stood above her, and she looked up at him. His face was doing funny things, it was going in and out of focus and twisting. He said something and she didn't understand it. His voice was a blur, a distorted sound. She pushed herself up to her knees and looked around. Everything seemed so peculiar. The waves were doing funny things on the beaches and the dune was changing shapes, getting bigger, then smaller. Loggins himself looked so strange. He seemed distorted. His arms grew longer, then shorter. He seemed to be talking but she didn't understand him.

She looked behind her. The music coming from Harry's was the craziest she'd ever heard. It seemed to be coming in great swoops and swirls. The sounds were swirling about her and the lights were flashing off and on, colors changing constantly. It was a strange distorted sensation, but she didn't care. She didn't care about anything. She just wanted to lie on the ground and listen to the beautiful sounds and watch the lights move.

Loggins had his hand under her arm and was pulling her slowly to her feet. "All right," she said thickly, her tongue making it difficult for her to speak. She felt so tired, but she looked back at Harry's place. The music sounded so nice, the lights were so pretty. Loggins was helping her. Why had she been so afraid? He was nice. She would do what he said. He was trying to take care of her. She felt so sleepy she wanted to lie down.

He helped her down the beach a ways and then up over the dune. Weakly, she walked along with him, trying to cooperate. Several times she slipped and stumbled in the sand. Silently he would lift her back to her feet. He is trying so hard to help me, she thought. How silly of me to have been afraid.

She sat contentedly in his car as they rode into the Florexco compound and parked near the helicopter pad. "You sit up straight and act right," Loggins told her. "Don't do anything to get anybody upset."

"No, I wouldn't," she said, sleepily. "I'll be very nice."

Loggins helped her into the aircraft and she smiled at the strange-looking pilot who gave her a peculiar look. A short while later they were out over the ocean approaching the well.

"It's so beautiful," she said to the others as she watched the red blinking light on top. The other lights seemed to change colors and move about at times. The shadows and latticework of the steel made it seem like a large piece of art. She felt at home. It's so nice to be back, she thought to herself, as she was helped down onto the deck.

She waved good-bye to the pilot who immediately took off again, and then she was in the dressing room where Loggins was helping her get into one of the suits. She giggled as she tried to put the helmet on herself, unsuccessfully. Following his instructions, she walked unsteadily across the deck into the doorway leading down into the sleeping area. He led her to the end of a long hallway and unlocked the door to a tiny room.

He took her in, removed her helmet and helped her lie down on the bed. "You can sleep now," he told her and left, closing the door behind him and locking it.

Jori put her head back on the pillow and, with a gentle smile on her face, drifted into a deep sleep.

Loggins climbed the stairs up to the main deck and then went to the control booth. Sumter was standing over the instrument dials and Hex St. Claire was sitting in the corner, snoozing. He sat up when Loggins entered. Sumter turned to look at him, his face drawn and fatigued. "What happened?" he asked.

"It was her," Loggins responded, "but we caught her. I don't think she had time to talk to anyone."

"Did you get the graphs?" Sumter asked.

"No, we didn't have time. Things got a little too sticky. She murdered Duval."

Sumter's mouth dropped open. Hex stood up and walked over to the two of them.

"She chopped him in the face with a hatchet. I've never seen anything like it in my life."

"My God!" Sumter exclaimed, the shock registering in his face. "Did the police come?"

"I don't think they know about it yet. We didn't call them, and there's no reason for anybody else to have found the body. It was on the beach behind her house."

"She killed him?" Sumter said again. "That's almost impossible to believe. Where did you find her?"

"We chased her down the beach and caught her."

"Where is she now?"

"Where do you think?" Loggins responded, irritated. "Here. I had to bring her back here with me."

"You're not serious!" Sumter cried. "You didn't bring her here!"

"We didn't have any choice. She'd go straight to the police if I hadn't. With Duval dead at her house and the graphs, she'd get too much of an investigation going. We have to stall."

"You idiot!" Sumter yelled. "Bringing her here— that's kidnapping. We'll have federal agents all over the place."

"No," Loggins said calmly. "I've got that covered. Nobody knows she was brought her forcibly. I drugged her—phencyclidine—a form of angel dust. She came cooperatively. The only person that even knows she's here is the pilot and she smiled at him and talked, so he wouldn't be able to state that I was forcing her to come."

"But what about Duval?"

"I'll just say that I didn't know anything about it, and she came a little drunk, but wanted to come to the well and talked me into it. I've got her downstairs locked up in a room. She's sound asleep by now, but she'll be awake soon."

Sumter put his hand to his head, his expression showing the anguish he was feeling. "You stupid fool, Loggins," he said. "All you needed to do was get the graphs. She's been acting so crazy, nobody would have believed anything she had said anyway. Let the police find her. They'll think she murdered Duval in a fit of insanity. Why did you have to involve us by bringing her out here?"

Loggins's voice rose, "I said I didn't think we could afford the risk of a big investigation right now."

"Oh my God," Sumter said. He turned again to stare at Loggins. "You've got to take her back while she's still drugged and drop her on the beach or something. We cannot have her on the well. That's final. That's an order. Just do it, and don't give me any static."

Anger flashed in Loggins's eyes. "Wait a minute, Sumter. You don't give the orders around here, I do. You may be the hotshot scientist, but I am in charge of this godforsaken well and don't you forget it."

"Since when?" Sumter shot back.

"Since Strombeck and I decided that we couldn't take a chance on you screwing this thing up. You make the scientific decisions and keep your opinion on other things to yourself. I know you want to be a scientific hero and that's fine, but I've got to make sure that this thing makes money for Florexco. You've got us in so much goddamned economic trouble now, as it is. We can't take a chance on this thing screwing up."

"You disgusting idiot," Sumter said.

"You say that again, I'm going to break your nose," Loggins responded and glanced at Hex, who took a step toward him. "Don't move, nigger, or you'll be sorry."

Hex's expression was unchanged, but his hands curled into fists. Sumter held out an arm to stop him.

"All right, Loggins," Sumter said, his tone softer. "You're in charge of the drilling, but I'm telling you right now that I'm washing my hands of this problem with Jori and the Coast Guard and everything else. Everything you do from this step forward, you do alone. You had better get rid of her. You're making a big mistake that could bring this whole thing down around our heads."

Loggins smiled sarcastically, "Let me worry about that, Doctor. If what you've been saying all along is true, this whole thing will be done in the next twenty-four hours anyway, right? Then we'll all be worth so much nobody will give a shit *what* Jori Ashe says about it."

"Yeah, that's right," Sumter said stiffly. "We're all going to be rich."

"That's what I like to hear," Loggins said. "So let's just bring this thing in like we started out to do."

Sumter glanced at Hex, then turned away and looked out the window at the activity below. "We're going to bring it in all right," the scientist said, "one way or the other."

"What do you mean by that?" Loggins said.

"I mean exactly what I said."

Loggins stared at the scientist, chuckling to himself at the implied threat the old man was making. "One thing's for sure," he said slowly and forcefully, "you two aren't going anywhere until this is all over. So don't get any ideas."

If there were any problems that developed, he was going to make damned sure that Sumter got his share of the trouble. He was going to take no chances with the old bastard. If the well blew, it was going to take Sumter with it. But he didn't think the man had the guts down deep to take any serious chances.

TWENTY-THREE

When Blain Robson left the OR it was past one A.M. He had been in surgery for almost five hours. A gunshot wound to the abdomen, a bloody mess. Almost everything had been torn up. The poor bastard, he might live, but it was going to be close. The man would need intensive care for a long time.

He walked into the dressing room and slumped exhausted into a chair. He leaned forward and rested his head in his hands. After a few minutes he got up, took off his shirt, rolled it into a ball, and shot a perfect goal into the clothes basket at the other end of the room. He reached to open his locker and then saw the note for him to call his answering service. He quickly dialed the number and received the message from Jori. It had been left around eleven, but it sounded impossible to believe. How could she have gone to the well, and what kind of danger could she be in. He dialed her number and no one answered. Perplexed, he called information and then dialed the night number of the Coast Guard station at Fort Pierce. The duty officer, a Lieutenant James answered. Blain asked him about Jori.

"Dr. Robson, I've never even heard of anyone named Jori Ashe, much less received a call from her tonight, and I can assure you she is not on this base. She wouldn't have gotten in at this time of night without clearance from me, and the switchboard operator doesn't put any calls through to any of the other officers after midnight without checking with me first. So we're sure the Coast Guard hasn't heard from her. Is there anything else we can help you with?"

"No," Blain responded and ended the call.

He got dressed and, after checking on his patient in the recovery room, he tried to call her again. Still no answer. Becoming increasingly worried, he decided to go out to her house and check on her. It seemed impossible to believe the message that she had left. He knew she really couldn't have gone to the well, but maybe it was some sort of code she was using to tell him something. He couldn't figure it out, but it made him nervous. It crossed his mind that she had relapsed into her earlier disordered psychological state. It wasn't an extremely remote possibility—she had been out of it for so long. Relapses were common after neurological injuries, particularly when the patient came under stress like she obviously was.

A great sense of relief came over him as her house came into view, down the road in front of him. Her car was parked out front. She was at home. But then his anxiety increased again. What if she'd been there all along, perhaps too ill to answer the phone or maybe even unconscious. Damn! He shouldn't have allowed her to be alone.

He parked the car, walked up on the front porch and looked with rising alarm at the front door. It was wide open and a big chuck of freshly splintered wood had been torn out of it near the lock. It looked as if it had been forced open. He walked into the living room and flipped

441

on the light. He called her name. No response. He walked into the dining room, picked up the one overturned chair and then into the kitchen. He turned on the light and called her name again, still no response. The back door was wide open. He walked into the bedroom and through the bathroom into the other bedroom, but no one was there.

The house was totally empty. Going back to the kitchen, he stepped out on the back porch. No one was in sight. He was worried. She would never have left the house wide open like this. And why was the front door damaged? Where would she have gone without her car? He called her name from the porch, but still no response. The beach was deserted. He quickly went back inside and called the police.

They came sooner than he could have hoped. By the time he had made one more search through the house, the patrol car was out front. The two sheriff's deputies came up onto the front porch, looking around cautiously. He went through the living room and stepped out to greet them.

"Are you Dr. Robson?" one of them asked.

"Yes. I'm the one who called."

"What do you think is wrong, Doctor?" The second deputy was bent over examining the damaged door.

He quickly told them about the message, emphasizing the part about her being in danger.

"No one was here when you arrived?" the officer asked and stepped into the living room.

"No, it was just like this," Blain answered.

"Have you touched anything?"

"Only the light switches and that dining room chair there. It was lying on the floor."

The officer walked through the dining room into the kitchen, then circled through the bedrooms. "There doesn't seem to be any sign of violence except for that front door. Do you know for a fact that that door was not that way before tonight?"

"I saw it this afternoon and it was fine."

"Now let me get this straight," the deputy said. "That message was left for you about two hours ago, and when you got here both doors were wide open and the lights were off. Nothing else, right?"

Blain nodded.

"Do you have any reason to believe that Miss Ashe was in some kind of danger? Had she had some trouble with anyone?"

Blain took a deep breath. "Yes," he answered after a pause. "There's been some real trouble. She's been sick. It's sort of a long story and it goes back several weeks." He spent the next ten minutes explaining in as much detail as he could about Jori's job with the company, her accident, the problems of the well, her suspicions about the dangers of the drilling, and her confrontation with the workers on the rig the previous night.

The officers asked very few questions and seemed confused by the whole story. Blain thought they focused on her illness and abrupt departure from the hospital more than on the problem at the well.

"Is it possible that she's still sick, maybe having hallucinations or something? Still acting crazy?"

Blain nodded. "It's possible. I doubt it, but it's distinctly possible. She could have relapsed into some kind of delirious state, considering the pressure she's under."

"So this whole thing could be just a figment of

her imagination?"

"Yes, I suppose you could say that. A lot of it could be, but not the accident and the strange goings on at the well. Those things I can verify."

"But do you really think she is in any danger from the people at Florexco? That seems a little far-fetched."

"I don't know," he answered. "I just don't know. I can't imagine them coming after her."

The officers seemed satisfied. "All right, here's what we'll do, Dr. Robson. Let's make a quick search around the house, walk down on the beach, make sure she's not down there. If we don't find her and she's not home by then, we'll put out an all-points bulletin and try to locate her. We'll go to work on it. I think we'll find her."

Blain followed the two officers out onto the back porch and stood there as one of them walked down onto the sand toward the water and the other went around the side of the house. It was then that he noticed the wet life jacket on the floor behind the open door into the house. He picked it up. It was still dripping wet. It was obvious that it had been in use not very long ago. Strange, he thought, and dropped it where he had found it.

The silence was suddenly broken by the frenzied yell of the deputy on the beach. "Sergeant Fulmer, over here, quick! It's a body!"

Terror seized Blain as he leaped from the porch and sprinted across the sand, followed immediately by the sergeant. It can't be, Blain thought with anguish as he saw the limp form at the deputy's feet. A moment later he looked down at the shattered remains of a dead man's face. A group of crabs moved back and forth across the body, clicking and clacking in defiance of the interruption of their meal. Fulmer quickly kicked them away as

Blain and the deputy stood by, stunned at the intense mutilation. The face was an unrecognizable mass of matted hair, blood and tissue. Spicules of white bone and teeth stood in marked relief against the dark brown clotted blood.

Knowing it was futile, Blain reached down and felt for a pulse.

"He's from Florexco," the sergeant said, glancing at the other officer. They both waited while Blain assured himself the man was dead.

"Doctor, it looks like she may be in more trouble than we realized," the senior deputy said at last.

Blain stared at him. "You don't think she could have done this, do you?"

The man shrugged, "I don't know. You said she was sick."

"Not this sick," Blain answered. "I don't think she would be capable of this kind of thing."

"I don't know," the sergeant responded. The other deputy was shining his flashlight around the sand near the body.

"Look at all these footprints, Sarge," he said. "They're brand new—there's been a big crowd down here." The three of them looked around at the numerous prints in the sand.

"Holy shit," the sergeant said. "We'd better call headquarters and get some people down here to help us. Stay with the body. I'll get on the horn." He turned and started up the beach.

While the officer went to the patrol car, Blain walked back into the house. He was sick with fear. Where could she be, he thought. Had someone taken her, or had she escaped down the beach? It was impossible to guess. He went into the bedroom and sat down on the bed, rubbing his face with his hands.

Glancing into the closet, he noticed for the first time the soaking wet clothes piled on the floor. They were still dripping with water when he picked them up. What did it mean? The wet life jacket, the wet clothes? She must have been in the water, but why? It didn't make sense.

Blain went back out to the porch and picked up the jacket again. This time he held it to the light and looked at the words printed across the front: Florexco Crew Boat No. 2. Oh, God, he thought. Had she jumped from the boat and then swum to the beach? Had the dead man been chasing her? But why? None of it made sense.

He went back into the bedroom and picked up the wet clothes. They gave no hint of anything. He looked around the room again and his eyes fell on the large black plastic tube lying across her desk. He had not seen it before. Then, beneath it he noticed a small pool of water. The tube had been wet and not long ago. He quickly picked it up, popped open the can and pulled out the graphs inside. He spread them out on the bed and looked at them curiously. They were obviously technical tracings of some sort. But he had never before seen anything like them. At first they were totally undecipherable, but then he realized that one of them was a footage recording. If he was reading the graph correctly, the tiny black tracing had crossed the 45,000-foot mark.

He stared unbelieving at what he had found. This was it. This was what she had been talking about. She must have gone to the well and, through some act of sheer idiocy, stolen the charts. That's why she was going to the Coast Guard. The people from Florexco must have chased her here. He rolled up the papers and put them back into the tube.

There was no way to know whether Jori was dead or alive. But one thing seemed very likely: the reason for everything was right there in his hands—the charts. Whoever had come after her had not found them for some reason, or perhaps they didn't care if they had Jori herself. In any event, she was probably still in danger, either out on her own, running, or perhaps captured, being held somewhere. It crossed his mind that she might already be dead. He suppressed the idea and took the tube out into the living room and onto the front porch. Wherever Jori was, she would want him to get to the Coast Guard as soon as he could with the evidence she had somehow obtained. Perhaps this was what they needed to stop the drilling, and maybe—just maybe— with some luck they could find Jori.

Fulmer had just finished his radio call for help when Blain opened the car door and sat down beside him. Ten minutes later, after a detailed explanation of the possible significance of the charts, Blain and the sergeant were on their way to the Fort Pierce Coast Guard Station. A radio message had already been sent ahead alerting the commander of the station as to their impending arrival and the significance of what they were bringing with them.

TWENTY-FOUR

The men in the control booth of St. Lucie One stood silently over the panel of gauges and printouts. The depth indicator slowly crawled toward 48,812 feet and stopped. Their eyes glanced up and through the window to the working platform below. Methodically, skillfully, and silently a new section of pipe was swung into position above the turntable and quickly made secure. Slowly the great engine started up again and the pipe began to descend, spinning its way through the small opening in the deck.

The tool pushers stood back uneasily beyond the protective shield around the spinning pipe. They waited. Anxious, tense, and apprehensive. The word had come down—tonight was the night. Whatever it was that the men driving them were after, it was going to happen in the next few hours. It had been a strange job and, in its own way, frightening. But it was lucrative and because of that, the men drilled on. With occasional nervous glances up toward the men hidden behind the glass of the big booth above, the men worked. They kept their mouths shut and their ears opened and they worked. Soon it would be all over and they were glad.

The three men in the booth looked back down at their instruments as the footage began to roll on. But now their eyes watched something else, the electromagnetic force indicator dials. Both the vector and the amplitude measured by the advancing bit had been changing dramatically in the last twenty-four hours. It looked now as if they were about to peak out. The vector had swung around 180 degrees and its oscillations had ceased. The direction of magnetic forces had completely changed and were no longer variable. The amplitude had been climbing steadily and now indicated a magnetic field strength higher than any of them had ever witnessed. It would soon reach its maximum theoretical reading.

"I think this is it," Sumter said and stood up and walked across the room to reexamine the geological diagrams there. "I think this is it." He turned to Hex and Loggins. "Let's cut back to one-half speed."

The black man's expression was unchanged. He looked at Sumter silently and then back again at the men working below.

"That's more like it," said Loggins, rising and stepping to the intercom. He flipped the switch to the engine deck and depressed the talk button. "Cut the power back to one-half and stand by for further reductions. We're getting ready to bring this thing in." He released the talk switch and turned again to Sumter. "Let's just take these last few hundred feet nice and easy, okay? We don't want to end up like the Ruskies, do we?" He grinned.

Sumter ignored him and walked back to the control panel. The reading was 982 degrees. "The temperature is higher than I like. I didn't expect it to be this warm. It doesn't leave much margin for safety."

Hex stood beside him, looking at the gauge. "You didn't really think there would be much room for error though, did you, Adrian?"

Sumter frowned. "No, I knew it was going to be a tight squeeze."

"Let's just not let it get too tight, eh?" Loggins added.

Hex turned to look at him disdainfully. "What's the matter, Mr. Loggins? I thought you were anxious to get this project completed."

"That I am. I just don't want it to wind up as another sad chapter in the good doctor's book."

"I see," Hex responded. "I didn't realize you don't like to see your name in print. I've already got several chapters about you in my book."

"What book are you writing?" Loggins looked suspicious.

"My working title is *Great Asses I Have Known*," Hex replied. His expression became a defiant smile.

The muscles in Loggins's face tightened, but he said nothing as he stared at the big black man.

A moment later the intercom came on carrying the voice of the chief mechanic. "Mr. Loggins, you better come down here. We've got some kind of peculiar vibration. I don't know what it means. But we've never had it before."

Loggins pressed the talk button. "I'll be right with you." He looked at Sumter. "What do you make of that?"

"It's probably nothing," the scientist replied and glanced again at the dials in front of him. The magnetic force amplitude was continuing to climb slowly and the temperature had gone up two more degrees. "Let's go to a quarter speed," he said.

Loggins spoke into the intercom once more. "Skip, cut it back to one-fourth. I'm coming right down." He went to the desk, picked up his helmet and snapped it into place. He opened the door, started out, and then looked back at the two of them. "You'd better teach this nigger boy of yours to watch his tongue, Sumter, or somebody's liable to cut it out for him." He pulled the door shut and was gone.

"I don't think it's necessary to prod him like that, Hex. He's hard enough to work with as it is."

"I don't trust him," the black man said. "His motives are evil."

"Everyone's motives are evil," Sumter replied briskly. "He wants money, that's all. It's the strongest motivating force in the world, but whatever it is each of us wants, we all have our motives. We each have a reason for being here. Some better than others, but all are basically selfish, I can assure you."

"I think that's an overly harsh view," Hex answered softly. "I'm here out of friendship and loyalty to you. I don't think you can label that a selfish motive."

Sumter's cold expression went away and his voice took on a warmer tone. "You're right, Hex. Everyone's not selfish all of the time. I know you're not here because you want to be. You think I'm wrong, don't you?"

"No, I don't," Hex replied. "There is no right or wrong on issues such as these. It's all in the balance between the gain and the risk. I know what you're after and I think it's worth it. I simply have ill feelings about what might happen. I wish we weren't here. But I wouldn't leave without you."

Sumter smiled. "Just like your momma, huh?"

Hex grinned back and nodded. "Just like my momma. Nothing could have pried her from you."

"I know. I still miss her. I think about her almost every day." He thought of the beautiful black Bahamian

451

woman who had been his mistress and housekeeper for almost twenty years—Hex's mother. He had raised the woman's small infant boy as if he had been his own son, and now, almost ten years after the woman's death, the two were still inseparable. As far as he was concerned, Hex was his son. "I understand what you're saying, Hex. But I want you to understand that if you want to leave, you're free to go. I wouldn't hold it against you. It's just that I'm so far along here now. I'm too committed. I've got to take this chance and see if we can do it."

"I understand," Hex said, his expression more serious again. "Don't worry about me." He glanced out the window for a second and then back to the scientist. "I think you ought to worry about the girl, though. I think Loggins may harm her. She's innocent, and she doesn't deserve to die, especially at the whim of that bastard."

Sumter grimaced. "Make sure that she's okay, would you? Take care of that. My feelings about Loggins are the same as yours. I only cooperate with him because it seems expedient for the present."

"I understand," St. Claire replied. "It's going to be a great moment if this thing works the way you want it to."

"That it will be, Hex." Sumter picked up his helmet and snapped it into place. "I'm going down to see what this vibration thing is all about. Keep an eye on that temperature, will you? Let me know if it goes above 990. Somewhere around a thousand degrees is the critical point. I don't know how much leeway we have there." He stepped through the door and closed it behind him.

The night was overcast, but the wind seemed to have died down a little and the sea was becoming calmer. He started down the stairs thinking about the delicate task before him. To avoid the risk of pushing the Balthorium to the point of a self-sustaining reaction, he had to take the drill right up next to it and then stop. It was going to be touchy, but at least he knew what he was dealing with. That was why the Russians had lost their bet. He was convinced of it. They had not understood the necessity of gentleness. But in any event, tonight success would be his. It was inconceivable that anything could stop them now.

As with many great discoveries, it had been the combination of chance and perceptive observation that had led them to the threshold of this achievement. An ordinary man might have missed the significance of this strange softness in the earth through which they were drilling, but his knowledge of the Russian episode and the great drilling machine he had created put him in a position to take advantage of it. How this defect in the earth's crust came to be was of no matter. Whether it was a rare natural geological occurrence or the remains of a previous drilling operation from ancient times, he didn't know or care. There would be plenty of time in the future to decide that. He looked up into the sky above him. It titillated his imagination to think that perhaps some other civilization had visited here eons ago. But that would be for the philosophers to consider, not him. He was interested only in the here and now and the fascination of what he was about to discover.

By the time he reached the drill table, almost all the tool pushers and Loggins and chief mechanic Skip Majors were inside the protective shroud studying the giant revolving clamp that held the pipe in place. It didn't take long to see what the concern was about. On every rotation when the turntable reached a certain spot, there was a small, very minor, but definite clanking vibration.

It was almost as if the drilling was out of alignment, stressing the clamp at one point. The giant hoses from the mud pump would tremble ever so slightly as the turntable reached the point of vibration. Sumter had never seen this exact type of problem before. It was difficult to understand how it could be happening in the absence of a major defect in the turning gear.

Skip Majors was on his knees looking closely into the bearings and their surrounding casing at the point of the maximum vibration. He finally stood up. "I don't know," he said. "It doesn't make any sense to me. The gears are all in good condition. They're brand new. It's almost as if there's some sort of lateral force on the drill pipe that tends to put everything under stress right at that point." He glanced at Loggins and then toward Sumter. "I don't really think there's anything wrong up here. What we're seeing is probably a transmitted vibration from below. Maybe the drill bit's lost a cutting edge or something."

Loggins shrugged. "Could be. Could be some lateral shearing forces down there, too, that are putting some stresses on the bit as it advances. That would make it tend to dig into the side walls of the well at one point more than the others. I don't know if it'll get any worse or not."

The men looked at Sumter. "Okay," he said. "Whatever it is, there's nothing we can do about it now. I doubt if it's going to get any worse. Especially since we're slowing down anyway. Let's just keep an eye on it. It may improve as we get a little deeper. Give us a call up in the booth if it starts to get worse."

He walked out from the protective screen and went toward the crew office. The peculiar vibration made him nervous. None of the explanations offered really made much sense. But one thing was clear, there was nothing wrong with the equipment here on top. Whatever was causing the odd motion in the rotary gear, it was being transmitted from nine miles below. Whatever the explanation, he hoped it wouldn't get worse.

Adm. MacMahon and Kemper Daniels studied the strange-looking graphs spread out on the desk in front of them while Blain waited impatiently in the chair across from them. Sergeant Fulmer of the sheriff's department occupied himself with the nautical charts and graphs displayed around the room.

"And you're sure these came from the well?" MacMahon said, glancing up at Blain.

"No, I'm not sure," he said. "I just believe they are. Like I said, Jori left a message with my answering service that she had been out to the well, that she had something for the Coast Guard. We assume this is what it was."

The commander appeared perplexed. "And, Sergeant, you can corroborate this story that these tracings probably came from Florexco?"

"All I can say, Admiral, is that the girl's missing. There was a dead Florexco employee near the house. There were some wet clothes and a wet life jacket from a Florexco boat, and then there was this tube of charts that looked as if it had just recently come out of the water. Those are the facts. I would certainly say, considering the message that Dr. Robson got, that there's a reasonable chance these items came from the well."

"Do you think the girl's in any danger?" MacMahon said.

"I always think someone's in danger when their house

looks like it's been broken into with a dead body on the premises and they're missing."

The commander sat back in his chair, annoyed at the snide reply.

"Reggie, I think we've got clear evidence to move now," Kemper Daniels said. "Nobody could possibly fault us for taking action, even if we're totally wrong."

The admiral nodded. "I'm forced to agree. Show Dr. Robson the telegram we got last night."

Kemp Daniels opened the file cabinet and pulled out a folder from which he removed a sheet of paper. He handed it to Blain. "We ordinarily wouldn't show a civilian communications of this sort, but since you and the young lady have been so intimately involved in bringing this thing to light, I think it's fair and reasonable to let you know what's coming out of this."

Blain looked down at the paper in his hand. It was a telegraph from Washington, D.C.

TO: *U.S. Coast Guard Station*
        Fort Pierce, Florida
        Rear Admiral MacMahon

FROM: *United States Coast Guard Headquarters*
        Washington, D.C.

RE: *Deep Subsurface Drilling: In Particular*
        Regard to Subcrustal Penetration

In regard to your inquiry about the Florexco Drilling Operation under Offshore Oil Exploration Contract with the Department of Interior #4581-Z, the following facts are reported:

456

1. *There is no limitation within the contractual obligations of Florexco as to the extent of drilling or the depth obtained. Additionally, there is nothing in U.S. Statutes prohibiting deep drilling of the type you have described.*

2. *The Department of Interior as well as CIA information indicates that no successful perforation of the earth's crustal structures has as yet been accomplished. In a report to Congress which was declassified last year, the CIA noted several failed attempts on the part of the U.S. Government and other Western nations to drill a so-called Mo Hole through several selected spots on the floor of the Pacific Ocean. It was also noted that some evidence exists of an abortive attempt by the Russians in the early 1970s to penetrate the crust somewhere in Siberia. Information about this particular effort is extremely sketchy, but the attempt apparently ended in a disaster, with resultant loss of thousands of lives and many millions in equipment. The causes of the accident are unknown, but theories center around hypotheses regarding the existence of a previously unknown element.*

3. *Dr. Adrian Sumter, about whom you inquired, is a highly respected geophysicist known well to the lay public because of his publication,* Seek the Distant Shore. *He has received no major scientific awards or honors, although he is considered to be an expert. In his book, which discusses a number of scientific disasters, he summarized the known facts about the Russian drilling accident.*

4. *Based upon information from the CIA and the U.S. Army Corps of Engineers, the Defense Department has established an internal policy regarding the likelihood of unacceptable consequences of crustal perforation. In brief, considering the unknown aspects of this type of operation, it is at present considered a very hazardous endeavor and should be attempted only under the strictest scientific and governmental control. Risks are said to include the induction of geological accidents as well as the creation of undesirable geological formations. A small, theoretical risk exists of the possibility of radioactive contamination.*

5. *Considering the above facts, you are authorized under federal law to act to protect the public interest. Should it become evident that Florexco is engaging in activities which may be dangerous in the light of the foregoing statements, it is recommended that you act immediately to cause them to cease and desist until further examination of their operations can take place.*

6. *You are instructed to keep this office fully informed on all aspects pertaining to this matter.*

> *Adolph Kerner*
> *Admiral*
> *United States Coast Guard*
> *Chief of Staff*

Blain looked up and handed the sheet back to the commander. "Jesus Christ! According to this thing, she was right."

"We almost shut them down last night," MacMahon said, "but I decided to sleep on it. I wish I hadn't now. I just hope she's okay." He turned to the captain. "Kemp, put the base on full alert. I want three rescue copters scrambled. I'll lead the mission myself. Tell the crews we may have to evacuate the rig." He turned back to Blain. "We'll have this whole thing resolved in the next hour and a half. If she's out there, we'll find her."

Blain frowned. If she is there. That's the question, he thought. He hoped that wherever she was, it was not too late to help her. This situation was obviously much worse than he had realized.

Jori opened her eyes and could see nothing in the dark room. Her head was splitting and she was nauseated. She felt as if she had been sick for a year. Where am I? she wondered. She remained motionless on the bed listening to the familiar throbbing sound coming from outside the room. The well—she was on the well. But how and when had she come? She felt confused and disoriented, but then, slowly, she began to remember. She had been on the beach, caught by Loggins and injected. Injected with something that had only now worn off. She felt lucky to be alive, but scared. Scared at what might be happening.

She sat up, continuing to listen to the sound of the great engine outside. It was going slower, much slower than usual. She stood and felt around the wall until her hand found the switch. The light hurt her eyes, but she felt better being able to see. She looked around the room. It was one she had slept in many times before.

She put her ear to the door, listening for the sounds of

any nearby workers and heard none. Slowly, she turned the handle, but then it stopped. It was locked. She was a prisoner, trapped on the well, and at the mercy of the man who brought her. She felt herself breathing harder and her heart was racing. She was scared. It was frightening to be locked in this small room, waiting. She wanted to demand her release, but she was too afraid to attract the attention.

She looked at herself in the mirror. Her eyes were bloodshot and her face tired. There were still small spots of blood—Duval's blood—scattered over her cheeks and forehead. She looked at her hands and could see blood caked around her fingernails.

She sat back down on the bed. It all seemed like such a bad dream: a nightmare that would end soon. God, she thought, if she could just start all over, she would let the well and everyone who worked here alone. She sat perplexed, frightened, and wondering how she was going to make her escape.

She first realized someone was coming when she heard the metal door at the end of the long hallway squeak slowly open. Then came footsteps. Slow, heavy, ominous footsteps that grew louder and louder until they seemed to be pounding inside her head. And then there was silence. She could feel the presence of a person just outside her door. He was listening to see if anyone was stirring within. She could almost hear him breathe. She wanted to scream, but she was too frightened.

Then there was the sound of a key in the lock, a rattling sound, ominous and full of dire implications. She looked around the room for a weapon, anything to defend herself. But the room was bare. She held her breath as the door knob began to turn.

The large silver-suited figure stood silently looking at her. He stepped toward her and closed the door behind him and then slowly removed his helmet. She let out a deep sigh of relief. It was Hex.

"How are you doing?" the black man said, his tone sympathetic.

"I'm scared to death," she said, her heart still pounding.

"You should be," he answered solemnly. "I think you're in great danger here. Loggins has become irrational."

"Can't someone stop him?"

"It's too late for that. The man has gathered too much power unto himself and there's no time to get outside help that we can trust."

"The Coast Guard, the police, they can help," she answered.

"Not now they can't. They would ask too many questions and want to know too many things. There are simply too many answers we are not prepared to give anyone right now."

She started to lose hope again. "What's going on out there, Hex? How come the engines sound so slow?"

"We are about to reach the mantle, and maybe with it the Balthorium. Dr. Sumter has slowed everything down to a snail's pace. He wants no accidents here."

She shook her head. "He can't do it, Hex. You've got to stop him. It's too dangerous. No matter what he does, it may be disastrous."

"I'm afraid that that is something we are going to have to find out," he answered solemnly. "I have bad feelings about this place, too. But we have no choice now. Dr. Sumter's going to finish what he started."

461

"Even if it kills us all?"

"You should have more faith in him," Hex said and smiled. "He's a brilliant man. I know that he is aware of what he is doing. I trust him. My intuition tells me that he is wrong, but I listen to him with my heart. He deserves this chance. Whatever the cost. He has earned it."

"But God, Hex," she replied. "Even in his book he talked about the dangers. What about the Russians?"

"His book was written for the past, Jori. He has learned from their mistakes. Maybe he can do what they couldn't. He is taking us into the future. Perhaps it's his destiny."

"If he wants to find his destiny, fine. But why should he take the rest of us with him? I don't want to die. And what about the others? Help me stop him, Hex. You've got to."

"That's why I'm here," Hex responded. "The doctor wants to make sure you are given your chance to decide for yourself. The men working here know it's risky. But they're getting big money, more money than they could ever earn anywhere else. So they're making their own choice. It's a roll of the dice for them, don't you see?"

"Are you sure they know all the odds though, Hex?"

"They know it's risky, and they choose to stay for money, that's enough. But you don't have to. I can help you escape. But we must move quickly. Loggins feels very harshly about you. Put on your helmet and come with me."

She did as she was told, and then followed him out of the room, down the long hall and up the stairway where they stopped just inside the door leading to the main deck beyond.

"There is some risk in what I am going to have you

do," Hex said. "But I believe you've got to take it. It's your best chance. I'm not sure that either I or Dr. Sumter can control Loggins. You're willing to try, aren't you?"

She nodded and followed him through the door into the open air. They walked quickly across the deck, past the crew office, beyond the stairs leading up to the control booth and around to the far side of the platform. He stopped when they reached the railing adjacent to one of the great legs that supported the rig. He first unlatched and then removed the cover of a large steel container attached to the rail. She realized what he was suggesting. Within the box was a self-inflating life raft, one of several posted around the well. With it she could float her way to freedom. She looked out at the sea. It was rough, but she had no choice. She would have to chance it. The rafts were designed to withstand storms, so she felt sure that she would be all right until rescued. There was even fresh water and food aboard if she had to wait several days to be picked up.

The wind was coming from the south. That was good. It, along with the prevailing four- or five-mile current of the Gulf Stream would push her north at a pretty good clip. In less than an hour she would be miles from the rig.

Hex finished preparing the raft to be launched and then looked at her. "Are you too afraid to try it?" he asked. "It's going to be hard. After a decent interval, I'll make sure the Coast Guard is alerted. You should be rescued by morning. That will give us enough time to complete our work here as well as guarantee your safety."

"Let's go," she said, grateful for any chance she might have. She had almost abandoned hope when she had realized how trapped she was in the locked room below.

Hex was taking a chance with his own safety in helping her to escape and she appreciated it. She knew that Sumter was playing a role also.

"Climb down the ladder on the leg," Hex said, "and when you get near the water, I'll launch the raft. It will remain hooked to the well by a tether that slides down toward the base of the leg. Pull the raft toward you and, after you're aboard, unclip it and you'll be off."

She climbed over the railing onto the ladder going down the side of the giant leg. Ninety feet below was the dark, turbulent water. She looked into the silver reflective shield behind which was Hex St. Claire. She wished desperately she could change his mind. "Hex, listen to me, please. We've got to do something. This drilling has to stop. It's soon going to be too late. I've seen Sumter's notes. I know you believe in him, but he might be wrong. Can you take that chance? Can you let this many men be risked? And what if something even worse happens? Don't you see that we've got to change his mind? Let me talk to him, please. Just give me one chance to convince him to wait."

"Jori, it's no use. He's going to do it."

"Can't you do something? What about the others? They'd help if they knew the truth."

"You'd better go now," Hex said sternly. "We may be seen."

"Come with me then. Save yourself while there's still time."

"No. I have to stay here. I have faith. Now go quickly before we're seen."

She started carefully down the ladder but then stopped after a few steps to peer intently into his faceplate. "Thank you, Hex," she said with conviction. "You told

me once you would be my friend. Tonight you proved it."
He stood motionless above her while she continued the
downward trek. Soon she was standing just a few feet
above the waves. She looked up, waved, and then
watched as Hex pulled the lever next to the raft.

It sprang loose from the rail and fell toward her,
opening up and inflating as it came. A shiny, steel ring
attached to a long cord from the raft slithered down a
steel cable anchored along the leg only a few feet from
where she was. She reached out, grabbed the rope and,
with a great deal of effort, pulled the raft toward her.
Finally, carefully timing herself as it heaved and bobbed
in the sea, she lifted herself into it. She unclamped it
from the cable and set herself free into the ocean.

On the platform high above she saw Hex wave, and
then he disappeared from view. The raft was jerking and
bobbing, but it was not as rough as she had expected.
Fortunately, she was going to have very little problem
keeping it upright. It was obviously designed for sea
conditions much worse than the one she was facing. Her
biggest concern now was wondering how long Hex would
wait until he notified the Coast Guard, and how readily
they would find her. She looked around at the food and
water supplies contained in various compartments of the
raft. There were enough provisions to keep ten men going
for a week. She could survive indefinitely. There was
even a small kit filled with fishing equipment and
apparatus designed to catch fresh rain water.

In the last compartment she found the key to her
quick rescue. At first she thought the foot-long cylinder
was another packet of food, but then the words on the
side caught her attention: "EPIRB" in capital letters,
Emergency Position Indicator Radio Beacon. The

instructions said that, upon breaking the seal, an automatic distress call would be sent out on an international emergency frequency monitored by all ships, planes and the Coast Guard. She followed the instructions exactly and noted gladly the faint humming noise that began. As she watched the distance between herself and the well grow larger, she thought about Hex and felt sorry for the man who may have saved her life. He was obviously a very devoted and loyal friend to Sumter. She wondered why.

Hex turned away from the rail feeling an odd combination of loneliness and guilt. He couldn't deceive himself. She was right. The men aboard, the workers, were innocents in this undertaking and weren't truly informed of the potential cataclysmic results of their work. They took their bonus money and incentive pay as an inducement to take extra risks, risks which they thought were not much beyond those normally entailed in a fast-paced drilling operation. They had no idea of the dire suspicions of Jori, his own anxieties, and the suppressed vague fears of Adrian. Maybe they should be given a chance to leave now that the drilling was getting closer. He would mention it to Adrian, but it was probably too late. For sure Loggins would veto the idea. He was uncaring and selfish. If the opportunity ever presented itself, it would not require much incentive to destroy a man like that.

As he rounded the large storage shed and started in the direction of the stairs, he glanced back out to the ocean below. The raft was in plain sight, moving slowly, but steadily, away from the rig. It had already drifted more than fifty yards, and in a few more minutes it would be gone for all practical purposes. Jori, at least, was going to be safe.

A movement to his left caught his eye, and he stepped back into the shadows to avoid being seen. It was Winston Loggins. He recognized the insignia on the arm of his suit. The man was walking along the rail, not more than fifty feet away. He seemed to be studying the raft, clearly visible below him, and even worse, he was carrying a weapon—a small hand gun of the type that all the security guards wore. As he watched, Loggins raised the gun, pointed it in the direction of the raft, then lowered it and moved down the rail a few more feet. He seemed to be searching for the best vantage point from which to take his shot. Hex had no idea how Loggins had spotted her. Perhaps it was just bad luck. But it was clear that any action to save her life must be taken immediately or not at all.

He looked about for a weapon, but there was none. On impulse, he started quickly toward Loggins, the sound of his steps obliterated by the wind, the sea and the throbbing of the engine. By the time he reached him, Loggins's arms were outstretched, supported against the rail, the gun held securely in both hands as he took aim. A few seconds and it would be too late.

He hit Loggins from the side with a charging body block that sent the man sprawling onto the deck, the gun skittering harmlessly away under the rail and out into the ocean.

"What the hell!" the man yelled as he looked up to see who had hit him. Hex's heavy boot crashed full force into the front of his helmet. A crack appeared in the faceplate, and a small trickle of red blood came out from the opening as did a soft anguished moan. Quickly Hex had the man's body in his arms and, with one massive heave, lifted him up and over the rail and set him into the salty, windy air above the sea.

Hex watched as Loggins slowly tumbled over once and then hit the water on his back and disappeared. He came to the surface, floundering face down. Hex watched until he disappeared again in the waves and the darkness.

"Who's the nigger now?" he muttered quietly, and then stepped back from the rail, still surprised at his own precipitous action. He looked around. He was alone. What he had done had been accomplished silently and anonymously. He had been totally undetected. Hex was filled with anger and animosity, but also with a sense of relief. Winston Loggins was gone. The man would practice his evil arts no more.

He gazed out to the raft, now disappearing in the distance and wondered if Jori had witnessed what happened. He stood, entranced, staring into the empty waters below and then finally walked across the deck and started up the stairs.

When he entered the booth, Sumter didn't look up. "The magnetic amplitude is reaching a peak now, Hex. We're essentially there. But the temperature is much higher than I expected. We're going to have to stop soon. If we can just make it a little farther, we'll be done."

Hex walked across the room and stood looking out over the rest of the platform. He had never before killed a man, even by accident, and now, as he contemplated what he had done, it was beginning to weigh on him. He had killed a man willfully, wantonly, and with a desire to see the man dead. It did not match the reasonable, compassionate image he had always held of himself. It was at variance with his notions of decency: even if a man were evil, it was hard to justify the ultimate elimination of his existence. In hatred, he had done it. Hex had committed a murder for hatred, excusing it in the guise of protecting an innocent. But he had gone further than necessary for mere protection.

"Loggins is dead," he said firmly. "I just killed him."

Sumter turned around abruptly, his face filled with disbelief. "What are you talking about!"

"He would've shot her. I put Jori Ashe in the life raft and set her free, but he would have shot her. I had to kill him or she would've been dead."

"What happened?" Sumter asked quietly.

"I tossed him into the sea. I threw him overboard. He drowned."

Sumter buried his face in his hands. "Oh my God," he said softly. "I just can't believe it. Another man dead. We can't go on like this, Hex. The price is getting too high. I don't understand this slaughter. First Duval, now Loggins, and the others. I don't understand this senseless destruction. Accidents are one thing, but this intentional violence. There's no call for it, Hex. What's happening to us out here?"

Hex stared sullenly out over the well. "It doesn't matter any more," he said finally.

"It always matters, Hex," Sumter said, and turned back to look at the controls. "We can't go much farther. Tell them to slow down to one-tenth speed."

Hex depressed the talk button on the intercom and quietly gave the order. They heard the engines slow down, and shortly the chief mechanic's voice came into the room. "I don't know if we can go on much longer. The vibration's getting worse down here. Maybe one of you should check on it."

Sumter went to the intercom himself. "It can't be getting worse now. We're slowing down."

The mechanic's voice was emphatic. "I don't care. It's getting worse. I don't think it's in any of our gear. It's being transmitted from below. Something's happening down there and I don't like it."

Sumter didn't answer the man, but walked back to the dials. "Damn," he muttered almost under his breath. "We've got to be so close. We can't quit now."

He glanced at the gauges in front of him. The footage indicator was going much slower now. As his eyes moved across the other dials, suddenly what he had been hoping for happened. The amplitude of the magnetic force, which had been moving toward its peak intensity, suddenly dropped to almost zero and stayed there. The vector of the magnetic waves, instead of remaining at 180 degrees, as it had been for the last ten to twelve hours, became erratic, swinging wildly back and forth over the entire range of the meter.

All other thoughts were instantly swept from Adrian Sumter's mind. "This is it!" he yelled excitedly, his hands held high for emphasis. "The magnetic field's gone. It's just like I said it would be, Hex. Look, it's been obliterated. Just like at the center of a bar magnet. The magnetic force is gone. We're there, Hex! We're there!"

He hurried to the intercom and gave the order. "Slow to one foot per minute and keep it at absolute minimum speed. Stand by to cease operations." He turned back to the controls.

"God bless it!" he said excitedly. "I knew we could do it, and not a minute too soon, either. Look at that temperature!"

The joy and success of the moment overcame Hex's personal concerns, and he broke into a smile along with his friend. "I can't believe it," he said. "I was expecting something different. I don't know what, but more of a dramatic endpoint."

Sumter laughed. "How much more dramatic can it get? We're right in the middle of an intense magnetic field and suddenly it vanished. That's drama, Hex! That's drama."

In their jubilation they almost missed the green flash which shot out from the turntable on the deck below. "What was that?" Hex said as they both turned to look out the window.

"I don't know," Sumter replied. "It looked like some kind of light."

There was a muffled shout from the intercom and then it went dead. At the same instant, two figures burst into view from behind the screen erected on the drilling apparatus. The green flash came again. It was more like a glow that reached out to envelop everything within ten to fifteen feet of the spinning pipe and then, as quickly as it had come, it retracted. But it had reached the two running men. They crumpled to the deck and remained motionless. An instant later, the well went dark, the lights blinking off in sequence from one section of the rig to the other. The rig seemed swallowed up in blackness. Only the distant sound of the engine remained.

Both Sumter and Hex experienced a disquieting, skin-tingling sensation. For a moment, there was a ringing in their ears.

Out of the darkness came the greenness again, a faint scintillating glow that reached out from the area around the turntable to shimmer momentarily, and then it was gone. But this time before it disappeared, it climbed for a brief instant to the top of the derrick. For one microsecond the entire platform seemed bathed in shimmering phosphorescence. Then once again darkness returned. Several more figures could be seen running across the deck, and then they stumbled and didn't get up.

As their eyes became accustomed to the dark, they realized that a number of bodies were scattered, motionless, in the working area.

"My God! We're going too far!" Sumter muttered. "Stop the engine!" He depressed the intercom talk switch, but it was obviously not working. The sound of the engine roared on, joined now by a strange new vibrating sound. More than a sound. They could feel the vibration beneath their feet. The entire platform was shuddering perceptibly.

Sumter glanced at the gauges. The vector indicator was still swinging wildly. The magnetic force amplitude was on zero, and the footage meter continued to move slowly forward. "We'll have to stop this before it's too late. We're going too far," he said, frightened. "We must stop the engine, Hex."

"I think it's too late."

"No! I'm going down!" Sumter yelled. "We were supposed to stop, damn it. It was all going to work just right if only we'd stopped. It's all going wrong." He pulled on his helmet. "If we can just shut down now, we can still save it."

Hex picked up his helmet. "I'm going down with you. We can give it a try."

"I'm sorry, Hex. If I've made a mistake, I'm sorry."

Hex said nothing as the vibrating noise grew louder.

The whole rig seemed to shudder in short bursts separated by pauses of stillness. They left the booth and went quickly down the stairs, started across the platform and then up one more level to the engine deck. They passed at least ten motionless bodies. Sumter was near panic, muttering, "Oh my God," over and over again.

The chief mechanic was standing over his engine controls, both hands locked tightly in a death grip around the main lever, his body weight slumped forward holding the engine in gear.

"Stop," Sumter screamed hysterically at the dead man, and lunged forward as Hex reached out to stop him—too late.

The mechanic's body was layered in a very thin pale green glow. As Sumter grabbed him and pulled him away from the machine, the dead man slumped backwards, the glow gone. But as Sumter pulled the lever back, shutting down the great engine, he let out a muffled scream, glimmered with the radiation for a moment, and then stumbled backwards over the body of the mechanic and lay lifeless on the floor beside him.

The sound of the engine stopped and the rig turned silent, but the emptiness was punctuated by the prolonged echoing scream of Hex St. Claire as he ran to Sumter. He bent over his dear friend, then picked him up and, carrying the limp body in his arms, walked defiantly past the giant silent engine, down the steps onto the main platform and out into the open air. He gently placed the scientist's body on the cold steel and, crying softly, took off his own helmet and threw it across the deck. After removing Sumter's helmet, he supported the dead man's head in his hands.

The scientist's face was in gentle, quiet repose. His

eyes partially opened. Hex carefully pushed each eyelid shut and sat sobbing over his dead friend. "I love you," he said. "You were a great man. You were the only father I ever knew and I loved you. I want you to know it." Tears ran down his cheeks and fell onto the older man's still face.

The quietness was broken by an intense vibration from the drill pipe in the turntable. It stopped and then started again, and Hex looked up just as the sparkling, shimmering burst of green glowing radiation burst forth to envelop the rig once more. For a moment he was inside it. There was a roaring noise in his ears and his skin tingled and then the glow was gone. He heard the vibrating noise once more. He felt himself becoming dizzy. The well began to spin around him. Everything started to go black. He tried to stand, but he had no strength. Finally, he slumped backward and lay motionless on the floor beside his old friend. He felt himself going away into a long, dark tunnel. The light at the end blinked out, and he was gone. Hex St. Claire's eyes became dull and lifeless and, like the others around him, he experienced the loneliness of death.

The well was quiet except for the intermittent vibrations and rattles of the drill pipe against the grip of the quiet and still turntable. Glowing fingers of green radiance leaped out from around the pipe, but they grew less intense and less frequent as the minutes passed.

The exhausted, almost lifeless man clinging to the steps of the ladder began the slow, painful climb to the landing platform above him. His helmet was cracked and his broken face ached, but his desire for revenge pushed him onward. The struggle against the wind and the sea had been immense, but finally, all hope gone, his hands had clutched the ladder. Without the strength to pull himself entirely out of the ocean and up onto the rig, he had clung there for what seemed an eternity. He had felt the surges of energy sweep across the well, and had seen the shimmering glow.

Now was his last chance for survival. He felt his strength ebbing even further. There was a peculiar ringing in his ears and he felt nauseated. Slowly, painfully, he raised himself up and slid defiantly onto the deck. Across the way, slumped at the bottom of the stairs, was the guard. He looked dead.

What has happened, he thought. What has gone wrong? He waited and rested, struggling to regain his strength. He wanted to make the climb to the well. He wanted it for two reasons. First, to get Hex St. Claire, and second, to find out what had gone wrong. He would wait just a little while longer and make the attempt, but he knew he had to move soon. He was getting sicker and sicker. He would be dead soon. The feelings he had were unmistakable. Already, his toes and fingers were getting numb and cold.

Finally, he struggled to his feet and painfully made the long ascent to the main deck above. Never in his life had he felt as strange. There was a ringing in his head and his skin was tingling. He felt a peculiar faint vibration from within his own body. It was almost as if he was receiving small electrical shocks over and over.

Carefully he edged to the top of the stairs and peered through the portal out onto the deck. Even in the darkness he could see bodies of men scattered over the rig. High above in the derrick, one man slumped precariously over the rail. A number of forms could be seen around the turntable, and in the middle of the platform two bodies were slumped together.

He stepped carefully up onto the deck and walked toward the two bodies nearest him. He felt an isolated, almost floating sensation. He seemed enclosed in something which he didn't understand. Unmistakably he was alone, the only survivor. He looked down in horror at the two dead men. It was what remained of Sumter and Hex St. Claire. Sumter's face was wrinkled, contracted and looked like old burned leather. His eyeballs had swollen and popped, and thick, viscous jelly bulged through the corneal cracks. The expression was one of agony. The corners of the lips were torn and cracked, the edges of the wound were dry and crusted.

Hex St. Claire looked the same way, only worse. His black skin had been dried and stretched taut across his bony face. Large dry splits gathered across his forehead with one deep fissure going down across his nose clear to the bone. Loggins bent over and put one finger onto the coarse-looking skin. It was hard and dry and leathery, as if it had been cooked in a microwave oven.

Loggins stood up and moved away from the bodies with revulsion. He had never before seen anything like it, and he felt panic creeping up on him.

The crackling noise from the turntable continued, and occasional small green arcs leaped out to touch the surrounding structures. It looked like lightning in a dark storm. He realized he was beginning to feel very warm. His skin tingled. His eyes burned. His hands and feet were becoming increasingly numb and his face began to feel as if he'd had a bad sunburn. It's happening to me, he thought. I am burning! I am beginning to cook with radiation.

He turned toward the stairs, stumbled across the platform. It became increasingly difficult to breathe. His legs got weak. He fell once, and then slowly stood up. He took off his broken helmet and threw it away from him. He rubbed the skin of his cheeks. It felt firm and rough and it hurt to touch. Oh, God, he thought and looked around with horror, hoping for some escape. His chest was beginning to ache and he was becoming more confused.

The boat, he thought, I can get to the boat. He started toward the portal leading down to the landing dock. His legs were becoming unmanageable. He stumbled forward again and then tried to push himself up with his arms, but they were too weak. I'm going to die, something inside his head was screaming as he tried to crawl forward using his elbows and knees to push against the deck. He felt his face and chest and back burning even more.

"Oh, no," he groaned, "please not me." He started to cry, but no tears came. The ringing in his head grew louder. His eyes felt swollen, tense. He reached the edge of the stairs and, locking his arm over the rail, slowly pulled himself up to his knees. The ringing noise in his head rose to a fever pitch and he felt himself spinning. He grunted loudly and pathetically, and felt darkness creeping into him.

Loggins slumped forward, his arms still dangling over the rail. The cornea across the front of his eyes cracked with dryness. The skin across his face began to wrinkle. His heart beat on, but a minute later faltered and then stopped. His face split and his eyeballs ruptured. Thick viscous fluid oozed out and then began to harden under the influence of the intense energy.

TWENTY-FIVE

The three giant Coast Guard air-sea rescue helicopters were ready for departure by the time Adm. Reggie MacMahon reached the airfield. They waited, illuminated brilliantly by the lights surrounding the small terminal, the blades above them turning slowly, engines throbbing and their running lights blinking. The second and third aircraft had their cockpit doors closed and locked, the pilot and co-pilot within rechecking their flight list. The main cabin door of the first was still open. The pilot, Lt. John Palmer, blond, short-haired, about thirty, stood on the ground below the ladder leading upward to his craft talking idly with his chief mechanic. He came to attention and saluted as the commander, in a bright orange flight suit, exited the building and strode briskly toward him.

"Good evening, Lieutenant," MacMahon said and returned the man's salute. "Let's get moving. We've had a change in flight plans." He went up the ladder and into the cockpit, followed immediately by Palmer.

The second officer and navigator of the craft, Lt. Allen Winters pulled the door shut and sealed it with the assistance of the third crewman and then went forward with the other two officers.

The commander was terse. "The operations room has

just informed me that we are getting an emergency radio beacon signal not too far from where we're headed. Instead of scrambling another crew, we'll divert into that area and see what needs to be done before we proceed with the primary mission."

Palmer acknowledged the orders, made a quick visual inspection of his control panel and then checked to see that his crew was in proper position for take-off. MacMahon was flying the co-pilot slot and Allen Winters had moved back to the third crew position at the navigation table and radar screen. The seaman, back in the cabin, had strapped himself into one of the bucket seats there. The crew members all had their helmets on and each wore an inflatable life vest. Palmer glanced at his instruments for one last check, looked toward MacMahon and held one thumb up. The commander returned the signal and then looked at his own instruments.

The pilot reached forward, flipped the radio switch and then spoke into the microphone extending from the side of his helmet to a point just an inch in front of his mouth. "Seabird Fourteen, Coast Guard Four-one-one-seven requesting clearance for departure."

The response was immediate as the large speaker overhead crackled to life. "Seabird Fourteen, you are cleared for take-off. Seabirds Eight and Seventeen are cleared in that sequence following the departure of Fourteen."

Palmer pushed the throttle forward and the jet engines above them began to roar and the giant propeller accelerated into a thunderous whine. A moment later the craft was airborne, ascending rapidly and then, making a wide sweeping turn to the east, continuing to climb above and away from the lights of the Coast Guard base. Five minutes later the small fleet was out over the ocean, still accelerating toward cruising speed and moving away from the beach into the darkness ahead.

"Seabird Fourteen, this is Fort Pierce Coast Guard. Your course will be one-one-five. Estimated distance of suspected emergency radio beacon—twenty-seven miles. Do you read me?"

Palmer turned the craft onto the indicated vector and responded to the message. "Fort Pierce Coast Guard, this is Seabird Fourteen. We read you loud and clear. We have turned into vector one-one-five. Anticipate overflight within eight minutes."

"That's a roger, Seabird Fourteen. We will be standing by for confirmation and visual report. Coast Guard Fort Pierce, clear."

Palmer spoke again, "Seabird Eight and Seventeen, this is Command Craft. Please check in, then stay with me until we are over target. And stand by for further instructions."

"Seabird Eight checking in to Command Craft. Steady and clear. We acknowledge your instructions."

A moment later the third helicopter checked in. The voice was slow and had a Texas drawl. "Command craft, this is Seabird Seventeen checking in as requested and what I wanta know is what in tarnation are we doin' out here at four in the morning when all good Christians are in bed?"

John Palmer smiled and glanced at the commander, who shook his head in mock exasperation. "Sounds like Dawson's in his usual form tonight," Palmer said. "I don't think they should let Texans loose until they teach them how to talk."

480

MacMahon smiled and then Palmer spoke into his radio again. "I acknowledge receipt of your question, Seabird Seventeen, and I will refer it to Admiral MacMahon, who is sitting right beside me at this moment."

The Texan's voice came over the speaker again. "In that case, I withdraw the question. I'm not as curious as I thought I was. I'll just sit back here and follow instructions. Seabird Seventeen, over and clear and mindin' his own business."

Palmer chuckled and then rechecked the instrument readings in front of him. The cabin was dark, lit only by the glowing dials and meters on the panel in front of the two pilots. The sky was overcast and moonless, and they could see the reflections of the running lights of their craft on the water below. They sat in silence, listening to the hypnotic sound of the engines above them and the air outside rushing past.

"That's funny," MacMahon said, picking up the binoculars and looking to the southeast. "I don't see the lights of the rig out there."

Palmer peered out in the direction of St. Lucie One. "Neither do I. I can usually see it from here pretty easily. Must be some fog."

"I guess so," MacMahon replied. "Doesn't seem like the kind of night for it though." He turned back to the second officer, Allen Winters. "What've you got on the radar, Lieutenant?"

"Nothing yet, sir," the baby-faced officer reported. "I'm getting some interference. I'm checking the circuits now, though. Should have it working in just a minute."

MacMahon carefully scanned the area in front of them from which the emergency signal was coming. He could see nothing.

Palmer spoke into his mike. "Control tower, this is Seabird Fourteen. We should be nearing the position you indicated. We have nothing visual yet."

"Seabird Fourteen, this is Coast Guard Fort Pierce. Cross vectors from us and the Lake Worth station indicate that you should be reaching the point of transmission any moment. Stand by and I will confirm your arrival on radar."

"Roger, Fort Pierce. We request permission to descend to five hundred feet to facilitate visual surveillance."

"Seabird Fourteen, you are approved for descent to five hundred feet. Seabird Eight and Seventeen stay at assigned altitude and stand by to assist."

The pilot eased the throttle back, the craft slowed and he pushed it into a gentle descent. He switched on the spotlights beneath the craft, and they continued their look out as they moved forward along the assigned course, but saw nothing in the turbulent sea below.

The Coast Guard base called again. "Seabird Fourteen, radar vectors indicate you have overflown the target. Please turn to two-nine-five degrees, stay at five hundred feet and resume searching."

Palmer made a quick turn to the assigned vector, then reached over and flipped a switch above the words "Illumination Flare." There was a small explosion to the left and behind the cockpit. An instant later a giant flare shot into the sky and exploded a thousand feet in front of them. As it slowly descended, it cast a faint illumination on the waters below. They waited and watched and were rewarded when their target came into view.

MacMahon spotted it first and pointed it out. The pilot immediately alerted the Coast Guard station. "Coast

Guard Fort Pierce, this is Seabird Fourteen. We have made visual contact with what appears to be an inflatable life raft, unlighted. There's an occupant moving and waving at us. We will initiate pick-up sequence at this time."

"Good job, Seabird Fourteen." The voice which had been professional in tone now carried a trace of excitement. "We put you right on it, didn't we? Coast Guard Fort Pierce standing by awaiting further report."

Palmer put the helicopter directly over the small craft below and began a slow descent toward it. Lieutenant Winters and the other crewman attached safety harnesses to themselves, then carefully opened the side door of the helicopter and prepared the rescue harness to be lowered. About 75 feet off the surface Palmer brought the craft into a steady position and authorized Winters to begin the pickup.

MacMahon was leaning over the back of the pilot to get a better view of the rescue operations. "What kind of a goddamned suit is that guy wearing?" he said. "That's not a flight suit. Where the hell did this guy come from anyway?"

"I don't know." Palmer was puzzled. "I just assumed we were dealing with some kind of boating problem. There's been no report of aircraft down."

"Especially one that would require flight gear like that," MacMahon added. "We would have known about that."

"Holy cow!" Palmer said as he got a better look. "That's the kind of thing they've been wearing on the rig. That's one of those Florexco outfits."

"I'll be damned," MacMahon responded. "I think you're right. That is from Florexco. What the hell's he doing way out here?" They watched as the figure below got securely into the rescue harness and was then slowly lifted toward the aircraft.

"It's a woman!" Winters shouted from the rear. "It's an honest-to-God female. No kidding!"

"I think it's that Ashe girl," MacMahon said incredulously. He rose and walked back into the cabin area as she was lifted into the doorway. She was dripping wet and looked exhausted. Her face was pale and at first she could barely speak.

"I thought you'd never come," she whispered at last, but she was smiling. They laid her on a pad of blankets and unzipped the uniform to loosen it around her neck and chest.

MacMahon was down on his knees leaning over her. "Are you all right?"

She nodded. "Yes, thank you. I'm doing better. I'll be all right. Give me a minute. It's been torture in that little raft." She closed her eyes and took several deep breaths and then pushed herself up to a sitting position. "Wow, I was never so glad in all of my life to see a helicopter as I was when you guys showed up. I guess that radio worked, huh?"

The crew standing around her were smiling. "You're very lucky," MacMahon said. "You'd have drifted forever out there if that radio hadn't alerted us. What happened to you? How'd you get out here in that raft? We were headed out to the well to search for you."

"Oh, thank God," she said. "It's a long story."

"Everything's under control. You can rest awhile. Dr. Robson brought the charts you had. We're going to stop the drilling. That's where we're headed now."

"Hurry, please," she said. "I'm afraid something's happening. The lights on the well just went out a few minutes ago and I saw a couple of peculiar electrical flashes. They may have had another accident. They've been drilling hard and heavy all night. I hope it's not too late to stop them."

"It'll be okay. We're only eight miles away. We'll be there in just a few minutes. You actually saw the lights go off? We thought they were in a fog."

"No, no!" she said emphatically. "I had a clear view of them until just a few minutes ago. The rig just went dark and then there was kind of a green flash and that's all. I haven't seen anything since." She put her hand on MacMahon's arm. "Believe me, Commander, something's wrong out there. All the things I was trying to tell you are true. The place is ready for a disaster. You've got to stop them quick."

"We will. You just take it easy and relax. We've got a handle on this thing now."

"I hope so," she said and looked up at the others. "Thank you for coming. I don't think I could have made it much longer."

MacMahon smiled and went forward, and almost immediately the craft accelerated in the direction of the well.

Winters held her hand and grinned. "This is the best part of our job when we pull somebody out of the water like that. As soon as we get this well problem taken care of, we'll get you back and have you checked over by one of the docs."

He pulled the big door to the cabin shut, removed his safety harness, then went forward and sat down in front of the radar screen.

Palmer was talking to the other helicopters as well as the Coast Guard station. "We have completed our secondary mission. We have the subject, a female named Jori Ashe, with us and she appears to be in good condition. We are proceeding now to the oil rig. Be alerted that the lights of the derrick are no longer functioning, and we will have to use radar approach. Seabird Eight and Seventeen space yourselves widely and follow us in."

"Admiral, you'd better come back and look at this radar yourself. There's something very strange. . . . I don't understand it," Winters said.

The commander walked back and stood beside Winters looking into the big screen. "We should be picking up the well right there," Winters said pointing to a large, irregular, fluffy-looking tracing on the scope, exactly where there should have been a much sharper, more distinct image. "What we're seeing here doesn't look like the well at all, it's way too big. It looks more like a dense thunderstorm ahead. I don't understand it." He looked up at MacMahon who continued to watch the screen.

"It must be the equipment," MacMahon ventured. "It's some sort of malfunction."

"That's what I thought at first too," Winters replied. "But I don't think so now. The circuits all check out okay. I think we're getting a true reading. I just don't know what it means."

"Let's check with the other choppers, see what they're reading," MacMahon said and stepped forward into the cockpit and plugged in his own mike. "Seabird Eight and Seabird Seventeen, this is the commander speaking. Please give me a report of your radar tracings of the St. Lucie rig."

Ron Dawson from Seabird Seventeen spoke first, "Admiral, I'm embarrassed to tell you this, but we're having a little trouble with our equipment here. I think we have a problem with our fine tuning. We're working on it, though, and we'll get back with you as soon as it's doing okay. Seabird Seventeen, clear."

Seabird Eight checked in. "Sir, this is an odd coincidence. We're havin' the same sort of problem. We're just getting a big fuzzy image up ahead. More like clouds or somethin'. I don't know what's wrong. The circuits seem to check out, but obviously it's goofing up somewhere. Seabird Eight, clear."

"Communications received," MacMahon said. "Seabird Fourteen over and out. Standing by." He unplugged his mike and looked at Palmer. "I don't know." MacMahon threw up his arms in a questioning gesture and then went back to reexamine the radar. He took one look and stuck his head back up front, "Lieutenant, hold up. Let's mark time right here until we get this clear. I want to know what's happening ahead of us before we blunder into anything."

Palmer gave appropriate commands to the other two helicopters and pulled back on the craft's speed until their forward motion came to a halt. The three large helicopters hovered at an altitude of 2000 feet. It was an unusual formation. The lack of forward movement at such a high altitude, the reflections of their running lights off the sea below and the curious mystery of what lay ahead fueled a mild uneasiness in the men.

MacMahon leaped over the scope beside Winters and studied the image there. The bright, irregular shape which lit up with each sweep of the constantly revolving radar beam was very large, more than 1000 feet across. It did not look like anything they had ever seen before. MacMahon walked forward and stared out the front windows of the craft. "Do you see anything?"

"Not a blasted thing," Palmer responded. "It should be sitting right out there. From here it usually looks like a giant Christmas tree. It must be entirely unlit."

"There's no fog either; that doesn't explain it. The damned thing's lights are just out." MacMahon walked back into the cabin and stood beside Winters. He looked at Jori, still seated, but who was now watching the officers intently. "You saw the lights go out? You actually saw that?" he asked her.

She nodded. "One minute they were on and the next minute they were off. Something is wrong. It's just like when I got hurt."

"When you were injured," MacMahon said, thoughtfully, "it was just the breakers that went. They thought it was some kind of electrical accident. Nothing else was damaged. By the next morning things were back in operation. I guess the same thing could have happened again."

"But that doesn't explain the radar," Winters interjected.

"I know," MacMahon responded. "Miss Ashe, do you feel up to looking at this radar scope a minute with us?"

She stood up and looked over Winters's shoulder as he pointed out the radar findings and explained them to her. "You know what I think," Winters said when he finished. "I think the size of this thing is growing. It's more than twelve hundred feet wide now. That's twenty per cent bigger than it was a few minutes ago."

MacMahon looked at the scope once more and then straightened up. "What do you think, Jori?" he asked.

Jori's eyes remained on the scope while she deliberated her answer. Then stepping away, and pulling her hair back from across her face, she took a couple of deep breaths and looked at MacMahon. "I think you know what I'm thinking."

The admiral let out an exasperated breath, "But that's ridiculous."

"This whole thing sounds ridiculous," she said. "But I'm not afraid to believe anything any more after what I've been through. I think they've finally done what we've been afraid of. They've drilled into something, and I think that we're seeing the effects of some kind of release of radiation or something. I think that's what we're seeing. If Sumter's right, we may be seeing the effects of a Balthorium reaction. It may be a new form of radiation. As I told you before, that's what he was after."

"I don't believe it."

"Neither did the Rusians in '74," she said. "But you give me a better explanation. There are a lot of things we don't know about radiant energy and if Sumter's right and they've drilled into a new element—one that's capable of fission reactions—there's no way to know what kind of radiation it emits. It could be anything— radio waves, x rays, heavy proton radiation—you name it, Admiral, and it's a possibility."

MacMahon did not respond but went back into the cockpit. He plugged in his mike again. "Coast Guard Fort Pierce, this is Seabird Fourteen. Come in please."

"We receive you, Seabird. Go ahead."

"Fort Pierce, this is MacMahon. Give me a radar report in the vicinity of the Florexco St. Lucie rig, please."

"Roger, stand by." There was a short pause and then the message continued. "Seabird Fourteen, this is Coast Guard Fort Pierce. I have been advised that, as of a few minutes ago, we have had a radar systems failure. They are having some kind of imaging problem and have lost contact with the St. Lucie rig. I have been told to advise you to stand by."

"Coast Guard, what kind of images are they receiving from this area. I don't care if it's erroneous or not."

"Seabird, I am advised that they have images which resemble a large thunderstorm more than anything else. This was not present just a few minutes ago and, in the absence of any surrounding weather conditions, is considered a technical error. I repeat, they have advised me to request that you stand by until their circuitry problems are corrected."

MacMahon unplugged his mike and returned to the cabin. "Something's wrong," he said quietly to the others. "The base radar is showing the same sort of thing that we are. Something's happening to that rig."

"Whatever's happening, it's getting larger," Winters said. "It's almost sixteen hundred feet across now."

Jori's face was drawn. "It's some kind of radiation effect. There's no other answer. They've done it. Whatever the hell's gonna go wrong now, it's under way. I don't think there's anything we can do."

MacMahon let out a deep sigh. "Lieutenant. Advise the base of our findings. Tell them we suspect this is some kind of radiation accident. Have Captain Daniels notify Washington immediately. Tell them we have no idea what's going to happen next, but that we're standing by, temporarily, just observing this situation. Whatever the hell is out there, we're not flying into it until we know more about it. I'll wait till daybreak if I have to. We've got plenty of fuel." He turned to Jori, "I should have stopped them yesterday, just like you said."

She shrugged helplessly. "How could anybody know for sure," she said softly. "It's all done now."

They looked down at the scope. The image seemed to have grown even larger.

The sky in front of the three hovering, lonely helicopters remained empty and dark.

TWENTY-SIX

Maj. Gen. Sam Weg rose from the command controller's desk at the North American Air Defense Command Headquarters buried deep within Cheyenne Mountain, Colorado and took the cup of coffee offered him by Sgt. Evan Elliot. The general yawned and stretched and glanced at his watch. Just a few hours until the end of his shift. He was bored and tired. The stress of being shift commander at NORAD was fatiguing. The days of sheer boredom, punctuated by occasional brief moments of crisis, were stressful. Even working the eight-hour shift only four times every seven days was more than most men could tolerate. He was charged with the responsibility of coordinating the incoming data from the multiple early warning systems in the Air Defense Command.

He took a sip of the hot, black coffee and looked around. He had a good team tonight. Most of them were young, but they were well experienced. They were alert and conscientious. They knew they had to be when he was in charge. He wanted no snafus. So far, he had avoided the embarrassment of false alerts that had plagued the center in recent years. That was partially by luck because the giant Honeywell 6000 Computer and its backup sister had never screwed up while he was in command. But more than that, it was because of his obsessively compulsive nature. He never relaxed during his shift as many of the commanders did. He kept constantly abreast of every signal, every indication. If there was a plane off course or an unexpected sunspot he knew it, and he knew it quickly. None of this responsibility was ever passed down the line. He watched everything himself. He made every decision himself, and his men knew he wanted instant responsiveness at the first sign of even the tiniest deviation from normal.

General Weg believed in the system. He believed that it was nearly impossible to initiate an attack against the United States without the commander in this room becoming aware of its progress within just a few minutes. As far as he was concerned, the key to that success was the satellites. Sure, there were the radar systems—the ballistic missile early-warning systems in Greenland, Alaska, England, Otis Air Force Base on the east coast, Beal on the west, as well as many other radar installations including the old Distant Early Warning System covering the Atlantic. But he knew the real secret to the accuracy of the modern warning system was the satellites. The three early-warning geosyncronous stations 22,000 miles above the earth relaying their signals constantly to NORAD—that was the key. That was where the real early warning would come from. With this system he could practically detect a car backfiring in Moscow, and there was no way the Ruskies were going to slip anything in on him. Not with the equipment he had.

He closed his eyes and stretched once more, and when he opened them he received the shock of his life. The panel in front of him which had been filled with darkened lights was now dominated by a single red blinking signal. The startling aspect was that the information in front of him was not an indication of a potential launch of missiles from Moscow, or from subs in the Atlantic, or even an indication of low-flying Russian bombers coming in over Canada. The signal was a statement that a nuclear attack was already under way with at least one nuclear detonation having already occurred.

Before General Weg could even respond, Capt. Burt Blizoro, sitting ten feet away in front of a computer-printout screen, turned and addressed him. "General, we have evidence of a nuclear explosion in Florida."

Other men in the room were starting to stir. Lights were coming on everywhere. "What the hell!" Weg screamed. "Reconfirm!"

As Blizoro hit the keys of his computer terminal, the general began to flip switches in front of him verifying the integrity of the warning circuits. Everything came up green. All circuits were intact. The red warning light continued to blink. A soft bell was ringing in the room. On the panel, another large red light was illuminated: "Hotlines activated." He eyed the red phones in front of him. They were communications with headquarters of the Strategic Military Command Center in Maryland, the controlling center to which the Pentagon officers and the President would go in the event of nuclear war.

Still in a state of disbelief, Weg looked at Blizoro. The captain's voice interrupted his thoughts. "Sir, everything checks out. We have satellite indications of a nuclear detonation off Palm Beach, Florida."

The general swung around to the radar control officer on his right, Lt. Alisha Bradford, the only female member of the team. "Bradford?" he said questioningly.

"We have radar confirmation," she said. "Otis as well as the Caribbean bases confirm detection of radar

493

densities consistent with thermonuclear detonation."

The general turned to Blizoro. "Reconfirm. How could anything get in there without us knowing about it?" Without waiting for a response, he addressed a group of technicians seated in front of panels far to his right, "Anything coming in from the north?"

"Nothing yet," one of them responded. "It's all quiet."

"Shit!" he said and swiveled completely around in his chair, and fired his next question at a technician sitting in front of a large computer terminal, "What does the computer say? Give me the possibilities."

The man hit several buttons and the monitor above him lit up. Three lines immediately flashed on the monitor:

1. *Data reliability factor—100%*
2. *Circuit reliability—100%*
3. *Valid attack conclusion—78% reliability*

Weg studied the readout. Even the computer had a slight doubt about the validity of the conclusion. As he watched, the 78 per cent changed to 91 per cent. As the seconds passed the computer was becoming more confident in its answer. He directed the question to his right again, "Still nothing from the north?"

"All clear."

"I don't know what the hell's happening here," he said, "but it's time to act." He checked his watch. It had been forty seconds since the first alert.

Weg picked up the red phone and was in instant communication with the acting commander of the Strategic Air Command and the coordinating commander

494

of the U.S. Armed Forces at the National Military Command Center. He knew they were each aware of approximately the same data. The elaborate and complicated defense computer network by now had already transmitted everything the gigantic NORAD computer had determined. He knew they would be awaiting his call. The first voice answered, "Gen. Richard Knowles, acting SAC commander." A moment later, sounding slightly more distant, "Gen. Les Marshall, acting commander National Military Command Center."

There was silence as the two men thousands of miles away waited for General Weg's message. "We have satellite evidence backed by radar confirmations of a thermonuclear detonation in Florida," Weg said, looking back at the printout terminal of the computer behind him. "I have a data reliability of 100 per cent and an attack conclusion reliability factor which is now at 95 percent."

"General Weg, this is difficult to believe," Marshall said. "What could have been the source of the attack, and why do we not have evidence of other missiles or planes coming in? It doesn't make sense. It's bound to be another computer foul up."

"I don't understand it myself," Weg said. "I'm limited to judgments based strictly upon the data we receive here. We have two separate reporting systems confirming the reliability of the detonation. But as you know, no evidence at all of the manner of the attack." He glanced at a big board on the far wall in front of him. "We have no data putting enemy subs in the area, none of our own subs are in the vicinity, and our system integrity information indicates that all warning systems are functioning properly. I suggest we bump ourselves to

495

condition red and stand by. According to my estimate, assuming that the attack is not somehow evading our detection, we are still outside of the eight-minute warning zone for additional hits. England, Alaska, and Greenland still report negative, as does the Arctic. Otis sees nothing over the Pacific, except that they do confirm the blast effect as noted."

"SAC agrees," General Knowles said.

"National Command agrees," General Marshall said.

Maj. Gen. Richard Knowles at Offutt Air Force Base in the Operational Command Center, pressed the "red alert" button bypassing the lower two stages. Because of the ominousness of the situation, he picked up the orange phone to the side of his desk and listened as the various SAC bases checked in. Finally, "This could be the real thing," he said. "We have a nuclear detonation in Florida."

At thirty-three SAC bases around the world bomber crews scrambled. Within minutes, fleets of B-52s and a dozen brand new B-1 bombers were screeching toward the stratosphere turning onto course vectors leading them toward Russia. At the alert level which had been called, they would proceed only to their checkpoint about halfway to their target, at which time they would go into a hold pattern until either authorized to attack or called back. One step up in the alert and the attack would be on.

In central Oklahoma, Capt. Billy Sanders stared, unbelieving, at the red light blinking in front of him.

"Initiate Attack, Phase I." He checked with his partner across the room, Lt. Bob Pittman whose console light was blinking the same message. They were seventy-five feet beneath the surface in a Minute Man ICBM Launch Command Post. They had only two steps to go through to launch the missiles and the first had been ordered. They, and ninety-nine other two-man teams across the country's prairies had now been ordered to ready the one thousand missiles for potential attack.

Sanders quietly withdrew the key from the container strapped onto his belt. Pittman did the same. They each inserted their key into launch control locks in front of them. The captain then twirled the combination on a locked box in front of him and removed a card upon which was printed a code word. If Stage II was ordered— an attack—the code word would be with the attack orders. If everything matched, he would turn his switch, the lieutenant would turn his switch, and if a coordinating team at another site fifty miles away concurred with the same action and turned their keys, giant doors covering fifty nuclear minutemen missiles in their silos would blast open, and the missiles would begin their half-hour voyage toward the enemy. Billy Sanders blinked nervously. He and three other guys were reaching into their guts to get the courage to launch a nuclear holocaust against an unseen enemy. What could possibly have happened out there, he wondered. What in hell is going on?

At the North American Air Defense Command in Colorado, General Weg studied the information coming in to him. Confirmation and reconfirmation of the blast was made. There seemed to be no question. The computer's attack verification conclusion was shaky though. It kept oscillating between 90 and 95 per cent. It refused to go to the 99 per cent level, which was required to advance to the next stage of retaliation. The radar network still indicated that the air space over the north and the east was still empty. Nothing was coming. He glanced at the data pouring in from all the other early warning systems. Nothing. Only the one explosion in Florida.

From the phone he was holding loosely at his ear, he heard the voice of Richard Knowles, SAC commander of the hour. "We are at maximum readiness and standing by."

Weg kept an eye on the clock on the wall in front of him. Four minutes into the alert. By now five hundred aircraft were in the air as nuclear technicians prepared their deadly cargo for possible use. Les Marshall's voice on the phone interrupted him. "The National Military Command Center is at full alert and the President is being informed at this moment. Gentlemen, I think we sit back and hold our breaths for the next two to three minutes."

"Agreed," Weg said. "Just a moment!" He read the computer printout handed to him, and his eyes flashed in the direction of one of the satellite printout consoles. "Gentlemen," he said into the phone, "we have just received satellite data that the Russians are scrambling their bombers. This may be it."

"Goddamn!" General Marshall responded. "What in hell provoked this!"

"This could still be just an alert," Knowles cautioned. "They might be putting theirs in the air because they know we're scrambling ours."

498

"That doesn't explain the bomb," Weg interjected.

"No," Knowles answered. "I think we're only a few minutes from a locked-in engagement. We need some local information."

"We have reconnaisance aircraft coming out of Miami and Jacksonville right now," Marshall said. "In a few moments I should be in touch with the Coast Guard station in Fort Pierce, Florida. That's the nearest military installation to the point of impact. I'll get back with you as soon as we have some information there."

"Better make it quick, Les," Weg said. "We need to have the President on the hotline to the Kremlin within the next three or four minutes, or we're going to have to pull out the cork."

"Agreed," Marshall responded. "Everybody just stand by. I hope to God they don't have STEALTH. If they're coming in radar-invisible, we're finished."

TWENTY-SEVEN

Seabird Fourteen and the other two Coast Guard helicopters waited, hovering at 2000 feet, slightly less than six miles from the expanding radar abnormality in front of them. Admiral MacMahon was perplexed. He had made many difficult decisions in his career, but they had each been totally different from what he now faced. In those earlier circumstances there had never been a question of exactly what to do. The only decision had been as to whether to do it or not. In this case the situation was different. He had no earthly idea as to what to do, or even why. He waited, hoping something would change or some new information would arrive that would show a clear-cut necessity for action. It had always been his style to make no decision until he was positive that a decision was called for. He was conservative by nature and held in disdain persons who jumped into precipitous, uncalled-for action. He firmly believed that doing nothing was frequently the safest course.

He stood with Jori looking over the shoulder of Winters at the radarscope. "The son of a bitch is still getting bigger," Winters said. "It's almost 2000 feet wide."

The commander and Jori went forward again, and he took his place in the co-pilot seat while she stood behind, resting one hand on each of the two seats. They both looked silently into the total darkness in front of them. On each side of them, a few hundred feet away, another copter hung suspended in the night air, its red and white running lights blinking continuously.

"All right," MacMahon finally said, impatiently, "let's move in closer. Let's get a better look if there's anything to see."

"Better be careful," Jori said. "There could be some risk if this is some kind of energy field, like I suspect it is."

MacMahon agreed. "We won't go into it, we'll just move in a little closer." He motioned to Palmer who passed the word to the other two pilots and then nudged the helicopter into a slow forward speed.

Several minutes passed silently while nothing changed. The water passed beneath them, but the darkness ahead remained empty.

"We're two miles off," Winters said. "It's still expanding a little."

MacMahon held his hand up and waved slightly at the pilot who slowed the craft's forward motion somewhat.

"Hey, wait a minute!" Winters yelled. "I've got two high-speed aircraft coming in from the south. And they're really moving, too."

MacMahon jumped out of his seat, pushed quickly past Jori and stood beside the lieutenant. Jori stood behind them, being careful not to get in the way of the two officers who were intently studying the radar.

"Jesus Christ!" Winters said, "those sons of bitches weren't even on there a second ago, and now look at them!" They watched for a few seconds longer. "I think they're headed into this thing, whatever it is."

"I think you're right, Al," MacMahon said. "They must be Air Force, out of Homestead. We'd better give them a holler, tell them to stay out of this thing until we know what it is."

"It's too late now," Winters said. "At the speed they're going they'll be in it in another five seconds." The three of them watched as the tiny white blips continued to move rapidly across the screen and then disappeared from the scope into the white, irregularly shaped radar density they had been watching.

"We'll know in just a few seconds what this is all about," the commander said, and then turned to call to the pilot, "John, we've got two high-performance aircraft in from the south and they flew right into this thing, whatever it is. Try the Air Force frequency and see if we can reach them. I'd like to get their observations. They went through it."

"Right," the pilot replied, and they could hear him flipping frequency controls and then broadcasting a call to the two craft. An instant later, two white blips emerged from the large mass on the scope. They were directly in front of the helicopter and headed straight for them, but at a lower altitude.

"Oh no!" MacMahon yelled, and stood up to look out the forward window.

"I got two aircraft right on our nose about five hundred feet below us," the pilot yelled. "It's going to be a near miss!" Straight in front of them, about a mile away, they could see the lights of the two planes.

"Surely, they can see us," Jori said nervously. "They're not going to hit us, are they?"

"God, I hope not," Palmer answered. "They are starting to descend."

They could see the outline of the craft now.

"They're F-14s!" MacMahon yelled, "and they're sizzling!"

"Something's wrong though," the pilot responded. "They're wobbling too much. I think they're going down!"

"Holy shit!" the commander cried, as the plane on the left suddenly put one wing down and rolled 90 degrees. It held steady for a second, and then suddenly a large object hurdled from the cockpit. The plane itself then rolled another 90 degrees and turned into a steep arc toward the water. It buried itself into the sea almost directly beneath them. There was a bright flash and then a fireball on the surface of the water, which rose slowly up toward the helicopters.

Acting reflexively, Palmer pushed the throttles full forward and the copter lurched forward rapidly. It then came around to the north away from the fire and dropped down to less than 500 feet off the water, no more than 1000 feet from the burning plane.

They saw the other aircraft speeding away from them but wobbling and turning irregularly. It quickly disappeared into the darkness, and they watched its running lights until they abruptly disappeared. A second fireball lit up the night not more than two miles away. The one in the distance formed a billowing red burst of flames with skyrocketing pieces of burning metal glowing yellow and red in the dark. The major explosion was followed by a number of smaller ones sending tiny fingers of flames shooting up from the surface.

The plane beneath them continued to explode violently. The fireball expanded rapidly forcing Palmer to bring the copter around and retreat an additional 500 feet. Huge balls of black, angry smoke hurtled up toward them as the flames devoured with spectacular fury the remains of the craft and fuel. The helicopter shuddered perceptibly with the shock wave from the explosion, as its crew watched in stern silence the awesomeness of the accident. The clouds above them glowed red in reflection of the inferno below.

Finally, the twin fires began to ebb, each alternately being renewed by an occasional repeated small explosion, but the worst was over. Like two hot cinders glowing in the night, they receded into quiet, strange-looking, silently burning interruptions in the black surface of the sea.

Palmer was the first to react. "Seabird Eight, proceed to the distant crash site, search for survivors. Seabird Seventeen, stay with me and assist in search and rescue. I think I may have seen a pilot come out of this plane."

The two other copters acknowledged their orders. One of them peeled off from the others and headed toward the distant fire.

Jori was the first to sight the strobe light of the downed pilot. "Over there," she said, pointing to the east. The others peered into the darkness and about 1000 feet away found the brilliant white flashing light—possibly the emergency strobe beacon attached to the pilot's flotation gear, a self-deploying device.

"Let's go," said MacMahon. "I don't think he's got a chance in hell of being alive but let's get him out of the water."

"I don't know how fast he was going when he ejected," Palmer said, "but I guarantee you it was too fast. If he's alive, it will be a miracle. I don't think there'll be a bone in him that's not broken."

In the cabin of the helicopter, Lieutenant Winters and the Seaman First Class, Bobby Merrill, had both begun to put on their diving gear. They were preparing to go into the water if necessary to assist the downed pilot. The helicopter was brought over the flashing strobe, and as they descended to within seventy-five feet of the surface they could see the man clearly. His life jacket was doing its job of holding his head and face above water, but he was not moving.

"I'm going to take you down closer," Palmer said and let the copter slowly descend down to within thirty feet of the surface.

"I'm going in," Winters yelled. "Bobby, stay here and work the winch. If I get into any trouble, you can assist me." He sat at the edge of the open door and quickly put on his flippers and then leaped forward into the water. He and the lowered harness reached the pilot simultaneously, and he hastily fastened it underneath the man's arms and then waved to the seaman above. The limp body was brought up and swung into the cabin and the harness lowered again to retrieve the lieutenant.

Seaman Merrill concentrated strictly on bringing Winters back into the safety of the aircraft, while Jori and MacMahon worked on the motionless pilot. The man was gently placed on the floor of the cabin and his helmet unstrapped and pulled off. Jori could not muffle the startled gasp that escaped from her when she saw his face. MacMahon, startled, reeled backward and almost lost his balance. Seaman Merrill and Lieutenant Winters were now with them staring in horror down into the destroyed face of the dead pilot.

The skin across the man's face was parched and dry and cracked like old leather. It was stretched taut across his nose and cheekbones, and the corners of his lips were lacerated and distorted by the dead-looking skin. The teeth and gums were exposed and looked burned as did the eyelids and eyelashes. The eyes were pulled open by the contractures of the shrunken skin. The eyeballs had ruptured along the margins of the cornea. A thick, dry-looking gelatinous mass exuded from within what had once been delicate structures. The face looked as if it were a hundred years old—mummified.

Jori bent down hesitantly and touched the man's cheek and then pulled her hand back in revulsion at the coarse, dry feeling. All she could think of was pictures she had seen of thousand-year-old pharaohs pulled out of Egyptian tombs and unwrapped. The deep cracks and tears of the man's skin were not moist and there was no oozing blood. It was more like old, hard leather or meat cooked too long, but it was not like any burn she had ever seen before.

She felt a wave of nausea run through her but suppressed it as she looked into the horror-stricken faces of the men with her. Gently, she pulled the gloves from the hands of the pilot. His hands were contorted, twisted. The dried skin was pulled tight around all the bones and joints. The fingers were flexed and pulled by contractures, dried muscles, and tendons into what resembled a claw more than a hand. She tried to straighten out the fingers but could not do so. The man looked as if he had been dead and dried a long, long time. He was like the victims of the first accident on the well, but much worse.

She slowly stood up as the understanding of what had happened and what was happening began to come clear in her mind. The man had been destroyed by radiant energy. He was a victim of massive exposure to some sort

506

of very intense radiation.

Merrill turned away, gagging, struggling to keep himself from vomiting. He gained control of himself and then got busy closing the outside door to the copter and putting away the rescue gear. MacMahon's face was drawn and serious. He looked shocked, but in complete control.

"What do you think, Jori?" he asked. "This doesn't look like any kind of burn I've ever seen."

She shook her head. "I don't think it is, at least not in the conventional sense. I think it's the effect of a very heavy exposure to radiation. It's almost like he's been cooked. His skin feels completely dried out."

"I've never seen anything like this," the admiral said slowly. "I don't understand it at all, but we've got to do something to stop it. If that well is emitting some kind of radiation, what would make it all so visible on radar?" He glanced at Winters.

"That's very unusual," the lieutenant said, "but not entirely unheard of. Some types of ionizing radiation can cause things to happen that will disturb the atmosphere enough to create a radar image."

"The thing I'm starting to worry about now," said MacMahon, "is how far out the radiation extends. Even though it may not be as intense out here, we may be getting heavy exposure right now."

"We'd better back away from it," Jori said. "There's a good possibility you're right."

The commander looked back down at the dead man. "Poor bastard. He probably never knew what hit him."

Jori stared at the body and shuddered to think of being cooked alive.

The pilot's voice interrupted their conversation.

"Commander, I have Captain Daniels back at the base on the radio, and he needs to talk to you. He's got some strange news."

"Wait till he hears what we've got to tell him," MacMahon said to the others and then went forward. "John, let's get out of here." The pilot nodded and spoke into the radio while the commander plugged in the mike on his helmet. The three helicopters, having for the moment given up the search for the other pilot, were moving rapidly away from the enlarging field of radiation. They set a course for the base at Fort Pierce.

"Fort Pierce Coast Guard, this is Seabird Fourteen, MacMahon speaking. Come in."

"Seabird Fourteen, this is Coast Guard Fort Pierce, Daniels speaking. Admiral, some very odd things have been happening here in the last few minutes. We have just intercepted a few messages on the Air Force frequencies that seemed to indicate that an all-out alert has been called by the National Military Command Center. Over."

"Why, for Pete's sake? Do you have anything else on it? Over."

"No. I think the SAC bases have been scrambled and there's a couple of things that make me think the ground missiles have been put on alert. We intercepted a coded message from Norfolk, but we can't interpret it. We just know that it was a high priority message to the strategic submarine force. We've not received official notification of anything, but about a minute or two ago a message came in on the VLF for us to stand by for important communication from Maryland. Nothing's come through yet, but I understand from the radio operator that the communications around here are getting a little shaggy. There's apparently been some kind of electromagnetic interference. What do you make of that? Over."

"It's hard to say, probably just an exercise. Have you been able to get through to headquarters about the problem we're having out here? Over."

"No, sir, I haven't. All communications circuits have been blocked out by outgoing messages from Maryland and Washington. We can't get anybody to pay any attention to us right now . . . I'm assuming because of the alert."

"Damn, we need to get some help. We're into something real bizarre going on out here. We just pulled a pilot from one of those F-14s out of the water. He was burned to a crisp by something, but not fire. Jori Ashe thinks it's radiation. I guess that could be what's screwing up the radar too."

"Yes, sir, it's possible. I wonder if that has anything to do with some of the communications difficulties."

"Could be. Look, we're coming in with this pilot. I'm worried about the radiation levels out here. You continue trying to get through to headquarters and see if you can communicate with Homestead Air Force Base—hell, any Air Force base, and let them know about the downed F-14s.

"In the meantime, alert the Coast Guard up and down the coast so we can start blocking off all air and sea traffic into this area. See if you can get us some equipment that measures radiation levels. We've got to get a handle on this thing, before too many people get hurt. We'll be in in about fifteen minutes. In the meantime, get hold of the Pentagon and get the word through that we've got a whale of a problem down here. We're going to need lots of assistance, but to do what, I frankly don't know. At the very least, we're going to have to get some navigation aids down here till this thing calms down. Seabird Fourteen

509

clear and out."

"Roger. Will do. I'll be standing by to keep you posted if we get any new information. Coast Guard, Fort Pierce, clear and out."

MacMahon turned to the others. "What a ridiculous time for them to be pulling off some kind of alert. We finally have something down here we can't handle and need a little advice and some assistance and we can't even get through to the bastards. I don't know what good it does to have all these communications systems if they're not going to be useful when we have a crisis. I don't know what the hell to do about this thing, but whatever we are going to do, we've got to get on with it."

He shrugged. "Sometimes I think our defense system is too complicated to work if anything really did happen." He turned to look at Jori. "Assuming everything you've said is true and all the things you showed me from this Dr. Sumter are true, then what are we going to do, Jori? How are we going to stop this unholy thing? You helped to drill it, so how are we going to undo it?"

She looked into his eyes for a moment, wondering if anybody knew the answers to his questions. "I don't know," she said reluctantly. "If Sumter is right, and if this is what happened to the Russians, I wonder how they stopped theirs."

"It's a cinch we're not going to find out from them!"

She nodded, wondering if this is what really had happened in Siberia in '74. Maybe. Maybe not. She glanced back toward the dead body. It could be there wasn't a person on earth who knew anything at all about the problem or how to solve it. It might be something that was just going to have to be allowed to run its course, like a hurricane or an earthquake, beyond the control of man. She shivered at the thought, and wondered again—for the millionth time—about the defect in the crust they had stumbled onto, and why they had been able to drill so deep so quickly. At that moment, she felt quite positive that neither she nor anyone else would ever know the answer. It was one of those things that just shouldn't have happened. She hoped they hadn't unleashed a natural phenomenon that would be self-perpetuating and maybe even one that would get worse before it was all done.

She looked at the men around her. It was obvious that none of them—nor anyone else—understood as she did at that moment what tremendous adverse consequences could be in store for them and the rest of South Florida in the next few hours if whatever this thing was didn't quit. Balthorium, she thought. Sumter had been right. It surely existed.

"Mayday! Mayday!" The startling words from the radio speaker obliterated all other thoughts from their minds. The message came again, "Mayday! Mayday!"

Palmer flipped his transmitter to "On." "This is Coast Guard Seabird Fourteen receiving a mayday message. We are standing by for further information."

"Coast Guard, oh, thank God! This is the *Linda Sea*." The radio signal came in strong and clear, but the man's voice sounded weak and shaky. "We are a 65-foot drift fishing boat headed home from the Bahamas into the St. Lucie inlet approximately fifteen miles offshore. Something's happened in the last five or ten minutes to my passengers and crew. Everyone's sick . . . some dying. I have about twenty persons that I think are dead and the fifteen of us that are left are too sick to do anything. Everyone's weak and vomiting and I think we may have more deaths in the next few minutes. I don't know what's happened. . . . Please help us!" The man's voice sounded

511

weak and scared.

"*Linda Sea,* this is Coast Guard helicopter, please give us your exact location."

The man read off some Loran coordinates. "Please help us, I don't think we can make it much longer. . . . Something's wrong."

"Stand by, *Linda Sea,* we are on our way," Palmer said. And then with his radio off, he checked with Winters. "Do you have them on our radar?" he said.

"No," Winters answered and spent a second or two plotting the coordinates. "This location puts them on the other side of the well from us. The energy field or whatever it is, is blocking them out from us. If these coordinates are right, they're not really into it yet, but getting damned close."

"Well, tell them to stay out of it," MacMahon said, looking at Palmer.

"*Linda Sea, Linda Sea,* Coast Guard helicopter, come back please," Palmer said.

"This is the *Linda Sea.*"

"*Linda Sea,* I have some very important instructions for you, I repeat, very important instructions. Please do exactly as I say, if not, your craft will be in immediate danger. Turn your vessel onto a direct easterly course, that is 90 degrees. Turn your vessel immediately onto an easterly course, 90 degrees and proceed on that vector until we intercept you. Is that clear?"

"Roger, Coast Guard, we receive you and I will follow your instructions. I am turning the vessel due east and will proceed in that direction until you have found us. Please hurry."

Palmer glanced at MacMahon, waiting for his orders.

"Okay," the admiral said, "let's make a wide swing around whatever the hell this thing is until we can come in from the north. I don't want to approach any closer than six or seven miles. We'll get in where we can intercept the *Linda Sea* as she's outbound from the well. From there we can recover the surviving passengers and get them into the hospital. I don't want to endanger our crew any more than necessary, so we'll have to use a little restraint."

Palmer nodded and quickly communicated with the other craft. He took the helicopter around in a wide arc and put it on an easterly course, planning to swing widely around the danger until he could turn south to intercept the course of the distressed boat.

Jori forced herself to breathe slowly. She was scared. And she knew the others with her shared her feelings. Their faces were tense and drawn and the helicopter seemed filled with anxiety and a strange dread of the unknown. Clearly, a potential for uncontrollable disaster existed. God only knows what would happen if the radiation field continued to grow.

The night air whistled around the sides of the copter as it roared along at top speed. Trailing out to the northwest were the other two craft, silently hanging in the distance, moving through the darkness with them, the ever-present red and white lights blinking ceaselessly. The cockpit in which they were riding was darkened except for the control panel and no one spoke. The radio was silent and they waited. They had no choice. They were headed toward a rendezvous with a boat filled with the dead and dying. To their right was an invisible ominous presence which they did not understand, but which they feared. Each man would have preferred to be heading north, homeward and away from this danger.

Winters's voice broke the silence. "We have incoming aircraft from the north, a fleet of four very high-performance craft at an altitude of fifteen thousand feet. They're moving real fast. Admiral, could be more F-14s. They're on a course which will take them right over the well."

"My God!" MacMahon said. "What do they think they're doing? Get in touch with them and tell them to keep their asses away from that well!"

Palmer broadcast a message on the Air Force channels and they waited. No response. He tried again with the same result, and then finally a third time. He tried several channels and was unable to get any response. "Admiral, if we're in the middle of an alert," he said, "they might be in radio blackout . . . just using combat frequencies."

MacMahon frowned in exasperation. "What in the hell is going on around here? Call the base, see if they can get hold of the Air Force somehow and get the idiots to stay away."

Palmer switched back to Channel 16.

"You'd better hurry," Winters said. "They're closing fast. I don't know if they're in any danger at that altitude but they're going to be making an overflight of that well in less than five minutes."

The crew looked out to the north and after a minute of seeing nothing, finally far in the distance they could see four tiny blinking white lights.

"Here they come," Palmer said.

"Shoot up a flare," MacMahon said. "Maybe that will attract their attention."

Silently, the pilot reached forward and flipped the second flare switch. An instant later above and in front of them the brilliant ball of flame shot into the sky. A few seconds passed and the aircraft they were watching broke into a long dive and then thundered overhead at 5000-foot elevation. Two of the planes broke off and circled back around to the west and came in for a second pass, presumably to inspect the helicopters. The other two roared south toward the well.

The helicopter crew watched with horror as they thundered by, the tails of the jet engines glowing brightly in the dark.

"They're going in," Winters said quietly. "It's too late for them to turn. They're almost there now." He paused and then continued. "I lost them. They're in there somewhere."

The two aircraft that circled came by, their speed reduced and their altitude 3000 feet. They made their pass about a quarter mile to the north. One of them tipped his wing back and forth several times as he went by, and then the two continued in their slow turn and once again took up their southerly course.

John Palmer was frantically trying to contact them but to no avail. The tails of the jets lit up an even fierier red as they accelerated back to their cruising speed.

"They're going to follow the other two!" MacMahon cried. "Do something, John!"

"What else can I do?" the pilot responded angrily. "I'm calling everyone!"

The commander frowned and clenched his fists. They sat silently watching the planes disappear into the darkness.

"They all went in," Winters said. "All four of them. Why do they keep flying into it!"

"It must be some kind of reconnaisance mission," MacMahon said. "It may have something to do with this alert. They're probably on some practice runs. I know they see this thing on their radar. They must think it's just some kind of weather. You'd think they'd try to go around it."

"Not those guys," Palmer said. "A pilot who is man enough to get hold of an F-14 is fearless, and that hotshot aircraft is capable of anything. They're not going to slow down just because of a little squall or something, which is probably what they think it is."

No one responded to the pilot and they waited, hoping what they feared would not come to pass. Then it happened. First one, then a second fireball rising from the darkness miles away.

"Poor bastards," Palmer said and the others sat dumbfounded and shocked. Two more explosions joined the others. The disasters were far off in the distance; it seemed like fifteen to twenty miles, but they could be clearly seen lighting up the overcast sky above them and glowing like tiny torches miles away on a black night. The flames flared and went quickly out. The brilliant glow on the distant horizon turned again into empty blackness.

"Should I send one of the choppers over to them, Admiral?" Palmer asked.

MacMahon shook his head. "No, it's no use. Let's just go see if we can save any of the people in that boat."

Jori felt hopeless, almost as if she were in a nightmare. It seemed impossible to believe that six planes had gone down and now there might be a boatload of people dying all because of the well. "It's insane," she muttered.

MacMahon turned and stared at her, wordlessly. Almost in a trance, he reached forward and flipped the transmitter back to the Coast Guard frequency. "Coast Guard, Fort Pierce, this is Seabird Fourteen. I would like to report some additional downed aircraft."

As he continued to describe what had happened, Jori turned away. Her head felt as if it were splitting. She closed her eyes and buried her face in her hands. She felt as if she'd been awake for a week. The throbbing between her temples was intense, just as it had been since she had awakened from the drugs Loggins had given her. She didn't want to think about what all had happened; it was too terrible. She wished it had been just a nightmare, one that she could forget, but the memory of Duval's bleeding face was irrepressible. It was etched in her mind in vivid color, a scene of unforgettable terror.

Why, she thought, why had things degenerated into such horror? What had become so important about the well that even violence was thinkable? She wondered what had happened during the great void in her memory during the time she had been drugged. Thank God for Hex. She would be out there now, undoubtedly dead, if it hadn't been for him. She thought about the face of the body in the back of the craft and then remembered the friends she'd had on the well. Everyone out there must be dead, cooked, burned, in some horrible way destroyed. She felt sick and wanted more than anything to run away, be away from it all. Too much had happened to her. She wouldn't be able to stand up under any more. It was not the sort of thing she was used to.

She sat still for a little while longer, her face still covered, her eyes closed. She was afraid and withdrawn. She wondered where the courage had gone that had led her through the early portions of the night . . . the dangerous voyage out to the well, and then the killing on the beach. It was all more than she could stand to remember.

The voice of the pilot broke through into her thoughts and she looked up. "That may be the *Linda Sea* coming now," he said. Ahead out the front windows they could see a tiny distant light far away in the darkness. It seemed to be moving toward them slowly.

"Let's wait here for them to reach us," MacMahon

said. "I don't want to go in any closer."

"Let me see if I can reach them on the radio," the pilot said. He began calling to the boat, but no answer was forthcoming.

Jori got up, walked back into the main cabin and looked at Winters, who was intently watching the scope. She stood by the large door and looked through the big window out to the east. On the horizon could be seen a thin line of early morning; it would soon be dawn. She watched the comforting early morning glow as it crept ever so slowly into the sky. She hoped the new day would bring better news. She wished somehow she could be anywhere except in this helicopter preparing to see more death. She didn't think she could cope with what she knew was inevitable. If somehow the boat could just go away.

Finally, she returned to the cockpit. Just in front of them, 500 feet below, a large fishing boat was churning slowly through the dark waters. The pilot was still trying to establish radio communications but no one was answering. He turned and stared grimly at the admiral. MacMahon put one hand to his forehead and rubbed it dejectedly. His face expressed his fatigue and disheartenment. He stared rather absently into Jori's eyes for a long moment and then down at the lifeless vessel beneath them.

"I don't know what to do," he said quietly. "I guess we ought to go down and take a look."

The pilot obeyed and the craft started to descend slowly. Jori heard the big door behind her being swung open—the door through which the bodies would be lifted.

TWENTY-EIGHT

Ed Wallen looked at the big clock suspended above the long wall of meters, gauges, and control panels. It was almost 5 A.M. One more hour and the first big surge of electrical demand for the county would begin as the overnight lull in power needs ended. But he still had a half hour to relax before beginning the process of bringing the nuclear reactor up to the necessary energy level. Until then, it was sit tight and wait.

It had been a quiet night. The vibrating pump on the auxiliary cooling system to the reactor had been repaired by 2 A.M., and the mild concern this had caused was now gone. All the lights on the big board were green. Things were calm; it was business as usual. But that was the way it usually was at the Martin plant. This nuclear reactor, one of the oldest in the Florida Power Company, had experienced very little down time during its ten-year on-line life. One of the older models, it had turned out to be one of the most reliable. But one never knew. As a controlling engineer, Ed was fully prepared for the day when something would go wrong.

Unexpectedly, a soft bell began to ring, and a blinking red light came on underneath a series of six gauges at the far left of the room. It was the first time the alarm bell had rung in six months, and, although not loud, it was

519

quite startling. Even more surprising was the source of the abnormality: the outside radiation detectors. He hurried across the room to get a better look at the readings and stood beside the chief engineer who was studying the printout, which was being automatically displayed beneath the gauges. He quickly looked at the six meters, each of them giving ambient radiation readings from a site outside the physical compound of the nuclear power plant. He had never seen one of these read abnormal. Each of the twenty or so meters which took readings within the nuclear compound had on one occasion or another registered mild elevations. These had all been temporary, very simple problems, which had been solved long before the radiation levels had reached a point considered even remotely dangerous. But the outside gauges had never wavered away from normal.

The plant, situated almost equidistant between Fort Pierce and Stuart, was along the beach. When it had been built, no outside radiation monitors had been considered necessary. However, four years ago environmentalists' demands had led to the construction of six small buildings positioned between 500 and 1000 yards outside the plant itself. In each of these had been placed a very sensitive radiation indicator which was linked to this control room and the alarm system. Presumably they would be useful in the event of a major accident in order to determine if radiation leakage from the plant had occurred. It had never happened, but now, incredibly, three of the gauges had risen above their normal levels— not much—but a definite change had occurred. The two on the east side toward the beach and one on the south were definitely in the abnormal range. The one to the north had lifted slightly away from the zero line, but was not yet abnormal. The two to the west had not moved.

He looked quickly across the rest of the big board. All of the internal monitors were within normal limits. All the temperature gauges were within normal. The reactor itself continued to function at only a 15 per cent maximum capacity level. Finally, he checked the circuit integrity indicator switches. They were all fine. He flipped several of them back and forth and got safe readings each time. There was no equipment malfunction. There was no circuit malfunction. The readings seemed to be true, but just as strikingly, they seemed to be impossible. He couldn't imagine a circumstance where radiation levels outside the plant were abnormal while those within were unchanged.

He looked at the printout closely. The three meters had definitely slowly crept away from their zero line into the abnormal range over the previous five-minute period. The alarm had finally gone off when the preset abnormal range had been reached. The level was still incredibly low, of no possible danger, but the more serious issue was—why? What kind of leak was occurring?

"I don't understand this," the chief engineer said, looking up inquisitively.

"I'm with you, Pat," Wallen said. "It doesn't make any sense. It's bound to be a circuit failure or something."

"We've never had any circuit failures like this before."

"That doesn't mean it can't happen now." Wallen looked again just to be sure, at all the other indicator gauges in the room. Nothing was abnormal. Absolutely nothing.

It seemed impossible that radiation leakage outside the

521

compound could have occurred. If it were true, a serious breach in containment had occurred. It was the exact sort of thing that he and the other operators of the nuclear power plant feared: radiation leakage, no matter how inconsequential. It was the sort of thing that brought consumer groups to their feet. Whatever was causing it, he had to bring it to a halt immediately. And in addition to that, he had to have an adequate explanation for it. The public would have to be informed. He looked at the dials once again. There was no question at all; they were distinctly in the abnormal range. Every other way of verifying the validity of the readings seemed to check out.

He seemed to have no choice but to shut down the reactor. He glanced again at the water temperature of the cooling system. No problem. Everything was running smoothly.

"Pat, I'm going to shut the reactor down. Let's drop the rods back in." The engineer nodded grimly. He agreed completely, although he hated the commotion that an emergency shutdown always caused. The chief engineer began to pull the levers that would very quickly bring the reactor activity to a halt. Within less than a minute the fission reaction going on less than 200 feet from where they were sitting would be ended.

Wallen walked back to the desk, picked up a phone and spoke tersely into it. "We have an outside radiation leak, emergency shutdown procedure initiated."

The safety engineer in another room would receive his message and flash the word to the reactor crew so they could begin the long sequence of bringing the reactor to a cold stop after the nuclear reaction had been squelched. Ed Wallen considered the emergency button to his right and decided there was no need to use it. Everything was calm and under control. The reactor would soon be stopped. There was no need of alarming all the non-nuclear employees within the facility.

He continued to watch the big board. The cooling temperatures were fine and the core temperature was already starting to drop. Everything was going to be okay. Before calling Cyril Rodsbury, the vice president of FP in charge of operations at the Martin County site, he went once more across the room to look at the readings from the outside monitors. The red alarm light was still blinking. Incredibly, the radiation levels, instead of beginning to taper off, had actually gone up. Four of the readings were now in the abnormal scale, and the other two had moved away from the zero line and were slowly climbing. The two sensors located on the beach side had moved well into the abnormal range, although still far from the level that would constitute a danger.

"Damn," he said to himself and went quickly back to the phone.

Cyril Rodsbury would be unhappy. He was very much of a PR man and absolutely hated this sort of thing, not because of the power shortage brief shutdowns created, but because of the public image it gave nuclear power plants. Rodsbury was one of the few executives in the company who would have preferred to keep all incidents private and quiet. Fortunately, he was overridden by better sense within the company. FP's record was clean and they wanted to keep it that way.

After three rings, Rodsbury answered. He sounded only partially awake. "Cyril, this is Ed Wallen. I've just ordered the reactor shut down. We have some kind of radiation leak."

"You what?" the irritated response came.

"I said I've shut down the reactor. We have some sort of outside radiation leak. I don't know the source of it yet, but four of the outside monitors just bumped into the abnormal range, so we've got a problem here. I don't think it's going to get any worse."

"Oh my God!" Rodsbury said. "You realize what this is going to cost? We're going to have the press all over our backs for a month now. How bad is the leakage?"

"Not bad. Hold on a second. Let me look at it again."

Wallen crossed the room and checked the gauges again. What he saw gave him a sick sensation. He had never seen nor heard of this sequence of events. The readings, almost unbelievably, were continuing to climb slowly.

He picked up the phone. "Cyril, I don't know what's happening. The readings are still going up. They're not bad yet, but they're climbing. We may have a bigger problem than I thought. You'd better get over here."

"Okay. Get it under control, Ed."

"I will," Wallen replied. "And one more thing. I'm going to alert the governor."

"Are you sure that's necessary?"

"There's no question in my mind about it. With an outside leak that's still going up, if we don't alert him, we'll catch hell about it later."

"You're in charge, Ed, and you'll have to answer for it, but go ahead."

Wallen put down the phone and scanned the other dials in the room. Absolutely everything was perfect. The core temperature was dropping fast. Every indication was that the reaction had come to a standstill. The cooling temperature was normal and getting cooler. Everything was fine. Everything. There was not one indication anywhere of trouble. The interior of the plant was absolutely radiation free. No abnormal readings had occurred anywhere within the plant walls. The only abnormality was with the outside monitors. It seemed incredible.

He took one last look at the meters before taking his final action. This time all six of them had moved to the abnormal range, and were climbing steadily. Even though the radiation level was significant, fortunately it had not yet become dangerous. He walked slowly back to his desk. What he was going to do now, he had never done before.

Following the protocol everyone had agreed upon after the Three-Mile Island accident, he was going to alert the governor's office of a break in radiation containment. It had been a unanimous decision that public officials should be notified immediately of any conceivable danger to the environment or the public. Radiation, beyond the containment walls of the reactor, would certainly be viewed as a dangerous consequence by everyone involved. It seemed impossible that something like this had happened without other indications of abnormalities, and Ed continued to hope, way down deep, that electric circuitry was the cause and that the readings were false. It seemed the only plausible explanation.

He looked again at the radiation levels within the plant. They remained normal. It was almost as if the safest place to be was within the confines of the nuclear power plant behind the radiation-proof walls. It was ironic that he was receiving less radiation than persons on the other side of the shield designed to protect the outside environment.

Ed Wallen heaved a big sigh and looked up the number for the governor in the emergency procedures manual he had helped write. He quietly dialed and got a switchboard operator at the governor's mansion in Tallahassee. He identified himself, explained that he had an emergency message for the governor and was immediately connected with Will Barnes, the governor's executive assistant.

"Mr. Barnes, this is Ed Wallen. I am controlling engineer at the Florida Power nuclear facility in Martin County. We have just initiated an emergency shutdown sequence, and I regret to inform you we have indications of a radiation leak outside the confines of the plant. I don't think we have any immediate danger. However, we definitely have abnormal readings on our radiation monitors which test the outside atmosphere."

"Damn it! I thought you guys said we couldn't have a Three-Mile Island here."

"Well, sir, I don't think this is a Three-Mile Island. Hopefully, we'll get it under control quickly. At this moment, I don't think there is any public danger. The whole thing just happened less than five minutes ago."

"All right, I'll tell the governor. You'd better just hang on the line."

Ed waited almost five minutes and then heard the governor's voice. "Ted Hartley here. What kind of problem have you got?"

Wallen explained the circumstances again.

The governor listened without interruption, but when the explanation was finished, he asked the tough question. "Is this problem going to get worse, or is it going to get better?"

"I have to say I don't know, sir," Ed responded. "The

problem is we don't exactly know what's causing it or where the leakage is coming from. That's why I can't give you more specific information."

"Exactly how much radiation is leaking out?" the governor asked.

"It's very small now. A man standing a thousand yards from the plant would probably get the radiation exposure equal to a chest x ray approximately once every six hours."

"And you think there's a chance it may get worse?"

"Unfortunately, sir, I cannot answer that question with any reliability at all. We are in the middle of a paradox. Our radiation levels within the plant are absolutely normal, while only those outside of the plant are going up. I am completely mystified as to the cause, but we're working on it, and I'm sure we'll have some answers for you in a very few minutes."

"The leakage is still going on, right? It wasn't just a one-shot deal and it's over with? You have ongoing problems at the present time? Am I correct on that?"

"Yes, sir, you are. Our meters indicate continuing elevated radiation levels outside the plant."

"That's it," the governor said, softly. "I don't have any choice but to order an immediate evacuation. You let the other FP officials know, and I'll take it from here. You can tell them we'll try to keep this thing low-key. I don't want a lot of panic. I'm going to call out the National Guard right now. Just get this thing under control as quickly as you can, and keep me informed, understand!"

"We will, sir." Ed heard the phone being hung up at the other end and then quietly put down his own receiver. He picked up the red phone and again spoke

527

with the safety officer. "Let's find out what's going on and quick. We're still having elevated readings outside the plant. We've got to get it stopped. The governor has been notified and he's going to begin an evacuation." He put the phone down and again surveyed his vast array of instruments. The reactor temperature continued to drop, the cooling water was almost at ambient temperatures. Everything looked perfect. With a feeling of helplessness and dread, he went over to the six gauges. Nothing had changed, except one thing: the radiation levels had climbed even higher. What in the living hell is going on? he wondered.

TWENTY-NINE

The National Military Command Center in Maryland, far outside the capital, was functioning with near perfect precision. All military information analysis and command defense functions had been placed under the control of the Center from the moment the alert had begun. The total command structure of the United States military was located here and would remain so until such time as the alert ended or the center was rendered inoperative as a result of enemy action, in which case the necessary command functions would be shifted to "Looking Glass"—an airborne SAC 747 command plane on station somewhere over the Midwestern plains at 40,000 feet.

As Army chief of staff, Gen. Lance Mendell cleared the last security check point and entered the large operations room, the place was literally humming with activity. Giant electronic maps of the United States and the world completely covered one long wall. Two other walls were covered with constantly changing electronic displays of the status of all United States combat units. One large bank of monitors indicated the exact position of every nuclear attack unit. The place was a flurry of moving men: changing charts, graphs, maps, and situation reports. The back wall was occupied entirely by the giant

Honeywell computer system linked via satellite communications with a similar system at NORAD headquarters in Colorado.

Maj. Gen. Les Marshall, along with two other members of his staff, rose from the large table at which they had been sitting immediately behind the last row of display consoles occupied by busily working communication specialists.

Mendell scanned the room quickly as he approached the table, noting particularly the time clock which had been running since the moment the alert was called. It had been almost 30 minutes. "What the hell is happening, Les?" he said. "Are the Russians hitting us or not?"

"It's a toss-up, General," Marshall replied as they all sat back down. "The computer attack reliability index is down to 50 per cent and I frankly don't know. It's the most bizarre sequence of events I've ever seen. It doesn't fit any predictable pattern."

"What about this nuclear explosion in Florida?" Mendell asked, impatiently.

"I can't confirm it," Marshall replied.

"What do you mean, you can't confirm it?" the chief of staff said, irritated. "It's been thirty goddamned minutes since this alert was called. You'd think we'd be able to find out for sure whether we are under attack or not!"

Marshall shrugged. "Our communications have gone to pot. There's not a soul outside the state of Florida that knows what the heck is happening down there."

"Electromagnetic interference?"

"Partly, and just very poor communications in general. I still have the ability to launch an all-out attack, but I've lost the opportunity to discriminate carefully

bout what's happening out there. We don't have enough
pen channels. Many of the ones reserved for incoming
eports have either broken down or are being filled up
with immaterial bullshit. Somehow, our setup leaves us
erfectly capable of getting any message out that we
want, but we can't get enough local data in. We're still
depending upon satellite reports and long-range radar
data. We cannot confirm the onsite conditions as yet."

"Goddamn!" Mendell muttered. "You spend a billion
dollars on electronics and the first time we really need
them it all goes to hell. What are the chances this is a
computer screw up again and the whole thing's a false
alert?"

"General, until we get onsite confirmation, I cannot
rule that out. It has to be a distinct possibility."

"What are the Russians doing?"

"They've scrambled all their bombers. We have
almost fifteen hundred planes headed this way. That, of
course, is of no immediate concern. They're still hours
off, but all of their missile bases—and we have
information it includes their nuclear subs—have been
put on top alert. There could be a launch at any
moment."

"But they've done nothing other than match our
response so far, have they?"

"That's right," the acting commander responded. "So
far, they've stayed with us. For every action we take, they
react, but no more. Both of us right now are armed and
bristling, and we are staring at each other nose-to-nose,
hoping the other one doesn't flinch."

The chief of staff shook his head. "It's hard for me to
believe they would wait this long to initiate the main
attack if they were planning one. What do we know about
the Florida situation?"

Marshall turned to his executive assistant seated at his right, Brig. Gen. Ham Collins, an intelligence officer. "Ham, fill him in on what we've got."

Collins leaned forward, "General Mendell, we have six or seven groups of facts, more or less unlinked at this point. It could be that several of them are related, but we just don't have enough data to draw firm conclusions. First, we have definite satellite indication of a nuclear detonation somewhere off the coast of Palm Beach. Or, if it's not a detonation, we have ultra-high ambient radiation levels in a very confined location approximately ten to fifteen miles offshore. There are some indications at this time that this might not be due to a conventional nuclear explosion. It's somewhat confusing.

"Second point, we have no definite evidence that any other attack by other modalities is under way with the exception of the airborne Russian bombers General Marshall mentioned. Our long-range radar profiles as well as satellite coverage so far is clean. Third, we do have six downed F-14s in the area of the postulated attack zone. Our information is sketchy, but it is clear that the aircraft went down in a precipitous manner without warning shortly after their arrival into the area of the presumed detonation. None of these planes were able to verify the occurrence of a nuclear explosion prior to their loss.

"Fourth—and this is a real hooker—we have just received verified information through the National Guard command post in northern Florida, that a nuclear power plant in the area has developed a serious problem with radiation leak. The reactor has apparently been shut down. There is conflicting data as to whether or not there was an explosion. There is some information, which we

532

cannot confirm, that the accident is a rather major one with the outside possibility that the reactor has detonated. The question has, of course, been raised that this is perhaps what our satellites have been picking up, but in any event at last word an evacuation of the area was under way. We're hoping to get more information on that momentarily.

"Fifth, we just received a report through Coast Guard headquarters at Norfolk that the Fort Pierce station has reported some kind of bizarre offshore oil well accident. I am told that the commander of the base there is on site and has passed along the information that there has been no nuclear explosion in the area, but that this oil well has drilled into some kind of radioactive material that is causing some kind of a radiation-emitting energy field in the vicinity. We're awaiting additional details on this, as well as a report that is supposed to be en route from the CIA regarding a similar Russian accident of this type."

"General Collins," the chief of staff responded, after a moment's sullen silence, "I can't believe that thirty minutes into a presumed nuclear attack, all we can put together is the nebulous crock of crap you just gave me. Two-thirds of what you have is speculative and based upon unsupported data. What we need are some facts, goddamn it. Hard facts. Things that we can use to make decisions on."

"General, we don't have them," Collins replied glumly.

"It's a hell of a way to try to decide how to defend this country," Mendell responded angrily. "What conclusions can we come to from all these half-truths and misinformation?"

"Mostly nonconclusions, General," Marshall responded. "First of all, whatever is happening, it doesn't meet any of our predicted attack profiles. Maybe this is an attack. Maybe not. Perhaps this is some kind of screening maneuver, maybe a decoy. Maybe this is preliminary to some kind of bizarre landing on the beaches of Florida. One thing is clear, it doesn't seem like a go-for-the-throat attempt by the Russians, which brings to mind another extremely remote possibility. Maybe we're under attack from someone else, perhaps some Third World nation. This could be the work of a single nuclear sub, or perhaps some kind of splinter group. An number of possibilities exist that we've had a nuclear detonation that is not the prelude to all-out war. We ever have to consider the possibility that a single commander has gone berserk some place and initiated this action. think we've got to be very careful at this stage so we don' do anything to force the Russians into a response. I don' want either us or them getting trigger happy. I think the risk of that happening has diminished since the first few minutes, but I believe we're still right at the edge."

"Good thought," the chief of staff said. "This really could be someone other than the Russians. What do the computers say about that?"

"It requests more data. Statistically, the only thing it can do is waver somewhere around the 50 per cent point about whether an actual attack of any type is under way. I don't think it's going to help us very much."

"Worthless pieces of junk! I knew we couldn't depend on them when the chips were down anyway," Mendell said. He looked up at the lieutenant who approached them and handed Marshall a communication.

Marshall glanced at it and then looked up at the others. "The CIA is bringing over a geophysicist who wants to talk to us about some possibilities regarding the well accident the Coast Guard is reporting. Apparently it has something to do with the Russians and a nuclear accident they had in 1974."

"Great," Mendell responded sarcastically. "We're right in the middle of a goddamn shooting war and the CIA wants to start talking about 1974. What a bunch of asses. All right, let's get on with it. The President will be here in just a few minutes and we're going to have to tell him what action we've taken. What have you done so far, and what are you going to recommend?"

Marshall cleared his throat, "First, I want to leave the alert where it is. I want to keep the bombers on course. We've still got two hours before they reach their callback point, so let's leave them there. The Russians know there's plenty of time and I doubt that they'll do anything that we're not doing. But I want to keep as tight an eye as possible on them. Whatever is going on here, I don't want them to get the idea that they can take advantage of some kind of unusual situation and go ahead and launch a preemptive strike."

The chief of staff nodded and Marshall continued. "Next, I want to throw everything we can mobilize into that south Florida area. I mean, I want air force, ground forces, and naval forces to close in. If something crazy is going on down there, I think we've got to anticipate every possibility. I want to scramble our entire air defense fleet, get them into the skies and see what's going on. I want everything the Navy's got put to sea—nothing in port like a sitting duck. And equally important, I want to mobilize as many airborne units as we can and get them on the ground in the Palm Beach area and set up a beach defense. We're going to look pretty goddamned stupid if a couple of thousand Cubans or somebody come marching right up the beach and take over the city. If we're not careful—if that sort of ridiculous situation pops up, we could wind up with half a million hostages looking down the barrel of some radical guns. And lastly, I want to work like hell to get our communications reestablished. I agree with you, we're totally impotent until we can get more information."

The chief of staff nodded, as a buzzer sounded in front of Marshall and the intercom came on, "General, a CIA officer is here with the geophysicist who wants to talk to you. They both have top priority clearance and we have firm identifications on them."

"All right," Marshall responded, "escort them in."

The door on the far wall opened and two MP's accompanied a weasely man in civilian clothes and a taller, but also skinny-looking Oriental man. They were brought to the table and introductions exchanged. The smaller man was Rick Simmons, an officer of the CIA and the Asian was Dr. Juro Nagaishi. They were quickly seated.

"Gentlemen, I don't have long. I'm going to have to brief the President in just a few minutes," Marshall said. "What is it that you've got to tell us?"

Dr. Nagaishi spoke first, hesitantly and then more forcefully. He had a Japanese accent. "General, I am a geophysicist. I was born in Japan, but I am a naturalized United States citizen. I have spent my entire career studying the continental drift theory and plate tectonics. I have also done a great deal of work involving the makeup of the crust which covers the earth, over the inner layer we call the mantle." The scientist paused.

"Yes, yes, go on," the chief of staff said irritably. "We don't have very long."

Nagaishi bowed his head. "For the past ten years I have been doing a great deal of work for the CIA, analyzing certain geological explorations being conducted by other countries. We have information that in 1974 the Soviet Union attempted to drill through the crust into the underlying mantle. The CIA has a great deal of evidence that there was some sort of accident which created a nuclear disaster in Siberia at that time. There were apparently no survivors, and it has been a very well-kept secret inside the Soviet Union."

"Yes, I've heard of such stories," Marshall replied. "But what has that got to do with our current situation, Doctor?"

"Twenty-four hours ago we were informed by the Coast Guard of some very deep exploratory drilling being done by an offshore oil well near Palm Beach, Florida. One of the scientists in charge of that project has written a book in which he discussed the Russian accident. We think it is possible that he may be attempting to do what the Russians failed at, and that is drill through the crust into the mantle." He paused and the military men waited silently, wondering what in the hell all this had to do with what was going on.

"There is some speculation," the scientist continued, "that such activities carry a hazard in that a previously undiscovered element, which has been mythically labeled Balthorium, might be present in small deposits right on the surface of the mantle. If this were the case, drilling into such a deposit could be extremely dangerous."

"Dangerous in what way?" Mendell asked, leaning forward intensely.

"If the hypotheses are correct, and Balthorium does exist, it could be that the material under certain conditions is radioactive and can even undergo fission reaction. It is possible that a nuclear reaction resulting in the release of large amounts of a form of radiation—

perhaps new to us—could occur. There is no proof, of course, but this is speculated."

The generals sat back in stunned silence.

Finally Marshall spoke. "Do you mean to say that it's possible that an oil well drilling too deep could drill through the crust and into the mantle and in some way ignite this Balthorium or whatever, into a nuclear reaction?"

"Exactly, sir. That is why I came. It is our understanding that the Coast Guard is reporting some kind of radiation accident early this morning at the site of the well."

"Dr. Nagaishi, this is very important." Marshall spoke very quietly. "Would it be possible for this reaction, which was taking place miles beneath the surface, to somehow work its way up and release radiation into the atmosphere?"

"General, that is exactly what is possible. The mathematical calculations show that, if Balthorium exists as postulated, when it does have a fission reaction, it breaks down into more inert elements. The type of radiation it releases could be of a very unusual form. It would be almost a cross between radiation as we understand it and electrical energy. This would mean that the radiation itself could easily be conducted up steel pipes and then emitted from the well using the steel structure almost as a transmitting tower. It would form sort of an energy field surrounding its point of transmission. It could exert tremendous electromagnetic changes as well as cause radiation damage to living organisms."

"How big could this energy field get?"

"I don't know, conceivably it could be miles across. It

would depend upon the intensity of the reaction going on. It would probably affect radar and radio communications, and would very likely be deadly to anything passing through it."

"Would it be visible?"

"I do not know. The radiation itself probably would not be, but its ionizing effect on the atmospheric gases might give it some kind of faint, glowing appearance in daytime because of absorption of certain wave lengths of light."

"Dr. Nagaishi, could anything else happen other than the creation of this radiation field?"

"You mean like an explosion or an earthquake? I simply have no experience upon which to base an answer, General."

"One more thing. What can we do to stop the reaction and get rid of the radiation once it started?"

The cold, barking voice of an MP at the front entrance interrupted. "Gentlemen, the President has arrived." Everyone not extremely busy at the moment immediately rose as the President came through the door.

"Dr. Nagaishi," the chief of staff said, "don't leave. We've got someone else you need to talk to." He looked at Marshall. "This beats me."

A small smile moved briefly across Marshall's face and then was replaced by a look of ironic humor. "I know I've seen this somewhere before, maybe in the movies. But how do I tell the President we're under attack by an oil well!"

The chief of staff grinned and then quickly brought his expression under control. He was sober-faced by the time the President reached the table and so was Marshall. Only Dr. Nagaishi was smiling.

THIRTY

The *Linda Sea* was larger than most of the fishing boats Jori had seen in the area—and nicer looking. In the pale light of the early morning, she appeared to be a well-kept vessel. But as they hovered above her, matching her slow forward speed, she seemed lifeless.

The pilot tried one last time on the radio, but no response was forthcoming. "Quit wasting your time," MacMahon said. "Let's put someone aboard her and get her stopped. Then we can see if there are any survivors."

Winters was already securely strapped into the life harness and, as Palmer eased the craft even closer to the rocking boat, Seaman Merrill helped him swing out the door and lowered him to the forward deck. There were anxious moments when the lieutenant dangled precariously just above the vessel as it moved unpredictably in the sea, but then he was safe. He quickly made his way across the front deck down along the side passageway and into the bridge. The boat's forward motion slowed and then stopped.

They heard his voice on the radio. He sounded scared. "Seabird, this is Winters. It's real bad down here. Several bodies on the bridge. They're dead all right. I've never seen anything like it."

MacMahon flipped on his radio. "Winters, come back

out on the front deck. We're going to put Merrill down to you and then you can search the rest of the vessel."

Winters helped Merrill into the boat and the two disappeared inside. A long five minutes passed and then Winters was on the radio again. "Admiral, it's just like you thought. They're almost all dead. It looks like it was pretty terrible before they went . . . a lot of them must have vomited . . . the boat's a mess. About twenty bodies lined up in the main cabin . . . the last ones to go must have put them there. The rest of the bodies are scattered all over the place. At least six of them are still alive. They're in some sort of coma, but they're breathing. We've got about 35 altogether. The captain and the crew are dead. Most of the ones that are still alive are younger . . . two of them look like teenagers."

"Okay," MacMahon said. "Bring them up to the front deck and we'll pull them aboard. Make it as quick as you can. I'd like to get out of here."

"Will do," Winters replied, and then was gone. A few minutes later the two could be seen struggling with a limp body. With a great deal of effort, they brought it out onto the deck and then quickly attached the safety harness lowered to them. The victim was rapidly hoisted up toward the craft where the commander with Jori's assistance swung the man through the big door and laid him out on the floor.

It took almost forty minutes to get all six of the passengers into the helicopter, and by the time they were through, the first had died. Jori bent over the others one by one, listening to their labored respirations. They looked like old George had looked the night of the first accident at the well. That seemed so long ago, and so much had happened since then.

As she looked at the unresponsive victims, she was sure that they, too, would soon be dead. The skin was mottled—it felt coarse to the touch. There were none of the terrible-looking splits and tears such as she had seen in the pilot's face, but one of them was not far from it. His skin seemed tight, stretched, and his eyeballs bulged as if ready to burst at any moment. He was the one who had already died. His mouth hung open, his tongue looked dried and parched. It was a grisly sight.

"I don't think they've got much chance if what I've seen before is any measure," she said, looking up at MacMahon.

"I'm sure you're right. We should get them to the hospital as soon as we can." They quickly retrieved the two Coast Guardsmen from the boat. While the winch was being pulled in and the door shut, Jori splashed water on a towel and draped it gently against the dried faces of the unfortunates. The body of the dead one was placed alongside the F-14 pilot and covered with a blanket.

Palmer put the helicopter into a steep climb and brought it up to its maximum forward speed as they headed for land. When Jori had done what she could, she went forward into the cockpit just in time to hear MacMahon order the other two aircraft to the base. He seemed to be having some trouble with the radio communications and was unable himself to make contact with the Fort Pierce station.

She hardly took notice, though, because of her shocked fascination with the view from the front windows. During their rescue effort, morning had arrived and the thin clouds had disappeared, revealing a pale blue sky; but startling beyond expression, and similar to nothing she had ever seen before, was the beautiful shimmering kaleidoscope around the well. It was not like a cloud; it was more a delicate wisp of haze which surrounded the faintly visible derrick in the distance. The strange veil, which seemed suspended against the clear blue background of the sky, was a constantly changing panorama of pastel colors. It was immense.

The early morning sun was reflected as if from a million rainbows, and, with the changing angles from the constantly moving helicopter, there was an endless evolution of flowing color and beauty. It was at once awesome and delicate. It should have been frightening, but it was not. It seemed almost to beckon.

From the sea below, its edges rose like tall, granite, dew-covered cliffs sparkling in the morning sun. It had a sense of graceful movement within a constant evolution of spectacular mammoth beauty. It was like nothing she had ever seen before or even dreamed of—an act of God.

Off to the northwest, the other two helicopters had almost disappeared. Being very careful to maintain a safe distance, Palmer took their craft in a great arc, slowly moving along beside the colored wall of thin air, and eventually turned beyond it and headed due west toward the city of Stuart and the hospital. No one spoke as they moved slowly past the astounding creation, and, as they began to fly away from it, all except the pilot went to the rear cabin windows to watch the sparkling panorama of glimmering colors. It was like a giant, glowing vapor framed against the blueness of the sky and the deep green of the sea. It was almost an emotional experience, and Jori felt a disconcerting sense of disappointment as the distance between them and the beautiful phenomenon increased. The strange feeling had overtaken them all, and no one spoke until they were over the beach, headed inland.

"Admiral, better come take a look at this," the pilot called, and they all went forward. From their vantage point in the sky, they saw that the highways and roads leading south and west from the nuclear power plant were jammed with cars, military trucks and people walking.

"What in the hell is going on down there?" MacMahon said, and tried the radio, but the instrument was useless.

Most of the traffic was coming down Hutchinson Island and turning west across the bridge and going toward the peninsula of Sewell's Point, and then beyond the St. Lucie River into the city. But a large amount of traffic was bypassing the route west and going farther south down to the dead end of the island toward the Florexco compound. Up and down the beach hundreds of cars were parked, and people were climbing over the dunes out onto the sand. They seemed to be attracted by the glorious shimmering radiation field in the distance.

"It looks like they're starting to crowd the beaches," the pilot said. He didn't need to say why. They all knew. It was crazy, but they all understood the unspoken urge to watch the glowing colors over the ocean.

"I don't think they should stay on the beach," Jori said. "It might be dangerous."

"You think the radiation reaches this far?" Mac-Mahon asked.

"I don't know," she answered, "but what if something else happens."

"Like what?"

"I don't know," she said slowly. "We don't have any idea what's going to happen, but what if it gets worse?"

She paused, then added, "I just don't think they should be there."

The admiral frowned. "Perhaps not, but you're going to have one hell of a time getting the beaches clear now. This is the show of the century."

She shook her head. "I'm just afraid, that's all. So much has already happened. I don't want any more trouble."

MacMahon was studying the streets below them. "It looks like there are National Guard trucks down there. I think they're doing some kind of evacuation."

The mass exodus beneath them moved steadily west. There were people carrying children, overcrowded cars, and occasional policemen or National Guardsmen. A few accidents had already occurred and the immobile vehicles had been pushed to the side of the road. There did not appear to be any panic, only a slow, constantly moving column of people.

The area around the hospital was chaotic, with vehicles and people going in all directions. It took several police officers to clear away the helipad so they could land.

To her great joy Blain Robson broke loose from the crowd and came toward them. Their eyes met and he gave her a big smile. He held his arms up to steady her and, before the ramp could even be lowered, she jumped out and was beside him.

"God, am I glad to see you," he said and put his arms around her, engulfing her in a tender bear hug.

"You can't imagine what I've been through," she said, as she squeezed him tight.

He pushed her back a little so he could look into her face. "I thought I was never going to see you again! After

545

we found Duval's body and everything, I thought you were a goner."

"I came so close," she said. "I did a lot of stupid things. . . . I'm just glad to be alive."

"This place has gone crazy. Everything you said might happen seems to be coming true."

"I know. We picked these people up off a boat. I think they're dying." She pointed into the helicopter. "There is a giant energy field out there. It kills anything that goes through it! Have you seen it?"

"Yes, from the third floor. All the patients and nurses are glued to the windows. No one seems to be able to take their eyes off it. I've never seen anything like it."

"We flew right by it. It's beautiful; it seems to call to you. I'm serious, Blain, the closer you get to it, the closer you want to get. It's unreal."

"What is it? Radiation?"

"I don't know. It must be that Sumter was right. It's got to be something totally new, something we drilled into that's creating a force field of some sort out there. I can't explain it. I just know it's deadly." She put her hand on his shoulder. "Come look at these people."

There were now only four. Blain stopped at the first one and looked carefully at the woman's dried-up face. He touched her skin and examined her pupils. He felt her pulse. "She's in bad shape," he said and looked up at the orderly. "Get her inside quick. We need to start some fluids."

In the same manner he examined the second. This one was closer to death, the respirations very weak—almost absent. The third one appeared to be in the best condition of all. An uneasy moan came from the lips of the patient as Blain ground his knuckles into the victim's chest to see

546

if he was responsive to pain. "This one looks hopeful. Take him in and give him top priority." He had almost finished with the fourth when a voice behind him called his name.

"Dr. Robson, may I have a word with you?" Dr. Hoyt Fieldman and the hospital administrator were approaching them.

"Blain, we need your help," Fieldman said, and Aaron Fischer nodded his agreement. "We have a real disaster on our hands with this well thing. It's going to be more than the hospital is equipped to handle. We need to have someone experienced with this sort of thing to take command, to run the show, and get us through this. You're the only one who knows enough about these injuries to do the job. You've produced the only living patient from this series of accidents so far." His eyes swept over Jori and then back to Blain. "What we need is for someone to take charge of these patients until we're able to transfer them to a more appropriate facility. You would have everything at your complete disposal. We would give you as much help as you need. The entire staff, surgical and medical, would be behind you and would function in whatever manner you see fit. The hospital needs you and these patients need you. We may have a lot more. What do you think?"

Blain looked surprised. "What about Wilcott? He's the chief of surgery, shouldn't it be his job?"

"Wilcott can't handle this situation," the administrator said. "He's a good doctor, but not for this kind of crisis."

"Blain, Wilcott doesn't like you," Fieldman added, "and you know it. You should be aware of the fact that he resigned as chief of surgery a short time ago when I told

547

him I was going to ask you to take temporary control, but he won't give you any trouble. He knows better than that. He's not a bad guy and I imagine he'll settle down after all this is over. But whatever he does, the rest of us don't care. We need your experience right now."

"Okay," Blain said, "I'll do it, but I'll need Dr. Hallam to act as my assistant, and I'm going to need your help too, Hoyt. The three of us together are the ones who brought Jori through. It wasn't just me."

Fieldman smiled. "I appreciate your saying that, and I'll be glad to help you in any way I can. Have you had a chance to examine these patients?"

"Yes, I have. One of them looks like he's about gone. The other three have a shot at it. One of them doesn't look too bad. It's going to take everything we've got to pull them through the next twenty-four hours, if we can do it at all. We're going to have to go the whole route, though, just like we did with Jori. We're going to need a lot of help from the blood bank."

"You'll get it," Fischer replied. "We're already starting to line up extra donors. We're discharging every patient this morning who doesn't really need to be in the hospital. We'll only be accepting other emergency patients until this crisis is over."

"Right," Blain answered. "Let's get these patients in and get started." He turned and took Jori by the hand and walked away from the others. "How are you sweetheart? Are you really okay?"

She managed a smile. "I'm exhausted. I feel like I've been hit by a Mack truck, but I think I'm okay."

"I hope so," he replied softly. "Why don't you just stay here and we'll check you out in a little bit to make sure you're all right? I'll get you something to eat, and maybe you can get a little rest."

"Blain, what can I do to help? I feel like I'm partly a cause of all this."

"Sweetheart, you're not the cause of any of it. You tried to prevent it. You just come in here and sit down. Let me get these patients taken care of and then I'll take a look at you." He took a step toward the emergency room.

"Okay," she said, "but let me talk to Admiral MacMahon a minute and then I'll come right in. You go ahead and do your work. I'll wait for you."

"Good. I'll try not to take too long." He hurried briskly toward the building.

She looked around for the Coast Guardsman and found him talking with the sheriff's deputy at the edge of the helipad. "Admiral," she said, "I want to thank you again for helping me."

"Nonsense, it was my pleasure and my job," he replied. "We owe you a lot for warning us about what was happening out there. I'm just sorry that I didn't pay more attention to you earlier."

"What's going to happen now?" she asked.

"I don't know. My communications with the base are completely cut off," he said. "The deputy here says they're having trouble at the power plant and that's what this evacuation is all about. No telling what the hell else is going on. I've got to get back to the base as soon as I can and try to get some help to deal with this well business. Where are you going to be? We might need to get some more information from you, depending on what develops."

"I'm planning on staying right here for the moment. What are you going to do about all those people on the beach?"

"There's nothing I can do. That's out of my authority. My responsibilities are to get a report out so that somebody who knows what the hell they're doing can get on it. The National Guard will have to worry about the people."

"You can't tell them to evacuate the beach?" she asked.

"Jori, I can't even communicate with them. The radio is not working. And even if I could, they wouldn't listen to me. They've got their own commanders. It's going to take a higher authority to get any kind of coordinated action."

She looked at the deputy. "Can't you do something? I think those people on the beach could be in danger. That well could explode. There could even be an earthquake. Nobody knows what might happen."

"Lady, I'm afraid you're talking to the wrong man," he said. "I've been told just to stay right here and keep the peace at the hospital."

"Can't you radio the sheriff and get some help to the beach?"

"The radios are out; so are the telephones. We don't have any way of communicating. Everything's gone to pot. Best thing for you to do is just stay here at the hospital and relax. Let somebody else worry about it. It's not your job."

She turned away from the two of them, frustrated and annoyed. It was hard to believe that no one was willing to help. If whatever was happening on the well got worse, thousands of people could be in danger.

MacMahon put his hand on her shoulder. "Jori, just relax. You've done your part; now take care of yourself. You're not in a position to do anything else right now.

It's totally out of your control and you shouldn't worry about it. The Civil Defense people and the military will do the best they can."

"Sure," she replied, her face expressing her unhappiness with the situation. "Thanks again, Admiral." She waved halfheartedly as he climbed into the helicopter and, after the crowd was cleared back, it rose quickly into the sky and roared away.

The crowd around her continued to mill about, talking and arguing in confusion. She thought about the things Sumter had said about the Balthorium and the possibilities of a serious reaction. She couldn't ignore the thousands of people lining the beach. It was unfair to stand by and let them be risked. She was the only one who appreciated the danger. It was up to her to do something. Anything. She was tired, but she had to make this last effort. She walked quickly into the emergency room, planning to speak to Blain, but it was obvious when she got there that he was extremely busy. She could tell from the activity that another one of the victims had died. She grabbed a piece of paper and wrote a message that she was going home and would be back after a while. One of the nurses promised to give it to Dr. Robson when he was free.

As she left the building, she remembered she had no transportation. She should have gotten Blain's car. Standing in front of the hospital, however, watching the traffic on East Ocean Boulevard, she could see that a lot of the traffic now was going toward the beach instead of away from it. The exodus was continuing, but at least a fifth of the cars were headed back toward the ocean. Surely she could catch a ride.

In less than ten minutes she was on her way, riding in

the back of a pickup truck and glad to be moving. Most of the crowd was just plodding along. There were many walkers now. The National Guard trucks that they had seen earlier were few and far between. The children appeared to be enjoying the whole thing. It was a great big party for them. Most of the others looked frightened or angry. Those headed east toward the water were excited, talking animatedly about the spectacle. In about fifteen minutes, they crossed the waterway, and the road forked into two directions. To the left, it went north along the beach to the power plant. To the right, south to the Florexco compound and the dead end. A sheriff's car blocked the southern route.

"Can't we go down there?" the driver of the truck asked, hopefully.

"Nope," replied the deputy, impassively. "This road's closed. For pedestrians it's okay, but no vehicles."

The driver angrily threw the truck into reverse and backed away from the blocked road. When he turned north and started forward, she jumped quickly from the back, walked around the patrol car and began the three-mile hike to her house.

The road was truly jammed with cars and trucks and vans, but they were all empty. She climbed up over the dune and looked down to the beach. It was an incredible sight. All the way south as far as she could see, the waterfront looked more crowded than she had ever seen it. Thousands of people were sitting, walking, standing, or just milling around looking out to sea. The top of the dune was lined with a row of spectators—all enthusiastically watching the strange marvel to the east.

She tried to yell to get their attention, "Hey, everyone, listen to me, please listen . . . it could be dangerous here.

Go back from the beach! There could be radiation!" But it was no use. The few people who did turn their heads just looked at her curiously for a moment and ignored her warnings.

She walked down to the beach and grabbed a few people, forcing them to listen to her message, but no one cared. They were too engrossed with what they were seeing. "Listen to me!" she said. "You're in danger! You've got to go away from the beach! There could be an earthquake. . . . You may be hurt by radiation!" A few people laughed at her, but most merely ignored her. She hurried on through the crowd exhorting them to flee for their own safety, begging them to take their children and leave this place. Some eyed her as if she was a little crazy.

She walked down in front of a group standing in the water so they would have to look at her. "Listen to me, please," she begged. "Go away! This well is dangerous. It might explode. If it does, you'll all be in danger. You've got to go back to the city." Empty faces, blank faces, smiling faces. No one heard or perceived her warning. They were mesmerized.

She continued down the beach for almost half a mile, alternately yelling from the top of the dune, or walking through the crowd, or standing in the water in front of them. After half an hour of the grueling ordeal, she had convinced no one.

She looked about for some authority—sheriff's deputies, the National Guard, anyone—someone who could help her convince this crowd that they were in danger.

Finally, exhausted, she dragged on numbly through the crowd, moving mechanically. A mile later she reached Harpoon Harry's. The deck was jammed with people. Harry, old Joe, and a new waiter were selling cold drinks as fast as they could. Harry was getting rich.

The proprietor looked up, surprised to see her. He grinned. "Can you believe this, Jori?" he said. "What a show! Here, take one. It's on the house." He handed her a soft drink and then disappeared in the crowd.

She took a long sip of the soothing liquid and it was good. She became aware of how tired and hungry and thirsty she was. Admiral MacMahon was right—it wasn't her job to warn them, and besides there was nothing she could do anyway. For the first time since reaching the beach, she took a long, satisfying look at the awesome spectacle in the distance.

It seemed even more beautiful than before. From where she stood, it was a shining mixture of pale reds and greens. Color changes seemed slowly to move from the center, working their way up and outside of the thin veil hanging silently in the distant sky. There was a faint pulsation that gave it a lifelike quality. Again, she felt the peculiar sensation she had experienced earlier when she had first seen it. But from this distance her compulsion to go closer was not as strong as it had been when flying along the awesome, towering edges of the mammoth glow.

As she watched it, she began to feel much better, more relaxed, calm. A spirit of tranquility overcame her. Why had she been so concerned anyway? It was such a pleasure to study this magnificent thing.

After fifteen minutes she decided to continue her journey homeward. It was a pleasant walk, looking at the happy people, and every few steps she would glance out again and drink in the vibrating colors.

As her house came into view, harsh memories of what

had happened the night before came flooding back. She stopped for a moment and looked around the area where she had fought Duval. Pushing that horror from her mind, she hurriedly covered the last few yards up the beach and climbed the stairs to her porch.

She went inside and a few minutes later emerged carrying a beer and a sandwich. She put them down on the small table in the corner, went back inside and almost immediately returned with a bag of potato chips and a large piece of cheese from which she took a bite. She sat down, propped her feet up on the rail, and devoured the food. Afterwards, she leaned back in the chair and gazed almost contentedly at the giant radiant spectacle before her.

She was exhausted, but an irresistible compulsion kept her from closing her eyes. The thing was a mesmerizing force, like nothing she had ever seen before. How strange it is, she thought, that there is really nothing out there to feel or touch. It's only energy, a force field, an emission of radiation, and a deadly one at that. The thought troubled her . . . deadly . . . filled with death. . . . She remembered the faces of the people from the boat and, with even more horror, she recalled the destruction that had been the face of the fighter pilot. Again she felt anxiety, a small fear, but it was so beautiful. As she watched, the glowing began to soothe her again, and then she realized what was wrong.

Jori jumped up quickly and, resisting the urge for one last look, opened the door and went into the kitchen. She sat down at the table, waited a minute, then got up and opened the icebox. She took out another piece of cheese and ate it slowly, concentrating on its mellow flavor. Anything to keep her mind off the colors. She went into

555

the bedroom and looked at herself in the mirror. God, she looked horrible. Her face was drawn and tired. Deep black shadows were under her eyes. Her hair looked like seaweed. She seemed pale. Something terrible had been happening to her. She kept busy. She thought about anything except the colors. With great effort, she forced it from her mind.

Finally, as the minutes passed, she overcame the spell as she escaped the near enchantment that had occurred while she watched the danger outside. It's incredible, she thought. Such a rare, beautiful thing that it overcomes judgment and good sense. Even she, the most knowledgeable of all, had been nearly hypnotized into euphoria while watching the beautiful display of light. She understood why no one would listen to her. They were moonstruck, like lunatics. The spectacular beauty of the dangerous emissions at the well was having a soporific effect. It was as if the observers were drunk on beauty. The spectacle of spectacles had an alluring quality which humans could not resist. It was a temptation that would lead many of them to their deaths.

Somehow she would have to get help. The people would have to be forced away from the beaches. The National Guard could do it, if only she could reach them. She picked up her phone; it was dead. She turned on the radio she had in the past used to communicate with the well. There was nothing. The electrical power was off. Of course, the reactor must have been shut down. It seemed hopeless. She hoped she was wrong.

She heard a car stopping out front and she walked into the small living room just as the door swung open and Blain came in. "Boy! I'm glad I found you. You should have told me you were leaving. They've been looking for you."

"Who has?" she said, frowning.

"Everybody: the police, the National Guard, you name it. When I got your note, I came straight out here."

"What do they want me for?"

"I don't know. They're trying to round up everybody who's had anything to do with the well. There's a military alert on. On my way out I saw ten or twelve big Air Force planes coming in. I don't know what the hell is going on."

"How did you get past the deputy in your car?"

"He didn't try to stop me, or anyone else for that matter. He was just standing there on top of his car, watching the fire out there—or whatever it is. Have you looked at that thing?" He walked past her and started for the back porch.

She looked chagrined. "A little too much. It's almost hypnotic."

"I've never seen anything like it," he said. "What do you suppose it is?" He opened the door and stepped out onto the porch. "Jesus," he murmured, "it's better than the aurora borealis."

"I don't understand what's causing it exactly," Jori said, "but it's spellbinding. You look at it for a little while and you don't want to stop. It scares me."

He was smiling, "I know what you mean. It sort of makes you want to get closer to it for a good look. You feel like you want to look into it as hard as you can before it stops."

"I guess it has the same effect on everyone. It's like a carnival or something out here," she said. Fifty feet south of them, standing knee-deep in the water, was a small group of Hari Krishnas. Their bald heads shining in the sun and yellow robes blowing in the breeze were a

557

startling contrast to the rest of the crowd. She could hear them chanting something over and over.

Blain looked at her, grinning. "I've never seen anything like this before in my life. Somebody ought to be selling tickets."

A group of teenagers, carrying a heavy cooler, came from around the side of the house and walked past them down onto the beach. They were laughing and smiling. When they had found a vacant spot near the water, they popped open the cooler and were soon passing beers around. The whole place looked like the Fourth of July.

The sound of music drifted toward them from the direction of Harpoon Harry's. "Jesus Christ!" Jori said. "He's even got a band going down there now. Everybody's gone insane."

"Yeah, but why not? This is a once-in-a-lifetime show, Jori. What do you expect people to do, shut their eyes and ignore it? People love a disaster—that's why they go to fires." He was smiling.

"See, it's even affecting you," she said. "This is dangerous, Blain. Somehow it makes everybody throw caution to the wind. What happens if it gets worse? What do you think is going to become of all these people? They're too exposed on the beach. What if it turned into some kind of huge explosion, what about that? There could be more radiation, even an earthquake, or something."

"Yeah, you're right," he said, frowning slightly, but continuing to stare at the dazzling lights. "Maybe someone ought to tell them to leave."

"It's no use. I tried that. They won't listen. According to what you say, even the deputy at the end of the road is so carried away with the thing he's not doing his job."

Blain walked down the steps and out on the beach and she followed. "It's just so damned impressive with all those changing colors and all," he said. "It's hard to take your eyes off it. It almost makes you feel good."

She looked at it briefly, knowing he was right. Understanding its appeal, she was no longer so totally mesmerized by it. The scene up and down the beach was almost as amazing. It was somewhat like the crowds at sporting events: people laughing, talking, milling around, drinking. She spotted a few kids down the shoreline passing a joint around. She thought again of the deaths she had witnessed and her mood began to sour.

She put one arm on Blain's shoulder, "Listen," she said.

He continued to look out to sea.

"No, damn it! Turn around and look at me. I want to tell you something."

He turned and gazed at her quizzically. "Listen," she repeated, "this may be a lot of fun and games to these people, but there is something wrong, dead wrong out there, and I think there is a significant hazard. We don't even know what the radiation level on the beach is right now. We may all be getting zapped silly as far as I know. They have no idea of the danger. We've got to do something to get the beaches cleared. I know you don't care as much as I do, but that's only because it didn't nearly kill you like it did me."

His smile faded. "You're right," he admitted. "I was getting carried away with it myself for a few minutes there. Let's go see what we can do. Could it really get worse?"

"I don't know." She sounded worn out. "I don't have any idea. I just feel sort of responsible. I helped start this thing, you know. I just don't want to see anybody else die." The music from Harpoon Harry's seemed to grow louder. And than another unusual sound, becoming more intense, caused them to look around to the west.

More helicopters than they had ever seen at one time were rising like angry wasps from beyond the trees on the other side of the river. They were a drab olive green. The large military craft fanned out into an almost endless formation and came swooping toward them. Jori and Blain ran up the sand, past the house, and stood in her front yard, watching them approach. A large group turned north and spread out along the beach while some veered south. Within minutes they were landing, and battle-dressed troops poured out and ran down onto the beach.

Behind the first wave of copters came a smaller craft, the sheriff's helicopter. It seemed to be coming straight at them. It hovered over the house momentarily and then slowly descended to the ground in the sand along the edge of the road.

An army major with a gun strapped to his hip got out along with a man in a business suit and walked toward them. "Excuse me, ma'am, I'm Major McDonald, United States Army, and this is John Franklin, from the FBI. We're looking for Miss Jori Ashe. Do you know if this is her house?"

She looked at the man intently. "That's my house and I'm Jori Ashe."

"Miss Ashe, a state of martial law has been declared in this area, and I've been ordered to detain you in protective custody. I also need to know if you have any knowledge of the whereabouts of a Dr. Adrian Sumter or Mr. Winston Loggins."

"They were on the well the last time I saw them. I imagine they're dead."

"All right," the officer said. "I'm going to have to ask you to come with us."

"What's it all about? Where are you going to take me?"

"The FBI with the assistance of the Army has been ordered to pick up all persons having knowledge of the Florexco drilling operations at St. Lucie One platform."

"I see. What's going to happen then?"

"Ma'am, I have no idea. I'm just the arresting officer."

"Okay," she replied and then looked at Blain. "I guess we had better go."

"I'm sorry, Miss Ashe," the FBI man said, "he can't come with us. You're the only one I've been authorized to detain."

"But he's my doctor. I've been sick. I can't go without him. As a matter of fact, I won't go without him."

The major looked surprised. "Miss Ashe, maybe you don't understand. This is a state of martial law. You don't have any choice about what you are or are not going to do. We will take you forcibly if necessary. This is not a game. You are involved in some extremely serious circumstances."

"No one knows that better than I do," Jori replied crisply. "You had better get your men to evacuate the beaches. These people may be in danger. As for me, you're going to have to take me screaming and kicking unless you take Dr. Robson with us. Besides, I know more about what this is all about than you do, and I can assure you that whoever wants to talk to me wants to talk to him, too."

The two men looked exasperated. They glanced at each

other and then back at her. "All right," Franklin said. "Both of you get in."

She didn't move. "Are you going to be able to evacuate all these people, Major? I'm telling you there's a real chance of something terrible happening here. I'm afraid that situation on the well could get worse any minute."

"Lady, let us worry about that," the Major replied sternly. "Just get in the helicopter like we told you to. I'm trying to be nice about this. You may be in a lot more trouble than you understand."

As he spoke her eyes were drawn to the beach where the troops were forcing the crowd at gunpoint back away from the water. The music from Harpoon Harry's had stopped. The crowd, which a few moments earlier had seemed happy, was now turning surly and angry. Taunts, curses, and beer bottles were being hurled at the well-organized soldiers, a few of whom were already beginning to be distracted by the dazzling display behind them out over the water.

In an instant, however, the confrontation ended— brought to an abrupt halt by the blinding, brilliantly intense flash of light from the distant ocean. Several seconds later, as everyone stood motionless, stunned, and silent, the heat wave reached them. A searing blast of intense heat and pain that was gone the instant it arrived, leaving thousands with first-degree burns.

The dancing lights on the horizon were gone. In its place was a boiling, red inferno of liquid fire. It rose slowly from the surface of the sea. It grew steadily for several seconds and then pulsated violently with the release of secondary light flashes and blasting heat waves which could be literally watched as they shot out in great concentric rings from the red ball and rushed to the beach. By the arrival of the third withering blow from the distant conflagration, everyone was on the ground, faces buried in fear and horror at the anticipated damage.

Then came the sound: a thunderous roar that burst eardrums and literally knocked to the ground those few persons still standing. It was a soul-numbing vibration that left senses scrambled and hearts pounding. When it and its echo were past, ten thousand faces looked up in fear.

The fiery red bubble in the sea expanded slowly and then broke open at the top as a giant plume of flame erupted upward, shooting thousands of feet into the sky. It formed a new, equally fearsome monster of flame and smoke on a second level. After a moment of expansion, another plume and a third level of the inferno developed. Each of the three spectacular displays seemed to pulsate and tremble, shooting out smoke and flame. After several minutes, as the shapes slowly enlarged and rose higher into the sky, the intensity within seemed to dim. All that remained was black and dark and foreboding.

And then the wind began to blow. From behind them it came rushing out to sea to replace the super-heated air that had been consumed by the fires. The wind whistled around their ears, roaring and moaning with the cry of a thousand banshees. Trees bent and bushes were uprooted and carried out over the ocean. Sand filled the air and the sky turned red. Everyone waited and hoped and prayed that the fury would end before their aching, blistering skin was shredded and torn from them by wind and sand. Finally, as mysteriously as it had begun, it ended. The storm was over.

Slowly and fearfully they raised their faces, sat up on hands and knees, and then cautiously pushed themselves erect, their eyes transfixed on the sight in front of them. A distant thunderous rumble continued to ebb and flow, but the silence was slowly returning. The burning, blowing horror was gone. All that remained was the towering giant of black smoke and heat gradually dissipating itself into the skies above them.

Children were crying and dogs began to bark, but it was over. What was done was done. The sensual, sparkling display of shimmering glory and light was gone, but it had died with an awesome, mighty stroke of violence. The innocent appeal of its haunting beauty had been matched by the ugly, angry temper of its ending.

Their enchantment over and their fear subsiding, the beach people stood in silence, reflecting on what they had witnessed. The unique experience they had shared created a sensation of common bond between them as wordless homage was paid to what they had seen. With rare exception, they did not notice or in any way concern themselves with the subtle, almost undetectable, shifting of the sandy earth beneath their feet. The tiny instant of quivering movement was unimpressive. It paled in comparison with the cataclysm just ended.

Jori alone among the thousands perceived the import of the ominous tremor. Silently, she stepped forward up onto the dune and gazed over the sea into the empty distance.

It was several minutes more of confused milling about and waiting before knowledgeable eyes began to perceive the meaning of the peculiar white line on the water, which was coming toward them from the distant horizon. At first it was only a murmur, a faintly whispered recognition of doom: "Tidal wave."

An instant later it became a pandemonium-producing

scream of terror: "Tidal wave!" They could see it coming—strong, delicately capped with a faint line of curling foam, growing larger and more massive by the second as the energies of the underwater explosion were forced closer and closer to the surface.

As with one mind, the masses hurdled themselves, screaming, up the dune. The weak were pummeled and stepped upon. The panic was universal. Army gun butts came down upon the heads of those blocking the retreat of the uniformed warriors, and the great battle for the safety of the helicopters began.

With no communication but fear to bind them, the major, the FBI man, Jori and Blain ran as one and entered the waiting copter.

With white-knuckled hands, the pilot pushed forward the stick to begin the assent. For a fateful moment the craft shuddered as its passengers looked into the doomed, terrified faces of the shrieking victims running toward them. A moment later they were fifty feet off the ground looking down at the sad, empty faces of those who had nowhere to go.

The army helicopter to the south of them came up first. Overloaded, it struggled and trembled as it made a slow ascent. A small mob at first hung on to the landing gear, and then, one by one, slipped away for the fall to the sandy dune as the craft began to pick up speed. There was finally one man left who had pulled himself up into a safe and secure position, clinging with tenacity to the support structures of the landing gear. To the north they could see copters starting sporadically to rise here and there, masses of humanity dangling beneath them, falling back to the ground. And then one, because of its heavy load, tipped over, fell off to the side and crashed in a blaze of fire, consuming all aboard and many nearby. Black smoke rose from the burning craft, and a secondary explosion engulfed others trying to flee the flames.

To the south of them there were now three helicopters in the air and still two more on the ground, while in the north most seemed to be coming up.

Thousands of the unfortunates below were running in panicked frenzy to and fro seeking some means of escape. A few others seemed to have become resigned to their fate and remained passively on the beach, watching with little reaction as the giant wave rushed toward them.

Jori and Blain stared in terror-filled fascination as the gray wall of water approached, sucking the sea ahead of it down from the beach, leaving it bare and exposed until the final instant of smashing destruction. With a furious roar, the fifty-foot giant stormed up the beach and over the dune. Thousands were instantly engulfed.

Both of the two remaining helicopters began a slow ascent as the wave roared toward them. The one farther south, less heavy, with only a few stragglers hanging on, accelerated quickly, and then shuddered briefly as the tip of the killer giant washed its bottom and stripped the landing gear free of those struggling to survive. Clearing the water by inches, it ascended safely into the haven of the sky. The nearer of the two was not so fortunate; it had only risen ten or twelve feet from the sand when it was smacked broadside by the power of the water which sent it reeling downward into a destruction of shearing forces. It disappeared beneath the wave almost immediately.

From their vantage point 500 feet up, the beach and Hutchinson Island seemed for an instant to disappear beneath the ocean's surface. But then it reappeared as the torrent of water went beyond it and, with most if its energy spent, collapsed into the river in a great foaming, churning mass of white water and smaller waves. Its force gone, the millions of tons from the sea quickly raised the level of the river almost eight feet over the bank beyond. Just as quickly, it began to recede. Some of the water crossed back over the island, while the rest rushed in a stormy torrent out through the inlet. In no time it was over and gone. The river was returning to its normal height and the ocean settling down.

But Hutchinson Island was different. What had been covered with vegetation, scattered buildings, houses and thousands of curious humans had now been swept clean. A barren, sandy peninsula remained. The fractured remains of the road were covered with sand. Jori's house was gone. Harpoon Harry's was gone. Palm trees and dune brush—all gone. The sand was clean and white, pristine and virginal. Only the river was dirty, filled with the debris washed clear of the island. Chunks of houses and boards, destroyed boats, and vegetation floated in its turbulent waters being carried by the tidal surge back toward the sea downstream to the inlet. They could see bodies everywhere bobbing, disappearing, some struggling to swim and others lying still. A few fortunates were hanging on to broken trees and other floating debris. Hundreds of overturned cars lay along the western banks of the island or floated in the water.

The bridge over the river was a terrific jam of thankful survivors who had made it off the island before the onslaught. The Florexco compound to the south was gone. Two of the crew boats floated bottom-up out in the middle of the river. Ruin and destruction were everywhere.

The sky was filled with military helicopters which

began to fly rapidly across the river to the airport. No one spoke as they studied and surveyed the tragedy below. The pilot finally brought their craft around through a slow arc beyond the tip of the island, and then turned out over the river heading for the landing area beyond the trees on the other side.

Jori felt Blain's hand in hers, and she squeezed it out of fear and relief and security. Their eyes met silently in painful communication. Without a word he pointed to the east out over the ocean. The sea looked calm and peaceful. The well was gone. The lights were gone. Only the distant smoke high in the atmosphere remained as a reminder of what had come before. The sky around them was blue and the air smelled clean as if after a great storm.

He turned back from the window and looked again into her eyes. He could feel her sense of defeat.

"They wouldn't listen," she said softly. "I tried. I really tried, but they didn't listen. No one would."

"Jori, they never do. No matter what, they never do— until it's too late."

"I know," she answered. "I wonder why?" She turned her tear-filled gaze out over the ocean. It was a beautiful deep blue, and the horizon was empty. The black ugliness of the smoke had faded into gray, becoming thin and whispy, as if from a distant fire.

EPILOGUE

One Year Later

The olive-green military car crossed the bridge over the St. Lucie River, moved slowly through Sewell's Point, and then beyond the waterway to Hutchinson Island. It turned off the road toward the tip of the peninsula and slowed, approaching the checkpoint. When the vehicle stopped, the MP came out of the guard post and carefully inspected the papers handed to him by the driver and then waved it through.

As the car passed, the guard bent down to get a look at the famous occupant riding in the back. Through the tinted glass he couldn't see much, but he recognized Jori Ashe even in the faint light. She was wearing sun glasses.

Traveling down the restored road, she moved closer to the window to look out at the terrain that she had not seen for almost a year. It was late afternoon and shadows fell across the road from the recently planted palm trees and pines. Small bits of vegetation and dune brush were beginning to spring up across the sandy land, but the island still looked clean and virginal. They went past the new Harpoon Harry's. The rebuilding was almost complete. It looked like it was still going to be an interesting place, much of the original flavor having been retained.

A few miles down the road, only a "For Sale" sign marked the spot where once her house had stood. Nothing else remained except, far off to the right, a few timbers still standing in the shallow water where once the dock had been.

They reached the boundaries of the old Florexco compound, and the gate was quickly opened by the army guards. The place was still a temporary army post, but was soon to become a public park. Reentering the area stirred an old uneasiness in her. She put her hand in Blain's hand and squeezed it tightly as he put his arm around her.

"You're nervous, aren't you?" her husband said as he pulled her closer.

She nodded. "A little, but more tired, really, than nervous."

Blain smiled understandingly. "We can let you sleep on the way home. We'll be back at the hospital in just a few hours." She closed her eyes and rested her head on his shoulders. "They really wanted you to come," he said. "I think the press is making a big deal out of this."

She smiled and looked up ahead as a giant monolithic memorial came into view—it was an obelisk. She was pleased to have been specially invited to this dedication honoring those who had died a year ago. She hoped the new laws would keep it from ever happening again. As they arrived at the base of the huge sculpture, she was surprised at the size of the crowd. She had expected a smaller gathering. There was a large contingent from the press, and TV camera trucks.

She glanced at Blain. "How do I look?' she asked, and quickly ran her hand through her very short and extremely thin hair. She was no longer embarrassed about her leukemia and the terrible effects of the chemotherapy, but she disliked the awkwardness it provoked in others, and she always tried to look the best she could.

The car stopped and the officer driving opened her door and Blain got out quickly to assist her. She knew she looked pathetic as she walked toward the stage, but she held her ninety-three pounds erect and tried to walk as independently as she could, but she needed his help to climb the stairs.

The crowd stood in silent respect and then spontaneously applauded as she took her seat beside the governor. She smiled and waved, and the applause grew louder as the cameras clicked and lenses zoomed in on her emaciated but still very pretty face. With her arrival the cermeonies began.

As the politicians and government officials droned on about what had happened and what they had accomplished, her thoughts drifted off as she remembered what had been. In the early days, no one had even dreamed about the leukemia, except maybe Blain and a few of the other physicians close to the problem. It seemed so obvious now, considering what had happened after Hiroshima and Nagasaki. But nevertheless, the immediate concern had been about the massive destruction the incident had caused—and the incredible loss of life, of course.

It had taken almost a month after the St. Lucie One accident before even a resemblance of normalcy could be restored along the coast, but the reins of power had finally returned to civilian authorities just after the new year. In a ceremony conducted along the beach in the early morning hours of a chilly, rainy day, the acting military commander had formally declared the cessation of martial law and demobilized the National Guard. She remembered well his farewell statement to the audience, which was mostly newsmen. The general had warned of future tragedies if human judgment did not soon develop restraints on advancing technology.

The army had helped a lot, before its role in the restoration had ceased. A judicial tribunal had taken a number of significant actions to render whatever justice was possible, considering the uniqueness of the disaster. The civilian court system of Florida had later concurred with every recommendation from the tribunal. The surviving executive staff of Florexco had been punished—found guilty of negligent manslaughter, homicide in the third degree. They had been given sentences ranging upwards to five years, and the appeals court had let the lower court decision stand. Poor Matthew Downing had suffered a massive stroke during the first week of his confinement and died. Craig Strombeck failed to present himself for incarceration and was found dead in his bed from a self-inflicted gunshot wound of the head. Walter Jenkins, still protesting his innocence, was serving time at the state penitentiary at Raiford.

The civil litigation that arose from the incident was unprecedented in scope, mostly coming from Palm Beach county to the south because of the enormous destruction of the extensively developed ocean front there. But areas as far away as Miami Beach had also experienced quite severe damage to some of their older structures along the water's edge.

Almost ten billion dollars in lawsuits for property damage and wrongful death were eventually filed, although most had been quietly dropped when the assets and insurance of Florexco were gone. The company had recently been put into receivership and sold piecemeal to satisfy the early judgments. Because of the nature of the damages, the stockholders had also been held liable and their individual estates attached. The total loss of life had never been accurately determined.

The rumors that had circulated widely about the etiology of the crustal defect through which Florexco had drilled were partially laid to rest by a statement from the International Society of Geophysicists. The strange opening was described as a very rare but naturally occurring phenomenon which most likely represented ancient vent holes which had formed during an early cooling period of the earth's crust and mantle. It made good sense and Jori believed it.

The controversy about the existence of Balthorium was still unsettled. No residual radiation had been detected despite the massive fish kill which had occurred immediately after the accident. Navy drilling efforts to find the original defect had failed as she had known they would. The opening had surely been closed by the earthquake which followed the explosion.

The international outcry about the disaster had been overwhelming. She had been swept up by the controversy and had become an object of tremendous public adulation. As a result of the actions she had taken to try and stop the well, the press had lionized her. She had been turned into a veritable folk hero and had even been asked to testify before Congress about the accident. Her name had become a household word known even by children, much like an astronaut or an Olympic hero. She had worked hard during those first few months and, with the support of almost every ecology group and consumer organization in the country, had mounted a tremendous campaign to outlaw deep wells of the St. Lucie One type. She was proud of her role in the creation of the legislation that was finally enacted in the United States and endorsed by the United Nations.

Apparently spurred on by military as well as commercial interest, however, efforts continued on a global scale to discover new areas of crustal defects. Fortunately, so far, no evidence had surfaced of positive findings. But a recently released report, delivered last spring by the CIA to the Senate subcommittee on energy and military affairs, indicated that a new massive drilling project by the Russians was to be initiated in Siberia by next summer. Sadly, the Israelis were also preparing to undertake a well-guarded drilling attempt of an unknown nature in the desert west of Jerusalem. The future was uncertain.

But now, for her personally, it didn't mean much. The leukemia, which had come as a surprise to Jori, was getting worse and she knew it. She had felt so well in the first few months, but now the drug treatments were becoming less and less effective each week; she could feel it.

As the ceremony ended and Blain helped her back into the car, she was exhausted. She could see in his face that he, too, was tired. She felt so sorry for him. He had been so good to her. She knew he loved her—very much. He was going to be hurt when she was gone, but she almost wished it would come quickly, just for his sake. It had to be hard for him to see her wasting away. She would have hated to see Blain die this way.

He climbed in beside her and put his arm around her as the car pulled out of the compound and started north up the road she had once known so well. She sat quietly secure next to Blain for several minutes and then suddenly looked up as the old location of the house came into view. "Captain," she said to the officer driving, "could you stop, just for a few minutes? I want to take a look at something if you don't mind."

The car was slowly pulled to the side of the road and Blain, understanding without comment, helped her out. Steadying herself with his hand, she made her way over the dune and then carefully down the other side onto the beach. They took off their shoes and together walked to the edge of the water and stood in the wet sand as the waves splashed over their feet. The far horizon was growing dark as the sunset was ending behind them. The full moon had already risen and glowed beautifully in the early evening.

She looked up and down the beach and back at where the house had once been. "Memories," she said softly as Blain hugged her. "So many memories."

He smiled. "I love you, girl. You need to always remember that." He glanced down the beach toward Harry's new place. "And it all started for us right down there, not much more than a year ago. So much has happened . . . so incredibly much." His eyes were wet.

She put her head on his shoulder. "Blain, my sweet Blain. Why did it all have to happen this way?" she said as big tears rolled from her saddened eyes. "It could have been so different for us, so beautiful. What we have is so special." She choked back a sob. "I don't want to die like this. It's not fair. I don't want to leave yet."

"I know," he replied, his voice quivering. "I don't want to be away from you, ever."

They clutched each other tightly and cried together softly as the wave-washed sand continued to gather about their feet.

The Army captain stood high upon the dune, watching

them as he smoked his cigarette. He wondered what they were saying and was glad he was not ill.

Within three weeks Jori Ashe-Robson was dead, a victim of myelogenous leukemia. The incidence of the disease was rising sharply in south Florida and within four months of her death over six hundred cases had been reported, including the deaths of the crews of the three Coast Guard rescue helicopters. It was predicted that many hundreds more would die before the final effects from St. Lucie One were felt.

Blain Robson left Florida soon after Jori was gone. He presently lives somewhere in the mountains of Colorado, but each Sunday a dozen red roses are delivered to her grave and placed beside the large stone bearing her name and the quotation from Adrian Sumter that seemed to mean so much to her in the last few weeks of her life:

There inevitably will come a recognition that not all things are reasonably possible. For the present, our frail species—bold, energetic, and adventuresome—is filled with dreams and visions of glory which we pursue with vigor. Sadly, however, there exists waters deep and dark across which we cannot and must not sail.

Like a child untaught, we blunder onward, not yet understanding the dangers of our limitless explorations. Some day we will learn.

Until then, like our fathers before us, we will seek the distant shore.